✤✤ ✤✤ ✤✤ ✤✤ ✤✤ ✤✤

The
Rising
of
the
Lark

by Ann Moray

WILLIAM MORROW AND COMPANY · NEW YORK, 1964

Library of Congress Catalog Card Number 64-11270

What is longing made from?
What cloth is put into it
That it does not wear out with use?

Gold wears out, and silver wears out,
Velvet wears out, and silk wears out,
Yet longing does not wear out.

The moon rises and the sun rises,
The sea rises in vast waves,
But longing never rises from the heart.

WELSH, *Seventeenth century*

I wakened to the smell of burning leaves, lay still, and breathed it in, sharp on the frosty air. Suddenly I remembered it was Guy Fawkes Day. Through the window I could see the blue smoke rising through the almost bare branches at the edge of the orchard, just behind the vegetable-marrow patch. It rose upward, straight as a birch, on the cold, windless air. I pulled on my bloomers and kilt and a thick dark green jersey and hurried downstairs.

"Emma!" I called while I ran down, two steps at a time. "It's Guy Fawkes Day and I want my breakfast. Can you smell the leaves?" But the smell of bread, baking, filled the kitchen.

"Close the door, Miss Catty-fach. You know how Miss Withers is about kitchen smells."

"Lovely kitchen smells and lovely burning leaves . . . Emma, let me have breakfast in here today . . . just because it's Guy Fawkes Day." Emma pursed her lips, but she couldn't stop the corners of her mouth from turning up. She scooped an unused heap of flour that was on the pastry board back into the flour bag and tied it up tightly.

I followed her, chanting:

"Or flour in a bag
Or flower in array . . ."

She took the pastry board to the sink.

"Or flower of warriors
Gallant and gay.
With flour and flower
You've now done away."

"For goodness' sakes alive, now be off with your chatter. I've no time this morning for your stories. And Miss Withers will not like it if you have breakfast in the kitchen."

"Where is she?"

"In the sewing room."

"I'll be quiet as a mouse."

"You'd better be." Emma put my porridge on to heat and went into the larder for milk.

"But, Emma, it was in the days of Bran the Blest . . ." I sat on the edge of the kitchen table—the edge that wasn't floury.

". . . And there had been a great battle, and so that the land should not be laid waste a truce had been called. Bran sent his page, Efnisien, to see if the truce was an honorable one, and he came to a pillared hall, the place where the parley was to be held. There was a lone warrior there, who greeted him, and they talked. Everything seemed to be quiet, and Efnisien was about to leave, when he noticed that on each of the pillars there hung two large sacks—"

"Now, Miss Catty," said Emma, bringing a tray with my breakfast on it and putting it down on the small table by the window, "come and eat your porridge while it's hot."

I got down from the kitchen table. ". . . And Efnisien wondered why there were so many sacks. 'What's in those sacks?' he asked. 'Flour,' answered the warrior. Now, wouldn't you think it odd to have so many sacks of flour in a great hall, Emma? Where a parley was to be held?"

Emma sat down opposite me. "I don't know as I'd think

anything about it at all," she said, "but I know that once
you've started on one of your stories I might just as well sit
down and listen."

I took a spoonful of porridge, with honey and cream, and
some milk.

"Well, Efnisien did. He thought it was odd. 'Flour, indeed?' he said. 'Then it will bear kneading.' And the young
Welshman began to knead the first bag with his mailed fingers, and when he felt the head of the man inside he squeezed
until his fingers sank through the bone into the brain—"

"Now, that's enough, indeed to goodness." Emma shuddered. "And, Miss Catty, you'd better eat your breakfast,
and that's not a ladylike story at all, at all, look you."

"And, Emma! He squeezed all their heads, except the last
one, and that one was saved because his hands were tired."

"Please, eat your porridge."

"All right. . . . With flour and flower we've now done
away . . . and I think the bread is baked."

"It is, indeed." Emma opened both oven doors and pulled
out the trays of hot bread. Then she took the flour bag and
lifted it. "And I'll never open it more, but I'll think of a
squeezed head inside of it," she said, and put it on the shelf
in the cupboard and closed the door.

The kitchen window was open, and I could only faintly
smell the leaves because of the baking, but I could hear the
scrape of Mr. Evans's shovel as he put more of them onto
the blaze, and then without warning there was shouting, and
the sound of young voices, gay and high-pitched, shrill and
clear, from the Hill Lane, outside the garden wall.

"It's the children," Emma said. "And I do believe they're
coming here. Goodness, gracious to me, I must get some
pennies . . . some of these gingersnaps, too." She took a
big, square, gold and blue tin from the high mantelpiece; it
had a picture of two collie dogs on it. I left half of my por-

ridge and hurried upstairs to my governess. She was sewing. The sewing room was over the front porch and had a big bow window; from there I could see everything that happened.

When the children reached the wall door, they banged on it and then knocked loudly with the heavy iron knocker, and then rang the bell, shouting:

"A penny for the Guy. A penny for the Guy." It had never happened before. I went to the window. I heard Emma come from the kitchen to open the front door. Then tying her apron up around her waist, she went along the gravel path to the wall door and opened it. The children came running, jumping and tumbling into the garden, dressed in rags and all kinds of funny clothes and hats, and they had blackened their faces with soot.

"Jane," I said, "please let me go down." I'd seen some of the children in church, on the first Sunday in the month, when we took eggs and flowers and vegetables, but Jane never let me speak to any of them. Only to Ellen, who came to stay with Grandma Rhys-Evans when she had her rheumatics and Jane and I had taken her some of Emma's calf's-foot jelly. Ellen had talked about rabbits. I told her about my big Brindley-Flopsy, and she said that her brother had a white one, with pink eyes. Today they would smile at me. They wouldn't look down, as they did in church.

When Jane said, "No, dear, I don't think you should go down. They look very rough. Emma will give them some pennies," I went to the middle window, where they could at least see me. And one boy did. That's Nana's grandson, I thought. He told the others. They stopped shouting and looked up at me; then they looked down again, as they did in church.

"I'm going down, Jane," I said, and before she could reply I was halfway downstairs.

The front door was open, and Emma was bending over a child who was crying. I saw Nana's grandson. He kicked a stone along the gravel path. He had seen me again. This time he did not tell the others, but they had seen me too, so I couldn't go back. I felt awkward.

"Hello," I said. Emma looked up. The child was still crying. She was only about four years old. I turned and went to the tall chest in the hall and found a big red and yellow ball that had been there since three Christmases ago. I went out again and gave it to the little girl. She stopped crying so suddenly that I laughed. When I looked up, some of the others were laughing too. Then a rough boy tried to take it away from her, but Nana's grandson stopped him.

He said to me, "That's a beautiful ball, indeed, Miss Catriona."

"Well, it made her stop crying." Then eagerly I asked, "When will you have the bonfire?"

"At the darkness. On the Mochdre Hill," he said. I looked for Emma. She was sitting on the iron seat, on the grass near to the path. I ran to her.

"Emma," I asked, "please take me to the bonfire tonight? Please." She looked surprised, and then doubtful, and then she laughed.

"My goodness to me, indeed," she said, "and who'll ask Miss Withers?"

"I'll have to . . . and I've been disobedient, too."

"And you'll be punished."

I nodded. "But we'll go, Emma . . . I just know." The children were leaving. I went to the wall door and held it open. "Good-by," I said to them. I was excited and happy. "I'll see you tonight, on the Mochdre Hill. Emma's bringing me."

And Nana's grandson said, "Don't forget to bring something to burn, to throw onto the bonfire." I didn't know about that. I was grateful to him.

"Thank you for telling me," I said. Then the children were all shouting again, some already running down the Hill Lane and others crowding through the door. I waited until they were away down, and then I closed it. When I turned around, I saw that Nana's grandson was still inside. He was talking to Emma as they stood in the middle of the path. They stopped talking as I walked toward them, and I heard him say, "Good-by, Mrs. Higgins, and thank you, indeed." And then, "Good-by, Miss Catriona." And he left us. I wanted to know why he had thanked Emma, but I didn't ask. I put my arm as far as it would go around her waist, and we went back into the house.

"You didn't eat your porridge."

"I'll eat it now."

"It'll be stone-cold."

"It doesn't matter." After I'd eaten it, I went upstairs to the sewing room to ask Jane about the bonfire. She was making small lace-edged sheets for the Mothers' Union Baby Fair. She looked up, thought for a few moments, then answered:

"All right, this year you are old enough to go."

"Oh, Jane! I'll go and tell Emma."

"And I think I'll come with you."

"I'm sorry I was disobedient about running downstairs to the children just now."

"Never mind, it's Guy Fawkes Day." We laughed, and I wished Jane could always be as nice as she sometimes was.

Emma was delighted. I told her I wanted a flour bag for the head of my dummy.

"Now then, Miss Catty . . ." she said, but she went to find one.

I spent the afternoon stuffing an old jacket that we found

in the attic with newspapers and pieces of cloth from Emma's rag bag, and anything else I could find; sewing it together with a large darning needle, threaded with twine; thinking, as I pulled the worn tweed together and stuck the needle through the cloth, of Nana's grandson, talking to Emma, and then of Nana. Nana was dead. For a whole year the cottage next to the wall had been empty. A whole year, I thought. *"Sili fritt, Leisa bela,"* the Faery woman sings in the Dyffryn Wood at dusk. *"Sili fritt, Leisa bela."* Nana had known the Faery tongue and all the true Faery stories. I pulled the twine stitches tightly together, remembering again that day a year ago.

"The child is far too young to see a person who is on the point of death, Mrs. Gwynne-Thomas." Jane and the District Nurse had been in the hall, and the library door was open. I did lessons in the library. They were easy. I hurried through them so that I could spend the rest of lesson time reading the books on the shelves. At the point of death? I had wondered. Who is at the point of death?

"No!" Jane was saying. "It would be most unhealthy."

"All right, Miss Withers, you are Catriona's governess"—I had heard the District Nurse walk to the front door—"but Nana . . ." Nana! Nana is dying. I didn't hear the next words. I listened again. ". . . And Catriona hasn't been to see her for three days, you know."

"I know very well, Mrs. Gwynne-Thomas. I forbade it."

"Please, Miss Withers . . . they love each other very much."

"No."

"Please, Nana is near death."

"Exactly. Why, she might die while the child was there."

"And what would be so wrong?"

"Unthinkable!"

"Indeed?"

"No, Mrs. Gwynne-Thomas! No." Jane's voice had grown higher and shrill. "I'll send Emma with some calf's-foot jelly."

" 'Tis not calf's-foot jelly that Nana is in need of."

I had heard the District Nurse's firm steps as she walked to the wall door and the scrape of it against the gravel path as she closed it. Jane had gone upstairs to dress. She was going for her Thursday-morning coffee with the Vicar's wife. I sat still, holding my pen, looking at the small red lines, in squares, all over the page of the arithmetic exercise book. Jane had come downstairs again, wearing her English tailor-made coat and skirt. It was navy blue, and her hat was navy blue, with a small red feather in it. She had come to the library door and was holding the knob.

"Have you finished your geography?"

I couldn't speak. I nodded.

"Then go and do at least three quarters of an hour on your Czerny and finish the arithmetic I set for you. What a beautiful autumn day it is. We'll go for a walk this after-noon."

Then she had left. Nana was dying. I had listened till Jane shut the wall door, then I dipped my pen in the ink. She would see the sums, but she wouldn't know whether I had practiced the Czerny or not. I finished the arithmetic, quickly and neatly, drawing double lines at the bottom of each sum with the ruler, as Jane liked, and then I went to the broken place in the orchard hedge and climbed through, as I always did when I went to the back door of Nana's cottage.

Nana's bed was in the kitchen-living room, at the front. It was made of dark wood, and the head of it was carved with arches like the ends of the front pews in church. It had been brought downstairs the day that Dr. Fraser told her that she must not get up again. She lay propped up on pil-

lows that looked white as one night's snow, in the autumn
sunlight streaming through the cottage door.

"You look like the Snow Queen, Nana," I had said. "And
your pillows are made of hoarfrost."

"Kishli!" It was her name for me, and meant "Little Thin
One" in the Gypsy language. She and Codger had been
friends to the Welsh Gypsies since they were children, and
old Matthew Bock had ridden horseback all the way from
Bettws-y-Gwerfil, when he heard she was ill, to play "The
Rising of the Lark" for her on his fiddle. "Kishli," she said,
"wonderful it is, indeed. . . . Indeed, and it is wonderful
that you are here." She held out her long, thin hand. "Sit
here beside me on the chair as you ever do." And I had sat
down on the wooden chair, between the fireplace and the
bed. "That's better. Now I can see you clearly, indeed." Her
voice was deep and young. I loved the sound of her voice. I
loved the stories she told and the words she used in the telling. " 'Tis not long that I have, Kishli, and much to say . . .
and indeed to goodness, the words have left me." She held
my hand. Hers was dry and cold. It felt like smooth stone. I
listened. Then a boy had come up the garden path. He stood
in the open door, shutting out the sunlight. "Go away,
Grandson . . . Come later, please," Nana had said.

"Surely to goodness, and that I will . . . and is there
aught that I can bring for you?"

Nana had smiled and shaken her head. He had run away
down the path, and the sunlight flooded the room again.
"He is a good boy, indeed . . . a gentle boy, and understanding"—Nana looked at me—"and you will be friends."
Then holding my hand, she talked softly. "Remember,
Kishli?" Again she told me the stories of Faery and the
Twylyth Teg, the Fair Family, who dwell in the mountains
and inside the lake islands and under the rivers. Snatches of
story, reminding me of the whole; waiting for me to add the

next words; smiling when I did. "You have remembered, Kishli . . . And you will always remember. . . . And now," she said, "which of my pictures will you have?" I had turned to look at the pictures on the wall left of the doorway. Two of them were caught in the sun's rays, but I knew each one of Nana's paintings. Three small views of the mountains, but though the pictures were small the mountains looked huge and rugged. One of Snowden, of Wyddfa, and Llyn Llydaw, with shining water and dark hills, and two of her beloved Cader Idris. Nana had the *hireath,* the longing, for her own mountain; she had been born in a stone cottage, in the depth of the valley that stretches from the sea to Tal-y-Llyn, near to the Rock of the Birds, where the cormorants nest inland; and near to Llyn-y-Cau. Llyn-y-Cau, where, just under the huge, sharp ridge that faces Craig Llwyd, about three feet above the green-gray tarn water, there is a door to the Faery world. Nana said that the door had opened to mortals on the Eve of All Souls, each year, until Goronwy ap Dafydd had become greedy and had stolen a rose from a tree with golden leaves, and had abused the hospitality of the Faery people. Since that day, Nana said, the door on Cader Idris had never opened again.

"May I have the one of Llyn-y-Cau, please?"

"It is yours, Kishli. It has always been yours." And still holding my hand, she had talked again of her Gypsy friends; of Saiporella, her soul-friend, who had thrown old Jasper Boswell's harp into the river just below the bluff, where the current was strong and the water deep, so that no one else should ever play on it. After he died, she had traveled the mountains, her belongings, fire irons, bellows, and copper pans, packed on her donkey's back. I looked at the big brass kettle on the oven at the side of the hearth and the long-handled bellows, with dancing figures carved on them in wood and brass. I knew that Saiporella and Jasper Boswell

had given them to Nana and Codger when they were married, and Jasper had played the harp at their wedding,
when Nana was eighty-two and Codger seventy.

I listened to her voice, and knowing her pain, I had leaned
my cheek against her hand.

"Look up, Kishli." She took her hand away from me and
pointed to the big stone fireplace. "Look you at the kettle-
hook, hanging low to the flames. See how it is changed."
She took my hand again. "See how it glows, Kishli, when it
is touched by fire." Her bright gray eyes caught the firelight.
"Iron is an ancient and magic metal. There is iron in our
blood, Kishli, and love is like fire." She had put her hand
on the plaits, pinned up on my head. I remembered her
touch; strong and gentle, and not light. "Look, Kishli, at
the kettle-hook. See it; and when it hangs, cold and black,
over an empty hearth, and longing is in your heart, remember it as we see it now, together. . . ." It glowed, flame-
golden against the sooty darkness of the chimney back. "And
remember, Kishli, there can be no radiance without love,
and no longing where love has not been." And Nana's eyes
were brighter than the sunlight and the firelight. "Kishli, do
you remember Einion's song?"

Holding her hand, I said:

> "What is longing made from?
> What cloth is put into it
> That it does not wear out with use?
>
> The moon rises and the sun rises,
> The sea rises in vast waves,
> But longing never rises from the heart."

And we had looked at each other. I leaned my cheek again
against her hand.

"Thank you, Kishli." She smiled. "Yes, Kishli, you will

remember." She lay back on the pillows, still smiling, then she closed her eyes. After a while I left. That night she died.

A year and three weeks had passed without her. I finished sewing the dummy and began to stuff the clean flour bag that Emma had found for me with cotton wool. Nana . . . My tears fell on the thick, dry ticking. I worked hard to push the needle through it. When the flour bag was sewn up, my eyes were dry again. I drew a disagreeable face on it, with down-slanting black eyes and a turned-down mouth, with one big tooth and a black mustache. I was proud of my work, and Jane was pleased to see me doing even that much sewing. The dummy was clumsy and fat. I took it downstairs to show Emma.

She was in the little room off the pantry, standing on a chair, taking down from its shelf the large cardboard box in which she kept her Paisley. She never called it her shawl, nor even her Paisley shawl, but always her Paisley. And no one dared to tell her to put on a coat, or even a jacket, when she wore it, however cold the weather; it was too well known that Emma could go to the North Pole in it and be as warm as toast.

I waited while she carried the box to the kitchen table and untied the string carefully, knot by knot, and opened it. She removed all the layers of tissue paper, folding them neatly, and then shook out the heavy, soft folds and laid it, warm and silky, rust-red and brown-green, brown and gold, across the high wooden back of the rocking chair. Then I showed her the Guy I had made.

"Why, indeed to goodness, whatever, and if that isn't a real wicked Guy Fawkes . . ." She laughed and held it aloft. "A real fat old Guy Fawkes, if I do say it . . . and I don't know how we're going to the bonfire at all, at all, and I'm not going to ask." She gave it back to me. "And I think I shall wear my Paisley. It blows cold on the Mochdre Hill these nights."

We set out at dusk in the governess cart. Jane and Emma and the Guy and I. Emma sat across from me, stiffly, almost as stiff as the Guy at my side. Jane sat in front of me, driving. Molly-fach, our pony, began to trot as soon as she was in the Lane, but she made her usual fuss about the cobblestones in the coachyard. There was no one behind us as we went up to the Rise, and the air was still and cold and clear.

I had never seen the countryside after the sun had gone down, except from the garden, across the river to the mountains. I couldn't believe I was out in the dusky world and it was Guy Fawkes Night. I laughed, quietly because of Jane, but Emma saw me and her mouth curled up at the corners and she unstiffened with a sigh and shook her head.

The Lane was unfamiliar in the half-light, and the sounds were different, softer, yet sharper on the ear, and they seemed closer than sounds do in the daylight. Stars came out suddenly, like sparks, and Molly-fach's hoofs on the stony road made a noise I had not heard before, a hollow sound, that echoed. The hedges and trees were almost leafless against the twilight gray, and the Mochdre Hill rose widely dark to the left of us. It looked near and huge. I asked Jane why mountains were like that, sometimes near and sometimes far away, but she only said that the Mochdre Hill was far enough away and that she really didn't know why we were going there at all. So I thought it better not to talk any more for a while.

When we turned the crest of the Rise, Molly-fach trotted faster than ever, and I thought that she, too, liked to be out in the darkness. "Our sister between the shafts," Nana said the Gypsies called the horses that pulled their vans. I laughed again, and watched her fat, silky-round rump moving up and

down as she trotted. From the crest we could see the Old
Roman Road, and a lot of people from the Village, and
from the Mochdre Village, driving or riding or walking toward the Hill, and the night was no longer still. There were
traps and carts and brakes and two milk carts from Myfanwy Jones's Farm, all full of people; bicycles and tandems,
with bright acetylene lamps and hundreds of people on foot.
Those who were walking carried torches that shone, honey-
scarlet, in the gloom. Everyone was talking in singsong
Welsh voices, and laughing, and soon we were caught up in
the throng; Molly-fach settled down to jogging quietly behind the second milk cart, and Emma said to Jane, "Miss
Withers, if I might be so bold as to mention something that
isn't, as you might say . . . that isn't . . ."

"What is it, Emma?" Jane looked at her and turned back
to her driving.

Emma stroked her Paisley, pulling it tight over her large
bosom; then taking a long breath, she said, "Well now, and
it has come to my ears that Mr. Evans has, for no little
time past, look you, been saying that he could do with some
help in the garden . . ." She stopped. I knew then what
she and Nana's grandson had been talking about on the
garden path this morning and why he had thanked her. I
hoped Jane would listen.

"Yes, Emma?" she asked. Emma took another breath.

"Well, Miss Withers, now . . . and Archibald is a good
enough lad, indeed . . ." Archibald, I thought. I hadn't
known his name. "And a good worker, too . . . Well,
Miss Withers, he would like to have the job." Emma sat
back.

Jane, without looking away from the road in front of
her, said, "Thank you, Emma, for your suggestion. Mr.
Evans's sciatica is troubling him, I know, and he does need
help. I know very little about the boy, but I will consider

what you have said." Emma took another breath, and we smiled at each other and did not speak till we reached the foot of the Mochdre Hill.

Jane reined Molly-fach in to the side of the road, by a gate that led into a field, and we all got out. She tied the reins around one of the stumps, leaving enough slack for Molly-fach to eat the grass if she was hungry, and then she told Emma to carry the dummy, but I wanted to carry it myself. Now people were coming from all directions and there was movement and noise. Voices were all around us and we could hear singing on the clear air, coming from the hilltop. The naked flares of the torches made bright swords of flame all up along the dark slopes. I was happy, more excited than I could ever remember. Every other Guy Fawkes Night, I had watched the glow behind the Rise, from the sewing-room window. We began to climb the Hill. As it became steeper, Emma held one arm of the Guy and I the other. When we had almost reached the top, Jane said that she thought we could see everything we wanted to see from where we were, but I said I couldn't throw my Guy onto the bonfire from there, nor dance around it, nor roast chestnuts, so we scrambled to the top, and there we saw the huge pile that was to be the bonfire. Everyone was heaping more and more things onto it. Wood, old chairs and tables, stacks of newspapers, worn-out clothes; anything that would burn, as well as all the Guys. I wondered how they would be able to build it high enough; then I saw Mr. Jones, the butcher, with a stepladder. He leaned it against the strong stake in the center of the heap and climbed halfway up.

"Come up! Come up! One and all! Come and put those Guys where they belong," he shouted. "All Guys this way."

"I'm going to take mine now," I said. Jane still hadn't enough breath after the climb to say "No" or "Wait" before I had run up to the ladder, clutching my dummy proudly.

"Hello, Mr. Jones," I called as loudly as I could. He didn't hear me, but he took it and stuffed it between the legs of a broken chair, about three quarters of the way up.

When all the odd, stuffed figures were on the pile, Mr. Jones climbed down, pushed his way through the crowd, and disappeared. A minute later he came back carrying the biggest Guy I had ever seen, and never even thought of. Everyone began to cheer as he mounted the ladder again, and called out warnings to him as he reeled under the weight of it. Some people were singing. He put it high on the top. It took a while to make it firm, and when it was settled in its place a great shout arose and rolled like thunder around the Hill as the people on the summit and those still climbing the slopes all joined in. Mr. Price, from the White Horse, brought two cans of petrol, and his son, Dylan, followed him with another. Mr. Jones came down the ladder and let Mr. Price climb up. He climbed almost to the top and began to soak the enormous Guy. I had been standing near, to watch.

There were a lot of children, but I couldn't recognize any of them with their black faces and it was now quite dark. After Mr. Price came down the ladder, people began to join hands. I remembered Jane and Emma and turned to look for them. As I turned, I saw the boy, Archibald, at my side.

"I saw you put your Guy on the pile. It was a right big one," he said, and smiled at me for the first time.

"I made it this afternoon. It was big, wasn't it? And ugly?" We laughed, and then Jane and Emma came up. Emma said, "Good evening," to Archibald, and I asked Jane if she had met him. She smiled and said that of course she had. She was looking disapproving again.

Two rings were forming. I wanted to be in the inner ring where the children were, so I pushed through the crowd, away from Jane and Emma. When I held my right hand to the girl next to me, Archibald was there to take my left hand, quickly, and I was happy. He was going to say something, when another huge shout arose, and we formed two circles round the tall pile, and then twenty or thirty people, men and women, ran toward it, each carrying two torches, and stood in a close circle around it, with torches held high above their heads. A second later they had put fire to the pile and another shout arose that must have echoed all through the valley to Conway.

The flames licked and roared, and the two rings of dancers were now going in opposite directions, laughing and shouting and holding hands. The flames were mounting to the top and the dance grew wilder and faster and I thought my legs would give way, but I didn't let go of the girl's hand and Archibald held on to me tightly. The flames rose to the Guy at the top. Now no one was shouting, the pace of the dancing was too fast, and as the fire rose to the body of the wicked Guy Fawkes, suddenly the dance stopped and all the people fell to the ground, still holding hands, and there wasn't a sound in the whole valley except the roar and crackle of the flames until the figure had been burned to ashes.

Then a glad cry sounded through the night and the rings broke and everyone rushed here and there with chestnuts to roast. The boy was still near me.

"What were you going to say?" I asked, but he laughed and said that his pockets were full of chestnuts.

"I'll go and roast some for you."

I wanted to roast my own, but Jane came up and took my hand and I thought it better to stay with her. I looked at the people on the Hill. They looked strange in the light from the fire. One side of their faces, the side turned toward the glow of the bonfire, was bright and all the lines showed clearly. The side away from the flames wasn't there. The half-faced

people, a strange race of magic people, a tribe of the
Bendith-y-Mamau, Faeries, who come out of the hills only
on Guy Fawkes Night. I stood lost in my thoughts.

"It's cold . . . really quite cold, Catriona, have you got
your scarf round your neck?" Oh, Jane, I'm warm. I would
always remember the half-faced people.

I said, "Yes, I have . . . and thank you for bringing me."
Jane smiled; her good smile, so that I knew she had enjoyed herself too. I was happier than ever, and squeezed her
hand; and then Archibald came with hot chestnuts. I had to
drop them quickly from one hand to the other, even with
woolen gloves on, but he could hold them all the time with
one bare hand. Jane ate some too, and a group of men began to sing wildly, and some of the people from the Mochdre
Village began to dance again, wildly too, until the flames
died down, and then the singing was soft and sweet and deep
and everyone listened quietly.

I don't know how long we listened, but when the music
ended the bonfire was just glowing and the top of the Hill
was cold.

"Come along, dear. It's time to go now," Jane said, and
she went across to Emma, who was talking to Mrs. Eyeball,
who washed for the Vicarage, and who had cooked for us
when Emma's sister died and she had to go to Bethesda for
two weeks. People were already turning away happily,
laughing when they missed their footing or trod on a stone.

I said to Archibald, "Thank you for the chestnuts." And
then, "I hope Jane will let you work with Mr. Evans." He
was standing on the slope above me and looked taller than
he was. "How old are you?"

"Thirteen. I left school last summer."

"I'm nine," I said. He looked shy and turned away, and
then Jane and Emma came back.

"May we give you a lift home, Archibald?" Jane asked. I thought he wasn't going to answer, but he did.

"Thank you, indeed, Miss Withers, and I'll go and untie the pony and bring the governess cart to meet you." Jane looked surprised, and then pleased, and said that it would be a great help. Archibald ran quickly down the hillside.

I wondered how he knew where we were tied up, and supposed he'd been in the road as we drove along. We went down the slope, scrambling where it was steep and half running, half walking, as we reached the bottom.

"Try not to stiffen your knees when you come downhill," Jane said, and as we came to the level ground we saw Archibald leading Molly-fach toward us.

I turned and looked back at the Mochdre Hill. It was high and dark and the edge on the Mochdre side was lit by the moonlight, and looked as though frost had fallen along it. The embers gave a warm, pale glow as the bonfire died and the men were still singing a low chant. We climbed into the governess cart.

"Indeed, and I'm sure that I don't know what I'd do without my Paisley," Emma said as she settled into her seat. Archibald took Molly-fach's bridle and led her off the grass onto the road; then he climbed in next to Emma. The singing sounded far away, above the voices of the people, all preparing to go home. Now there were no torches, just the lights of the acetylene lamps on the traps and carts and bicycles. Molly-fach broke into a trot, and Archibald leaned over and put some warm chestnuts into my hand.

When the hard months had passed and the blackbirds began
their song with the first streak of dawn and the bare
branches were covered with a thin veil of pale green, Archibald and I began to race our four swiftest homing pigeons.
We had been caring for them during the winter with good
barley, beans, and grits, and giving them short tosses from
the time they were three months old. We carried them,
sleek and smooth-winged, blue-gray, dun, yellow and blue-
checkered, up the Rise in our hands, their round, black, far-
seeing eyes bright and watchful, and walked for almost a
mile across the sloping Mochdre fields. Then for two miles,
three, and later we took them in a cardboard box with holes
in it and a leather strap around it in the governess cart to
Llanberis. They didn't mind the cold weather, but we never
tossed them when it was wet and misty, which was often;
now the four best had flown twenty miles, and Archibald on
his day off took them up the valley in the cardboard box and
we couldn't wait for Saturday afternoons. We saved our six-
pences for the fare, and Archibald loved the train ride, because Morfran Griffith, the engine driver, let him climb up
into the cabin and drive the train. When he got out, he freed
the birds, leaving fifteen minutes between each toss. Then he
went to visit his uncle and caught the train on its way back.

I waited on top of the coop, huddled in my waterproof Welsh tweed coat against the raw late March winds. Last Saturday the birds had flown forty miles; they would fly the same race today, but the wind would be against them. Sitting there cross-legged, I thought that since Archibald had come to Bryn Llithrig, I had been happier than I could remember. He had been with us since Guy Fawkes Day, five months ago, and he was my friend, as Nana said he would be when he had come to her cottage door on the day she died. Everyone seems happier, I thought.

Mr. Evans was less dour. "He doesn't seem to be forever moaning about his sciatica like he used to, look you," Emma said, "and that lightens the day, indeed to goodness." He left most of the everyday work to Archibald and gave his time to the fruit trees and the rose garden, the lawn borders that were his pride, and his vegetable marrows. Three years ago he had won the first prize at the Agricultural Show, but since the English artist and his wife had come to live beyond the Mochdre Village she had taken the trophy away from him. Mr. Evans was determined to win it back. The honor of the Village was at stake, and now Archibald could trundle all the barrowfuls of manure that were needed. As he tipped it out, mound after mound of it, Mr. Evans spread it carefully with his pitchfork and tended and pruned, while Archibald weeded and troweled, cut the logs and the small wood for the fires, cleaned the stable and harness, and kept Molly-fach well groomed.

I watched the sky, holding the big silver watch that Codger had lent to us. It had black Roman figures and a red minute finger. I timed the first bird from the moment the train arrived at the chosen station, and each fifteen minutes afterward. It was Morfran Griffith's pride that he was rarely a few seconds late. I could hear the loud tick, human-made, exact, among nature's sounds, wind gusts and the cry of wild fowl from the waters, as the thin red minute finger sped around the face of the watch, and suddenly, where a moment before the sky had been empty, there was a tiny speck beyond the empty stone cottage on the bluff. Straight as a dart, the pigeon flew toward the scarlet-painted tarpaulin on the roof of the cote, nearer and nearer till I could see the ring on his pink foot. Then with a swish of strong wings the blue-gray cock bird settled on the ledge. He was always first, but for all our patience he stayed there, fussing and cooing, and wouldn't go inside through the wire trap. The female, dun and white, tall, with a long, graceful neck and high-placed white-ringed eyes, though smaller and slower, alighted and was through the inward-swinging wires in a trice. I was happy when they were all home and fed. We flew them as far from the falcon's haunts as we could, but there were hazards from the peregrines and other stranger prey birds. When one of the homers was late and weary, I knew he had been pursued and had avoided peril. We hadn't lost a pigeon to the hawks, but this was only the third Saturday, and we were training the blue-gray cock bird and the dun female for the Show.

When he had time, Archibald helped Tessie to polish the heavy oak furniture with beeswax, and Jane was delighted with him. "Really," she said one morning at breakfast, "Archibald has become quite indispensable . . . and that reminds me, Catriona . . ." She spoke the words slowly, and I was wondering what she was going to say, when Tessie came into the dining room and stood there with her hands behind her back.

"Miss Withers, begging your pardon, but Emma says would you like a lemon spongecake for tea this afternoon, or a simnel?"

I liked Tessie. She was fifteen and had come to work at Bryn Llithrig last year when she left school. Emma had known her since she was a child, and she was plump, had curly brown hair, brown eyes, and pimples on her face, but she was pretty.

"Oh, Tessie, lemon sponge, I think, thank you."

Then Jane turned to me. I wondered what I had done. Her face was set and disapproving.

"Catriona, I have something to say to you." She poured herself another cup of coffee, with milk, and took four lumps of sugar. "There is something you do not seem to realize." She sipped her coffee, put the cup back firmly in the saucer, wiped her lips on her napkin, and said, "Archibald is paid to work for five days a week. Five days, Catriona."

I waited.

"These Saturday pigeon races must stop. Archibald is a good-natured boy and he must not be asked to do more then he is meant to do, more than it is right that he should do. It is an imposition, Catriona, to send him all the way up the valley with those birds in a box."

"But, Jane, he loves to take them. We have tossed the birds, trained them, and nurtured them since they were three months old."

"Nonsense!"

"And, Jane, Archibald's so happy because when he built the pigeon cote Mr. Evans said he was right handy with his tools, indeed, and now he lets Archibald build more things in the garden, and Archibald likes to build things, and if he hadn't built the cote Mr. Evans wouldn't have known he was handy, and—"

"Catriona, please!" Jane sighed. "You do run on so. Archibald only takes the wretched birds because you ask him to and he feels he cannot refuse."

"That's not true, Jane."

"Catriona!"

"But, Jane—"

"Enough! From now on Saturday pigeon races are out of the question. Archibald must have his day off to do with as he wishes."

"But it is what he wishes."

"How dare you answer back to me, Catriona? You will learn six verses of 'The Inchcape Rock' before lessons. I will hear them at lunch time. I am tired of your insubordination." She poured herself a third cup of coffee. "Furthermore, there will be no walk with the puppy this afternoon."

"Jane, but—"

"He gets all the exercise he needs in the coachyard and chewing up the kitchen rug, as well as everything else he sees. And remember, it is Wednesday. The Vicar's wife is coming to tea." Jane put three more lumps of sugar in her cup. "You are excused," she said.

The Vicar's wife had come to tea every Wednesday for as long as I could remember. I folded my napkin, stood up, and pushed the heavy oak chair against the table. As I walked across the hall to the library, I wondered how I could tell Archibald. He would be as disappointed as I was, but not as angry, I thought. Archibald was slow to anger. I took the clean, new-looking book of *Collected Poems* out of the drawer in my desk and sat down with my elbows on the blotting pad and my chin on my hands.

"The Inchcape Rock." I hated it. "Sir Ralph the Rover sailed away . . . "! I couldn't keep my mind on the words. I looked up at the library windows. Five tall windows, low onto the carved-oak, crimson-cushioned window seat. Beautiful windows with small diamond-shaped panes, leaded, with pictures in the glass; animals, griffins, and a knight; a lady, old-fashioned letters, and a unicorn, their colors clear in the rain-washed light of the April morning. I looked down again and tried to learn the verses. "Sir Ralph the Rover sailed away, and scoured the seas for many a day . . ."

My mind wandered. Owein . . . the prince who does not grovel . . . Trystan . . . and Esyllt sang this englyn . . .

> There are three trees that are good,
> The holly, the ivy and the yew.
> They keep their leaves while they last
> And Trystan shall have me as long as he lives.

The book of translations from the Welsh was in its place on the shelf. I was careful now. Jane's annoyance about my reading the books in the library had grown, and I no longer left them on the small round table by my red plush chair, where one day she had found the *Mabinogion* and opened it at the page where Arthur ". . . seized the mouth of the cave, and from thence he took aim at the hag, with Carnwennan, his knife, and struck her through the middle till she was like two tubs, and Arthur's warrior took the witch's blood and kept it with him . . ."

"Those uncouth, horrible stories," Jane had said.

I looked at the book on the shelf, faded with age, the gold letters of the title almost rubbed away. After a while I learned the verses and began lessons.

That afternoon I didn't take Paddy for a walk, but we went out, down the coachyard steps, Paddy stumbling and tumbling and slipping on the damp stone and then running ahead through the archway to the rose garden. He waited for me by the sundial. I picked him up and ran past the vegetable-marrow patch and the birch grove; then I put him down and we went together through the orchard to the river path, but not out onto the path, that would have been a walk. Up to the end of the orchard was still part of the garden. The river was in thaw spate. I called Paddy back from the wave-lapped edge. He came, wriggling and yelping and wagging his tail. He was a Welsh springer, liver and white, with wide shoulders and strong pads. His long curly ears were low down on his head and his eyes, which showed white at the corners when he had chewed something he shouldn't, were like brown velvet. Myfanwy Jones had given him to me. I thought it was because she had heard about big Brindley-Flopsy. I turned to walk back, thinking of my rabbit, speckled brown and silky-soft, her nose twitching while she nibbled long leaves of London lettuce, all around the tender stalk; her ears tall and straight and her little front feet together. I had been helping her to have her babies, and when I was gently rubbing her stomach and the third one was coming out Jane had found me. "Vermin!" she said. "And you've got blood on your hands. It makes me quite sick." The next day she had told Mr. Evans to drown them. "When you learn to keep animals in their place, you will be allowed to keep them—and close to your person is not their place."

I had been in the kitchen when Merfyn Jones put Paddy into my arms. "Myfanwy sent him to you," he said.

The puppy pushed away from me with his damp pads. He felt strange and afraid, twisting about in my grasp. I talked to him, and he looked up at me. Then he licked my face, and I couldn't believe he was mine.

"Thank you, Merfyn Jones . . . and please thank Myfanwy, and tell her I'm going to call him Paddy because of his big strong pads. Tell her I'll come over to the Farm tomorrow."

Merfyn Jones patted the puppy's head and pulled his ear. "He's a dog, so there'll be no trouble about breeding," he said.

Myfanwy and Merfyn Jones owned the Farm. It was called the Farm because it was the largest for miles around.

Myfanwy Jones and Merfyn, and their cousin Penry, who was the Village builder and carpenter, had always smiled at me in church, as Ellen did; since Guy Fawkes Day almost everyone smiled, but Jane was strict about it, and didn't let me stop and talk to the children after the service.

Now Paddy came around my feet, biting my ankles, and I stopped thinking to play with him. In and out of the trees and around the raspberry and gooseberry bushes we chased until suddenly, as I paused to look at the first tiny green shoots, I saw that the light had changed. I looked at my watch. It was five minutes past four. "Come on, Paddy. We're late." I ran on, but Paddy was tired now. I went back, picked him up, and hurried to the house.

"You'd better be quick and get changed, look you now," Emma said, and Tessie took Paddy in her arms and stroked him.

I ran upstairs, took off my bloomers, and pushing my sandals off with my feet, pulled my jersey over my head. While I was pinning my plaits up more tidily, the outside bell rang. I heard the scrape of the wall door on the gravel path. Why couldn't the Vicar's wife come at the right time, just once, and not ten minutes early? I took my navy blue velvet dress from the wardrobe. It had buttons down the back. Small, round velvet buttons. I ran to the bathroom and scrubbed my hands and hurried downstairs.

"You know, the child uses the most outrageous language," Jane was saying, and I stopped behind the Japanese screen, outside the drawing-room door. "Sometimes I hardly know what she is talking about."

"Her eyes, too," the Vicar's wife said. "It can't be good for her eyes, all this reading."

"Such tiny print . . . and the horrible words in those musty old books. Really, I'm so worried."

"Yes. The fine print is very injurious. My dear brother,

Sir Phillip, you know, he blames absolutely the studying he
did in his youth for his bad eyesight now."

"But your brother is such a handsome man, the eyeglasses
don't matter in the least. For a girl it's different, as the District Nurse said."

"Indeed?" The Vicar's wife sounded cross. "Well, I
wouldn't pay too much attention to what that woman says.
The Vicar calls her progressive, but I told him he'd do well
to ask the Mothers' Union what they think of her, with her
sterilize this and sterilize that."

"She seems to be a good woman, I think, but meddlesome.
She annoyed me very much at the time of old Nana's death."

"I remember that. On a Thursday morning, wasn't it?
You came for coffee. That was about the child too."

I stood there, quiet as a shrew mouse. I knew it was wrong
to listen, but I couldn't move.

"It most certainly was," Jane said. "The District Nurse
actually wanted Catriona to go and see the old woman on
the very day she died. Thank goodness I put a stop to it."

"I should say so." I heard the Vicar's wife drink her tea.
She had big, long, stuck-out teeth. Her lips never covered
them, so that she looked as though she were laughing when
she wasn't at all. "Very odd, Miss Withers, that friendship
between the child and an old Village woman . . ."

"Most detrimental," Jane said, "and there seemed to be
nothing I could do about it. Catriona sneaked away to see her.
I couldn't be watching her every moment. I'm sure it was all
the stories that old woman told her that started this reading
nonsense."

"Certainly the child needs discipline. Particularly, if I
may say so, Miss Withers, being the child of her parents."

"You're so right. I often think of that myself . . . so
spoiled and reckless . . . hunting in Ireland, polo in India,

parties and balls . . . not a useful day in her whole life."

She birthed me, I thought; then listening to Jane's cold voice, wondered if that was useful at all.

"Drowned, weren't they?" the Vicar's wife asked.

"Yes, in a mountain lake. They were up at a hill station . . . Naini Tal. . . . My cousin brought the child back to England, you know."

"Really? No, I didn't."

"She was governess to a neighboring family—the Colonel's family—she said the dinghy smashed like matchwood in the fury of the sudden storm."

"Such a tragedy. I saw her pictures at the time, in the newspapers. She was quite beautiful."

"Irish," Jane said, and I held my stomach.

"Well, the guardians seem to be responsible people . . ."

"If they were ever in England."

"I must say, Miss Withers, they were most fortunate to find you."

"Through my cousin, and of course, my own credentials . . . and I must say they are completely to be relied upon, and of course, Mr. Amphlett, the solicitor, is a charming man. But it isn't easy. I'm very upset. Catriona is willful and disobedient. I'm really at my wit's end."

"Be firmer, Miss Withers. Be stricter. As we said . . . her heritage . . ."

"If only there were no *library* in this house . . . all those books . . . far beyond her years."

"My dear, remember what my dear brother always says: 'Where there's a will there's a way.' And remember how he lived up to his maxim last year, when he dealt with those revolting factory workers."

"Oh, I do! Yes! He was splendid."

"The iron hand in the velvet glove," his sister said.

"But dealing with Catriona is different. I never actually catch her reading those books. At times I think she's thoroughly underhanded and deceitful."

"There's just one thing to do—"

"Oh dear," Jane interrupted her, "I wonder where she is. I told her to change her clothes and come to tea. If she's taken that puppy for a walk . . ."

"Just one quite simple solution, Miss Withers. Lock her out of the library. Just simply lock the library door."

My breath caught in my throat, I almost choked. Jane wouldn't do that. Often she didn't understand, but she wasn't cruel. I knew I couldn't go into the drawing room for tea. I turned and crept along the hall and up the stairs to my room, took off my dress and hung it up, and then took off my slippers and socks and lay on the bed, thinking. I had never known anything but this house, Jane, Emma, Mr. Evans, and Betty Eyeball, who had worked for us before Tessie came. I had been a year old when the accident happened.

After the Vicar's wife left, Jane came to my room. "Why didn't you come to tea? Did you disobey me and take that puppy for a walk?"

"No, Jane. I felt sick. I'm sorry." She put her hand on my forehead.

"You've no fever, but you'd better stay in bed this evening and I'll send Tessie up with some camomile tea. I shall be out to dinner. I'm playing whist at the Vicarage." She left me, and after she had changed and gone to her party I went downstairs and read for more than two hours, curled up in my red plush chair. When I put the book back on the shelf and went to bed again, I thought that Jane was right about my being deceitful, and I was sorry.

Mr. Evans sent the pigeons to his nephew in Beddgelert, and Archibald used the wood and wire netting of their cote, with two panes of glass, to make a cucumber frame. When I told him what Jane had said, the blood rose to his face and went away, leaving it white. His eyes looked dark blue. He didn't say anything, and we never talked about the pigeons again.

We went bird's nesting in the woods and among the rushes and moss-covered rocks along the streams, we searched for otter holts. We tried to teach Paddy to retrieve, but he still chewed everything he fetched, and Archibald said, "He's still a small puppy, Miss Catty, look you, let him play while he can." So training stopped, but Paddy rarely left my side, and lay under the desk while I did lessons.

Spring had come early. There was a morning haze on the full river, the days were balmy, and the orchard grass was bright with wild flowers, and on a May afternoon Jane asked Archibald if he thought he could clean the chimneys. He waited a moment and then said, "Surely to goodness, and why not, indeed?"

There was an old flue brush in the tool shed, and when we went to look for it he said to me, "I'll ask Penry Jones how to clean them without making too much mess; I've never done it before, look you."

About two weeks later, when the weather was mild enough to be without the fires, he set about his task. Jane said she was driving to Capel Curig in the governess cart to lunch with the Girls' Friendly chairwoman and discuss the joint bazaar.

"Now cover all the furniture with sheets, Emma," she said as she put on her yellow wash-leather gloves, "and see that there is as little mess as possible . . . and that you and Tessie have everything shipshape on my return."

"It's a dirty job, Miss Withers."

"It needn't be," Jane said, and buttoning her gloves, left the house.

I followed Archibald to each fireplace. Tessie had covered everything, and Emma and I and Mr. Evans and Idris Williams, the post, who had come to deliver a letter for Jane from Mr. Amphlett, the solicitor, waited till Archibald had climbed inside the hearth; then we held two heavy blankets across the opening while he scraped all the soot he could reach with his scraper into a sack. Then he handed the sack to Mr. Evans and we gave him the flue brush. It was made of two jointed rods of cane, like a fishing rod, and there was a stiff-bristled brush at the end of it that stayed furled, like an umbrella, while it was being pushed up the chimney and opened as it came out at the top. When it was hauled down, the stiff bristles loosened the soot, which Archibald caught in a big sack.

As soon as he was ready to push the flue brush up the high, narrow part, I ran outside to watch the round stiff bristles burst open at the top of the long, slender chimney. There were four in the big center stack, with wide decorated rims around the mouths of them, and others, single and in pairs, and different lengths, stood out of the uneven sea-green, purple-blue slated roof. The stone chimneys were not whitewashed, like the half-timbered walls of the house. I watched the sooty brush bob up, open, waver, and disappear inside the two that served the dining room and Jane's bedroom, and then I went to watch the center stack over the high pointed porch. I loved the gay timber patterns on it, in squares and triangles, and the straight front-lawn path, flanked with poplar trees leading to the heavy carved-oak front door. By the time the center stack was cleaned, I had a crick in my neck, so I didn't stay to watch the others on the right side of the roof, and went back to the kitchen.

Emma was smiling and merry. "I've never seen a neater job, look you . . . not even when the real chimney sweep came from the Junction, years ago. The lad's a wonder, he is, indeed."

Archibald did the kitchen chimney last. We all helped, holding the blankets and taking the bags of soot and getting blacker and blacker.

"'Tis a pity we can't use it to make floors like they did in the old days," Emma said, "and Miss Catty-fach, you'd better go and get cleaned up and your lessons done. I'll send Tessie up to the bathroom when you're through."

I nodded, but waited till Archibald stepped down from behind the iron bars of the grate, bringing a last cloud of soot with him. His eyes looked china blue in his black face, and when he took off the soot-caked peaked cap he had been wearing his hair shone bright, orange-red. Emma said, "That was a fine morning's work, Archibald," and then, "Tessie, put the kettle on; we'll all have a cup of tea before we clean up ourselves or anything else."

"What about a drop of that rhubarb wine that's in the dresser cupboard?" Idris Williams, the post, asked, and Emma turned to him.

"And for what would you be deserving that, indeed? I haven't seen you exerting yourself overly, look you." Then she said, "Miss Catty-fach, you're about the cleanest of the lot of us, and it's no use spreading the dirt." She laughed. "I don't know as you are, at that . . . anyways, get it out for me and then away you go. Lessons, Miss Catty; there's no use courting trouble."

I took the rhubarb wine from the cupboard and put it on the kitchen table, and then I went upstairs and bathed and changed my clothes and went down to the library. I finished lessons quickly and went to my chair and read till lunch time; after lunch too, with Paddy on my knee.

When I heard the sound of Molly-fach's hoofs coming

down the Rise, I put the book back on the shelf, and as Jane came in I was at my desk, doing algebra, Paddy at my feet.

Since the day Merfyn Jones gave him to me, Paddy had slept on the window seat in my bedroom, and whenever Jane came to look he was curled up on the cushion, asleep. By the end of the day he was tired, and he looked small and young, lying there. But one morning, after I dressed, we were playing together and he jumped up onto the bed. "Paddy, down! Here, Paddy, come down." I was about to pick him up, when Jane came in.

"I knew it! I knew it. I should never have allowed that puppy upstairs. He has been sleeping on your bed."

"No, Jane. He hasn't. We were playing. It's the very first time he's ever been on the bed—truly, Jane."

She looked down at me and shrugged her shoulders. "I should have known . . . give you an inch and you take a mile. Take him downstairs immediately, and come to breakfast," she said, and that night she closed him in the kitchen. There was no need to lock the door that led from the kitchen to the hall, it had a large iron bolt, which was rarely used. Jane used it.

Paddy whined and cried for me even though Emma tried to comfort him. I listened as long as I could; then crept down, avoiding the creaks on the stairs, onto the cold flagstones, and to the kitchen door. Paddy knew I was there. He stopped scraping along the bottom of the door with his claws and crying, so that when I pulled the stiff, heavy bolt the rasping sound echoed through the house. I heard Jane strike a match, and then saw the candlelight from the landing as she opened the door of her room. I hadn't time to latch the door. I sped across the hall and up the stairs, three at a time. My bare feet made no noise, and when Jane came to my room I was in bed. She stood above me. I could see the light from her candle through my closed eyelids. Please let

her go to bed again, I prayed. Paddy, hush! Quiet! Or she'll
go downstairs and find the kitchen door unlatched. She
didn't speak, and the light went away. I listened to her steps,
holding my breath. She went downstairs. She trod on every
creak. When she tried the latch on the kitchen door, I knew it
was no use to pretend any longer. She closed it with a firm
scrape. I sat on the bed and waited for her.

"Catriona, you have been downstairs . . . and in your
bare feet, I suppose." She was wearing a blue crepe-de-chine
dressing gown and Indian slippers with turned-up toes and
golden embroidery on them. Her fair hair was in a plait. It
had fallen over her shoulder. She looked pretty and young.
Her eyes were pale blue, like the dressing gown. "If there's
any more nonsense about that puppy, I shall send him away
till he is grown-up and properly trained."

"Jane! No!"

"Keeping the whole household awake with his whining . . ."

"He wouldn't if—"

"You are nine years old, and all this reading of adult
books and childish fairy stories is absurd and must stop. It is
bad for you, and it must stop."

That's not fair, Jane. I didn't say it, but I wanted to say
that reading had nothing to do with Paddy and Brindley-
Flopsy and the pigeons, that always when she scolded me for
other things it was my reading the books in the library that
made her angry.

"I can't think why they don't send you away to school like
any other child. . . . Tomorrow you will do arithmetic
and algebra all morning and maps in the afternoon, and
don't try to get out of it."

"Jane, I won't . . . and I promise faithfully that Paddy
never slept on my bed . . . and he doesn't wake up the
house when he sleeps near me. Jane, please, couldn't he sleep

outside my door? On the floor, outside . . . it couldn't do any harm, and he'll be good as gold, I promise. He's small and lonely and afraid. Jane, let him."

"No!" Jane put the candle on the bed table. "Get into bed." She tucked the bedclothes in at the foot. "No, Catriona, once and for all, and remember what I say." She straightened up and stood at the foot of the bed, stiff in the flickering candlelight. "The place for a dog is out of doors. While he is a puppy, I will allow him in the kitchen, but if I find him anywhere else in the house—anywhere, do you understand? —back to the Farm he will go." She picked up the candle again and stood over me, and as she held it one side of her face was lit and the other dark. I thought of the half-faced people on the Mochdre Hill on Guy Fawkes Night, but Jane was not one of them.

And she did send Paddy away.

It was my own fault. While she was at the bazaar meeting, I had him on my knee again, in the library, while I was reading. When Jane came to see afternoon lessons, she found white hairs stuck in the red plush of my chair. Next day, Merfyn Jones came to take him to the Farm.

He came into the coachyard, leaving the small milk cart outside the wide gateway. I had been giving Molly-fach her sugar. I ran across the cobbles to meet him.

"Good morning, Merfyn Jones."

"Why now, look you, Miss Catty." He looked down at me. He was tall and broad-shouldered and dark, and he had all his own teeth, which was a good thing because he laughed a lot, like his sister, Myfanwy, but he wasn't laughing now. "Where is he, Miss Catty?"

"Who? Archibald, Mr. Evans?"

"No. The puppy." I was standing near the kitchen steps. I sat down on the second one because the earth seemed to stand up. "It won't be for long, Miss Catty-fach . . . and you can see him every day." He was awkward and uncomfortable. Jane seemed to cause so many people to do what they didn't want to do.

"He'll soon grow up, won't he?"

"Before you can say knife. He will, indeed."

"I'll go and fetch him." I got up and turned away just in time, and the tears splashed down the front of my jersey. I ran through the archway to the rose garden and leaned against the ivy-covered wall, pressing my head against the stone. I felt the cool, smooth leaves, and after a while something crawled on my face. I remembered that Jane said if an insect went up my nose it would eat my face away from the inside. I jumped away and the insect fell to the ground. It was an earwig.

I found Paddy chewing on one of Jane's buckskin shoes. She had left them in the kitchen to be cleaned. I picked him up, but he wouldn't let go of it. He was warm and soft and silky and fat. He kicked and wriggled; then he licked me and the shoe dropped. My tears fell all over him. I looked at the shoe on the ground and knew it was wrong to feel as I felt. I turned and walked to where Merfyn Jones was waiting. He held out his strong hands and took Paddy gently, and stroked his head. Paddy licked his chin. I stood there and watched him walk away, up the cobbled slope to the gates, and still holding Paddy in the crook of his left arm, untie the reins and get up into the milk cart. He drove away without looking back.

I sat down again on the kitchen steps, and after a while the hot, quiet tears spilled over. I wasn't crying, but the tears wouldn't stop. I wasn't thinking, but I could feel Brindley-Flopsy's thick, fine, silky fur; the smooth, strong wing quills of the pigeons, their velvet backs, and the warm, fat softness of Paddy and his hard, big pads. Paddy . . . I put my head in my arms against the stone side of the steps, and the sobs came up from my stomach.

It seemed hours later that I heard a loud honk. Then two more. It was Mr. Jones, the butcher, in his Ford motorcar. I remembered, he was coming to pick up Jane. She and the Vicar's wife were going to Llandudno, shopping. I sat up, pulled a handkerchief from the leg of my bloomers, blew my nose and wiped my eyes, and listened. Mr. Jones charged by the hour, and his motorcar was used for weddings and christenings, Bank Holiday picnics, honeymoons, and other special journeys. It was the only car in the Village. I heard the wall door open and close. Then the metallic clang of the car door and the voice of the Vicar's wife. Mr. Jones cranked up the engine. I listened till the sound of it died away down the Hill Lane.

Jane had gone. My head ached with crying, but I thought of my chair and my books. I'll do arithmetic and other lessons like lightning, and no piano practice at all, I thought. Then I can read for hours and hours. I tucked the handkerchief back into the leg of my bloomers, got up from the steps, and hurried in to begin lessons.

The library door was locked. I tried to turn the large wooden knob. The oblong oak panels blurred in front of my eyes. I tried again, this time with both hands, and pushed with all my strength. I don't know how long I stood there, outside the strong barred door, seeing through the dark solid wood into the forbidden room. My red plush chair, the small round table, the books, ". . . and Excalybur gave a light like thirty torches . . . and the Damozel came to Arthur and saith, 'King, this Sword is mine. . . .' " Standing there, still clutching the doorknob, I thought of Culhooc at Arthur's gate, " '. . . and if you do not open to me, I will bring ill-fame and dishonor to your lord, and I will give

three screams before this gate and all the pregnant women
in this court shall miscarry . . .' " Three screams. My
hands turned the knob again, hopelessly. I stayed there till
my fingers were stiff and cramped. "Just simply lock the library door." I could hear the high, busy voice of the Vicar's
wife. I moved my hands from the knob. As I opened and
closed them to ease the stiffness, I could see the lines inside,
shining with damp. My thoughts seemed to stop. I felt cold
and clear and tall. Everything looked small and bright and
far away, and there were no shadows. Emma called from
the kitchen, "Miss Catty, do you want your milk?" The
crevices between the large stone flags in the hall looked like
problems in geometry. Thoughts came back. The library
windows. One of them would be open. Jane would not have
closed them all. "For goodness' sake! Who's closed all the
windows? The fug in this house." Jane would not have
closed all the windows, it was almost June. The stairs looked
near again, and the shadows came back. "In a minute,
Emma," I called, and ran out of the front door and around
the house onto the side lawn. Five windows, low to the
ground. All closed. Were they locked inside? I walked
slowly to the first one. When I came close, I could see
through the small golden-yellow pane. The iron fastener
was snug and secure in its socket.

The rays of the morning sun threw dapples on the shiny
dark-wood floor boards, aslant the white skin rug in front of
the fireplace, and halfway up the bookcase on the left wall,
lighting the fawn-colored bindings of the English novelists.
The sunlight was almost touching my chair. My crimson
chair, with its curved carved legs, like a griffin's. "Arthur
. . . Owein, easy in adversity . . ." Now the light touched
the claws of the chair foot and lit up the place where Paddy
had sat at my feet. Sitting on the stone sill, I cupped my
hand around my eyes. My chair looked brown through the

dark green pane. I lowered my hand and leaned my forehead against the cool glass. "Owein . . ." I wondered how it was to be, easy in adversity. "Owein . . . the prince who does not grovel . . . Banner of Arthur with Black-banded Shield, sinisterwise across a fair gold ground. . . . 'Here, let me tell you what I saw . . . O Shield and Sword of Arthur . . . in my swooning, I saw that which I saw . . . In my swooning . . .' "

There was no sound on the still, early summer air. "Peredur, Einion . . . Efnision . . . He whose hand and eye are gentle . . . Locked away . . . Forbidden." Paddy . . . Forbidden . . . I turned and rose slowly from the window sill. Forbid. Forbid. Always forbid. My face felt stiff, and the roots of my hair were tight. I could feel every hair separately. A slow shiver crept through my body, and I felt the damp across my forehead and above my ears, cool in the breeze.

I walked across the lawn and down the steps to the rose garden. There were large uneven stones along the edge of the path. I looked for the smallest. It was large, but I moved it easily. I didn't drop it when I saw the crawling things in the earth that stuck to it. Without strain or hurry I carried it up the steps and across the lawn, back toward the library windows. A new pane would be colorless, ugly. I came to the first window. I saw the small knight in armor, his long-toed feet turned outward, looking at the coat of arms in the russet pane above him. I smiled at him and lifted the stone. It had no weight in my hand. I held it for a moment; then there was a sound, silvery-sharp, and silence. I put my hand through the jagged hole and lifted the strong latch from its socket, opened the window and climbed into the room.

3

The scraping sound of the wall door on the gravel path made me remember the world I lived in. Jane was back from Llandudno. My heart beat in my throat. I looked at the marble clock on the library mantelpiece. It was ten minutes past one o'clock. I had been reading for four hours; I had forgotten lessons. Jane came into the hall and went upstairs to her room. I looked at the broken windowpane. ". . . and the Eagle said, '. . . I have a stone, and from its head I pluck the stars at evening. . . .' " A stone . . . My heart stopped and started again. I put the big book on the small table next to my chair. Now it didn't matter if Jane found it. She was coming downstairs. "Catriona," she called. Then she called again, louder and more slowly, "Catriona." I heard her go into the kitchen. She would come back into the hall; soon she would go into the garden, and then she would see the window. I knew I should never be allowed in the library again. I looked for a book to take with me before I left. The Welsh ones were big and hard and worn. Too big to hide in my bloomers. The poems! Keats and Shelley, Wordsworth, Tennyson . . . They were small and soft. I went to the poetry shelf. They were smaller than I remembered, and bound in wine-colored leather.

"Catriona." Jane had come back into the hall. My heart was beating as though I had been running. "Catriona, where are you?" I tucked Shelley into my left bloomer leg and Keats into my right and went to the window. My fingers trembled as I lifted the latch. I climbed out, ran across the lawn, down the steps and through the rose garden to the broken orchard hedge. I clambered through it, stumbling, and ran to the back door of Nana's cottage.

I leaned against the door to get my breath, then I went into the front room and sat on the chair by Nana's bed. I had a stitch in my side. The pain was sharp. I bent over and pulled my knees up to my chin, clasping my hands around them, but the stitch didn't go away. I wished I had waited in the library for Jane, that I hadn't broken the window. The stone! It must still be lying there on the ground, where I had let it fall from my hands before I climbed inside. I began to tremble, and held my knees tighter. Boys run away to sea. Where do girls run to? I looked at the hearth. The kettle-hook was almost lost in the blackness. I tried to remember Nana's words, to remember the golden glow of it, but it was gray-brown and cold. I felt alone and afraid. The stitch had gone. I climbed into Nana's bed and pulled the patchwork quilt over me. For a while I lay there, sick with the thought of what I had done. Then I fell asleep.

It was almost dark when I wakened, and remembered. It's late, I thought. Jane will be worried. I didn't want her to be worried. I sat up. I must go and confess. My heart began to thump again. I took a deep breath and climbed off the big bed. Then I heard voices in the Lane. The gate creaked open. I got back into bed and pulled the quilt up over my head. The shaking began again. My teeth chattered. There were footsteps on the path, and then the door opened. I lay as flat as I could under the thick quilted patchwork. Jane came in.

"Bring the lantern, Codger, it's dark in here." I heard her walk to the windows.

"She wouldn't be here, not now that Nana is dead." It was the Vicar's wife. Then I heard Codger's slower steps.

"Kishli comes here, I know. I come here myself."

"Please don't call the child by that silly name." Jane went into the scullery.

"Here, give me the lantern," the Vicar's wife said, and I heard her coming toward the bed. There was silence for a moment, then I felt the quilt move. She pulled it off me, onto the floor. "She's here," she said, holding the lantern over me. "Here in the bed, and with her shoes on . . . all muddy . . . Just look at the bedcover . . . the dirty, wicked girl." Jane came back and stood at the end of the bed. I could feel her rage.

"Get up, Catriona." Her voice was hard. "Get up." I sat up. "Get off the bed." I moved to the side near to the fireplace, away from the Vicar's wife.

"What's this?" The Vicar's wife caught hold of my right leg. "Why, the child's got something stuck inside her bloomers." She put the lantern on the floor and tried to hold me while she took the small book. I fought. I almost hit her teeth. I could have. They were in front of me and my left arm was free. Instead I kicked with both legs and got away from her, and sat on the wooden chair. Jane came between the fireplace and the bed. I clasped my hands around my knees.

"What have you got there?" The Vicar's wife was holding up the lantern again.

"It's a book of some kind."

"It would be. Give it to me." Jane pulled me out of the chair, and then holding my shoulders, she shook me till I was dizzy and my eyes felt as though they would fall out. I thought my head would leave my neck. "Give it to me," she said again. I pulled the volume of Shelley out of the left leg of my bloomers and gave it to her. She threw it on the bed. "Now go home. Go to your room and wait for me there." She pulled me into the middle of the floor and thrust me toward the door. I stumbled and almost fell. Codger was looking out of the window, into the darkness. He didn't turn around. I went through the open gate and up the Lane to the wall door. It was open. Emma was sitting on the iron seat near the path.

"Emma!" I ran to her.

"Oh, Miss Catty-fach . . . Miss Catty . . ." She held me for a moment, warm and safe. Then she got up and pushed me away. She held my shoulders, and her hands were gentle and firm. "Miss Catty-fach . . . Oh, Miss Catty . . . I've been that worried . . . All day . . . And that library window . . . Oh, Miss Catty, she was that mad." Emma's round, fat, jolly face was pinched and gray.

"Oh, Emma, I'm sorry . . . Please forgive me. I'll never do anything, ever again, to make you look like this." She sighed heavily, as she always did. Then she smiled.

"There's nothing to forgive, Miss Catty . . . nothing at all . . . but look you, Miss Withers mustn't find me here with you. She'll be here in a minute." Emma gave me a quick, tight hug. "You're going to catch it." She sighed again.

"I know."

"You'd better go to your room and wait for what's coming to you."

Jane didn't return for an hour. I supposed that she'd gone to the Vicarage. I had no supper, and she didn't come near me that night. The next morning Emma called me from halfway up the stairs. She never even went down the wide, shallow coachyard steps if she could help it. "I'm all right on the flat," she would say, but she was heavy and her varicose veins gave her more pain than she would admit.

"Don't come any farther, Emma," I said. "You shouldn't have come this far."

"Good morning to you, Miss Catty-fach."

"Good morning, Emma."

"Well, and it's not such a good morning at that," she said. "Miss Withers is in a fine royal rage, and that's for sure to goodness. She says that you are to report to her in the sewing room at nine o'clock, so you'd better get dressed."

"Do I have breakfast first?"

"No, you don't . . . and indeed, I never saw the like of it . . . a growing child and no supper and no breakfast."

"Oh, Emma, never mind. I won't die."

"That you won't!" said Emma, pulling a package from the pocket of her apron. "Here, take this . . . and it's me that'll be a-dying if I have to come up these stairs again." We laughed quietly. It was good to laugh. I wanted to help her downstairs, but I knew she wouldn't like me to. I went back to my room and opened the packet. It was a sandwich. Two slices of Emma's bread, spread thickly with Myfanwy Jones's butter and filled with two almost hard-boiled eggs mixed with crumbled bacon.

At nine o'clock I went into the sewing room. Morning sunlight flooded through the garden side of the big bow window. Jane was sitting on the window seat. She was wearing a blue and mauve striped shirt blouse, and the bright beams lit up her fair hair. She looks pretty, I thought.

"Stand up straight and don't slouch," she said, and her teeth barely opened as she spoke. She stood up. "Catriona, you are disobedient and destructive." Her small pale blue eyes became narrow. She wasn't pretty now. "I am utterly disgusted at what you did yesterday. Utterly disgusted. The

violence of it. That you could even lift that piece of rock"—
I had known she would find it—"let alone carry it up from
the rose garden"—she shuddered—"and to hold it, all
crawling and dirty, in your hands, and then deliberately . . .
with intention . . . to smash the window." She stepped
toward me. "Catriona, you are worse than a thief . . . a
hooligan. Children not so fortunate as you have been sent to
Borstal for less." Her breath whistled through her clenched
teeth. "I've been far too lenient with you"—she walked to
the sewing table—"far too lenient." She turned to look
down at me. "From now on you will be most strongly disciplined." Her voice rose, and was shrill. "And now you
will apologize to me for your violent and disgusting be-
havior."

"Oh, Jane, I'm so sorry. I'm truly sorry."

"Say it again."

"I'm sorry, Jane. Please believe me, I'm so sorry." She
smiled at me. Her bad smile.

"So it's as easy as that?" She sat down on the chair near
to the table. "Well, I'm unable to believe you. With your
head full of nonsense as it is and your bad, deceitful disposi-
tion, Catriona, I can't believe a word that you say." She
picked up a lace camisole. "And look at you . . ." She
looked at me, all the way down and up again, slowly. "You're
a sight. Your hair badly plaited. Your kilt on back to front.
Sandals on your feet instead of the good ladylike shoes that
are in your wardrobe . . . You are disgusting." She put
the camisole on the table and began to thread a needle, then
stopped. "Now listen carefully, Catriona." She spoke
slowly. Every word was clipped and clear. I wanted to tell
her again that I was truly sorry. "You will be isolated. Do
you understand? Isolated. For seven days you will not
leave your room, except to bathe. You will make your bed
and clean your room. At half past nine you will commence

the lessons that I shall set for you. At noon, for half an
hour, you will do physical exercises with me. You will learn
by heart six short, or four long, verses of a suitable poem
that I shall choose each day. . . ." I thought, She didn't
find the Keats in the other leg of my bloomers. She looked
at me sharply. "Tessie will bring you a slice of dry bread
and a glass of milk twice a day, and you may have an orange
or an apple"—she paused—"and you will not see Paddy for
a whole month."

"Oh no! Please, Jane . . . a whole month . . ."

"Hush." She threaded the needle and picked up the camisole. "And you will not speak one word, except to recite the
verses to me. Not one single word to anyone. Not one word
aloud to yourself." She looked up. "You are on your honor,"
she said. Then looking down at her sewing again, she
shrugged her shoulders. "If you have any honor. If you
even know the meaning of the word." I felt the blood rise to
my face. She stitched for a while; then she reached for the
scissors, cut the thread, and put them on the table again.
Without looking up, "You are dismissed," she said.

I went back to my room and sat on the bed. I felt sick. "If
you have any honor." Her voice had sounded as it did when
she had said "Irish." My blood rose again. "If you even
know the meaning of the word." I thought again of
Brindley-Flopsy, the pigeon races, and Paddy. I knew I had
honor. I had done a violent thing. I had been disobedient, and
I was deceitful about reading in the library. I sighed. Why
didn't Jane want me to read? Why did it make her so angry?
Why did she always forbid? Paddy, reading, Brindley-
Flopsy, and the pigeon races; they weren't wicked things. I
turned on my back and looked out of the window. The sky
was clouding and overcast, and the sun was hidden. I sat up.
I knew I deserved to be punished, but seven days, and not to
see Paddy for a whole month.

We both waited eagerly for Tuesdays and Fridays, when I was allowed to go to the Farm and take him for a walk. Myfanwy Jones said that on those mornings he was excited from the moment he woke up, and he came running to meet me across the meadow as I walked down the road from the Rise. I leaned back against the hard carved-wood bed head and thought of him. Sometimes we went to the Mochdre Hill, climbing and scrambling in the stubbly heather roots. Other times we went down to the river. Paddy was afraid to swim, but he liked to paddle and to chase the gray wagtails, flying low over the gravelly water's edge. Or we would climb the bluff and look in through the window of the empty stone cottage. I loved the big old-fashioned hearth that took up all one side of the room and had stone seats built into the wall, inside it. When we went to the Dyffryn Wood, he sniffed at and fussed about and worried every small bush, and if he saw a rabbit or a squirrel or a hare he was away like a streak of white lightning. He never caught one, but he trotted back, proud of the effort, and stood a little way off, his head on one side, with one ear cocked and his front pads wide apart. When he got his breath, he would run to me, wriggling with excitement and pleasure and wagging all the back half of his body. I thought of him by the trough. It was his favorite place at the Farm. He liked to watch the animals when they came to drink.

Then I remembered that I must clean my room and make my bed. I'd only made my bed once or twice before, when Tessie's mother was ill and she went to look after her. I'd only straightened the top bedclothes, as I was doing now. It looked quite neat, unless Jane looked underneath. I got an old petticoat out of the drawer and used it as a duster. It was white linen with two rows of tucks and lace around the bottom. I nearly dropped one of the china candlesticks that were on the mantlepiece. The flowers wreathed around it had caked dirt behind them. I dusted quickly, not touching the small Staffordshire hound on the left. I dusted the mirror and frame and tidied the dressing table, sweeping everything into the two top drawers with the duster. I took down Nana's painting of Llyn-y-Cau from over the head of the bed and looked at it. I wiped it carefully and hung it up again, and as I put the duster in the bed-table cupboard I heard voices on the stairs; Archibald's and Mr. Evans's. They were carrying something heavy. Jane was on the landing outside the sewing room, giving instructions. Mr. Evans's back appeared in the doorway. He was holding one end of my desk, from the library, and Archibald the other.

"Good morning," Mr. Evans said, although he was breathing heavily. "A rainy morning it is, indeed." I didn't reply. Archibald looked at me. I shook my head and put my finger to my lips. He understood and didn't speak, but he looked angry. I was surprised. It was the second time I had seen a look of anger on his face. Then Jane was outside the door. I turned my kilt around so that the buttons were at the side and twisted my hair in a knob on top of my head. I couldn't find a big hairpin in the untidy drawer, so I let it fall down again.

"Put it there for a minute," Jane said, "and move the dressing table to the wall at the opposite side of the fireplace." I went and sat down on the bed. The dressing table was heavy and difficult to move. It was a chest of drawers, the mirror was separate. It had two little drawers in it where I kept my silver bracelets and the brooch, made out of one of the military buttons that my Grenadier guardian had sent to me, and some coral beads. "Put the desk where the dressing table was, but slanting away from the wall. The light must come over the left shoulder."

"Yes, Miss Withers," Mr. Evans said. Archibald didn't speak.

"I do hope this has not affected your sciatica, Mr. Evans."

"Nothing to speak of, Miss Withers, and will that be all?"

"Yes, thank you." She turned to Archibald. "Will you bring in some wood for the drawing-room fire, please. It is still quite chilly in the evenings."

And Archibald said, "Yes, Miss Withers."

"Thank you both very much." Jane looked about the room as she spoke. She ran her finger along the mantelpiece and picked up the candlestick I had nearly dropped. She didn't look in the dressing-table drawers, nor inside the bed. She followed Mr. Evans and Archibald down the stairs and came back a few minutes later with lesson books and put them on my desk.

"When you have plaited your hair tidily, you will do algebra and English history till twelve o'clock." I thought, I don't have to say, "Yes, Jane," or "Thank you, Jane," because I'm not allowed to speak. She looked at me as though I had spoken my thoughts aloud; then she left the room, closing the door firmly behind her.

I sat down at the desk and looked out of the window, across the orchard to the river and the mountains. They were familiar. The books on the desk were familiar too, and the lessons seemed friendly after the long day and night. How can everything change so in one day? I tried to remember how I had felt. I couldn't. I could only wish I hadn't broken the pane. I opened the history textbook, so dry after the historical books in the library. Dates. William Rufus . . . Hengist and Horsa . . . Edward the First . . . the Tudors. They were Welsh. Jane was English. She was a B.A., and had been to the Royal College of Music. I learned the dates and the lesson, almost three pages on the feudal system; but it didn't tell that the Normans subdued the English in seven years, and that it took two hundred years to rule the Welsh, and then the people were always rebelling. I thought, Like my people. . . . But we hated Cromwell more than the Normans. I had learned these things reading the *History of Wales,* in two large worn volumes, in the library, and a translation of a *History of Ireland* that had been written a long time ago. I thought, History is strange. I am Welsh-Irish, and each country tells the same story in a different way. And then Jane came into the room.

She had changed and was wearing a navy blue pleated skirt and a white blouse.

"It's noon. Time for exercises. You may just wear your bloomers and blouse," she said. "Roll your kilt neatly and put it away." She was standing up very straight. "Now then! Stand in front of the fireplace, where there is plenty of room . . . and watch me. Do as I tell you." There were six exercises. For arms and legs and stretching and bending. We did them ten times each. They were easy. I could put my palms flat on the floor in front of my toes. "That is not necessary, Catriona. You will be stiff enough tomorrow. Just touch the tips of your fingers to your toes . . . Up and down. Up and down . . ." Jane looked young in her skirt and blouse. "Hands to the shoulders. Up and out. Forward. Down. One. Two. Three. Four. . . ." For half an hour. I was tired. Then Jane said, "You will bathe after your exercises, and you'd better make it a hot bath, Catriona, you have been using muscles that walking and running about with Paddy don't touch. . . . Afterward you may have your milk and bread."

I bathed. Then I drank the milk. I didn't eat the bread because I had half of Emma's big sandwich left from breakfast time. Afternoon lessons didn't begin until two o'clock.

I had an hour to read. I took the volume of Keats from under the window-seat cushion, where I had hidden it, and sat down on the seat.

Tessie came for the tray. I was reading *La Belle Dame sans Merci* and thinking, "The sedge is wither'd from the lake,/And no birds sing . . ." And I am woebegone. . . . Jane came in. I was lost in the poem, and hadn't heard her. I pushed the book up the back of my jersey.

"In future you will eat—" She came across to me. "What are you trying to hide in your jersey?" She pulled the small book away from me. Her eyes narrowed with anger. "Deceitful child. Disgusting, deceitful child." She held the book tightly in her hand, so that the soft suede cover was almost bent in half and the golden-edged pages sprayed out. "You must have had this up the other leg of your bloomers," she said. "Well, I know there are no more books in this room. I searched it yesterday. I know you, young lady . . . and in future you will eat every morsel of your bread. Do you hear?" She put afternoon lessons on the desk and then a book with a marker in it.

"These will be your verses for today," she said, putting it on top of the others. She held up Keats's *Poems*. "As for this, it will go back to where it belongs. In the library. And now, get on with lessons and the verses that are suitable to your age."

I got up from the window seat and looked at the verses. "The Eve of Waterloo." By four o'clock I had finished the French translation. "*Le petit Paul dit, 'Maman! Le savon pique quand il entre dans les yeux.*" Stupid little Paul. The map was untidy. Maps were difficult and uninteresting. I sat on the window seat and waited for the twilight. I could hear Molly-fach in her stall. She would wonder why I hadn't come with her sugar and rubbed her hard nose with my

knuckles. I thought of her shiny red-brown rump. Of the
Mochdre Hill on Guy Fawkes Night; of the half-faced
people and roasted chestnuts. It seemed to have happened
in another world. Next Guy Fawkes Day, I shall be ten, I
thought. Ten years old. Then I thought of Jane. "If you
have any honor." And the Vicar's wife. "She's got something
stuck in her bloomers." I hated her. I wished I had knocked
her big stuck-out teeth down her throat and choked her.
Perhaps Jane is right. I am violent. I sighed. Seven days'
punishment was enough. And not to see Paddy "even afterward . . ."

At six o'clock she came in to hear the verses. I had
learned them. ". . . and Belgium's capital had gathered
then, her beauty and her chivalry . . ."

"You will brush your hair for twenty minutes before you
go to bed, Catriona . . . a full twenty minutes." She sat
down on the window seat. "Now! The verses." I stood in
front of the fireplace and recited them. "The words are
correct. A little more expression would be welcome. You
have no feeling for poetry, I'm afraid." She got up. "Your
supper will be sent up to you. You may go to bed at any time
that you wish . . . after you have brushed and plaited
your hair. Tomorrow I shall expect the whole poem to be
memorized . . . and with some meaning in it, please." Her
voice was cold. She looked down at me, her lips tight together; then she left.

I went to the window and sat down. I tried to think of
Nana. To remember the lines from the legends and the
poems I loved. "But hark! that heavy sound breaks in once
more. It is! It is! The cannon's opening roar." I couldn't get
the verses out of my head. I went to brush my hair, timing
myself by the small china clock on the dressing table. A
shepherd and a shepherdess held it between them, with

curving arms and tiny fingers. The shepherd had his legs crossed, and his smiling lips were rosy-red. She had a flowered skirt and a pale pink petticoat and pointed green shoes with pink rosettes on them. They're holding time in their hands, I thought, and time was passing very slowly. When the twenty minutes had gone by, I plaited two braids, and as I finished the second Tessie brought my supper. After I had eaten it, I went to bed, but I couldn't sleep. I tossed and dozed, and wakened, remembering; ached with being sorry, turned over and slept a little, dreamed and wakened to memory again; turned the pillow to the cool side and lay there, awake and miserable.

Toward morning I slept, and when I wakened daylight was streaming in between the curtains and the wall. I got up. But only halfway. I was too stiff. "You will be using muscles that walking and running about with Paddy don't touch." I could hear Jane's voice; then I heard Tessie coming with my orange. I hadn't dusted, nor made the bed. I couldn't lift my arms to pull off my nightdress. I got out of bed, slowly, painfully, and tried again. Tessie knocked and came in. I pointed to my nightdress and shook my head. She laughed. I didn't. She put the fruit on the bed table and took hold of the hem and pulled my nightdress over my head. I nodded, Thank you, and she went out of the room.

I put on my bloomers and jersey—slowly. I couldn't bend. When I lifted my leg to get into my bloomers, the backs of my thighs felt as though a knife were slitting them open and cutting the muscles, one by one. This is extra punishment, I thought. I wasn't hungry. I hid the orange in the bed-table cupboard. I kept the duster there, too. The duster. I must do the dusting before Jane came with the lessons. I was even more careless than yesterday. I straightened the bedclothes. I couldn't lean over. I walked to each side of the bed and back again. I was tucking the quilted bedspread under the pillow when Jane came in. She watched me until I finished.

"Well, here are your lessons. I'm going to the Girls' Friendly. I shall be back at noon, for exercises." Lessons! Arithmetic! Exercises! I couldn't write. I could hardly hold the pen. My back and chest felt like a huge stitch. I threw the pen down and jumped up, angry, and knocked the ink bottle over. The ink covered my papers on the desk, spilled onto the floor and the rug, splashing the cushions on the window seat. I stood there; my teeth were clenched. I took a deep breath and closed my eyes. I felt hopeless and helpless. Then I looked at the mess and thought, Something must be done before the stains sink in. The duster? The bath towel? The ink bottle had been almost full. A full oval bottle of blue-black ink! I leaned over the window seat to look for Archibald. He was nowhere to be seen. Then I thought of the bathroom. It was over part of the kitchen. Fortunately, I was allowed in the bathroom. I took one of my best shoes, with the hard square heels, and banged on the bathroom floor. Emma, please hear me. I banged again, as hard as I could. Emma heard. She came into the downstairs hall. "Miss Catty . . . Goodness, gracious to me . . . What's the matter?" I stood on the landing and made signs that meant "Send Tessie," and pointed to the bedroom. She understood and called, "Tessie, come here a minute." Then said, "What's happened? . . . Oh well, Tessie will tell me . . ." She shook her head, muttering, "What a business this is, indeed to goodness . . . what a business," and went back to the kitchen.

Tessie came and looked, and then went downstairs and came back with a pail of hot water, soap and soap powder, and a scrubbing brush. In half an hour the desk and the floor boards were clean. The blotting paper had saved the textbooks, and only the arithmetic and essay books were ruined. She scrubbed the cushions on the window seat and turned them over, but the stain on the rug, though fainter, wouldn't come out.

"Let's turn the rug around," Tessie said. "Look you, I'll hold up the foot of the bed and you pull it out from under." The big rug would have been clumsy to move even if I hadn't been stiff and sore. "Just a minute," Tessie said, and let the foot of the bed down. "It's heavy." We looked at each other. Tessie laughed. And now I laughed with her. "Up we go again," she said, and this time I got the whole rug from under the bed. "It's happy I am that the head legs weren't on it too." She got hold of the rug. "Come on, let's turn it around; then you pull it under the bed again." We pulled and tugged at the rug. "Pull it a bit harder, Miss Catty, if you can, I've got work to do, and I don't want Miss Withers on my back . . . begging your pardon." I pulled hard, and thought, This is how prisoners on the rack must feel, and Tessie said, "Up we go. Pull it under." I pulled it under. She let the bed down, and we straightened it out. "None that wasn't looking for it'd notice a thing," she said. Then she looked at the desk. "I'll bring you a new blotting pad and two new exercise books . . . and a bottle of ink. I know where she keeps them. . . ." I nodded, Thank you . . . More than thank you, and she laughed. "The other books are all right. She won't notice anything." She put the soap and scrubbing brush into the pail and picked up the soap powder in one hand and the pail in the other. "Don't worry, Miss Catty. She won't see a thing."

When she brought the books and blotting paper and ink, I started lessons again. Though my whole body was stiff and painful, they were neatly done when Jane came in at twelve o'clock.

"You'll find exercises more difficult today," she said. "Ready now? . . . Don't be a baby . . . Stretch! . . .

Now we'll bend . . . Aha! Just as I thought." I couldn't get the tips of my fingers lower than my knees. "You are even stiffer than I thought you'd be. Come along now. . . ." She kept me for the full half hour. I was nearly crying. When we stopped, she said, "I'm going to play tennis on the Vicarage lawn this afternoon . . . and you'd better run your bath hot."

I was as hungry after eating the bread and drinking the milk as I had been before. I forgot the orange in the bed-table cupboard. I sat on the window seat and looked out at the mountains. They were hazy and far away. I was hungry and sore. There were lessons to do and verses to learn and long months of strong discipline to look forward to, and a locked library door. For the first time since I had broken the yellow-gold pane, I cried. I put my head on my arms against the hard window sill and sobbed till my nose was full and my eyes were red and swollen. After a while I went to the bathroom and splashed cold water on my face and blew my nose. Anyway, Jane didn't notice the ink stains, I thought, and was grateful again to Tessie.

Jane came in, after playing tennis till dusk. I had learned the verses. I stood by the fireplace to recite them.

When she said, "Shall I light a lamp?" I shook my head. She shrugged and sat down by the window. "Now, Catriona, recite as though you understood what you were saying, please, not like a parrot." I wanted to shout the lines, to scream the words. I wanted to stand there with my teeth clenched together and not speak at all. "Come along now." Jane was waiting. I said the whole poem. In the half-dark-ness she didn't notice my swollen eyes. "Better, not good, but better." I wanted to write down, "I'm hungry! I'm hungry!" But I didn't, and Jane said, "Good night." Last night she hadn't.

I ate all the bread and drank all the milk and felt as

though I had eaten nothing. I wished I hadn't such a good appetite. Brushing my hair was painful and tiring. My shoulders and neck ached, and the tops of my arms felt like the backs of my thighs when I lifted them, but the sharp pain made me forget how hungry I was. I made two plaits, and then there was nothing else to do. I went to bed. My head ached with weeping. I thought of Paddy, and wondered if he had waited for me. I lay on my back because lying on either side made my shoulders stiffer. I cried quietly. The tears wouldn't stop. They trickled into my ears and around the back of my neck. Soon my pillow was wet and hot and felt as hard as a rock under my throbbing head.

By the third day of punishment I was hungrier than ever. When I had finished lessons, I thought of the tastes and smells of foods, the meltings and the chewiness. I couldn't believe that I'd eaten so much between meals. Gingersnaps from the big blue Collie tin and pieces of Emma's sponge-cake; fresh peas, stolen from the kitchen garden behind the tool shed, tomatoes, radishes, and cresses; my mouth watered, and the hunger pulled my mind down into my stomach. It was hard to learn the verses. I wanted to scream, "I can't bear it. I'm hungry." I tried to think of base creatures that kill much more than they can eat, for the lust of killing. The weasels and stoats that suck the blood of the young lambs and stalk rabbits, watching them run around and around in circles, till they are too weak to run any more and just sit, still and stiff, waiting to die.

That evening, Jane went to a whist drive at the Parish Hall, and Emma sent Tessie up to me with chicken breast, mashed potatoes and peas, and gooseberry fool.

"Miss Withers will never know," Tessie said, "and Mrs. Higgins is that worried about you."

The smell and the sight made me drool, and I got a

sharp, prickly feeling under my tongue. I held my breath. "If you have any honor," I heard Jane's voice.

Tessie put the tray on the window seat. "Eat it, Miss Catty, for Mrs. Higgins' sake, look you." She was at the door. If she left, I would eat it. She turned to go. I whistled. She turned around, and I signed to her to wait. I wrote on a page of my notebook, "Dear, dear Emma. Thank you very, very much, but I can't. I'm on my honor." I tore off the page, folded it, and gave it to Tessie; then I picked up the tray and handed it to her. Her eyes and her mouth opened. "Why, miss, you're loony as a coot," she said, and then, "Beg pardon, miss," and hurried out, leaving the smell of roast chicken behind her.

She returned with the dry bread and milk and left, without a word. I ate the bread and drank the milk, and that night I couldn't sleep for the gnawing, grinding pain in my stomach.

Then on the fourth evening, after Jane had heard the verses, the hunger went away. I was sitting on the window seat, watching the river mist veiling the fast-fading fruit blossoms in clouds of milky vapor and thinking how beautiful the orchard was, and the world outside. I vowed never to do anything, ever again, to deserve being locked up. As I sat looking out, I found that my lips and tongue were caked and there was a nasty taste in my mouth. I went to the bathroom to get a drink of water. It tasted like metal. I felt dizzy, and went to lie on the bed. After a while I remembered that I must brush my hair. Still giddy, I undressed, brushed my hair and plaited it, and got back into bed. Everything in the room looked tiny and far away. The foot of the bed was distant, and my feet looked like doll's feet. My flesh and skin felt hard, like a crust around me. Like the shell of a crab. I lay there and half dreams came; vivid

swift moving pictures, lopsided landscapes, huge evil faces
that glowed and grew in swelling red and dissolved into a
green decay; and then a huge white stoat was sucking the
blood from my heart, and as it sucked it grew pink, like its
eyes, and as it drank every hair became a darker red, so that
its eyes looked pale and glared with cold light, and I wakened, sweating and terrified. Then the half dreams mixed
with real dreams, and at the end of one of them there was a
white light that wakened me. It was high daylight. I had
forgotten to draw the curtains. I sat up in bed and looked
out at the blue sky. I had never seen it so deep a blue, and
there wasn't a cloud. Thrushes sang, and blackbirds. I
heard the cuckoo. I feel well, I thought. I couldn't believe it.
I feel happy. I listened. The singing was joyful and loud,
filling the air, and clear kitchen noises, like cymbals, mingled
with the bird song. I can hear each bird, I thought, and
listened, still holding my breath in wonder. Thrush, black-
bird, and the missel thrush sang as she soared to the high
birch branches. I rose and went to look at the mountains.
They were close. I could see every patch of sunlight and
every jagged shadow, and in between the light and shadow
colors, yellow-gold, green, russet, rosy-pink, and white,
where the deep crevices held the snow, unmelted. I sat, en-
tranced. Then I looked at the china clock on the dressing
table. It was a quarter past eight. The dusting! The bed! I
dressed. My bloomers felt fleecy-soft, my blouse smooth
and cool against my skin. I pulled all the bedclothes off the
bed and shook the bottom sheet out of the window. Then
I turned the mattress over and played with the soft feather
bed, laughing as I pummeled it. I wasn't stiff. The soreness
had gone. I made the bed carefully, tucking in each sheet and
blanket neatly, without a crease, and smoothing them with
the palms of my hands. Cool woven linen. Warm woven
wool. The quilted bedcover was a wonder of color and pat-

tern. It must have taken a hundred years to make. I laughed
again, and felt the stitches around a triangle of blue and
white cotton, with checks so fine that it looked like a triangle of plain blue cotton, and the ends of my fingers tingled
as I felt each even cross-stitch. Then I dusted. I picked up
the candlestick I had nearly dropped, and saw that it was
shaped like the Grecian columns I had seen in *Stories from
the Greek Myths,* and was about twelve inches tall. Tiny
flowers, blue forget-me-nots, crocuses, and rambler roses
twined around it. I dusted it carefully. I licked the place
where the petticoat was around the end of my finger and
tried to clean behind the garlands, but the old caked dust
remained. I'll wash you both with soap and water, I promised, and I polished the Staffordshire hound till he shone.
Then I tidied the dressing-table drawers and took all the
pins out of the purple velvet back of the silver swan and
brushed the velvet with my clothesbrush. I put the pins back
again in circles, the big ones in the middle and the small ones
on the outside. I dusted the mirror and the fine-grained,
light-colored wood around it; then the high chest at the
other side of the bed, and tidied the drawers from top to
bottom. They pulled out smoothly, as though they had been
oiled, and the wood of them was dark and polished, and
carved, like Nana's bed, with pointed arches. I broke away
the wax stuck in the bowl of the brass candlestick on the bed
table and the drippings from the top and sides of the candle,
I rubbed the metal till it shone and then shook the petticoat
out of the window. There was still not a cloud in the sky. I
put the duster back in the bed-table drawer and found the
orange I had put there three days ago. I took it and went to
the window seat. I held it in my hand and looked at it, seeing
the tiny holes in the red-golden skin. They formed a million
patterns all streaming toward the center, where there was a
green star, with four points and a circle in the middle of it,

and rays going out of it, in ridges, down around through the patterns of the skin. O green star in a red-gold firmament . . . green field on the ball of the sun. My fingers pressed it and felt the fruit inside, hard with juice. O Orange! My mouth formed the words. O Orange of Oranges. I laughed and thought not to eat it, then, but it would rot. It had grown, blossomed in flower, and burgeoned into fruit, to be eaten. I made a Grace. O Heavenly Father, thank you for Thy gift of the orange, grant that it will be part of me and I part of it, to Thy glory. I laughed and silently said the Grace again, and ate the orange; the golden juice spilled down my chin.

Each thing I saw and touched seemed to have a life of its own. Even lessons were different. Algebra was clear. The problems slipped together and resolved, and geography was the living world: the sun, the moon, and the stars that shone upon it. The plants that grew in the earth and the animals that walked its woods and wilds. Pine trees in the north. Palm trees in the south. Daytime here. Nighttime there. Through the center of the earth to starlight, I thought, laughing.

Exercises at noon were a joy. Jane looked puzzled. "You're very graceful today, Catriona, but let us do them a little faster." I stretched. Upward with delight. Downward with reverence. As though I were in church. I wanted to dance. I can dance. I long to dance. "You are doing your exercises well . . . quite well, but in a very odd manner." I laughed merrily without making a sound. Jane looked shocked, and then worried. "You'd better have your bath," she said.

The water gushed from the long, narrow taps, clear and cool, welling up in the bath. I put the two china candlesticks on the floor, turned both taps full open, and stepped into the bubbling water. I lay down in it and watched the silver spray. "And they came to a place of fair well-being, to a

fountain in a sapling wood . . ." The water lapped against
me, rippling along my skin. "And I will wrap thee in the
fondnesses . . . Esyllt . . . and they keep their leaves
while they last . . . Arthur . . . and the Golden Eagle
rests no more on the crags of Llyn-y-Cau, but Arthur shall
awaken and the Golden Eagle return to the crests of Cader
Idris . . ." Nana . . . *"Sili fritt, Leisa bela,"* the Faery
woman sings. . . . I stretched my limbs. Then I took one of
the candlesticks and with the end of the loofah, soapy and
wet, sought out the dirt in the tiny crevices and in between
the flowers. Soon it was clean. I put it back on the floor and
took up the other one and washed it. The long, deep bath
was nearly full. I put the other candlestick on the floor and
lay back. The sky was a paler blue outside the tall window,
but still there was not a cloud. I turned off the taps and lay,
half floating. Nana . . . "Smooth thou, soft thou . . ."
She used to sing the words to me in the light of rush tapers
hanging from the cottage rafters and in the glow of the fire.
"Smooth thou, soft thou, soft as silk, well we love thee,
soft white, red bright . . ." Nana was close to me again. I
heard Tessie on the stairs. ". . . And then he rose out of
the bath and put one foot on the edge of the tub and the
other on the he-goat's back . . ." Laughing, I wrapped
myself in the bath towel and picked up the candlesticks.
Tessie had left the tray on the bed table. I put the candlesticks on the mantelpiece and went back to the window. I
felt feather-light—as though if I tried I could fly. I let the
towel drop to the ground and sat, naked, on the window
seat. Quiet shivers went up and down my spine and seeped
into all my veins, cooling my blood. I closed my eyes, feeling
the shivery flow. When I opened them, I saw the ivy leaves
growing along the sill. Three hearts in one heart, smooth
and shining with a light that was not from the outside. I
saw the clear green of the veins and the tiny rivers of sap

inside them, and my thin breathing seemed to be the flowing
of the sap in every ivy leaf and stem on the wall. The rose
garden was part of the ivy leaves and shining from within,
crimson, white and gold and green, and I saw each rose—
each petal, leaf and stalk, polished thorn and tiny, golden,
honey-holding stamen. The smell of roses filled the room,
and I felt the velvet touch of petals against my face and
body. The birch trees came close enough to touch, had there
been need to touch. I knew the markings on the silver bark
and saw the welling life inside. The rustling of their leaves
filled the air with whispering. They swayed and gently bowed
their branches and I danced with them, all around the room.
With the birches and the fruit-bearing trees. Towering pear
trees and cozy apple trees, plum trees and cherry trees, and
the bushes, raspberry and gooseberry, all danced. I laughed.
I can count the hairs on the gooseberries. I sat down again. I
was not breathless, held in the flow of the dance and the
light. In the light from the sky and the light from the garden
and the orchard and the birch grove and the light that
filled the room. I closed my eyes and stayed there. Still as a
star, yet moving as the stars do, seeming still.

After a while the shivers seeped away. I opened my eyes
and looked. The ivy leaves were ivy leaves and there were
clouds in the sky, blown by the wind. I put on my bloomers
and jersey and took the towel and hung it on the rack in the
bathroom. I ate the bread and drank the milk with thanks-
giving. I thought of Emma and white flour, and of Myfanwy Jones's cows, driven home at evening, and the smell
of the cow shed at the milking. I went to the window again
and put my elbows on the sill. I looked at the garden, the
orchard. Did it happen? It wasn't a daydream. Could I
remember? It was clearer than anything else that had ever
happened to me. It did happen. . . . "The Happening," I
thought. I didn't understand it. I could have told Nana. The

cuckoo called, and called again. I laughed, remembering
the old poem "And the cuckoo said most kindly that she
would send her servant to seek without ceasing, for him
whose hand and eye are gentle . . ." I sighed. Please seek
without ceasing, I thought as she called again with her
early summer double notes, because I cannot go to search.
I must wait here for him whose hand and eye are gentle. I
smiled to myself, as always when I thought of the poem. I
sat there, at ease and without thinking, till Jane came in
with afternoon lessons. I did them without effort. I learned
the verses and recited them.

"Quite good . . . really not at all bad," Jane said.

That night, I sat on the window seat. The air was
memory-soft and warm. I thought of Nana. Of her shining
gray eyes and her long, veined, shapely old hands. I remembered clearly every story she had ever told me, and
wondered, looking across the silver-gray river to the dark
mountains, if somewhere on their slopes, too, there was a
door to the Faery kingdom, as there was at Llyn-y-Cau. A
door to the "Lovely Land that is beyond the World's Age,"
where the Fair Family feasted and made merry, dancing,
singing, and telling the ancient tales to the music of golden
harps. I thought that the mermaids must be singing to the
harp music of Jasper Boswell, seven fathoms under the
water, at the place where old Saiporella had thrown his
harp into the river. I laughed in the balmy darkness. I
needed no books tonight. "Gware of the Golden Hair . . .
and Peredur. Never will this iron tunic come away from
him . . . And Owein could see a yellow-haired lady, with
her hair all about her shoulders and many a gout of blood
on her tresses . . . Efnision . . ." I laughed again. ". . .
then they will bear kneading." Dafydd ap Gwilym's words
flowed about me. "And he was friend to the birds in the
hearts of lovers . . . Fair sea gull on the seething tide,

swift proud bird, whose food is fish . . . and he lit for ap
Gwilym, the rush lights of the Twelve Signs, and their
glow was bright as sparks from the furze-fires of the
Saints, to banish my dire anxiety . . ." The words made
clear pictures in the dark garden. ". . . and the cock-thrush
advised me to have faith and hope, that he himself would
take a message to him whose hand and eye are gentle . . ."
I slept awhile, sitting there. When I wakened and looked at
the time, it was three o'clock in the morning. I went to my
bed and lay on it as I was, in my bloomers and jersey.

The last two days of punishment passed swiftly. Too
swiftly. Since The Happening everything had a solemnness,
like taking the eggs and flowers to the altar on the first
Sunday in the month. Everything was full of ease. Dusting,
lessons, exercises, verses, were all part of the offering. I
didn't want to eat anything. I waited for the times I could
be alone in my room. I didn't want punishment to end. I
wanted to live in my room till I died; to die there. I thought
that death would be like The Happening.

On the last day, after exercises, Jane said, "You look
pale. Emma has some fresh sole. You shall have it for
lunch, with a boiled potato." I shook my head and smiled.
Jane seemed more puzzled than ever. I couldn't explain that
I had no hunger, that I didn't need food. "Have your bath
and come downstairs for lunch." I shook my head again.
My lips formed "No." Jane walked to the door. "All
right then, Tessie shall bring it up here to you," she said,
and left me alone to bathe. But I didn't. I felt strange and
thought of death again. "Easeful death . . . to cease
upon the midnight with no pain . . ." Midnight or midday
. . . I sat on the bed. My head was reeling. My forehead
was damp and cold with tight shivers, like bands of steel. I
held my head in my hands and tried to think. Think! Stop
spinning. I went to the window and sat down quickly, dizzy

and weak. Think. I tried to breathe deeply, but the effort
made my heart race. The Happening. I made myself think.
That was good . . . good, like the feeling about the eggs
and flowers. . . . The lightheaded emptiness came again.
I longed to lie on the bed and daydream; to close my eyes
and watch the unfolding brilliant colors fold away, and un-
fold again, with the landscapes and the faces. I knew I
mustn't. I remembered Nana and took three deep, long
breaths. Eight in, hold, eight out. "Catriona," I said aloud,
and the sound of my name steadied me. I breathed again,
slowly, and soon, although I did not understand why, I
knew that I would eat the sole and the boiled potato and
anything else that Tessie brought for me. Then I remembered I hadn't brushed my hair on the night of The Happening. I got up. The room spun around me. I sat down
quickly on the dressing-table chair and began to brush my
hair. My arms didn't hurt. I could hardly remember the
stiff soreness, but after raising them three or four times I
was breathless. I changed the brush from the right hand to
the left and thought, The clock is ticking, but the fingers
have stuck. The shepherd and the shepherdess smiled. I
made two plaits and then lay on the bed, panting as though
I'd run up the Mochdre slopes with Paddy. Paddy . . . I
would have smiled at the thought of him, but it was easier
not to. I saw him in my mind, after we had been running,
panting too, his tongue hanging out a little between his teeth
on one side and his ear cocked.

After a while my heart stopped thumping against my
ribs. I heard Tessie's footsteps on the stairs and sat up.
When she opened the door, the smell of fish made my whole
stomach come up into my throat. I lay down again. Tessie
put the tray on the window seat. After a sick while I got up
and ate the food. All of it, and drank the milk. All afternoon I fought to keep it down. When afternoon lessons

were finished, I couldn't believe I had done them. I tried to learn the verses. I couldn't. I tried again. The mind pictures wouldn't come.

When Jane came in to hear them, I stumbled through the first three. They were easy verses, but I couldn't remember a word of them.

"Didn't you try to learn them today? Perhaps you thought the last day of punishment didn't matter." I shook my head. "You may speak, Catriona," she said, but somehow until tomorrow I could not speak to anyone. I wrote in my notebook, "I did try. I don't know why I couldn't."

"Well then, we'll let it go for today." My heart sank. For today? I thought. Not verses every day after punishment, too? But I was too tired to think. Jane looked worried. She has no need to be, I thought. I felt as old as Nana, and very tired, but I wasn't dizzy any more.

Jane sent up some warm porridge with honey and cream. I ate it. Then I put the tray outside the door, undressed, and was asleep as soon as I lay down.

ꕥꕥ 4 ꕥꕥ

The morning after punishment Archibald threw a piece of dirt at my window and wakened me from a deep, dreamless sleep. I started up, afraid, thinking that a bird had hurt itself against the pane. I jumped out of bed and went to the window to look and there, standing on the terrace steps, was Archibald.

"Come to the potting shed," he said clearly but not loudly.

"Now? Before breakfast?" He nodded. I dressed drowsily and plaited my hair and went downstairs and out through the kitchen. Emma wasn't there. I walked slowly down the coachyard steps and under the archway to the rose garden. Seven days of punishment and it is full summer, I thought. The morning breeze had left a haze, and everything was still in the sunlight. Mr. Evans was hosing his vegetable marrows; the sound of the water was cool, like rain on the eaves over the stables. Last year, again, he had won the second prize. The wife of the English artist had won the first, as usual. This year Mr. Evans was more determined than ever, in spite of his sciatica.

I went to the sundial and sat down on the damp carved stone. I felt quiet; strange in a familiar world. I closed my eyes and felt the faint warmth of the sun on my face. After a while I went to the potting shed.

Archibald was putting earth into the long, narrow boxes that came from the Vicar's greenhouse. He helped the Vicar and wouldn't take pay for it. He liked to learn about the plants and flowers that came from the south of England, and from foreign lands. "He writes his sermons in the greenhouse," Archibald told me, "and he leaves notebooks about on the benches and behind flowerpots . . . just anywhere." One day the Vicar had come to Archibald with a seed in the palm of his hand. "Look!" he had said. "It is tiny and dried up. Is it dead? . . . No, Archibald, in due season if it is cherished, stalks and leaves and flowers will spring from it, filling the air around with their scent." Archibald said that he had written it down in one of the notebooks, and we had listened for him to tell about the seed each Sunday from the pulpit, but until now he hadn't. Prayers were long and tiring, especially when the new Curate read them through his nose. "Bleated them out like a sheep," Emma said, but we liked the Vicar's sermons, and Archibald liked the words "due season," and used them whenever he could.

He heard me at the door of the potting shed and looked up.

"Miss Catty-fach!" He wiped his hands on the sack apron tied around him. "It's that glad I am to see you, indeed to goodness it is, and surely never did a week drag on so." He blushed, and his eyes were warm and bright blue. They called him "Carrots" in the Village, and his brows and lashes were almost white. "Miss Catty, you're awful thin, look you." He looked worried.

I wanted to thank him for missing me and caring that I was thin, but I said, "Why did you want me to come here?"

"A surprise."

"What is it?"

"Come and look." And he walked across to a piece of sacking that hung from two rusty nails on the wall and

bulged out over something at the bottom. Quietly he lifted it.
I looked underneath and there, lying on an old red blanket
in a washbasket, looking up at us startled, with huge golden
eyes, was a thin, small black and white cat.

"Oh, Archibald! Oh, Archibald." I knelt down by the
basket and gently stroked her head between the pointed ears.
She didn't move away. She had a small face, narrow below
and wide above. To make room for her eyes, I thought. She
had a small pink mouth and a short pink nose. I tickled her
ears lightly, hardly touching her, and then suddenly she
pressed her head hard into the palm of my hand, and I
picked her up and held her. Her fur was short and silky, and
I could feel her bones. She had long, down-curving white
whiskers and a fluffy little white beard under her chin. "Oh,
Archibald! She's beautiful!"

"I don't know if she's a she."

"I don't care. If she's a he, he's beautiful."

"I put butter on its paws. I think it's happy here."

"What shall we call . . . ?" The small cat stretched a
paw along my wrist and put out her claws slowly, looked up
at me, and drew them in again. "Archibald, look, she gave
me her hand . . . and listen, she's purring."

"You must think of a name."

"Let's both think." We sat on the bench between the seed
boxes and thought and talked, then we christened her Star.
For three reasons: because she was as black as a starling,
because she had a patch of white on her chest that was
shaped like a star, and I said, "Because Star will fit, whether
she's a she or a he," and we were pleased with the name and
laughed and sat talking, Star nestling into the crook of my
arm, warm against my chest.

Then Archibald said, "Indeed look you, and it's aways
past your breakfast time." I nodded. The small black and
white cat was still purring when I put her back in the basket.

The days and weeks of summer passed slowly; strongly disciplined, I learned, apart from lessons, the verses Jane set each day, and whole paragraphs from Dickens and Scott. Every Wednesday, I recited a poem for the Vicar's wife when she came to tea. Then one day, for the first time, I was to say a French one. Jane was excited. She was proud of her French accent.

We were in the drawing room. The Vicar's wife came at twenty past four, and Jane was ready for her, sitting in her chair by the fireplace, the large silver tray with the Spode cups and saucers on it, on the small table in front of her; the tea brewing. I had on my best pale green linen dress. "You'd better go and put a cardigan on, Catriona," Jane said, "there's an autumn chill in the air." I went to get it and came down and sat in the tall, straight chair, with my back to the window. I felt warmer. Jane is always right about things like that, I thought, and wished she would understand about other things.

"And after today we'll put away all the summer clothes. . . . I shall miss my tennis, the Vicarage lawn is such a pleasant place to play, with all the trees around it, so shady and cool. . . ." She was doing embroidery on linen stretched over a circle of wood. "And Emma and Tessie can put up the winter curtains." I thought of the crimson velvet ones that would be in the library, and found I was biting my lip. "And take the covers off the furniture in here," Jane said.

I loved the house in winter. Fires crackled in the grates, and there were heavy yellow damask curtains in the drawing room. The cushions under their faded dusters were made of velvet, tapestry, and brocade, with tassels. There were skin rugs in front of the fires, and crumpets for tea. Tea on Wednesdays. I wondered if I should have to recite a poem every Wednesday all through the winter, too. And always be locked out of the library. I sighed.

Jane looked up quickly. "That was a big sigh," she said, and pulled a thread of bright purple silk from the skein in her workbasket, which was on a round stool next to her chair. "And I'm sure I never knew a child with less to sigh about."

The early autumn sunlight shone through the long windows and lit up the pictures on the wall, pink peonies in an earthen pot, and the corner of the large oil painting of Cader Idris. I thought of Nana's small water color of Llyn-y-Cau above my bed, true and clear. "I have the eye," she used to say. "I see clearly." The oil was heavy and dull, with no mist, no light, and no shadows, just the outlines of the crags. Nana had taken me to Cader Idris when I was five years old. We had driven there in the governess cart. Molly-fach was younger then, and didn't mind the distance. Now if the way was too far for her, we hired Mr. Jones the butcher's Ford motorcar. Nana and I had climbed to Tal-y-Llyn and then ridden on small Welsh mountain ponies—Nana called them merlins—up to Llyn-y-Cau. Since then we had been twice again, and Nana told me that a painter called Wilson had painted the tarn in 1774, and of her anger as a young girl, living in the valley, when visitors had asked the way to Wilson's Pool. Now it was called Llyn-y-Cau again, even by the strangers. "And Wilson's dead and buried these hundred years and more . . . and his pictures all but forgotten, I'll be bound," she used to say, "but the tarn will be there till the crack of doom, and then the Faery door will open, and everything will be as it should be." Thinking of Nana and Llyn-y-Cau, I almost sighed again.

"I do wish Penry Jones would mend the library window."

Jane stopped her needlework. "It didn't matter while the weather was good, but now, with the winds coming on . . ." She looked at me. "Catriona, you never did get into the library, did you?" The jagged hole had been there all summer. "You could have quite easily, you know, while I was away from the house." She shrugged. "And I'm sure no one would have told me."

"No, Jane, I didn't."

"Not during the whole summer?"

"No, Jane." I was going to say that I had been on my honor, but I didn't want to see her smile and shrug her shoulders again. The hard feeling was gathering at the top of my stomach. She pulled another thread from the skein and held up the crewel needle against the light.

"Well, you've been a very sulky girl all summer"—the silk went through the eye of the needle—"but that's better than being deliberately destructive." The hard feeling felt as though it would burst. I closed my eyes and tried to think of The Happening. I took a deep breath and said:

"Penry Jones mended the window this morning while you were at the Girls' Friendly."

"He did? What color did he put in?"

"Plain glass—but he didn't like it."

I liked Penry Jones. Emma had told me he was there, and lessons were finished, so I had watched while he smoothed the putty with his trowel. "Come spring, and I'll be finding something more fitting, indeed. I'll not be leaving this ugly-looking job for the whole world to see . . . not in a fine-looking window like this," he had said, and turned away and gathered up his tools. He had looked at the window again. "It'll keep the winds out, anyway." Then he turned to me. "I see Paddy out at the Farm."

"I see him on Tuesdays and Fridays."

Penry Jones looked after everything in the houses and cottages except the drains and water pipes. When he laughed he looked like Myfanwy and Merfyn Jones, but he was tall and thin and fair-haired and Merfyn was dark and his broad shoulders made him look less tall than he was. They were both singers. Penry Jones's voice was rich and deep, Merfyn's high and clear. He sang the tenor solo in the Easter Anthem and the carols at Christmas, but Codger said, "There's none can weave a wittier web of words than Penry Jones in the Penillion singing." He was a good dancer, too, as good as Caradoc Ellis, the ironmonger, and he could do the lightest and fastest Welsh reels in the district, except the Pells, of Capel Curig.

"Tell Miss Withers that I'll not be collecting the five shillings till the job's better done," he said, and smiled down at me. "And you'll have a real nice yellow pane, come spring." Then he said, "And it's wondering I am, just how the pane got broken in the first place, indeed to goodness, whatever," and he threw his head back and laughed and picked up the bag, heavy with tools, swung it over his shoulder, and turned on his heel and walked away, whistling, across the grass to the gravel path. When he reached the wall door, he stood and waved to me, still whistling; then he went out, and I had listened to the high merry sound as he walked away down the Hill Lane.

"I must go and look at the new pane," Jane said. "Plain glass, not very nice."

"Penry Jones says he won't collect the five shillings until he puts the good one in."

"I should think not."

The outside bell rang. Jane put her embroidery down. I looked at the clock inside the glass dome on the mantelpiece. It was twenty past four. The wall door was open during the day. People rang the bell and walked in. I stood up by the chair and waited.

"Dear Miss Withers. Am I late?"

"Not at all. How are you?"

The Vicar's wife sat in her usual chair to the left of Jane and took off her white skin gloves. "You may sit down, child," she said, and began, as always, to talk about her brother. "It's just too wonderful, dear Phillip is so pleased and proud . . ."

"What about? Do tell me. Has he bought another factory?"

"Good gracious, no! And my brother never bought factories, you know . . . he just took them over to help the people who couldn't seem to make a go of them . . . that's why he was knighted, you know. . . . No, Miss Withers. My news is about Basil."

"Basil? He must be quite a big boy now . . . and if he takes after his father, very good-looking."

"Oh, he is, Miss Withers . . . fair-haired and brown-eyed . . . and huge, simply huge for his age, and—"

"Yes . . . but what happened?"

"Basil has been chosen to play rugger for his school."

"How splendid."

"Isn't it? Such a strong, handsome boy."

"Do give my congratulations to your sister-in-law when you write . . ."

"My sister-in-law! An ailing, selfish woman . . . no help to my brother at all."

"Such a pity," Jane said, and drank her tea.

"More than a pity, Miss Withers. A tragedy. My brother's position . . ."

"Yes . . ." Jane shook her head and sighed.

"I can't think how she ever had a son like Basil." She handed her cup to Jane. "And now let us talk about the Har-

vest Social, I'm really so far behind with my plans . . .
and it quite upsets me to talk about my sister-in-law."

The Vicar's wife was always looking for volunteers, and
every year Jane was responsible for the cakes and scones.
Emma made them. Mrs. Price, from the White Horse, pro-
vided the sandwiches. "The bread so thick, and so little
butter," the Vicar's wife said to Jane, "but what can you do?"
There were always sandwiches left over, but never a piece
of cake or a scone, "and just let there be," Emma said,
"just let there be a cake or a piece of scone left on the refreshment table, made as they are with Myfanwy Jones's
butter and fresh white eggs from the rose-combed Minor-
cas, and see if Emma Higgins bakes anything else for the
Harvest Social." But she was proud.

"Well, you may rely on me as usual for the cakes and
scones," Jane said.

"I know, and I'm always so grateful." She sighed. "I do
so hope that odious Mr. Morris, the plumber, will not take
too much to drink again this year—he can be very unpleasant. . . ."

Mr. Morris had done something peculiar to the Vicar's
wife, two years ago, at the Social. She had screamed, Emma
said, and no one knew what had happened. She went on to
dance with Dr. Fraser, but on the next Sunday, after
morning service, the Vicar had talked to Mr. Morris in the
vestry.

"He can be obnoxious, I know," Jane said, "but I don't
know what we'd do without him in the winter when the
pipes burst." Tessie brought in the sandwiches and a spongecake with lemon-cheese filling. Jane moved the cups and saucers on the tray to make a place for the plates.

"Yes, the wretched man is a good plumber," the Vicar's
wife replied, and I thought I saw Tessie almost smile,
"but a quite revolting person."

"Thank you, Tessie," Jane said, and when she had left the room, "Do you know, it wouldn't surprise me in the least if he takes the District Nurse."

"Really? I hadn't heard. I don't like her, as you know. The Vicar calls her forthright . . . but between you and me, I find her—well—frankly, vulgar."

"Anyway, let's hope there are no more contretemps this year." Jane turned to me. "Now, Catriona"—she put the quilted chintz cozy over the teapot—"stand up." Then to the Vicar's wife, "Today we have a French poem," she said, smiling. I stood up at the side of the chair, with one hand on the curved arm of it. "Hands to your sides, dear. Now! . . . *La Source* . . ."

". . . *et l'Ocean*," I said, "by Victor Hugo." And I recited the poem. It was the first French one, and the Vicar's wife didn't understand it but she pretended to. When I sat down again, she said:

"Miss Withers, I do congratulate you, really I do. What an unexpected pleasure . . . I had no idea . . . the child's accent is . . . well . . . really quite French." She laughed, and Jane was pleased.

"I was always very fond of French myself . . . at school and at college."

"And how do you like French, Catriona?"

I thought, *Le petit Paul* . . . stupid little boy.

"You've been asked a question, dear." Jane was pouring herself more hot tea. I watched her take four lumps of sugar and wondered how she could bear the sweetness. "Catriona!"

"Yes, Catriona," the Vicar's wife said, "you must learn to give a direct answer when you are asked a question." She turned to Jane. "I was very good at English, you know." Then back to me. "Now, child, once again, do you like French?"

I took a deep breath, thinking, I am not a child. I shall
be ten next week, and said, "Yes, I like it . . . I didn't like
le petit Paul."

Jane put down her cup and laughed, showing both rows
of her small, narrow teeth. "That was months ago. I'm
afraid we have left *le petit Paul* behind, he's quite forgotten . . . *le pauvre.*" The Vicar's wife held out her cup.
"Catriona is very quick to learn, you know, in some things.
And a little too quick in others." Jane poured away the
dregs and refilled the cup.

The Vicar's wife took it from her. "But . . . she has
been a good girl this summer. I know." She wagged a finger
at me. "A little bird told me."

It didn't seem rude not to answer; besides, I was seeing
a huge vulture on her shoulder, like the ones who pick the
flesh from the bones of the dead in round towers in India.
It was still and beady-eyed, and through its hooked beak
it was whispering to her, "Catriona has been a good girl.
Did you know? Catriona has been a good girl." It was a
stupid vulture, but I liked it. It was flapping its great wings
now and holding on to her shoulder with its claws.

"Hand the sandwiches around, dear."

"Thank you, child." The Vicar's wife took four tiny
sandwiches. I watched them disappear behind her teeth,
two at a time. Take one for the vulture, I thought, and
stood with the plate. "I think I'll have just one teeny one
more while you have the plate in your hand . . . cucumber
. . . so delicious, and almost over now." She took two and
wanted more. I went back to my chair with a large piece of
Emma's spongecake on my plate.

As I took a good bite, Jane said, "It has been decided
that you are to have a tutor." I swallowed the mouthful of
cake whole, but I didn't choke or cough. I nearly did both.
She turned to the Vicar's wife. "A retired college professor

would be ideal . . . a widower . . . or a bachelor . . ."

"Oh, my dear Miss Withers, what a wonderful solution that would be, really."

"It's awfully difficult, you know. Mr. Amphlett has been occupied with the matter since the beginning of the summer."

"He's really a first-class solicitor, isn't he?"

"First-class. Absolutely first-class," Jane said. "I don't know what I should do without him. The guardians are— Another cup?"

"If I may, but do go on." Jane emptied the leaves into the small china basin. "The guardians are . . . well, really so lax. Oh, the money is put into the bank regularly each quarter . . . but they are never at home. They can never be reached . . . India . . . Honolulu . . . and one of them is trying to climb that other mountain—you know, not Everest—with some Germans. . . . It may be a little strong, it has been brewing." The Vicar's wife took the cup of tea. "Really, Mr. Amphlett tries so hard to make up for them, and finding a tutor is not an easy task."

"You know, Miss Withers, I might just be able to help." The Vicar's wife was enthusiastic. "Basil is having a tutor this summer . . . he's not a studious boy, I'm afraid, as his father was . . . in fact, he's rather self-willed and simply loathes lessons." She laughed. "A real boy—but he must get into Cambridge."

"Oh, do give me the name of his tutor. I'll write to Mr. Amphlett immediately. I'm so grateful."

"Of course."

"Naturally, whoever comes, I shall continue with her French and music."

"Oh, naturally! You must! Your French is so good."

Jane nodded her head and smiled. "As you know, I went

to the Royal College, and"—she looked at me again—"Catriona is to begin dancing lessons this autumn."

The Vicar's wife smiled at me. "What a lucky girl you are." And she put her finger to the hollow in her cheek. "Now, I'm just wondering . . . I wonder if my brother has thought of dancing lessons for Basil." She nodded to herself. "Yes, he should begin to learn the social graces."

"He's sure to learn at his public school, don't you think?"

"I should think so. Nevertheless, I'm going to make a point of finding out." She laughed. "The rascal . . . the handsome young rascal."

I put my plate on the table. "May I go now, please?"

"I think you may," Jane said, and I held out my hand to our guest.

"Good-by." The vulture winked one of his staring eyes and kept the lid down. I almost laughed.

"Good-by, child." The Vicar's wife held the tips of my fingers as though she believed Jane, who said my hands were always dirty. She had long pointed nails, painted bright pink, with white under the ends of them.

I went out through the drawing-room windows and down the terrace steps and along the left side of the rose garden, to the potting shed.

Star was a she. Three kittens had been born last week. I couldn't come every evening to see them, because Jane often walked in the garden after tea, but on Wednesdays she and the Vicar's wife talked till six o'clock, and today they would be talking about the new tutor.

I went into the potting shed and quietly lifted the sacking. Star made a small welcoming sound and eased herself backward, then she proudly turned up her stomach for me to see.

"Oh, Star! You're beautiful!" She made a motherly

noise and pushed her first-born with her paw. He rolled over on his back and scrambled to his feet again. I knew he was the eldest because he was the only one who had a large black patch. It covered almost all his back and part of his left side, and I had seen him born.

Archibald had called to me from the terrace. I had been in the middle of lessons. I still did them in the bedroom because the library was locked. He had whispered clearly that it was Star's due season, and beckoned me to come down. I had crept downstairs because Jane was in the sewing room, and we had given Star warm cream and helped her to bear him. She had lapped it up, and her mouth and whiskers were all covered with cream when he was born. Then she had licked him and eaten his wrapping and there was cream on him, too. After cleaning him thoroughly she turned and licked the saucer till it was empty, and then looked up at us.

"She wants more cream," Archibald had said, and I went to the kitchen and warmed it on the stove.

"You should be at lessons . . . and what's more important, what about the trifle?" Emma complained. She was lining a cut-glass bowl with pieces of leftover cake. "A fine thing, indeed . . . cream for the cat . . . and warm at that, look you."

"She's not the cat. She's Star."

"Well, we'll see what Miss Withers'll call her if she ever finds out." When I took the cream to the potting shed, two other kittens had been born. They were white.

"She must have taken up with a snow-white tomcat, indeed to goodness," Archibald said, and laughing, I had hurried back to my lessons.

At lunch that day, Jane, dressed in a white pleated skirt and a loose pale blue jumper, was saying that there were to be tennis finals on the Vicarage lawn. She was helping herself to trifle. "If only the weather holds out for another week . . . the new Curate plays such a splendid, serious game . . ." She stopped talking and looked at Emma, who was serving the trifle to me. "There seems to be very little cream in the trifle today, Emma. It's very watery and uninteresting."

"Merfyn Jones brought but gill this morning, Miss Withers. Betsy-fach must be going dry."

Emma left milk and kidneys and sometimes an egg, and anything else she thought that Star would like, covered, on a small kitchen tray in the larder. Either Archibald or I took it to the potting shed. Star had been sleek and beautiful by the time the kittens were born.

I stroked the first-born, and then one of the others. Star made a proud sound and leaned over and licked them.

"Oh, Star, you are beautiful, with your kittens, on your crimson blanket—like a queen, Star." She purred. Her purr had deepened. The kittens were tiny and ugly, with long hairless tails and bony faces. Their eyes were tight shut. I wondered how they found their milk, the same teat again and again, after she'd pushed them away, licking them, and how they had the strength to knead at her belly as they did with their tiny paws. I watched them for a while and then lowered the sacking and went into the house.

Emma was asleep in her rocking chair. I didn't waken her. As I passed through the hall, I heard Jane and the Vicar's wife, still talking. I went upstairs to my room and closed the door. Then I put my hand behind the big chest of drawers and pulled out the worn book of ancient Welsh poems that I had taken from the library. I lay down on the bed, the book in my hand.

All through the long summer, when I passed the library window, I had looked at the jagged hole, and the iron latch, so easy to open, but though I longed to I had not opened it. Then one morning at the beginning of August, in the middle of lessons, I suddenly remembered that Tessie cleaned the library on Thursdays, and on Thursday mornings Jane went to the Vicarage. I ran downstairs to find Emma. She was cooking curry for lunch. The whole kitchen smelled of it.

"Oh, Emma! Curry. How lovely!"

"Well now, look you, and that's the first interest you've shown in your food for longer than I care to say, indeed . . . and shouldn't you be doing your lessons?"

I went to the stove and looked at the onions and apples and curry powder, russet-brown, in the big iron frying pan.

"There's nothing here for you to come tasting," Emma said, and then I asked her, "Emma, please call Tessie out of the library, just for two minutes, while I get three books?"

"I thought you gave your word of honor."

"I did. I promised not to get into the library through the broken window, and not to try to unlock the door."

"I don't know as this is any different."

"Please, Emma. I only want three books—only three, Emma. I need them. I can't remember all the lines in the poems, and I need to remember them." Emma stirred the mixture in the pan. "And I'm not breaking a promise . . . I didn't promise not to think up another way to get into the library . . . and I won't read a word while I'm inside the room . . . only three books . . . Emma, please."

Emma put the big wooden spoon to rest in the pan and turned to me, her hands on her hips, laughing. "Glory be to goodness now, and it's right glad I am to hear you talking a bit again, more like you used to, indeed, and it's missing those tales I've been, myself." She sighed and shook her head. "Miss Catty-fach, I've never in all my born days seen a girl as quiet as you since that punishment week." She pushed a lock of gray hair from her forehead and tucked it behind her ear. "And I'm thinking if it's these three books you need to liven you up a bit—"

"Oh, Emma! They will!"

"It seems they have already, at that."

"Oh, thank you, Emma." I gave her a big hug.

"Now! Now!" she said. "There's things to be done. Miss Withers is likely to be back at any moment. Get a brown paper bag out of the dresser drawer"—she went toward the pantry—"the top left-hand drawer." I found a medium-sized one and took it to the pantry. Emma had taken from its shelf the big red tin with the lump sugar in it. "I've never known anyone, nor young nor old, that sets so much store by books," she said, and took the lid off the tin. "Hold the bag open." She emptied the sugar into it. "Molly-fach doesn't know her luck, indeed." The red tin had been more than half full. "And 'tis an ill wind that blows none any good . . . and this time it's Molly-fach's the gainer."

"And me, Emma."

"You! Glory be! And goodness knows what you don't get me into." She put the empty tin back in its place. I laughed and twisted the top of the paper bag and followed her to the kitchen door that led to the hall. "Go and hide in the dining room, and for goodness' sake be quick about the business." I slipped past her and hid behind the dining-room door. "Tessie," she called.

"Yes, Mrs. Higgins?"

"Come here a minute. I can't get to the high shelf, and we've run out of lump sugar."

Tessie went to the kitchen. I ran across the hall and into the library. The travel books, which I never read, except for one called *Death Rites and Funeral Customs of Different*

Lands, were all stacked on the floor to be dusted. Quickly I took the two books I wanted from the shelf and then the *Mabinogion,* from the small table where I had left it when Jane was calling me the day I broke the window. I had not been in the room since that day. I sat for a long moment in my red plush chair, holding the three books in my arms. Then I stood up, leaned over the table, still holding the books, picked up the twisted top of the brown paper bag and within two minutes was back in my room.

I hid the books behind the chest, and through the slow, dull weeks of stricter measures the knowledge that they were there helped me to learn the things I had to learn. I sighed and opened the translations of Dafydd ap Gwilym's poems, losing myself in the familiar words: ". . . and there the skilled cuckoo, splendid, entrancing, sings his song of love-longing . . . and the young thrush, gay poet of summer . . ." The young thrush. I heard him in the orchard. Summer should be gay and happy. Sometimes it was. The heavy, musty-smelling book fell onto my chest. I thought of the thrush's song, and of the birds who stayed with us through the winter months. The sparrows and the robins, the ravens, who pair for life. The brown wren, with his short singed-off tail, hardly a tail at all, "But the spirit of Arthur, he is," Nana had said, "and you can't be an hour on the mountain but that he'll appear to you." She said the wren was the Druid's bird, and in some countries, king of all the birds, and not the eagle. I remembered the solitary buzzard that used to roost in the tallest pear tree in the orchard. "The farmer's friend," Merfyn Jones called them, and said the buzzards were not wanton killers and that they were often blamed for the cruel work of the sparrow hawks. I used to watch our buzzard flying upward in circles, its wings beating heavily, as though it could never rise, and then suddenly it was a speck in the sky. I lay thinking. Discipline left me little time for thought, and after a while I lifted the book from my chest. The musty smell of it made me sneeze. I laughed. I was already dressed for dinner. I began to read a long poem.

5

It was difficult to find a retired college professor, either a widower or a bachelor, who wanted to live in the Welsh mountains. Four people who, Jane said, seemed to be suitable were willing to come for the summer; one young man could come for as long as he was needed if pleasant and free accommodation was available for his wife and four children, and the tutor who had been teaching Basil Lockridge during the holidays was a permanent professor at Barnesworth School. Mr. Amphlett wrote almost every day, and Idris Williams, the post, every time he delivered a letter, had tea and gingersnaps. "It'll be the day when we find that teacher and the post himself doesn't live in my kitchen," Emma said. "The man's forty-odd, look you, why doesn't he find a wife?" But she made possets for him too when he had his stomach-aches.

Out of all the people who had written there was one, Mr. Amphlett said, who might come temporarily, and Jane agreed that it seemed to be the only solution left, until, inside one of the letters, there was a note from the oldest guardian that said, "A temporary arrangement is not to be considered. A permanent tutor must be found," and Mr. Amphlett had added at the bottom of the page, "Before you receive this, Miss Withers, he will be on his way to India, so there is nothing to do but to keep trying." Then on the last Tuesday in September, just after my birthday, there was a long letter, five closely written pages. ". . . and I am jubilant, Miss Withers—jubilant!" Mr. Amphlett had written. Jane read parts of it to me at lunch time : " 'He is the son of a cousin of mine, of extremely good stock, if I may say so, and although he is only twenty-five years of age he is a recognized scholar and has an M.A. degree from Oxford . . .' " Jane read on for a while without speaking, then she said, "How odd !"

"What is ?"

"Mr. Amphlett says that he spent some time in a Protestant monastery."

A monk, I thought. St. Francis, St. Andrew. I liked St. Andrew ; he argued. It was he who'd said that the loaves and fishes wouldn't be enough. The Vicar had read it in the lesson, and after church I'd looked it up to make sure. "But what are these among so many ?" St. Andrew had asked.

" 'He stayed in the monastery for two years,' " Jane was reading, " 'and then found he was unable to take his final vows.' " She looked up. "Of course, you don't understand what any of this means." "Final vows," I thought. They were solemn words.

" 'He wants to live in a quiet place, where he can write in his spare time, and fish. He also likes to live in the mountains.' " Jane shrugged. "That I can't understand." She frowned. "Twenty-five. I had a much older person in mind" —she sighed—"but he would be permanent . . . and he is an M.A."

"And he's lived in a monastery."

"I suppose that would make him a little more serious than most young men of his age."

"But, Jane! Twenty-five is old. He's not much younger than you." She didn't reply. She read almost the whole letter before she spoke again.

"Mr. Amphlett thinks it is a minor miracle," she said. "He says that he had almost given up hope and that he feels this to be a heaven-sent opportunity." She frowned again. "He already arranged for your aunt to meet his cousin while she was passing through London for a few days. He writes that the young man made a most favorable impression on her." Jane seemed to be annoyed. She shrugged again. "There seems to be little more to be said." She went on reading: " 'My cousin is delighted with the prospect of living quietly, and it remains only for you, dear Miss Withers, to interview him at your convenience.' Well . . ." She folded the letter and put it back in the envelope. "Everyone seems to be pleased. I shall have to see him and talk to him, of course."

"When will he come?"

"When I say that it's convenient."

"Soon, then?"

Even if the new tutor was stricter than Jane, it would be a different discipline. I wanted him to come.

"I shall get in touch with Mr. Amphlett this afternoon," Jane said, and she telephoned while I was in the Dyffryn Wood with Paddy. After dinner in the drawing room she told me, "The Vicar thinks it is a splendid arrangement and hopes the young man can play chess. He is quite upset that the new Curate takes no interest in the game. Of course, he plays whist."

"What did Mr. Amphlett say on the telephone? When's he coming? What's his name?"

"You really do ask so many questions all at once, Catriona. I have decided to see him as soon as possible . . .

and his name is Bernard Morgan." Then she said that he would take the train to Chester and walk from there to the Village. "I can't imagine why anyone would want to walk all that way." She thought for a moment. "That means he should arrive at the end of this week." She sighed and took up her embroidery. "Well, we can only wait and see."

The following day at tea Jane and the Vicar's wife could hardly listen to my recitation. It was a long poem. I said it slowly, with expression. They began to talk before I had come to the last verse, and didn't even say "Thank you, child," when it ended.

"A Protestant monk!" the Vicar's wife said. "How odd! Interesting . . . but really most odd, don't you think?" Jane nodded. "And why did he leave the monastery? Why couldn't he take his final vows?" She took the cup of tea Jane handed to her and some sandwiches from me. She didn't eat them. She put them on her plate, took a sip of tea, and then said, "Oh." She put her hand to her mouth, still holding the cup of tea with the other. "Oh, Miss Withers, a dreadful thought has occurred to me."

"Good heavens! What is it?"

"Oh, but he must be . . . and yet . . . Oh, Miss Withers, suppose he isn't—"

"He isn't what?"

"A Christian."

Jane was shocked. "Gracious! Mr. Amphlett is a church warden . . . the parish in Chester is a most important parish . . . Mr. Amphlett is a power in the church. Of course his cousin is a Christian . . . and the guardians, they'd never send an . . . an atheist." She said the word with horror, almost in a whisper.

Atheist? I thought.

"Of course they wouldn't . . ." The Vicar's wife

sounded doubtful. "I suppose you're right, but to be inside for two years, and then to come out . . . to want to live quietly, at his age . . . you must admit, it does make one wonder."

Jane remembered me. "You may be excused, Catriona."

"But I haven't finished my tea."

"You've had enough." I got up and put my cup and saucer on the tray. "We'll take your adieu as said, dear. Now run along."

I went upstairs and took down the dictionary from the top of the chest of drawers. "Atheism," I read, "disbelief or denial of the existence of a Supreme Being. . . . Atheist . . . a godless person." I put the heavy book back in its place and went to sit on the window seat. I knew Bernard Morgan was not an atheist, even though he couldn't take his final vows.

The next Friday was Paddy's last day at the Farm. I wakened and thought, Today I shall not have to leave him at the drinking trough while I walk away. I had taught him to sit, and not follow me, but I knew that it was as hard for him to watch me leave as it was for me to go. Archibald had built a wooden kennel, shaped like a house. It had a raised floor so that Paddy would not feel the damp, and it was painted bright emerald green. We put it outside the stable door, in the corner of the wall, under the oak tree and sheltered from the wind. That morning, before lunch, Jane and I went to the ironmonger's.

"But, Jane, he doesn't need a chain. He's good and obedient." Caradoc Ellis, the ironmonger, agreed with me.

"Spaniels don't need chains, Miss Withers." Caradoc Ellis was tall and thin, and even though he had six children he looked young. He was dark-haired and dark-skinned, and his eyes were almost black and almost always smiling, though his mouth wasn't.

Jane smiled at him and agreed. "Then we'll just take the two tin dishes for his food and water."

"That's all he needs, look you, Miss Withers . . . no chain . . . good food and drink . . . and no chain—" his black eyes smiled into hers—"and he'll never go roving. And if he does"—he put the two shiny tin dishes on the counter—"why, and he'll always come back again." And he looked at Jane as though the words meant something else. She blushed and looked away, and I thought that Caradoc Ellis was laughing to himself.

"Please wrap them up," Jane said.

He took a paper bag from under the counter and said to me, "And when's the home-coming?"

"This afternoon."

"So this is the great day, indeed?"

It was the day. I couldn't believe it, but when I went to the Farm after lunch, Paddy ran to meet me across the meadow, his long ears flapping backward, his pads barely touching the grass. He jumped up at me, wagging his stump of a tail and wriggling and yelping with joy. I wanted to see Myfanwy Jones, to thank her for keeping Paddy and training him and loving him, so we went over the stile, into the grassy lane, and ran past the cow sheds and up the shallow slope to the dairy. Myfanwy Jones was churning. It was hard work, but she was strong and loved her Farm. She loved her herd of Welsh cattle, small and black, with large bony heads and faces, and long, lean necks, and the ones with white faces, whose father was the Hereford bull. She saw all the calves born and cared for them. She looked around when Paddy and I came to the wide open doorway.

"Well, Miss Catty, so today's the day?" She laughed, and tucked her heavy dark blue apron up into her waistband. "Paddy knows, too . . . and look you, he'll be missed about here." She called to him, and he went to her. She patted his head and pulled his ears. He wagged his tail and licked her and came back to me. "He's a real nice dog," she said.

"Archibald's built a kennel for him. A big one. It's bright green, and the floor's above the ground so that he won't be cold."

"Cold? But he'll be in the house when it's cold."

"He will," I said, and thought of Jane. Then of Emma. "Don't cross your bridges before you come at them," she'd said when we'd talked about Paddy coming inside the house in the winter.

"Would you like some buttermilk?"

"Yes, please, I'd love some." She went to a big white bowl on the stone slab under the dairy windows and poured the thick, warm, sour milk into a white mug with blue rings around it.

"That'll do you good. You're too thin," she said as she handed it to me. "Doesn't Emma feed you?" She laughed as I drank and then gave her the empty mug. "Now be off with you. Both of you," but she called Paddy to her again and patted his head gently and smiled, and I thought of her in her wine-colored velvet dress, her fair wavy hair coiled at the nape of her neck, when she played the harp at the Annual Concert. She had the whitest hands I had ever seen. Strong white hands, and gentle, that soothed the cows when she milked them, birthed the lambs, and drew sweet, deep sound from the harp strings. She stood up.

"Thank you, Myfanwy Jones."

"What for? For the buttermilk?" She laughed. I shook my head. Tears came into my eyes. Paddy came back to me. After a moment she said, "Now be off with you. I've work to do," but she stood there watching us as we ran down the slope.

We went across the meadow and over the stile, onto the
road, and then up the ever steeper fields till we came to the
lower slopes of the Mochdre Hill. It was five miles in the
governess cart from the Rise to the foot of the Hill, but less
than half that distance across the fields. When we reached
the heather, I sat down, hot and breathless. Jane had made
me wear a thick jersey, and the afternoon sun was warm.
"Indian summer," she'd said, "but it turns cold when the
sun goes down. Now, don't stay till after sunset on the Hill."

I lay back on the heather and looked at the sky. It was
blue and clear, without clouds, and there was no wind. Only
Paddy's high, glad barks broke the silence and his rushes
from gorse clump to heather patch, to grass tuft, ruffled the
still air. I closed my eyes. My breath came out in a long, deep
sigh. The summer is over. Paddy is coming home. But nothing else had changed. Wednesday teas; verses; discipline. I
couldn't believe that Jane and the Vicar's wife would allow
Bernard Morgan, who had been a monk, and who was
twenty-five, to take "full responsibility" for my education.
Strong measures would continue. The library door would
stay locked. The thought of my red plush chair and the forbidden books on the shelves brought the hard, helpless lump
to my chest. I remembered the times I had been almost violent again. At Wednesday teas, when they talked in front of
me as though I weren't there. Once it had been about the
District Nurse. She had been helping a woman who had
twins, cleaning her cottage for her and washing the clothes.

"Just as she washed the sheets and pillowcases for that
old woman . . ."

"Nana . . ." Jane said. "The District Nurse is extremely meddlesome."

"At least Nana came from our village . . . quite mad,
of course . . ." I had almost thrown my cup and saucer at

her; but I had taken a deep breath and tried to think of The Happening and of Nana, and the sunlight and the firelight in her cottage, and the violence had passed. Discipline, all summer long. Distrust.

"Are you sure you never got into the library?" No picnics in the mountains, all part of the new, strong measures. Jane never wants to go to the mountains, I thought. She always has to be persuaded. Why do I always feel dull and tired when I am with Jane? Yet lighthearted and gay when I'm away from her for a while? With Emma or Archibald, or Paddy, or at the Farm. I wished she would not believe that I had been sulking all summer. I had only felt quiet. I lay feeling the pleasantly warm sun on my face, thinking of Nana, and death. I had heard the sexton's bell tolling the morning after I had been with her. Codger had seen the corpse lights, shining through the cottage windows, and then moving down the Hill Lane and up the Plas-y-Coed Road to the churchyard. Nana . . . *Sili fritt, Leisa bela.* . . . Thinking of her, I fell asleep on the hillside.

I wakened because Paddy had barked. A different kind of bark. The sun was sinking toward the mountains, and a wind had arisen. I shivered and was glad of the warm jersey. Paddy came running around the curved slope, stopping every few yards and barking. He was excited.

"What is it?" He stood in front of me now and barked again. Then I saw a man, away down the slope. He was climbing toward us. Paddy barked again. The man had a rucksack on his back. "Quiet, Paddy!" I watched the man. He wore breeches, the kind the mountain climbers used. He must be one of them, I thought. But the season was over. Whitsuntide and the early summer was the time for the normal mountaineers. He wore a brown tweed jacket and an old tweed hat. Like the one on Merfyn Jones's scarecrow. He was tall and thin. I waited for him to look up. Paddy was impatient, wriggling away from me and then coming close. The man climbed steadily. Paddy barked again, and he looked up. He looked at me for a moment, and then he smiled.

"Hello." Paddy ran toward him. He stood about five yards away. He patted his knee.

"Come here, boy." Paddy stood still. He held out his hand, and Paddy went to him. "That's a friendly fellow . . . Come on, then." He bent and patted him and pulled his ears. Then he stood up and looked down at me.

"And what are you doing on the lonely hillside? The sun will soon be setting."

"I came for a walk with Paddy, and I fell asleep." He came and sat by me. Then he looked up at me, eased the straps of his knapsack, and smiled. His eyes are the color of tarn water, green-gray, at dusk, I thought. He lay back in the heather. Paddy left my side and went close to him. Without looking at Paddy he stroked him and pulled his ears, gently. Tenderly, I thought. The mountaintops were golden-pink, and the river caught the sunset light into a golden pathway on the water. Soon the hills would be dark against the afterglow. I wanted to speak. I could neither speak nor move. I must be under a spell. Nana said that when you were spellbound you couldn't speak, nor move, nor hardly breathe.

"Are you always silent?" At the sound of his voice Paddy raised his head and wagged his tail. It was a deep voice, and quiet.

"I'm happy," I said. It was true. I thought, I'm happy.

"When you are happy, be silent, that the birds of happiness may nest in your hair . . ." He looked at me, and looked away again. "A Chinese poet said that a long time ago."

"Welsh poets said lovely things a long time ago, too."

"Did they? Tell me something they said."

"Fair sea gull on the seething tide, like snow,
Or the white moon in color.
Your beauty is unsullied, like a patch of sunlight,
Gauntlet of the sea . . ."

He turned to look at me. He was still stroking Paddy's ears; I could see the slow movement of his hand, although I was looking into his eyes. None loves a slim hound, or dog, like him . . . I closed my eyes and whispered the words in my heart. . . . "like him whose hand and eye are gentle." Heavenly Father . . . When I opened my eyes, he was looking at the darkening sky.

"You are Bernard Morgan."

"And you are Catriona." We sat awhile on the hillside.

"The sun has set. I must go. Will you come with me?"

"I'll walk a way along with you," he said, and getting up, he held out his hand to me. Then he pulled the straps of his knapsack into place and we half ran down the slope, and walked across the fields, without speaking, to the road. We came to Myfanwy Jones's meadow as the dusk light drained into the darkness. When we were at the gate, he said, "I'll sit here for a while and smoke my pipe." He pulled his pipe out of his pocket and held it in his hand.

"When are you coming to Bryn Llithrig?"

"Tomorrow morning at eleven o'clock. Is it far from here?"

"Just over the Rise there." Then I said, "Good night."

"Good night, Catriona." It was hard to turn away. I called Paddy to heel. He was tired and stayed by my feet as we walked up the Rise.

Archibald was waiting for us in the coachyard. "You're late, Miss Catty. Miss Withers has been looking for you. But she's gone out again."

"Let's show Paddy his kennel."

"Here, Paddy . . . Come on, boy." Archibald had seen more of Paddy than I had while he was at the Farm. We took him to his kennel.

"He likes it," Archibald said proudly. Paddy went into his house and came out again, then he took a long drink of water from his new tin bowl and came running to us, wagging his tail. He wasn't sure what it was, but he liked it.

"It's your house, Paddy."

"Let's bring him his supper; then he'll know."

"You go and ask Emma for it. I don't want to go into the house yet." Archibald went up the steps. I knew Emma had prepared a special stew for Paddy, and there was a leg bone of lamb with a lot of meat on it.

I sat on the mounting block, and Paddy jumped up and sat beside me. "Oh, Paddy! You're home." I remembered the morning Merfyn Jones had walked away with Paddy in his arms up the cobbled slope. I would never forget it; the hurt of losing him. Paddy put his head on my lap. "I was glad you chewed that buckskin slipper." I patted his head. "But you didn't do much harm to it. The cobbler mended it." He jumped up and licked my face. "Down, Paddy." He put his head on my lap again and looked up at me. "Oh, Paddy, I feel so much older. Do you?" At my words he jumped up again, and I laughed and pulled his ears. I wondered how he would like Star and the kittens. Archibald came down the steps slowly and carefully, carrying the tin dish in his hands. It was full of warm food. He walked across to the kennel.

"Come on, Paddy . . . Supper!" Paddy must have been hungry and he must have known where Archibald was going to put the dish, because he was there waiting for it. We laughed, and Paddy looked up at us. Then he didn't look up again until he'd eaten everything and licked the dish. Archi-

bald and I sat on the mounting block and watched him pushing the empty tin about.

"I'll go and get him his bone," Archibald said, and I
called to Paddy and patted him and stroked him.

"Good night. Tomorrow you will meet Star and the kittens," I said, and pulled his ears and left him. I went through
the arch to the rose garden as Archibald came down the
steps with the large lamb bone. I walked past the vegetable-
marrow bed to the birch grove. The moon was rising. I
leaned against the young, slender birch. Maiden of the
woods, I thought. Then in the quiet, everything has changed
again. It had changed when Nana died; then when Archibald
came, again when I broke the library window, and now today. Today . . . the day he came, walking toward me, up
the slope, on the Mochdre Hill, eveything had changed
again.

It was dark now. The moon had risen. The air was sweet
and heavy, save for the gentle breeze. The trees seemed farther apart than in daytime, to stand alone. There were no
shadows, only darker black and lighter darkness. The big
leaves of the vegetable-marrow plants looked strange and
fierce and thorny, as though they were standing guard over
the marrow. I loved the night. I loved this night. O Heavenly Father . . . I let the thought come at last, in all its
strength. Morgan . . . O Heavenly Father, help me to
deserve Morgan.

Jane did not know I had been in the birch grove till the
moon was high; she had been to a whist drive at the Parish
Hall.

At breakfast she said, "You were late yesterday afternoon."

"I went to sleep on the Mochdre Hill."

"Really, Catriona."

"And you were right about the woolen jumper."

"Of course I was right . . . I might have known that you would either go too far . . . or go to sleep . . . or something worse." I didn't tell her I had met Morgan.

"Paddy likes his new house. Archibald and I gave him his supper, and he—"

"He's not to be in the house, remember. I won't allow it."

"I know, Jane . . . and he—"

"Mr. Morgan is coming this morning." She was wearing her Saxe blue serge dress with the velvet collar and cuffs. "I will call you down to the library if it is decided that he is staying." Emma came in with the toast rack.

"I burned a piece for you, Miss Catty . . ."

"Emma! Catriona, please . . . How many times must I ask you?"

"Sorry, Miss Withers . . . I'm that forgetful, indeed."

"And please tell Archibald to light a fire in the library, and we'll have lunch at one, as usual."

"How many?" Emma asked, and Jane thought for a minute.

"Five, I think. The Vicar said he would come; he was quite reluctant, but I'm sure he'll come . . . and I suppose our visitor will stay for lunch, whatever the outcome. Yes, Emma . . . five." She turned to me. "And now, Catriona, hurry . . . your lessons are on your desk." Jane was what Emma called "all flustered up." I finished my toast, without marmalade so that I could taste the burnt parts, and then went upstairs to do my lessons. Jane doesn't want Morgan to stay, I thought. I was glad the Vicar was coming. I couldn't think about algebra. I didn't try. I sat on the window seat and thought about Morgan, the deepening sky behind him, his eyes, and the way he had looked when I said the lines of Welsh poetry. His face, when he stood, tall in the dusk, as I left him to walk up the Rise. After a while I thought I had better be obedient and do my lessons. Henry

the Fifth was better than the Norman Conquest. The algebra was easy. Suddenly the wall-door bell rang, loud and
clear. I ran to the landing and looked over the rail. Jane
came out of the library, where she had been waiting. I saw
Morgan's feet and legs walking up the gravel path. Then I
saw him. He was wearing a brown tweed suit and his old hat.
He took it off as he came into the hall. His hair was thick
and dark brown. Jane looked surprised. She stood still for
a moment and then touched her hair, patting it over her ears.
She smiled and held out her hand.

"How do you do, Mr. Morgan." Her voice sounded as it
did when she spoke to the Curate. I sighed with relief. She
likes him.

"How do you do, Miss Withers."

I remembered his voice. They went into the library.

After about ten minutes the bell rang again. It was the
Vicar and his wife. Jane came into the hall to meet them.
"How nice of you both to come. Mr. Morgan is already
here." I heard the Vicar's wife sniff, and they went into the
library and closed the door.

I went back to the window seat and finished learning the
history. I felt sick. Oh, why were they talking so long? I re-
vised the algebra.

"Catriona," Jane called from the bottom of the stairs. I
went out onto the landing. "Will you come downstairs,
please."

Then I was afraid; afraid that he wouldn't want to stay;
wouldn't like Bryn Llithrig, Jane, the Vicar's wife, me. He
liked me yesterday, I thought.

"Wash your hands first. I expect they're covered with
ink."

I went to the bathroom and stood by the washbasin and
took five long, deep breaths. Nana . . . I remembered her
words: "When the stress is in you, Kishli, breathe . . .

breathe deep." I washed my hands and went down to the library.

The Vicar was standing in front of the fireplace, his feet apart and his round stomach pushing out his clerical waist-coat. He was smiling. His wife was sitting on the dark green couch that faced the door. She was wearing her afternoon tweed and a velvet turban; purple velvet embroidered with black braid and pieces of jet. Jane and Morgan were sitting on the dark red couch on the other side of the fireplace. When she heard me come into the room, Jane turned around. "Well, here she is"—she looked at me from feet to hair— "and fairly tidy, for once. She's in your charge now"—she turned back to Morgan—"that is if you will stay with us." Morgan got up from the couch. If you will stay with us? My heart leaped to my throat.

"How do you do, Catriona."

"How do you do." He hasn't told them about yesterday, I thought. He was serious and polite. He turned to Jane.

"Catriona and I will walk for a while in the garden, and get to know each other a little."

"Of course," the Vicar said, but Jane seemed surprised and then displeased.

"It's quite chilly . . ."

"Brisk! Brisk! Just a little brisk." The Vicar rubbed his hands. "Good for them."

"Then you'd better get your cardigan." Jane turned to Morgan. "Lunch is at one."

"Thank you. It's kind of you to invite me."

I ran upstairs, and when I came down he was waiting for me at the front door. We walked around onto the lawn, passed the library windows, and down the steps to the rose garden, without speaking.

Then I said, "You didn't tell them we met yesterday."

"Did you?"

I shook my head.

"I understand that you broke the library window, Catriona."

Why did they tell him? I've been punished for that. He waited for me to answer. "Yes. I did."

"Why?"

"Didn't they tell you?"

"Miss Withers said that you were disobedient."

I didn't say anything. He believes them. He doesn't like me.

"And that you had taken one of these stones"—he pointed to one along the edge of the path with his foot—"and deliberately smashed the pane."

"I smashed the pane. I smashed the lovely golden-yellow pane and half the knight."

"And that since you were punished you've been sulking all summer."

I stopped and looked up at him. "That's not true." He looked down at me. "I promise that's not true."

"I don't think it is."

We stood looking at each other.

"No, I don't think it is . . . but why did Miss Withers think it was?"

"I don't know. I felt dull and quiet. I did everything I was told to do."

He walked on again, slowly. "Catriona . . . do you think that you are violent and disobedient?"

"No, Morgan . . . Oh, I'm sorry . . . I didn't mean . . . It's just how I've been thinking of you."

"Never mind, I like the name too." He smiled. "Answer my question, please." We walked toward the orchard. I tried to think truthfully.

"I'm not disobedient . . . but there are things I want to be disobedient about. . . . I was violent. Once. I've wanted to be again, but I only was that once."

"Why were you quiet and dull?"

"I was tired."

"Tired?"

"Tired of learning verses and reciting silly poems and no mountain walks and being strongly disciplined."

"I shall be stern with you if I decide to stay."

I stopped again. "Isn't it decided?"

"Not quite."

"You liked me yesterday."

"I like you today."

"Then why aren't you staying?"

"Catriona, why did you break the library window?" I closed my eyes, and thought, Whatever happens, I must tell the truth.

"Because . . . because . . . reading is the deepest joy I know and Jane forbade me to read the books in the library. She locked the library door."

"What books did you read in the library?"

"The *Mabinogion* . . . Lady Charlotte Guest translated it for her children, so it—"

"What else?"

"Oh . . . stories from the Greek myths . . . *The Life and Times of Akhnaton* . . . The *History of Wales* and *Celtic Folklore,* by Professor Rhys . . . it's all about the Faery people, here in the mountains . . . that Nana knew . . . and he's a professor and—"

"And what else?"

"Translations of the old Welsh poems and legends . . . the poems most of all . . ."

" 'Lightly you skim the ocean wave, swift, proud bird, whose food is fish.' Dafydd ap Gwilym?"

I was delighted. "You knew it! Reading these books is not wrong, is it?"

"No. It's not wrong, unless you do it when you should be

doing something else. What were the verses you called silly?"

" 'The Inchape Rock' and the 'Eve of Waterloo,' and 'We Are Seven,' and—"

"Did you learn them?"

"Yes."

"You may not like them, but you mustn't call them silly."

"Why? I think they are."

"Because that is only your opinion and may not be true for other people. Besides, the word 'silly' should be used with care."

"I'm sorry."

"But you did learn all of them?"

"Every one, except on the last day of punishment."

"The last day? How many days were you punished?"

"Seven."

He smiled. "A goodly number."

"But the fifth and sixth days were not punishment. They were wonderful."

"Why?"

"Because of The Happening."

"What was that?"

"Something beautiful, that was good. I shall remember it clearly till I die. I don't know what it was . . . but I knew that the daydreams that came before and afterward were not good, but The Happening was."

"What was the punishment?"

"I was isolated." He laughed quietly. "In my room for seven days. I cleaned it myself, and had to do exercises and learn verses and do lessons."

"Your meals were sent up to you?"

"Bread and a glass of milk, twice a day, and a banana . . . or an orange." I thought of the orange—remembered the golden juice.

"Did you do all these things?"

"Yes, and on the fifth and sixth days I loved to do them. I did everything except the verses on the last day." We had come to the birch grove.

"Did you feel hungry?"

"Terribly . . . and then not at all."

"I see," he said, "and The Happening was good? But the daydreams were not?" I nodded. "What was the difference?"

I knew, but I couldn't find the words. After a minute I tried. "The Happening was beautiful and . . . solemn, like the eggs and flowers in church"—I looked up at him— "but not quite the same . . . it was joyful . . . I danced . . ."

"And the daydreams? Why weren't they good too?"

"Because there was no joy in them . . . only dizziness and . . ."

"Go on."

"It sounds silly . . ."

"That word again . . . perhaps it isn't."

"I wanted to die . . . just to lie on the bed and think of dying . . . easeful death, only not as nice as Keats."

"I think I understand. You know, Catriona, that holy men and saints, and Indian wisemen, starve themselves."

"I read a book about that. There's one in the library called *The Lives of the Saints.*"

"And you were very hungry?"

I nodded. Then I suddenly understood. "I know, Morgan . . . I was starving." I stopped speaking.

"What are you thinking?"

"Morgan, The Happening was good." He smiled.

"The Happening was good," he repeated, and leaned against my birch tree.

"This is my birch grove."

"Oh, am I intruding?"

"No." We smiled at each other. Then he was serious again. He looked down at me.

"We shall study and learn together, Catriona." I closed my eyes. Then I opened them to look at him, but I shut them again quickly, to keep the tears inside. "I'll wait here and join you for lunch," he said, and I turned without looking at him and ran, across the rose garden and in through the drawing-room windows and up to my room. I pinned my plaits up on top of my head and put on white socks and brogues. I went to the bathroom and washed my hands. Then I came back to the window and looked out at the birch grove. Morgan was there, leaning on the birch tree, smoking his pipe.

At lunch the Vicar sat on Jane's right and Morgan on her left. The Vicar's wife sat next to him and I sat next to the Vicar. He was in high spirits. "We are delighted, Mr. Morgan. Delighted." There was a bowl of yellow chrysanthemums in the center of the table. Emma came in with the roast beef and Yorkshire pudding.

"Well, and did you get to know your new charge?" the Vicar's wife asked Morgan.

And Jane said, "You were in the garden for a long time."

"Catriona came in. I stayed in the birch grove."

"And did you decide, Mr. Morgan?"

"Of course he did, Miss Withers," the Vicar said.

"Yes. I shall stay and teach Catriona." He looked at me without smiling. "We shall work well together, I think."

The Vicar turned to me. "You are a very lucky young lady," he said.

His wife sniffed. "Let us hope that Catriona will try to be as good as she is fortunate."

"Really, Gladys."

"Mr. Morgan should know"—she turned to him—"she needs strong discipline. I suppose all children do—" And the Vicar interrupted.

"Not only children, my dear." His wife took no notice of him.

"And talking of discipline, Mr. Morgan," she said, "I understand that you spent some years in a monastery?"

Morgan didn't turn to her. Emma was handing the platter of roast beef to him. He smiled at her and said, "Thank you," then looking down at his plate, he said, "Two years."

"And how long were you at Oxford?"

"For four years."

"And it was after you were at Oxford that you decided to go into a monastery?"

"Really, Gladys!"

She tittered. "I know my husband is embarrassed, but it is so interesting."

Emma came to me. I helped myself to beef and pudding. She was wearing her black bombazine and an apron with eyelet embroidery and her cameo brooch. She had flattened her gray hair at each side of a center parting.

"But it was after Oxford that you decided?"

"It was after Oxford. Yes," Morgan said, then he turned to Jane. "Did my uncle . . . he's really my second cousin, but I always call him uncle—"

"Mr. Amphlett?"

"Yes . . . did he tell you that I am grateful for your invitation to stay at Bryn Llythrig, but that I should like to have my own cottage?"

"He did tell me." Jane smiled and shook her head. "I'm disappointed, really I am, but you will have your meals with us, won't you, and use the house—the library—as your own?"

"Thank you, I should like to have lunch with you, and we shall have lessons in the library."

Oh, Morgan. My heart leaped with joy.

"Oh!" Jane said, hesitating, her lips tight. "I had thought perhaps that the room next to the big guest room—"

"I prefer, very much prefer, Miss Withers, to work in the library."

The Vicar put down his knife and fork. "I'll wager you play a good game of chess, Mr. Morgan," he said. "You must come to dinner with us at the Vicarage."

"I should like to. I'm not an expert chess player, but I shall enjoy a game sometimes."

"Splendid! I'm sure you're much better than you admit."

"Do you know this part of the world, Mr. Morgan?" Jane asked. I wondered why she was smiling so much. More than even with the Curate.

"Yes, I do. I came here, mountain climbing and fishing, almost every year in my youth."

"Ah!" the Vicar said. "And so did I in mine . . . and that's a long time ago. But the mountains don't change . . . only we grow old and stiff in the joints, but"—his eyes were shining—"tell me, which are your favorite routes? Where did you start?"

"Like almost everyone else, I cut my teeth on the Milestone Buttress"—the Vicar nodded eagerly—"and I've been caught in the mists on the Glyder Fach."

"That can be frightening, especially the east gully. And Tryfan?"

Morgan smiled. "Tryfan . . . of this mountain, I am fond . . ."

"Ah!" the Vicar said again, and waited for Morgan to say more.

"A proud mountain . . . but never hostile, as I think the Glyders can be."

"Tryfan! Those extraordinary tongues and crags of rock . . . lava, you know, the upper part of the mountain, that cracked in cooling." Morgan nodded.

"Tryfan, and the twin heights of the Glyders . . . These are the roughest . . . and the best."

"Do you know Llyn Idwal?" I asked. "Where Prince Idwal was drowned by his foster father and since then not a single bird has flown over the waters of the tarn."

"Catriona, please speak when you are spoken to."

"That is the legend, Miss Withers," the Vicar said, then he smiled sadly, "but I'm afraid my climbing days are over . . . Tryfan . . . that stupendous pyramid of bristling rock."

"Stupendous pyramid of bristling rock," I thought. The Vicar likes words; that's why I like his sermons.

"I can't stand these mountains, myself," his wife said, "they give me the creeps."

Jane smiled at her. "I must admit that I, too, prefer a gentler, more rolling countryside." Her smile grew as she looked at Morgan.

"Is the fishing still free in Llyn Ogwen, Vicar?" he asked.

"Certainly. Small lake trout . . . delicious. Fewer eels, though." The Vicar was looking pleased. "My fishing days are by no means over."

"Then we shall spend some together. I always enjoyed fishing the high tarns and cold mountain lakes."

"That's a very special inclination, Mr. Morgan," the Vicar said. "You must be a philosopher." Morgan laughed, and was young.

"There is excitement, Vicar, in fishing these remote, locked-away waters." He turned to me. "One day we'll go to where the Ogwen flows out of the lake and joins the stream—"

"And then to the Benglog Falls?"

"You know Nant Ffrancon well."

I was about to answer, but Jane said, "We've driven there in the governess cart often." Not this year, we haven't, I thought.

"Well, you're no stranger to North Wales, Mr. Morgan"—the Vicar frowned—"not like our new Curate. Splendid young man, of course. Comes from the Cotswolds . . . finds the Welsh mountains slightly overpowering."

"I do so agree with him." His wife helped herself to more beef. "Delicious, Emma."

And Jane said, "I come from Sussex, myself. As I said . . . a gentler landscape."

"Civilized." The Vicar's wife looked up from her plate. "You see, we're English." Jane nodded. "And I don't mean to sound superior, as Miss Withers knows"—she put down her knife and fork—"really, I don't. Every country has its faults, after all . . . even England . . . but, well . . . it's simply a fact . . . we are more civilized." No one answered. She took her chance. "And now, Mr. Morgan, do tells us about your monastic life . . . so fascinating, and terribly ascetic . . . no decent food . . . Did they starve you so that you could pray better . . . or is that only in Roman Catholic monasteries?"

I looked at Morgan, thinking of his words in the garden, "Some holy men and saints . . . starve themselves," but he was looking down at his plate. The Vicar had lost his good humor. His face was stern. He is strong, I thought, even though he seems so jolly and spends so much time with his flowers and plants.

"Oh dear!" His wife said gleefully, "I've done it again. Look at my poor husband's face. But, Mr. Morgan . . .

it's just that I'm interested . . . purely and simply, interested."

"No, I didn't starve," Morgan said. Tessie took the plates away, and Emma came in with the sweet. The Vicar's wife tasted the gooseberry fool.

"You know, Emma has never given me the recipe for this." Then she turned to Morgan again. "Two years. You were inside for two whole years?"

"It wasn't a prison, Gladys." Her husband spoke quietly, but I felt him stiffening with anger in the chair beside me.

"Of course it wasn't a prison. A monastery is quite . . . quite voluntary. That's why . . . why . . . Oh, Mr. Morgan, do tell us why . . . just why you couldn't take your final vows?"

Even Jane seemed a little shocked. The Vicar put his napkin to his mouth. His fists were clenched under the linen. His face went as red as Archibald's did when he blushed. Morgan turned to the Vicar's wife for the first time during luncheon.

"When I am able to answer that question, I may return to the monastery."

Oh, Morgan. No! My heart stopped. I was cold.

"To turn to practical matters, Mr. Morgan . . ." Jane smiled again and leaned toward him, her elbow on the table. "There's a cottage just beyond here, on the bluff above the river. It belongs to Mr. Price, of the White Horse."

"I stayed at the White Horse last night," Morgan said. "He very kindly gave me the key and told me to go and look at it." The Vicar's face was pale, and he was calm again.

"Then after lunch we'll walk up there," he said. "A walk is what I need after Emma's Yorkshire pudding."

"You can get to the river path through the orchard," Jane said, and Morgan turned to me.

"Past the birch grove," he said.

"Yes!" Jane opened her pale blue eyes wide. "You have a splendid sense of location . . . you do go past the birch trees, along the left-hand path."

"It blows cold up there on the bluff, and there's no shelter from the wind," the Vicar warned.

"But there's a great stone fireplace, with stone seats inside it that are part of the chimney."

"And how do you know that?" Jane asked.

"I've often looked in when I take Paddy for walks." I wanted Morgan to live in the cottage on the bluff.

"Mrs. Eyeball will be delighted to look after you," the Vicar's wife said, and Jane agreed with her. I did too. I liked Mrs. Eyeball. "She is a very good cook. Miss Withers knows that."

"Yes," Jane said. "She was our cook for three weeks when Emma's sister died in Bethesda." Then to Morgan, "But you are having your meals with us . . . it's all arranged."

"Thank you, I should like to have lunch with you, but I should not like to feel that I was expected to dinner."

"Of course not . . . naturally . . . but sometimes," she laughed, "I shall insist."

"Sometimes I shall like to come, but I have work to do in the evenings."

"And you must ask for anything you need . . . please. There's a stack of furniture in the attic . . . rugs, tablecloths, towels . . . I shall be delighted to go up there with you and pick out the things you need."

"Thank you. If I need anything, I shall certainly ask." Morgan turned to the Vicar. "Were you serious about walking with me to the cottage?"

"Most assuredly."

Emma came in to ask Jane if she would like to have coffee in the drawing room.

"I think the Vicar and Mr. Morgan would like theirs in here." She looked at Morgan and then at the Vicar. They nodded.

"A splendid idea," the Vicar said.

"And we'll have it in the drawing room."

Emma left the room, and Jane got up.

"You must show Mr. Morgan your greenhouse, Vicar, and perhaps he plays tennis."

"There will be time. There will be time." The Vicar came and sat in the chair that Jane had left.

"I'm afraid I do not play tennis," Morgan said, and stood behind his chair. The Vicar's wife walked to the door with Jane.

"The new Curate plays well, doesn't he?" she said. Morgan held the door open for them.

"He does, and whist, too . . . so nice with the winter nights coming on." She looked up at Morgan. "I shall rope you in for whist, too, you know."

He smiled, but didn't reply.

"Catriona, I'll meet you on Monday morning, at nine o'clock, in the library. We'll plan our curriculum."

"Leave time for music and French," Jane said, laughing over her shoulder as she walked across the hall. Morgan smiled at me, and I followed Jane and the Vicar's wife, happily, into the drawing room.

I wasn't allowed to drink coffee, so after a few minutes I asked if I might go into the garden. They nodded and went on talking, about Morgan.

I knew that Archibald was waiting for me in the potting shed; we were taking Paddy to meet Star and the kittens. I went to find him; he was chasing the raised path of a mole that was ruining the lawn. He came when I called, and followed me. When he saw us, Archibald put his hand to his lips and took hold of Paddy's collar, then knelt down and held him by the shoulders. I went to the sacking, raised it gently, and looked into the basket. Star looked up, pleased, and began to purr. I talked to her and stroked her, and then picked up the first-born. She made a small noise, but allowed me to hold him, tiny, blind and weak, in one hand, and covering, barely touching him, with the other. Quietly I turned, and bending down, showed him to Paddy, who gave a loud, high yelp and jumped backward, but Archibald held on to him. At the sound Star leaped out of her basket, her back arched, spitting and hissing, her claws out to the skin and every hair bristling, her golden eyes bright with fear and fury, looking only at her kitten. I thought she would leap at my hands. Paddy was shaking with fear, and whining and squirming, and almost escaped. I put the kitten back in the basket. Star jumped in after him. She gave him a swift, strong lick and returned to the fray. She crouched low and then leaped in the air, landing about a foot from Paddy's nose, and before we knew what was happening, with a lightning slash, reached for it with her claws, scratched deep, and drew blood. Paddy wrenched himself free and fled through the door, Star at his heels. Then she stopped, and with her back arched and her tail stiff and quivering, she gave a last, wild, hissing spit, turned and walked past Archibald and me without a glance, and jumped into her basket. We looked at each other.

"Easy does it, indeed to goodness," Archibald said, and I went to the sacking and pulled it slowly down over the basket. Star was licking her first-born. I put out my hand to stroke her head, holding the sacking with the other. She looked at me, hissed mildly, and turned her back on me. I let the sacking drop back into place, stood up, and looked at Archibald. We laughed and went to comfort Paddy. We couldn't find him anywhere.

6

Two years after Morgan came to Bryn Llithrig, Mr. Evans
won the first prize for his vegetable marrow, and after the
presentation ceremony we all went back to his cottage, next
door to Codger's son and daughter-in-law, on the Hill
Lane. It was known as Mrs. Evans's cottage, and it was
neater than any of the others in the row. There were no
rambler roses climbing along the dividing lattice fence
and few flowers in the garden. "Breeding flies and insects,
indeed," she said, but she gave us cheesecakes and beer, and
everything in the cottage was polished and shining. The
copper kettle and fire-iron knobs, the brass candlesticks
and the Wedgwood plates on the dresser shelves; the window glass and the pewter mugs and glasses and cups we
held in our hands.

"Even the stones around the hearth," Codger said to
Grandma Rhys-Evans, who was rocking in the chair by the
fire.

She nodded. "She's got more elbow grease than any other,
look you, but she have her work cut out after this do, indeed," she chuckled, and Myfanwy Jones laughed and said,
"It's the time of her life that she'll have, spitting and polishing." It was well known that Mrs. Evans was "that house-
proud." Almost everyone in the Village was there, and

the loser came from the Mochdre Village with her artist husband. She was jolly and talkative and came from Cornwall.

"You won't win next year, you know, Mr. Evans . . . I'll see to that," she said as we raised our glasses and cups and mugs and Mr. Evans nailed the big royal blue rosette to the center of the wooden mantelpiece above the stone hearth.

"We'll see about that, indeed." Mr. Evans stood back and held up his own mug, his eyes gleaming with pride. "Indeed to goodness, and we'll just see."

So Archibald trundled barrowful after barrowful of good heavy manure to nourish the gourds, and one of them was bigger than ever.

Mr. Evans's sciatica had grown worse, and now he left most of the work to Archibald, but he came to the house when the weather was good, and the lawn borders were still his pride. From the early months, when the crocus, upthrusting toward the light, made a golden edge against the grass, and the violets, daffodils, and lilies of the valley gave to the cold, damp winds the smell of spring, he tended the borders and weeded and watered them until the summer flowers were all in bloom. The honeysuckle and the clove gillyflowers, the sweet briar and the matted pinks, too drowsy with their own sweet smell to hold up their heads; the golden-brown velvet wallflowers, standing up straight on their juicy stalks and the pale sweet peas. He sprayed the rose bushes and trimmed them, and walked about the orchard with Archibald, telling him where to prune and which trees to leave alone, but most of all, he tended his vegetable marrows.

Jane was strict. I never disobeyed her. Obedience was easy when I knew that at nine o'clock each morning I should be learning and studying in the library with Morgan. His

quiet authority ruled the hours of my day. The cottage on
the bluff had become "Morgan's cottage" to us, and "the
Reverend's cottage" to the villagers. Somehow everyone
knew of his stay in the monastery, and liked him for his
knowledge of the country and his love of the mountains.
They came to know his strength and understanding, so that
people went to his cottage when they were worried and
didn't want to tell the Vicar. They forgot that he was young,
and remembered only that he had Welsh and Border blood
and that he had been in a monastery. He had been one of
them since the first night, when he had stayed at the White
Horse. The Vicar was delighted with the nickname "the
Reverend" and said that though it "smacked slightly of
Popery," Morgan must "do his bit and live up to it." So he
was drafted to keep score when the Village men played
their game of fives, after Sunday morning service, against
the wall of the church. He helped to put up the heavy
wooden shutters over the stained-glass windows and to prepare for the game, and the Vicar went happily back to his
greenhouse.

When Archibald played for the Village team, Jane allowed
me to stay and watch until lunch time. Although he was
young and meager, he was wiry and learned quickly, and
Codger was proud of him. Codger had been champion fives
player in his day, and he never missed a game. There were
six seats in the churchyard, and each held four people. No
one ever sat with Codger on his seat unless he was invited.
It was an honor to sit with him and hear what he had to
say about the game and listen to the stories of his youth
and his Romany friends. On Sundays he wore his old-
fashioned black hat and his morning coat and gold watch
chain. The gold and green leaf-patterned waistcoat that
Jasper Boswell had given him for his twenty-first birthday,
he wore only, like Emma her Paisley, when he thought that

something different and special was happening. It was kept
in a tin box and smelled of mothballs. He wore it for the
opening game of the season and for the final game, at Christmas and Easter and at weddings and christenings, and he
had worn it for Nana's funeral.

Jane had now more time to spare, and she sewed the small,
dainty sheets and pillowcases for the Mothers' Union Fair
and did embroidery for cushion covers and tapestries for
chair seats and stools that were raffled at the Church
Bazaar. She made dresses for herself and crepe-de-chine
camisoles, with lace tops, that showed through the pale
blue and mauve georgette blouses that she wore when
Morgan came to dinner. She had tried, for a long time, to
persuade him to play whist; when he didn't, on the evenings
he played chess with the Vicar, she arranged, cleverly, to
play whist at the Vicarage, so that she walked there and
back with Morgan and spent the evening in his company.
She had cut her hair in a fringe across her forehead and
dressed it in coils over each ear.

By the middle of December we had all kinds of pin-
cushions, tea cozies, and pot holders and crocheted tammies
and children's bonnets ready for the Christmas Fairs, and
we began to make the Santa Clauses. They were stuffed, as
the Guy had been, but smaller and dressed in red velvet,
with imitation patent leather boots. They had merry pink
faces and cotton-wool beards. I liked to make snowballs of
cotton wool, with colored sequins sewn on to them, and
Jane came into the kitchen for the "first stirring" of the
mincemeat. "Three times round, clockwise, and wish hard,"
Emma would say. And all through the year we collected
silver charms to put in the Christmas pudding.

Codger came for Christmas dinner along with Grandma
Rhys-Evans and her son and grandchildren and Ellen; and
because Tessie liked to be at home on Christmas Day, Ellen

and I helped Emma, and Archibald carried in the turkey on a huge platter, with sausages all around it, and helped to wash up afterward. Emma sat down with us all, and Jane was at one end of the table and Morgan at the other. I loved all the preparations for Christmas—the gifts thought about, made or saved up for, and kept secret, and the Christmas dinner. Everyone was stiff and uncomfortable at first, but soon they were all talking at once, the children shouting and finding their presents under the small pine tree in the corner of the dining room. Every year it was hung with blue tinsel, and there was a blue tinsel star on the topmost branch.

Last year for the first time I was allowed to go to watchnight service. I had sat in the pew and looked at the altar rail and remembered Morgan telling me that in olden days dogs were allowed in church, and that Archbishop Laud had been the first to put up a rail to stop them from going near the altar, and that they had dog tongs to get hold of the ones who were fighting and carry them outside. I had wished that Paddy could sit in the pew with us; then I had looked at the colors in the stained-glass windows, fading into darkness above the glow of the candles and the lamps, and listened to the murmuring as the villagers settled into their pews. There was a louder whispering than on Sunday mornings, and then a deeper hush. The Vicar read about the shepherds and the Angel from the Gospel of St. Luke, and Merfyn Jones sang the carols: two Welsh, and one in English, about Herod's roasted cock that flew off the platter:

". . . three fences hence, and crowed . . ." Then we all sang "While shepherds watch their flocks by night . . ." but Merfyn Jones's clear, high voice rose above all the others. As Archibald and I walked up the Hill Lane behind Jane and Morgan, I could hear the ringing sound of it in the still, cold night.

Where is the golden cradle that Christ was rocked in?
A manger was the cradle, so sweetly He slept on . . .

Archibald had been living with us for a year. Codger's
daughter-in-law had given birth to her fourth child and
there was no longer room for him in the cottage. Emma and
I made a comfortable room for him, above the harness
room, in the coach house. Codger wanted to leave his
son's house too, but the "shrew from Shrewsbury," who he
said had caught his Emlyn on the rebound, told everyone
that it was her "bounden duty" to look after the old man.

And Codger said to Emma, "We'll let her have the pleasure of her bounden duty for a bit longer. Something will
turn up, look you." And he spent hours in Emma's kitchen,
rocking by the fire, with Star on his lap.

Star and her first-born, who had been called Rumpel since
the day he opened his eyes, had been part of the household
for three years, and Star and Jane had become good friends
since the day that Star caught a mouse and took it to the
sewing room and laid it at her feet.

"Really!" Jane had said at dinner. "I'd no idea we had
mice in the house—in the stables, yes—but in the house!
How fortunate that Star is such a good mouser . . . and of
course, Rumpel." Rumpel wasn't. He was a lazy, mischie-
vous, spoiled, and enchanting cat, and it was because of
Rumpel that Jane had discovered the family in the potting
shed. Morgan had been taken to see them, and had agreed
to keep the secret.

"But as soon as the kittens grow and get out of their
basket, your secret will be out too," he warned.

"Emma says we mustn't cross our bridges before we
come at them," I said, and Morgan had laughed.

"It's your bridge. You cross it."

And very soon the kittens were climbing up the sides of the basket, their thin legs taut with strain, or darting at the top edge and flopping back onto the red blanket and trying again. At first they all did the same things at the same time, playing, eating, and sleeping, always together; but soon each one began to teeter away about its own business, and it was one of the white ones, not Rumpel, who had first toppled over the edge onto the floor of the tool shed and began to explore the whole place, until his mother had taken him by the scruff of the neck and put him back in the basket.

Archibald and I watched the kittens for hours. They grew furry and soft, and Mr. Evans could tell which of them were tomcats. Rumpel was, and the one who had climbed out first. Morgan took him to his cottage. He christened him Columbus because he was always finding new places to explore and because he was pure white. He became Paddy's comrade.

It had taken Star about three weeks to understand that Paddy was gentle and affectionate. After their first encounter he had run out of the potting shed and hadn't stopped till he fell, panting, at Myfanwy Jones's feet in the dairy. She laughed when we told her the reason. Soon we all knew that though Paddy loved us—Myfanwy and Merfyn, Emma who gave him good food and bones, Archibald and me—and though when it was cold and Jane was out or upstairs in the sewing room he would sit on the rug in front of the kitchen fire with Star, his loyalty was given to Morgan. Almost every night he went home with him to the cottage on the bluff, and there he played with the tiny white kitten. As the months passed and Columbus, who was soon known as Colly, grew to be a fine strong cat, they went hunting together on the bluff and along the river path, and though Colly had chosen one of the stone seats inside the hearth for his own, when Paddy was at the cottage he left it and joined his friend on the rug.

Jane had found Rumpel when she was walking in the rose garden after tea, wearing her Harris tweed coat against the cold. He was jumping around the pump, his long fur blown by the wind. It was his special game. He would spit at the handle and dart away, and spit again, his back arched high, then crouch, his face between his paws, his tail switching, and creep on his stomach slowly toward it, box with it, leap in the air, twisting his body around before his feet touched the ground, stand still for a moment, and then wheeling around, jump into the air again and scamper into the potting shed.

Jane brought him back to the house, held under her coat, and put him on the skin rug in front of the fire in the drawing room. I was doing my piano practice.

"I've found the sweetest little kitten. He was fighting the pump. His fur is long enough for a Persian. I wonder where he's from . . . and if he's a he."

"He is."

She looked at me. "So you know him?"

"Yes, Jane." I turned on the piano stool.

"And how long has this been going on?"

"Since the day after punishment, when Archibald gave Star to me."

"Star? And who is Star?"

"Rumpel's mother."

"And I suppose this is Rumpel?" She looked down at the kitten. He was sticking his claws into the hair of the rug, then twisting in the air and landing the other way around, to see the brass handle of the poker that shone in the firelight, creep to it and touch it lightly with his paw, leap away and roll on the rug. Jane laughed and picked him up. He scrambled onto her shoulder and licked her neck.

"What a rough little tongue he has," she said. "And where have you kept them? Star and Rumpel and"—she looked alarmed—"how many more?"

"In the potting shed, in a washbasket under a curtain of sacking."

"Well, really! I must say—"

"Please let us keep Star. Please, Jane. Mr. Evans says that she keeps the mice down in the stables and that she wasn't frightened of a water rat that came up from the river. She didn't catch it, but she nearly did and she scared it away. Mr. Evans says he's never seen such a real game little animal, and she's beautiful and small and has huge golden eyes and—"

"Really, Catriona! Do stop talking. How many kittens has she?"

"Two more. One, all white, that Morgan took—"

Jane raised her eyebrows. "He did?"

"Yes, and he called him Columbus, but now he's called Colly and he's Paddy's great friend, and the other one, her name's Pusterkin, and she's had—"

"And where is this other one?"

"Tessie has her."

"Thank goodness for that."

"May I go and find Star now, please?"

"I suppose you may as well."

She wasn't in her basket. I called to her, and she came running around the vegetable-marrow patch. She was worried and made short mewing sounds. She was pleased to see me and rubbed herself against my legs. I picked her up and walked toward the house.

"It's all right, Star! I'll take you to him . . . he's quite safe . . . and you're both going to have a cozy winter in Emma's kitchen . . . and you can thank Rumpel for that . . . he's charmed Jane . . . so don't be angry with him.

Oh, Star! Isn't it wonderful?" I went into the drawing room and put her on the rug with Rumpel. She took no notice of anyone or anything else. She fussed over him and licked him and then cuffed him, hard, with her paw, so that he rolled over, and then she licked him again.

"She's a good mother," Jane said. "And now we'd better take them to the kitchen; we don't want them getting used to the drawing room." Jane was going to let them stay in the house. I hadn't believed it would happen. "It's your bridge. You cross it," Morgan had said. Well, it's crossed, I thought, and picked up Star. Jane carried Rumpel.

Emma was delighted. "Now, that's more like it, look you."

And Jane said, "So you were in it too?"

Emma laughed, and I couldn't wait to tell Morgan and Archibald. From then on Star stayed in the kitchen, but Rumpel had the run of the house.

We were happy during the changing seasons. Study was deep, and Morgan was stern. Whatever Latin declensions, English grammar, mathematics, or literature had been begun had to be well and truly learned before any time was spent on legends and ancient poetry. But he never allowed what I learned to become merely an exercise for memory. He said that I would never pull the meaning out of studies, like a fish out of the river, if I didn't feel it while I worked. The Greek dramatists, Plato, and the myths were part of lessons, and I enjoyed them, and he strove to make me understand; yet he never told me anything I could find out for myself by thinking, and one afternoon a week, if I had worked well, he let me choose the stories and poetry I liked best, to read and talk about. On Saturday, if the weather was reasonable, we went to the hills.

Jane had never liked the mountains, and what we called reasonable weather she called "practically a blizzard," and she was relieved when Morgan and Archibald and I took the governess cart to Beddgelert or Capel Curig, and went ridge wandering. But when Morgan and I set out together for a day's fishing, she hovered about the kitchen and the coachyard with tight lips and disapproving eyes. I thought Morgan would have to ask her to go fishing with us, but he never did. Sometimes he asked her to go for a short walk after tea, and sometimes, when she asked him to, he drove with her to Capel Curig for special groceries. But his quiet plans for climbing and fishing were rarely allowed to be broken and he would have no interruptions during study hours.

Usually he fished in Llyn Ogwen or in the Glaslyn stream, but sometimes when we didn't want to go too far afield we fished in the river under the bluff. One May morning when I was eleven, we were there at the water's edge and Morgan was waiting awhile before throwing a second time. He said that if the fish missed in making its first offer it was more eager for the delay, and he was about to throw again when, without warning, the weather changed from dull skies and a clinging mist to a slashing rainstorm. We scurried to shelter among the jutting rocks, and suddenly behind one of them I found the mouth of a cave. It was small, and we had to crawl into it, but when we were inside there was room enough to sit up and eat our picnic, and we had stayed there, warm and dry, till the storm had passed.

"This is our secret cave," I said, and laughed as Morgan crawled out, easing himself forward on his elbow.

"And I think it will flood when the water's high," he answered.

And I never told anyone, not even Archibald, about the cave.

When we went to Llyn Ogwen, we always started early, before Jane was awake, and drove to Beddgelert and then

walked along the dew-soaked springy turf of the easy route
to the mountain lake. It was set in a deep hollow, under Tryfan and the Glyders, and the small lake trout lay under the
shadows of the mossy boulders. There were eels in Llyn
Ogwen too, and the water was only ten feet deep, even in the
middle.

Emma liked pickled eels, and Morgan always brought
two or three for her. We ate them in the kitchen because
Jane shuddered and said she wouldn't have them on the
table. When Myfanwy Jones sent us a firsting mug, which
must never be sent back empty, Emma returned it full of
pickled eels. I liked the firsting custard. It was the thick
golden-yellow cream that came first from the cow after
calving. Emma called it natural medicine, and thinned it with
four times as much fresh milk and sweetened it with vanilla
and put it in the larder to cool. It set like egg custard, but
was heavier and richer and felt like satin to eat. Emma had
other natural medicines, but they weren't so good to taste.
She cooked mint leaves and flowers slowly, and then drained
off the water, bottled it, and gave it to Codger for his in-
digestion; and she swore that warm beetroot juice would
stop diarrhea in half an hour.

In wintertime the big kitchen was warm and gay. Emma
used the fire grate and oven, as well as the oil stove, and
they were both black and shining-clean, and the tiles on the
floor were brick red. The big copper kettle in the hearth and
the copper pans hanging behind the stove caught the sunlight and the firelight, and the lamplight when the blue and
white checked frilly curtains were drawn at dusk. The big
oblong rag rug spread in front of the fireplace was all the
colors of the rainbow and many more, and was made of all
kinds of stuffs: strong tweeds, pieces of sheepskin and cow-
hide, red flannel, and squares of bright blue ticking, like
Myfanwy Jones's churning apron. When it was rainy and

cold, or when the snows came, Merfyn Jones and Idris Williams, the post, always found reasons to stay awhile. Mr. Evans, after he had supervised Archibald's work, would sit on the bench under the window and say, "It's a pleasant thing, indeed, to sit in a place where a man can knock the ashes out of his pipe without vituperation," and Emma said, "Too much of that kind of carelessness and it's vituperating I'll be, and don't you forget it." Later, when she asked me, "Miss Catty, what's vituperating, anyway?" and I told her, she said, "Might just as well say nagging, and it's a good but nagging woman he's got himself, at that."

Whenever I could, between study and lunch or in the early evening, if Morgan had gone to his cottage and piano practice was done, I would sit on the rug with Star and listen to Codger's stories. Emma listened too, while she prepared dinner. I loved to hear him tell of his Romany days, while he rocked himself to and fro and smoked his Shropshire clay and spat into the fire. He told of the wild Dooval Bock, who traveled the roads of North Wales with a string of blood hunters and their colts and fillies, following behind his caravan. I loved the Romany words; Nana's name for me, "Kishli," and Codger called his tobacco pouch his *baccy-putsi*, though *putsi* really meant a pocket. He called Myfanwy Jones "Porni vast," which meant White Hand, and Emma "Dordi chai," but he didn't tell her what it meant.

Codger had been friend to old Abram Blood's great-grandson; Abram Blood had been King of the Welsh Gypsies and he had ridden a *porni grai,* a white horse, that was the best in the land, and he had worn a coat with swallow tails.

"Red and black and green, it was," Codger would say, "for those were his colors, and he wore a cocked hat, and a waistcoat that was embroidered with red berries . . . along the same lines as my own . . ." And Codger would look at me and then at Emma, and he would spit into the fire, clean to the center of the coals, listen for the sizzle, and then draw slowly on his pipe. "Save that the buttons on Abram Blood's waistcoat were silver coins from India and those on his swallow-tailed coat were silver and gold and his breeches were white as the early snow and tied at the knee with ribbons. His shoes were made of shiny black leather, and they had silver spurs on them, and he wore three golden rings . . ." And Codger would stop to look at us again and to catch his breath. "Only three, look you, and him the King of the Gypsies." And Emma always added for him, laughing, "And a gold watch of Continental making and a fine golden chain."

Codger had spent weeks and sometimes months traveling with old Abram Blood's great-grandson, or camped with him in a clump of dwarf oaks on the slopes of Cader Idris. "And it's him I can see now, sitting there on the steps of his *vardo,* with his fine dark skin and his eyes that were the gray color of the mist on the crags, and him playing on the old harp that wouldn't stand up by itself . . . and to the music he played, he'd tell of the Develesko mush, the God's dear man, his great-grandfather, the King of the Welsh Gypsies."

Emma would add, "Who came to Wales two hundred years ago, with his wife and two daughters," while she shelled peas or sliced runner beans or peeled onions, "and who was the first to play the violin in the land." And Codger would smile and wait.

"And what was it that Abram Blood had used to be saying two hundred years ago?" Emma asked, looking up from what she was doing. "Wasn't it that there's three things not easy to restrain?" And she would chuckle. "The flight of an arrow. The flow of a torrent. And the tongue of a fool."

Codger would take a long, slow pull on his pipe and wink at me, and answer, "And there's three things a liar must have, look you. A good memory. A bold face. And a fool to listen." And they would try to get the better of each other with words.

"And who's to say you're a liar?"

Emma would turn, with her hands on her hips, and look at him, and with his pipe between his teeth he would mutter, "And who's to say you're a fool?"

"Everyone in this house—if I don't have the dinner on the table when it should be." Then I would know that it was time to go upstairs and change my dress.

Jane didn't like the Gypsies, and was angry when Emma asked them to come into the kitchen. I remembered that when I was very young Saiporella had come to see Nana and Codger in the cottage. I had thought her beautiful. Morgan and I had seen her camp, when we were fishing, and had gone to visit her, and we often saw and fished with her grandson, Manfri, who, Morgan said, could "cast a line on a moonless night and play his fish without a ripple." He and Morgan talked about flies, and Manfri told him to use a small sober-hued fly on the left bank of the Glaslyn stream in the morning; and one twice as big, with a bold bright pattern, from the right bank at evening. Manfri said that the salmon would never take when the weather was about to change.

Morgan and I spent happy days scrambling over scree and rocks, and we walked the lower hill slopes, but it was not until my fourteenth birthday that he, for a birthday gift, took me for my first climb. It was in September, and the weather was good. He gave me the choice of climbing the Milestone Buttress or Moel Hebog. I chose Moel Hebog, Nana's mountain.

We set out at five o'clock, in the chill of the autumn

morning. I wore thick socks to my knees, my navy bloomers, and a thick green jersey and climbing boots. Morgan said that no one needed to have climbing sticks if he had good boots. I pinned my plaits firmly and tidily around my head and crept down to the kitchen. No one else was awake. Emma had left sandwiches and a thermos of tea in Morgan's knapsack on the kitchen table.

I drove Molly-fach, and as we came over the Rise, Merfyn Jones waved to us from across the meadow and we could see Myfanwy Jones's milk tubs and jars set outside the dairy, after scalding, to drip and dry in the wind. A mountain lark soared from the corner of the meadow.

"Like Jacob's ladder, only sound," I said, and Morgan smiled. He was sitting on the opposite seat, smoking his pipe. Molly-fach didn't like the last two miles because going downhill worried her. I thought of the words that every horse and mare said to their masters on their first day together. Nana had told them to me when I was very young: "Hurry me not down the hill, nor force me up an incline. On the level do not spare me, and feed me well on coming home." I laughed as Molly-fach held back and fussed and lost her easy trot, going down the hill to the sheltered Village, where the two steams meet and Moel Hebog towers above. Nana said that where two streams meet was always a Faery place. And often when Morgan stayed till dusk, fishing in the Glaslyn stream, I would sit quietly and listen for the Faery music that is heard only in the moment of time between the setting of the sun and the rising of the moon. I smiled, remembering, as we drove past the gray-walled houses to the Eunach's Head, and left Molly-fach with young Wynne Edwards. Then we went forth on my first true climb.

"Remember to climb slowly," Morgan said as we walked along the path by the stream, "and try, when we get to the steeper, rockier places, not to put your toes down first. But you know this from our ridge wanderings. Try to put your whole foot on the ground, and move from your hips."

I was excited. Our footsteps were silent on the turf. We crossed the field to the gateway. Always, before, I had only leaned on it and looked upward. Nana had been too old and I too young to climb, but the desire had been in our hearts. Today Morgan and I opened the gate, went through it, and turned up the steep slope above the half-seen gorge of Aberglaslyn.

"Though your legs are thin, they are strong with walking . . . but this will be different."

I was soon out of breath, and began to understand why Morgan said that these heaps and ridges of stone would be different. It had been a still, clear morning when we started, but as we climbed the soft mist that had been like a scarf around the brow of the hill descended and swirled about us. The rocks looked dim and distant, and I was no longer aware of height as I scrambled over boulders that loomed indistinctly in front of me. I couldn't go fast enough. I pushed on behind Morgan. We seemed to have been climbing for hours. We must be somewhere near now, I thought, and tried to put each foot down as flat as I could on the uneven steeps. Then, suddenly, we were in a gully, and the mist closed in. I felt a chill all through me as I looked at the high rocks above. The top of the mountain was lost in gray fog. Looking down, I saw the rocks below. The places we had climbed looked perpendicular, and the first boulders, miles away down, unreal. I was afraid. This was a new fear. I broke out in a cold sweat around my head. I couldn't believe I'd climbed the steepness I saw beneath me, and felt myself falling backward; saw my body hitting the jutting crags, bouncing from one to the other, until it landed, like a torn coat, on a small level patch of grass or

stuck in a crevice, like my Guy when Mr. Jones, the butcher,
had stuck it between the rungs of the broken chair at the
bonfire. I closed my eyes. Not as I had closed them on the
heights of Cader Idris with Nana, because of the vast majesty, but so that I wouldn't throw myself down. I screwed
my eyes up and tried to breathe slowly. My skin prickled.
My knees were like jelly.

"Morgan, stop a minute."

He turned. "Let's take a breather," he said, and we sat
down on a narrow ledge and leaned against the damp rock.

After a minute he put his hand over mine, on my knee.
"When you are afraid on the mountain, Catriona, you
should never force yourself upward—you should go back."

"No! Oh no!"

"It takes moral courage to go back before you try again.
If you are frightened you will not feel the joy of the hills,
and mountain climbing is a joyful thing. The straining and
the stress are part of that joy . . . and cannot, must not,
be spoiled by the discomfort of fear. There will be other
days. . . . We have done well."

My breathing was quieter. "Please, Morgan. I don't want
to go back. Please, it's my birthday . . . The fear has
gone. You know I love the mist."

He looked at me. "Come on. Perhaps higher up you'll see
the sunlight striking it and you will love the mist even more."

We scrambled upward again, going left around the crag,
skirting it closely. I found that I still had to stop myself
from clutching wildly at anything I saw, and the rocks
seemed to be upright in front of me; but the mist had lifted.
Morgan seemed to have no trouble at all, but I felt every
yard, and soon lost my breath again, so that every step was
a roaring in my ears and a knife thrust in my chest.

It seemed that I tore and scrambled after Morgan's heels
for hours; that all life was the need to put my foot where his

foot had been, to keep the stitches of his dark green ribbed socks at the same distance from my eyes. To forget the pounding of my heart against my ribs and the agony of taking a breath. I counted the stitches in each rib of knitting. There were eight. Knit eight. Seam eight. The green legs leaped ahead. The ribbed lines of stitches hazed in front of me and there was no place left in the dry, searing ache in my throat and chest to take another breath. Then suddenly the urge and the struggle dissolved into its own pain. I held on to a rock with my hands, leaned my stomach on it, and stayed there.

"Look up," Morgan called.

I looked up. We had crested the ridge. There, close above us, was the huge flat crown of the mountain. It was the roughest scramble of all, but I had breath and to spare. We reached the summit. I stood up straight and breathed. The air was clear and full of light. I closed my eyes. This time it was a gentle closing. When I opened them, I could see the mass of Snowdon to the north, and to the south, Cardigan Bay and Harlech Castle, and beyond, the long ridge of Nana's Cader Idris on the horizon.

We found a sheltered place, a crevice in the rock, with a view of earth and sky, and we rested, watching the clouds rise like steam and feeling the silence, after the inside noise of each step. It was hard to remember the tearing breath and thudding heart; now all was rest. A rest such as I had never known; gentle heartbeats and cool breathing, and a vast living quiet.

After a while, a long while, we unpacked the knapsack and took out the sandwiches and tea. Emma's special sandwiches, almost hard-boiled eggs and crumbled bacon, and some others with squashed banana and raspberry jam inside. This is like the food of the gods, I thought, but I didn't say it because Morgan didn't like extravagant similes.

When we had eaten and drunk the hot tea, Morgan lit his pipe and we sat in silence, Morgan with his eyes half closed, watching the thin smoke as it curled slowly upward till it rose above the sheltering rock and disappeared on the wind. Then he asked, "Can you hear the music of the mountain?"

I could hear only the silence. I was looking far away, over the peaks and valleys, to Cader Idris.

"Bring yourself back from the horizon, Catriona, and listen to Moel Hebog. Come back to this ledge and you will hear."

I looked at him and away again, but not afar. I saw the rock that shielded me; the bright green fronds of parsley fern and polypodies and the yellow-flowered roseroot in a crevice just above me. Then like a bolt from the sky a peregrine falcon came down, her talons lowered; she sheered up again with a rush of wings and a loud swish, came to a vantage point, and swooped down struck, and was away with her prey. I heard the winds rushing, halting a moment to change key, and rushing on again with new sound; and the mountain streams, slipping over smooth rocks; and bird song, wafted up from the valleys; the swift, high song snatches of mountain birds in flight, and I could feel the breeze on my face and the sun's warmth. My body rested. My mind soared with the mountain birds and mingled with the mists below. I moved with the tiny fern fronds and was still in the throbbing heartbeat of the rock I leaned against.

Morgan put his hand on the plaits pinned up on my head. As he put his hand on Paddy's head, I thought, the day we met on the Mochdre Hill. Then without moving or looking at him I spoke, for the first time since we had walked to the birch grove before lunch on Morgan's first day at Bryn Llithrig, of The Happening.

He was silent for a long while, and then I heard him say to himself softly, " 'When Beauty and Beauty meet, all naked fair to fair.' "

After the light had changed and the wind was stilled, Morgan knocked the ashes out of his pipe, refilled it, and cupping his fingers around the bowl, lit it. He smoked for a while, then he said, "Catriona, as we study and learn, we shall meet with people who have known moments such as you knew that day. You will recognize them, and as you recognize them we will talk again." Then he said, "And believe in beauty, Catriona, cherish the belief through your life"—he was silent, watching the soaring clouds—"and be like the mountain, whose beauty may be hidden by mists and driving rains, whose strength may be battered by storm and blizzard, and who may take her ease for a while under a soft cloak of snow yet will stand, tall and fair, when the mists have lifted and the storms have passed and there is only the changing light for a mantle."

Like Nana's face, I thought, against the white pillows, in the mingled lights of the sun and the fire. I listened to Morgan as I had listened to Nana on the day she died. I understood, and as I closed my eyes and heard his deep warm voice, Don't let him go away from me. Don't let him go back to the monastery, I prayed, and watched the clouds that had closed in on us in the gully, blown upward by the changing winds, hitting the ridges, and streaking away over the high crests.

We were silent again. I thought, I feel as I did when I was very young, and Nana took me to Llyn-y-Cau . . . as though I must keep my eyes closed or split up and dissolve into the vastness. . . .

"Morgan?"

He turned toward me quickly.

"What is it, this feeling, up here among the high crags, that isn't fear? Not the fear I felt in the gully. Is it dread? Awe?"

"Awe, I think. Perhaps both. And both are different from fear."

"Oh yes."

"And awe," he said, "awe is as old as living man and" —he smiled—"it never disappears with the growth of knowledge."

"And awe can be part of beauty." I leaned my head against the rock. I turned my cheek against it. It was cool and smooth. "Morgan, I heard the music of the mountain."

"I know."

"I love Moel Hebog."

"Yes. Why?"

"Because Nana used to say . . . 'She is my own dear love in a strange land. . . .' Nana longed for the high moorland reaches and the rush-grown bogs of her own hill, and when the *hireath* held her she would bring me with her to Moel Hebog, to the gateway at the end of the field, where the upward path begins, and say, 'Look up, Kishli,' and I was small and the mountain looked huge and high. 'Look up, and think, Kishli, if we were standing up there, on the top, we could see Cader Idris.' And, Morgan . . ." I looked at him. "Today, on my fourteenth birthday, I am on the heights of Moel Hebog, with you, seeing with my eyes the vision of Nana's longing."

"I wish I had known Nana."

"You know her mountain."

"And I know her through you . . . and Moel Hebog knows us. She has felt our scrambling feet on her sides."

We rested, lost in our own thoughts, until the touch of a chill wind aroused us. I shivered. Morgan turned to me.

"We'll go down the green slopes to the southwest."

"Oh, Morgan, I'd like to go by the Pass—by Moel-y-ogof."

"You've had enough for one day."

"I want to see Owen Glendower's cave."

"We have our own cave."

He laughed and knocked the ashes out of his pipe and put it in his pocket. We packed the knapsack, and he stood up, tall against the high rocks, and held out his hand. I took it, and he pulled me up; then I helped him with the straps of his knapsack and we scrambled down the ledge and onto the easy, muddy slope, making our way through the wet turf and the mosses till, with more careful footwork, we went across the boulder scree and onto the road.

We walked to Beddgelert and had tea at the Eunach's Head. Hot crumpets, oozing with salty butter and homemade strawberry jam, in front of the fire. Then Wynne Edwards brought Molly-fach around to the front door and we drove away up the hill, to the crest of the low pass where the road skirts the rocky stream, and home to Bryn Llithrig.

After a gentle autumn the winter was raw-cold, with heavy
skies and thick gray cloud, clinging yellow mists, and the
mountain sleet, a drizzling blanket, bringing night in the
daytime. We had lessons by the light from the oil lamps and
the flickering fire, except when the blown sleet came down
the chimney, dampening the coals and logs, so that they
gave up hissing smoke instead of flames.

Jane had decided to have tea in the library, so study had
to end promptly at five o'clock, when she knocked on the
door and came in, followed by Tessie with the tray. Only on
Wednesdays, when the Vicar's wife came to tea, and sometimes when there was whist with Dr. Fraser and the Curate,
were Morgan and I able to read and talk after lessons, as
we used to. I was angry, but Morgan said, "Jane is head
of the house, Catriona, and study is supposed to end at five
o'clock. If she wants to have tea in the library . . . well,
there's nothing to do about it."

And I smiled to myself, because now I waited for Wednesdays, when Morgan let me return to the ancient stories
that he loved as much as I did—Welsh, Irish, Egyptian,
Sumerian—and he taught me to recognize the threads that
were woven into the Indo-European legends and beyond
them, to a past almost too distant to imagine, where, he

said, there had perhaps been only two sources for all of
them, the hunters and the planters, in a world so old that
it seemed to have receded into the hands of the gods. He
explained that generally, the planters were more deeply
tribal, and their aspirations and inspirations were for the
group, while the hunters searched for truth in high soli-
tudes, on mountaintops, or deep in the caves.

"As we continue to work, Catriona, we shall begin to
recognize both these streams of myth and belief." And as
we read, he questioned me keenly and skillfully, and yet with
gentleness.

Sometimes I read with Archibald, between five and six
o'clock. It was Jane's idea, and she sent our tea and scones
up to us in Archibald's room, while she had tea with Morgan
in the library; and she chose the books we were supposed to
read, Dickens and Scott, but I took the books we wanted to
read from the library. The chimney served the harness room
and the big oblong room above. It had three windows and
thick oak beams and a big fireplace. Archibald had built a
workbench in the left-hand corner, away from the fireplace
and under the window that faced the river. When he came
back from having dinner with Emma, he carved figures of
birds and animals, in wood, with his penknife and a file, and
magic creatures from the old Welsh stories of Arthur's
Court, and he loved Goohir, Interpreter of Tongues to
Arthur, who could change himself into an eagle or into any
other bird or animal he wished and who understood the language of all living things, and Grugyn, Silver Bristle, the
magic pig, whose every bristle was a silver wing and who
could be seen at evening as he went, swiftly glittering,
through the woods and meadows.

Archibald carved Grugyn, cut and chipped and filed, and
while he worked I read to him from the old, worn copy of
the *Mabinogion,* which I had hidden behind the chest in my

bedroom four summers ago; and always he would say, "Read to me about Olwen, White-footprint, when she came and sat between Culhooc and the High Seat, and she was wearing a flame-red silken tunic . . ."

" 'And a massive collar of red gold' "—I knew the words by heart—" 'with precious pearls and rubies in it. Her hair was yellower than the flower of the broom. Her flesh whiter than the foam of the wave. Whiter her palms and fingers than the flowers of the melilot, among the pebbles of a welling spring—' "

" 'Pebbles in a brook,' " Archibald would say without looking up from his work. "I think of Olwen whenever I see water rippling over pebbles."

"And Culhooc?" I smiled.

". . . whose battle-ax was the four arms' length of a full-grown man from ridge to ridge and could draw blood from the wind, look you," Archibald always added.

His blue eyes were bright with wonder, and I thought of the changing winds on Moel Hebog and drops of blood from the ring ouzel's heart as the peregrine falcon soared aloft with her prey. Archibald worked for hours and days and weeks and Grugyn's bristles were never fine enough to satisfy either of us, but it was a beautiful and almost magic pig, and we felt that Grugyn was pleased that Archibald had tried to carve him in wood.

In spite of Emma's cooking Archibald lost his fat. He was tall now, almost as tall as Merfyn Jones, and thin, but he was never able to stop the red blood from coming to his neck and face when he was embarrassed or angry, and often when he was pleased. He was doing more and more of the work, and Codger told Emma that Mr. Evans had said in the White Horse, "It was a fine day for everyone, indeed, the day that Miss Withers gave Archibald the job at Bryn Llithrig," and that he was "the handiest lad with his tools in the district, look you, barring Penry Jones . . . and had a way with growing things." And I thought, It was a fine day for me, too, when he came to Bryn Llithrig; and with study, and reading to Archibald while he carved, walking across the misty fields and up among the heather clumps and brushwood of the bare hills with Paddy, and sitting on the kitchen rug, listening to Codger's tales of the Romany life, the winter passed quickly, and on a morning in March, Jane received a letter from Mr. Amphlett. He wrote that the guardians had decided that it was time I learned to ride. Jane read the letter at lunch time.

"The head groom from your uncle's stables in Berkshire will come to stay for the summer and teach you," she said calmly.

"Oh, Jane! How exciting! When?"

She read on. "And he will bring his own horse and a mare for you."

"Jane! A mare for me! . . . Morgan, can you ride?"

"No. These lessons will be quite apart from your studies with me."

"Naturally they will." Jane was smiling. "Perhaps lessons should begin an hour later."

"Not at all," Morgan said. "I don't want the hours of Catriona's studies to be interrupted. She can ride at eight o'clock and begin lessons at nine, as usual." Jane's mouth tightened. She shrugged and read the second page of the letter.

"Oh dear!" She put it down. "Really, Mr. Amphlett should have given me more time."

"Why? When do they come?" I asked.

"Next Tuesday," she said, her voice rising. "Well, I suppose he'll have to have Archibald's room over the stables."

"Oh no, Jane! He can't. Archibald has his workbench there. He's so happy . . . we can't move him."

"Perhaps the groom . . . What's his name?" Morgan asked, and Jane looked at the letter.

"Jackson, Edward Jackson."

"Perhaps he will prefer to stay in the Village . . . at the White Horse."

"Oh, I hope he will."

"I'm afraid he won't." Jane shook her head. "Mr. Amphlett writes that your uncle has told him there is a big room over the coach house and a lot of spare furniture . . . and that he expects to stay here. The letter says that he likes home cooking."

"Well, we can't move Archibald."

"Let's not cross our bridges . . ." Morgan said, and he hoped something could be worked out so that Archibald wouldn't be unhappy. "He's a very patient and obliging boy, you know."

Jane told the news to Emma when she came in to serve the bread-and-butter pudding. "Another mouth to feed," was Emma's reply. Then as she handed the dish to me, she said, "So you're going to be a horsewoman, Miss Catty?"

"Emma, please!" Jane was angry. "How many times must I tell you . . . Catriona . . . not Catty?"

"Sorry, Miss Withers," Emma said, and then to me, "Well now, and you'd better eat up. They're strong animals, horses are, and you'll be needing a little flesh on your bones if you're not going to rattle when you go bobbing up and down, look you."

After lunch I went to find Archibald. He was in the potting shed, working with the seed boxes. He was absorbed in what he was doing, and did not hear me until I stepped on a loose plank and splashed mud on my legs.

"Hello. What are you doing here?" he said, wiping his hands on his gardening apron. "What about lessons?"

"I have a few minutes; I wanted to tell you the news."

"What news, indeed?"

"I'm going to learn to ride."

"Ride what? A horse?"

I nodded. "Uncle Hamish's groom is coming and bringing his horse and a small mare for me."

"Well, and this is news, indeed to goodness." Then turning back to his work, "I've never been on a horse," he said, "and when's all this going to happen?"

"Next Tuesday."

"It is, indeed? So soon? And where will he stay?"

I looked at him and didn't speak. I wanted to tell him so that he wouldn't hear it from Jane or even Emma, but I couldn't say the words. I turned away and looked at the seed boxes, but I was seeing the loft room, the workbench, Grugyn and the other animals and birds he had carved. A swallow with long, outstretched, graceful wings, and another swallow, pretending to be hurt, as they do if anyone picks them up; a raven with a heavy, curved beak, and a stoat, its back arched and with tight-drawn lips.

"Oh, Archibald . . ." I turned to look at him, and he knew. He put down his trowel and turned to the shelves under the glass frame and brought out another seed box. I saw that the blood hadn't come into his face; it had gone away from it; he was white, but he knew that I was sad, and after a minute he looked at me and smiled with closed lips and then raised one eyebrow.

"Don't worry, Miss Catty-fach, it'll be fine. Mrs. Evans won't be against me lodging there for a while with her and Mr. Evans. I'll be packing tonight." Now he really smiled. "And it was real nice of you to come and tell me, Miss Catty . . . and now you'd better be getting to your lessons . . . the Reverend will be waiting for you." I wanted to put my arms around him. I went out of the potting shed, avoiding the loose plank, and across the coachyard and into the house, through the kitchen.

After lunch on Tuesday we went, Morgan and Jane and I, to meet the afternoon train. Almost everyone in the Village was there. The reason for Archibald's move to Mr. Evans's cottage had become known and been discussed and talked about in the White Horse, and interest in the English groom and the two horses had reached a high pitch. When we arrived at the station, the wooden fence that divided the platform from Mr. Price's meadow was lined with people. Merfyn Jones was there, as Emma had said he would be.

"Always on the lookout for a man for Myfanwy . . . as though she won't find a man for herself when the time comes . . . and it won't be John Thomas Davies, the blacksmith, either, look you." She was right about Merfyn Jones.

"We must make the stranger feel at home," he had said in the White Horse. Then Jane had come into the dining room and told Emma to talk a little less and to hurry because we had to go to the station.

From the platform we could see the train come around the curve of the Llithrig, about five miles away. Now some of the watchers were on the platform, forming into groups and talking. There was a raw March wind blowing, and they stamped their feet and blew into their hands against the cold. Codger sat on the seat nearest the entrance, wearing his winter overcoat and the royal blue woolen scarf that Emma had knit for his eighty-fifth birthday. He was smoking his discolored clay pipe, and his daughter-in-law and Mrs. Evans were sitting with him. Merfyn Jones went over to talk to them. Then the train was near enough for Morfran Griffith, the engine driver, to lean out and wave a sooty arm. It puffed to a standstill, with a screeching of brakes and a last big belch of smoke. Morfran Griffith looked around.

"What a welcome, indeed to goodness," he shouted above the spitting and crackling of the steam engine. "And you don't know the half, look you." He laughed and shrugged his big shoulders and jumped down from the engine cabin.

"Hello, Morfran Griffith," I said. We were friends. He had always been interested in Archibald's journeys with the pigeons, and our picnics to Llanberis in the summer, and once, when I was six, he had let me get up into the cabin and pretend to drive the train, but I got so dirty that Jane had forbidden him to do it again.

"Have you seen my mare?"

He looked down at me; he wasn't smiling now. "I've seen your little mare . . . and that's not all I've seen." He turned to Jane. "Good day to you, Miss Withers . . . Reverend." Then with a bang and a scraping noise a big flap fell open at the other end of the train, where the horse van had been hooked on to it. We walked toward it, the villagers following slowly.

"Look, Jane, the whole side of the van came down." I saw that narrow strips of wood were nailed across it to make steps.

"It's called a ramp," she said.

Morfran Griffith had been talking to Morgan; now he turned to go. "This time it won't be me that goes near that other horse," he said. "I need to have a word with the stationmaster." He called to Merfyn Jones. "You're big and strong and able, look you, Merfyn . . . you'd better go and help."

And Merfyn Jones crooked his arm and felt his muscle and said, "That I am . . . indeed to goodness, and that I will."

And we all laughed, and turned to look at the wide opening of the van, listening to the stompings and movement inside, and then, just behind us, the door of a first-class carriage opened and we looked around, to see a man step down. He was in riding breeches, and his brown leather leggings were polished so that they shone and his laced boots had pointed shiny toes. He wore a heavy mackintosh; it was unfastened, and I saw a bright yellow and black checked waistcoat under his jacket. He was tall and thin and had a long nose, the point turned down; his eyes were close to it. He looks like a sparrow hawk, I thought. He wore a black bowler hat and carried a long, thin switch. I didn't notice it then, but in the months that followed I came to know it well. It had a plaited leather knob and a wrist strap. It was long and strong and supple. For a few seconds we didn't speak. The Village people were quiet too. Then Jane stepped forward.

"How do you do. I'm Jane Withers, Catriona's governess." And everybody moved again. She turned to Morgan. "This is Edward Jackson."

Morgan nodded. "How are you?"

"Mr. Morgan is Catriona's tutor," Jane said.

"Pleased to meet you, I'm sure," the groom replied. His voice was harsh and high-pitched for a man. He looked around. He seemed to be sneering; then without moving his head he looked at me. Only his eyes moved. "And this must be the young horsewoman?"

I tried to smile.

"And how are you, miss?" He saw my doubt and seemed to be pleased.

"Very well, thank you," I said, and swallowed. "And how are you?" But he took no notice and didn't reply. Merfyn Jones came up to us.

"This is Merfyn Jones, from the Farm," Jane said.

The groom didn't know what a big farm Myfanwy and
Merfyn Jones had. He hardly looked at him. "I shall need
you to help with the horses," he said. "They sent a useless
idiot along in the van, and that engine driver had better
stick to his trade."

And he passed in front of us and walked up the ramp and
into the horse box, swinging his switch with a loud crack
against the wood of the van as he entered. We all waited
around the sides of the ramp, and Merfyn Jones followed
the groom, leaping lightly over the wooden slats and smiling happily; but the sounds inside the van were louder, there
was stamping, and the whinnying was an angry sound, and
so were the sharp claps of hoofs against the wood. We
heard a man's voice, and then the harsh voice of the groom.

"What the hell use are you if you're scared? You bloody
fool . . . get out . . ." Merfyn Jones had disappeared.

A little red-haired man ran out and down onto the platform. He looked up at us, and pointing with his thumb to
the wide opening, said, "That's the devil himself and his
familiar in there . . . that it is . . . that it bloody well
is." He put on a greasy cap. "And if I ever go near that
bleeding hunk of horse flesh again, my name's not Henry
Haskins."

He dropped all his aitches, and if he had not been scared
and angry I would have laughed. He turned and looked at
me.

"No!" he said. "It ain't fair . . . that it ain't . . . poor
bloody young tyke."

Jane, who had a horror of what she called "bad language," had been shocked into silence. Now she said,
"Really!" It was the wrong moment, because the strange
little man meant to be kind.

"When's the next train out of here?" He looked around.

"Six o'clock," Dylan Price said.

"I'm on it." The man looked up at the van. He had big brown eyes with veins in the whites of them. "I'd rather starve." He turned to us again. "Where's the nearest pub?"

"There's only one," Dylan Price said, "the White Horse."

"Lead on, Macduff," said the small stranger, and as he passed us he said, "Excuse me." And he and Dylan Price left the station together.

It all happened quickly, and now there was less noise in the horse box. We heard Merfyn Jones's gentle voice speaking.

"Quietly now . . . quietly, look you . . . gently does it . . ." In the Village it was known that he could soothe any animal. He had studied to be a vet in Llandudno and could cure any ill of bird or beast. "Gently, look you . . ." And he came onto the top of the ramp leading a large, almost black horse. "Come on now . . ." He held the halter rope and stepped a little in front of it. "Quiet now . . ." And then we heard the swift, stinging lash of the groom's switch, and the horse leaped forward and staggered, its forefeet spread out, shaking its head and whinnying. Merfyn Jones held on to the halter and was still talking to it, but suddenly the horse arched its strong neck and lifted its front legs off the ramp, and then with a downward sweep of his head it bared its teeth and banged its mouth into Merfyn Jones's face. He nearly fell, but still held on to the halter rope, though blood spurted from his nose and mouth. Then the huge animal lost its balance on the slope, tripped over the slats, kicked out viciously with its hind leg, just missing Llewellyn Davies, from the Mochdre Village, and caught Merfyn another blow on the neck and shoulder with its head. He fell off the ramp, loosing the rope as he fell.

Everyone scattered as the horse pranced and kicked till it reached the gravel platform. When it felt the level ground, it reared up again on its hind legs. No one screamed. Not

even the children. But everyone kept a safe distance.
Codger's daughter-in-law and Mrs. Evans and Mrs. Price,
from the White Horse, ran behind the fence and through
the gate at the other end of the platform, to help Merfyn
Jones. Mrs. Evans sent young Emrys Jones, the butcher's
son, to get Dr. Fraser and another child to the White Horse
for some brandy.

The dark-colored horse was now still and quiet. I saw Mr.
Jones, the butcher, move toward it. I didn't know he was so
brave, I thought. He put out his hand to take the halter rope,
and then as though it had waited, the horse reared again and
came down with a sideswipe of its head that knocked Mr.
Jones against the fence. Now everyone was angry and afraid.
Morgan held my hand, and Jane looked scared. Merfyn
Jones had stood up, and was leaning against the fence,
holding a handkerchief to his nose. Then the groom came
down the ramp, holding a bridle in his hand as well as the
switch. There was silence. Betty Eyeball was helping Mr.
Jones to wipe the dirt off his coat. The horse stood, quiet.
The groom walked up to it, slipped the bridle over its nose,
and forced the bit between its teeth, and then pulling its ears
through the head strap, he fastened the bridle and took hold
of the reins. He turned to look at Merfyn Jones.

"I'm sure I hope that you're not hurt. I didn't realize that
up here in these mountains you're not acquainted with the
ways of horse flesh. Unfortunate . . . but send the doctor's bill to me." Then he saw Betty Eyeball and stared at
her. She blushed and seemed pleased. She gave Mr. Jones's
coat a last, hard rub and gave him back his handkerchief,
and as she turned away she smiled at the groom. He watched
her for a moment.

"Where's Haskins?" he asked.

Llewellyn Davies said, "He went to the White Horse."

The groom looked around. "A ten-shilling note for any

lad that'll bring the little mare out." There was silence.
"She's real sweet-tempered," he said, and now I knew he
was sneering. Llewellyn Davies took the note, and a few
seconds later he led my mare down onto the platform. She
was red-brown, and put her feet carefully and daintily on
the strips of wood across the ramp.

"Oh, Morgan! She's lovely!" Llewellyn Davies brought
her to the groom.

"Now go and get the saddle traps," the groom said, "and
my portmanteau from out of the railway carriage. The crate
can be sent up to the house, I suppose." He turned to me.
"Here's your mare, miss. You'd better come and look after
her."

Loosing Morgan's hand, "In a minute," I said, and walked
over to Merfyn Jones. His nose was beginning to swell.
His face was white with pain.

"Oh, Merfyn Jones . . . Oh, Merfyn . . ."

He tried to smile, and said through the handkerchief,
"It's all right, Miss Catty . . . go and look after your
mare. It's a real beauty she is, look you now."

Dylan Price came himself with the brandy and gave it to
Merfyn.

"Oh, Merfyn . . . I do hope it isn't broken," I said.

"So do I." He drank the brandy and I went to the mare
and took the halter rope from the groom. She smelled
warm, and I could see the bones in her forehead and nose
and her long, straight black eyelashes. Llewellyn Davies
helped to saddle the big horse, and the groom mounted.

"Where's the house?" he asked as he moved away, and
Llewellyn Davies pointed to Bryn Llithrig on the hill.

"Go past the White Horse, turn right at the Square, and
go up the Hill Lane." Morgan spoke for the first time since
he had greeted the visitor. "You will find the coachyard
gates open, and Archibald will be there to meet you."

The groom turned in his saddle. Morgan's voice was low and clear, and held authority. They looked at each other.

"We hope that you will find your room comfortable. This evening," Morgan said, "I will meet you in the coach-yard at seven o'clock. There are two errands that we should do together." The groom touched his hat.

"Yes, sir," he said. "Seven o'clock, sir."

"Please tell Archibald to have the governess cart ready for us."

"The governess cart, sir?"

"The governess cart."

"Yes, sir." The groom turned forward again, and flicking the horse with his switch but keeping a tight rein, he walked it, prancing and fussing, out of the station.

We walked along the platform, following him. Codger was still sitting on the bench. He looked up without speaking, then he beckoned me to stop. I asked him how he liked my mare. He took a long pull on his smelly pipe, spat, and looked at me. His blue eyes were sharp and merry.

"And would you say now, Kishli, that Archibald was old enough, and able to look after an old man in the prime of health?"

"Of course he is." Suddenly I knew what he was going to say. He said it.

"Then we could live together in Nana's cottage . . . couldn't we just?" He chuckled. "Indeed, and we could, look you."

"You surely could. Oh, Codger!" Why hadn't I thought of it before? Or Morgan, or Archibald? I thought, Archibald can have his workbench again, and Codger's daughter-in-law will have to give up her bounden duty. I forgot Merfyn Jones's nose and my fear of the groom.

"Oh, Codger, you're wonderful." He spat again, and grinned.

"And the little mare . . . she's fine, indeed."

"I'll go and tell Morgan and Jane now, this moment," I said. I pulled on the halter rope and hurried to where they were waiting for me, just outside the station gate.

Morgan and the groom met at seven o'clock. A drizzle had begun with the darkness.

Archibald said, "I looked at his face when I put the rug on Molly-fach. He surely didn't want to ride in the governess cart . . . indeed he didn't." But Morgan had taken the reins and held the door open for him. They had driven to the Farm to ask how Merfyn Jones was, and if his nose was broken. It was. Then they had called on Mr. Jones, the butcher, who, Archibald said, "hadn't minced his words," and he said that when they came back and he was unharnessing Molly-fach they were standing together in the rain.

"You know," he said, "they're the same height. I would have thought the groom was taller than the Reverend . . . and the groom was that mad, Miss Catty. He shouted at the Reverend . . . he said that he took orders from none but Mr. Amphlett . . . and some other things . . . and the words he uses . . ." Archibald said that Morgan had stood quietly till he had finished shouting, then he had told the groom that my riding lessons were entirely his responsibility and that of the guardians, and walked away. Archibald had to clean the saddle and bridle and Edward Jackson's boots and leggings before he went home.

"I could have done them in the morning, look you," he said.

❋❋ 8 ❋❋

The groom stayed with us throughout the summer. He said that Archibald's room was not like what he'd been used to, but he seemed to like it well enough, and stayed there. Archibald and Codger settled happily into Nana's cottage, and riding lessons began.

At first I did suppling exercises while the mare stood still. She was a little under sixteen hands, and her name was Stray Moments. I called her Stray. I had loved her from the moment I felt her warmth at the station and saw her long, straight eyelashes. The exercises were hard to do, but she helped. She didn't move, nor shift about, but stood still patiently while I sat on her back, and the groom said, "Now circle your head. Four to the right, four to the left. Keep those shoulders erect. . . ."

I thought I could hear my neck creaking. Then with shoulders level I swung my arms in circles, first separately, then together, as hard as I could. The bending was the hardest. I sat on Stray's bare back because my saddle had not come, with my spine following the line of her spine, and though I tried not to move my legs and only bend my trunk, I shifted all over the place.

"Right shoulder forward. Keep that shoulder down. Your left hip's out of line. Your head's drooping. Forward bend, keep that line. Keep those legs still. . . ." My legs moved with every bend. My right shoulder wouldn't stay down. "Shoulders straight. Head erect." I heard the groom's harsh voice in my sleep.

For two weeks I could barely move. Then my saddle arrived. It was new and light-colored and comfortable. Archibald soon darkened it and kept it in good condition. I was glad of the first exercises, and now there were new ones. Ankle-rolling and leg-swinging, and the bending began all over again with the sidesaddle. Learning to mount took many days. Although Stray stood like a rock, I always seemed to poke her with my toe.

"You'd be halfway down the Hill Lane if you did that mounting any other horse," he said. "Keep your head up. Shoulders straight . . . and keep that left hip in line. You're leaning to your near side . . . you're leaning to the off side. Where's your vertical line? Your balance is gone . . . that right shoulder . . . that right bloody shoulder."

Neither Archibald nor I told anyone of the groom's language. I liked to ride sidesaddle. At first I had felt snugly held in the pommels. Later I learned that balance could be very easily lost.

Though I loved to ride Stray, I did not enjoy the lessons, and couldn't wait for the moment I joined Morgan in the library. My dislike and fear of the man who was teaching me to ride grew deeper every day, and to my shame, I was so frightened of the Other Horse that I felt sick when it came near me. When the riding master rode up behind me, or along by my side, I was afraid it would lash out at us, and when we went through gates or rode along narrow paths I tried to stay away from the reach of its hoofs.

Stray covered up my mistakes. Cantering in a left-handed circle, she would lead with her near forefoot at the moment he shouted "Aids! Aids!" before I had done anything. But soon I began to feel her rhythm, and to know the moment her head came up, with a gay nod, as though she were saying "Now!" I worked hard, and by the beginning of July, I could jump.

Stray loved to jump, and was gay and mettlesome. She collected herself, and soon I was able to feel the moment of her take-off and swing forward as I had been told to do. Jane was pleased, and sometimes looked out of the sewing-room window when I rode out of the coachyard into the Lane. She was worried because my habit hadn't arrived and because I rode sidesaddle in jodhpurs and a jersey, but I was comfortable and wondered how a skirt would feel. Codger would lean on one of the big stumps of the coachyard gate and watch, and Idris Williams, the post, and sometimes Merfyn Jones joined him. Mrs. Eyeball stopped on her way to "be tidying up the Reverend's cottage . . . if tidying's what it could be called," she said with a sigh, because Morgan left notes saying, "Don't tidy this table today," or, "Don't touch these papers." But she looked after him well and cooked for him in the evenings when he didn't come to Bryn Llithrig or play chess with the Vicar, and Emma would come out onto the kitchen steps and talk with her awhile.

"How a real nice woman like Mrs. Eyeball can have a snippy, disagreeable daughter like that Betty beats me, indeed it does," she said after one of the Parish meetings. "And that foreigner, for it's foreign he is to all that's normal in this Village . . . he bodes no good . . . take it from me . . . no good at all to that silly, flighty Betty Eyeball."

And because of the stories Henry Haskins had told before he had driven with Penry Jones to the Junction in the milk cart, and because the groom, himself, had been thoroughly unpleasant the few times he went to the White Horse, everyone was quiet and there was no talk at all. So he went to the pub beyond the Mochdre Village, along the Llanberis Road, and except Betty Eyeball, no one ever called him by his name; always he was known as "the Foreigner," but she called him Ted. She got a job in the Mochdre Village, and he rode over to see her every afternoon.

During the days of August we jumped higher and higher in Myfanwy Jones's meadow. She let the Foreigner show Archibald how to build two jumps, a picket and a chicken coop, and Merfyn had to dig a small pit for drainage that became the water jump. At first I grabbed Stray's mane with my left hand to try to keep my balance, but gradually I let her have her head over the jumps, allowing the reins to slip almost to the buckle and gathering them up again on landing. My balance was better, and my legs had begun to stay in the right place.

On Saturdays there were always some of the Village people leaning on the meadow gate or sitting on the stile, talking and watching Stray and me with interest and enjoyment, cheering us on and talking again. They greeted the Foreigner if he passed close to them, but they never talked to him. I could feel his sneering anger when we jumped well and there was a shout of gay approval and encouragement. The meadow gate had become the Saturday-morning meeting place instead of the butcher's shop.

Morgan was happy that I enjoyed riding Stray and walked by the meadow one Saturday with Merfyn Jones, to see me jump, and Archibald listened carefully to everything the Foreigner told me. Secretly he was helping Merfyn to train the colt, out at the Farm, and Myfanwy said that he had a way with horses. Stray and I were becoming quite famous. The summer visitors were brought to watch us jump on Saturdays, or walked past the meadow on their way to the White Horse. Although it was Stray who helped me to make a good showing, I had tried hard to learn everything the Foreigner told me and read the books he had sent to me on horsemanship and riding. He rode out every afternoon on the Other Horse and didn't return till I was asleep.

The months passed swiftly and almost as happily as before he came, until one evening toward the end of August when I was in the orchard near the river, watching the last quicksilver rays of the sun on the gray water, I knew. One moment everything was quiet and beautiful in the fading glow of the day, and the next, as a shiver scared up my spine and my scalp prickled, I stood holding my breath, knowing, aware at last of the full meaning of carefully chosen words; unexpected praise on Saturdays, when the people were watching. Praise that I didn't deserve. And sarcasm when we were riding up the Rise alone. Here as the light faded and the trees grew dark and solitary, I knew, with unspeakable fear and sick fright, that the Foreigner meant me to ride the Other Horse.

Thoughts, prayers, tumbled into my mind as I stood. O Heavenly Father . . . Morgan . . . Jane (even Jane) . . . Oh, Jane forbid . . . please forbid. I remembered Codger last Tuesday, when I had taken his loaves, had asked me when the day would be. I had thought he meant the day that the Foreigner would leave, and answered, "Soon now." With these thoughts came others. It would happen on a Saturday, when people came to the meadow gate; I held my breath, hearing Jane: ". . . and so they're bringing their guests to watch. He's a famous horseman, you know. He says Jackson has done a splendid job . . . and they'll come to lunch afterward. . . . He rides in shows. . . ." She had been to tea with the English artist and his wife. "It will happen next Saturday." I sat down at the foot of a tree. "Oh, light for me the Twelve signs . . ." He would show my fear to everyone who had pride in me; show that I wasn't a good horsewoman at all—worse, that I was afraid and a coward; that I could ride Stray only because she was well trained and good-tempered, that I hadn't taken to it like a duck to water, as Myfanwy Jones had told Jane at the Girls' Friendly. And another thought came: He will show the villagers they know nothing too; through me he will try to make them look stupid. Because they know him for what he is, I thought. He will make of their pride in me a stupid thing. I had never before been wretched with fear. Today was Thursday. St. Columba's Day. O St. Columba, you who love the birds and animals and talk to them, talk to the Other Horse. I sat on the dew-damp grass under the tree, shivering; and I knew this fear would grow.

That night I did not close my eyes. I lay with my heart thumping, quietening as I dozed and leaping to my throat again as I aroused from half-dreaming misery to the full fear. "The devil himself and his familiar." Henry Haskins. The Foreigner and his horse were a double harm. When the first bird sang the pale dawn, I had not slept. My eyelids were sore and stiff, and my eyes pricked. I got up and had a cold shower and splashed my face with cold water.

When I went to the stables at eight o'clock, the Foreigner was trying my saddle on the Other Horse. I came every day at the same time; I knew it was done purposely. I thought of the surprise and fear I would have shown, and wondered, How did I know? He looked at me, and the expression in his eyes was mean and angry.

"Your habit arrived yesterday," he said, then he looked at me from head to foot. "You can wear it tomorrow." I wondered how it would feel. How the skirt would feel about my legs. Tomorrow I would know. I was to be dressed for my downfall. I knew that a horse that is not used to a side-saddle dislikes it. The thought of mounting the Other Horse would not form in my mind. It stayed at the top of my stomach. I turned and went into Stray's stall. She was warm and friendly; I leaned against her. Then the Foreigner came in with my saddle and I went and sat on the mounting block till she was ready.

That morning we jumped beautifully. I felt glued to the saddle, head erect, shoulders straight, my loins moving rhythmically. I felt as light as a goose feather. Stray cleared the pit like a bird. The Foreigner called to us to canter to the gate, where he was waiting for us. His checked cap was pulled down over his eyes and a cigarette hung from the corner of his mouth. He was flicking the bars of the gate with his switch.

"Not bad! Not bad at all!" he said. "A remarkable young horsewoman." He opened the gate and held it. "Isn't that what they all say? A remarkable young horsewoman? . . . We must enter you for some shows, mustn't we?" At that moment I hated him. My thought must have shown in my eyes because he smiled and looked at me, tapping the top of his legging with the switch. "Quite the little woman we'll look in our new habit, won't we now?" I felt the hot blood rush to my face, and I wanted to bend double in the saddle.

For the last six or seven months I had been tying a wide black hair ribbon around my chest, so that I should still look flat under my jersey. This morning, with all the fear in my mind and the teeming thoughts, I had forgotten. I turned Stray and galloped away up the Rise.

Later in the afternoon Jane brought in my new habit. She was happy and excited. I changed and put it on. The boots were made of soft brown leather, and the jacket and skirt were of brown checked tweed. The checks were so small that it looked all brown. There was a bowler hat, and two pairs of khaki breeches. White shirts and yellow string gloves and two yellow jerseys, one with a low neck to wear with a shirt, and a polo jersey. I had to leave my plaits down my back. The bowler balanced on top of the braids.

Morgan called from the bottom of the stairs that he wanted to see me in my habit.

"You're not interested in my riding," I called back.

"Don't be cheeky, Catriona," Jane said.

"Come down here. I want to see you."

I went out onto the landing. Morgan was standing with one foot on the bottom stair. He was full of laughter and youth, and a strength I knew. I nearly sat down because of the feeling under my heart. I held on to the banister. He wasn't laughing now. He watched me walk toward him down the wide, shallow stairs. I had forgotten my new habit, the Other Horse, Jane. When I came to the last stair, we stood looking at each other in silence. I couldn't look away. I couldn't move. Like the first day on the Mochdre Hill, I thought, only this is a hurt, like a spear in my heart. I felt the blood rush to my face. A pulse throbbed in my throat. Still we stood and looked at each other, unsmiling.

"You should wear your hair coiled in the nape of your neck," he almost whispered. "It is a lovely way to wear it."

"Don't be utterly absurd, Morgan. She would look far too old for her years." Jane was standing just above us on the stairs. Her fury was like an ice-cold wind. I stood between them. No one spoke. I turned swiftly and ran past Jane, upstairs to my room.

I stood by the window. My heart was singing. I heard Morgan's steps on the terrace and looked out. He was walking with long strides, his head down, his hands in his jacket pockets, swiftly toward the orchard.

The evening passed uncomfortably, until Jane left for the Girls' Friendly Social, where she was to preside. She was wearing her royal blue taffeta semi-evening dress. She had asked Morgan to go with her, but he said he had work to finish. She had been angry and asked the Curate; but she had insisted that at least Morgan come to dinner, and she talked, laughing her thin laugh, about his "great tome," and of how tied to his work he was, and the rasp in her voice made the words more bitter. The Curate, with his usual uninterested politeness, asked the subject of the book, and after he had asked twice Morgan said, "Education." I hadn't known. He never spoke of it.

"Morgan—" I began to ask a question.

"Catriona! Please do not interrupt." Jane looked at me for the first time during the meal. "And do try to remember your manners. Though you may think you are grown-up, you are not, you know."

I didn't speak again, and the Curate changed the subject.

Afterward Morgan and I walked through the orchard and halfway along the river path. We didn't speak until as we turned back again I said, "Morgan, what about education? Has the book got a name?"

"As a matter of fact, it has. It might be changed, of course." He thrust his fingers through his hair. "A university press has taken it."

"Morgan!" I stopped and looked up at him. "How wonderful! What's the title?"

He hesitated. "So far . . . *Education, the Weapon of Progress.*"

"I didn't know. You never talked about it, even to me."

He put his hand on my shoulder. "Catriona"—he took it away again—"there's a great deal of work to be done yet; correcting the proofs and adding to the notation of it will take a long time."

"May I help you with research? Or make notes for you?"

"You may. I was going to ask you when the time came."

We began to walk again, in silence. When we came to the edge of the orchard, I said, "Morgan, must I ride the Other Horse?"

"So you know?"

"I knew yesterday. Suddenly I can't think why—or how —here in the orchard I knew." I looked up at him. "How did you know?"

"There's been great excitement about it, Catriona. Those horsy English visitors have been watching you jump Stray and talking about it in the White Horse . . . and they've been talking horses and racing with the Foreigner in the Mochdre pub." He frowned. "It seems the Foreigner is full of praise for you."

"Oh, Morgan! No! That's not true."

"Well, the villagers are; they're proud as Punch."

"Morgan, I can't ride the Other Horse."

"That is for you to decide."

"I'm so frightened."

"What are you frightened of? Think. What is the worst that could happen?"

"I'm just afraid . . . I'm so afraid of even going near it . . . and, Morgan, I'm not a good enough horsewoman yet. Even if I weren't afraid, I couldn't ride it . . . and the Foreigner knows."

"Yes . . . and you will, more than likely, get thrown."

"And look silly in front of all the people who are proud of me."

"Does that worry you?"

"That and getting hurt."

"You can't fall farther than the ground."

I smiled. I loved the earth. The smell of new-plowed furrows after rain. The fresh green meadow. The soft green meadow.

"That's a good thought. I'll try to remember it."

"And you think the people will laugh?"

"No, the villagers won't laugh at me. It's the Foreigner who'll laugh at them, for their pride in me."

"Catriona . . ." He was going to say something. He didn't. His dark gray eyes were serious. "Then do you think you should try?"

"I don't know . . . I don't know whether I should or not, Morgan. But I'm going to try to ride it if I can."

Morgan put his arm around my shoulder, and for a long moment the fear was lost in his nearness and the memory of his eyes when I had walked downstairs in my new habit. Then with a quick movement he took his arm away. I could see the shape of his clenched knuckles under the worn tweed of his jacket pockets. We walked in silence to the house.

I had hoped it would rain. I woke with the sunlight streaming into my room. Surprised that I had slept, I bathed and dressed. Except that dressing took longer because of the new habit, everything was normal. I had my breakfast and went into the sewing room to say good morning to Jane.

Then I went to the kitchen to see Emma. She turned from the stove.

"My! My! Indeed to goodness, and if it isn't a sight for sore eyes that stands before me . . . indeed, and it is."

I wanted to run to her and bury my head in her large, warm bosom and never go into the coachyard again, nor ever see another horse, not even Stray or Molly-fach.

"Oh, Emma . . ." I said, and ran out. Then I stopped, and walked slowly down the steps and across to the stables. The Foreigner was leaning against the trap-room door, reading the morning paper. The Other Horse was already saddled, tied up in his stall. My saddle was on his back. Stray was looking over her door. I gave her two lumps of sugar, and she nuzzled me. I gave two lumps to Molly-fach and rubbed her nose. I felt more alone than I had ever felt. There were no kitchen noises. Paddy wasn't in his kennel. Archibald was nowhere to be seen. I thought of Morgan. He would not come, but the thought of him gave me strength. The Foreigner was waiting for me to ask why my saddle was on the Other Horse.

"Do you wish me to ride your horse this morning?"

He didn't look up when I spoke.

"Looks like it, doesn't it?" he said, and went on reading.

He had never been openly rude to me before. I knew it had grown out of yesterday, when he had seen the hatred in my eyes and made me feel shy and ashamed at the meadow gate.

"Please help me to mount." I didn't know what to do with the skirt. I waited. He brought the Other Horse out of the stable to the mounting block. He held its head.

"Gather up your skirt across your left thigh while you mount," he said.

"Thank you."

I mounted. I felt dressed-up and absurd. I didn't know how to arrange the skirt over my knee. He showed me again, pulling it here and there, contemptuously, as though I were not wearing it, yet I felt the pressure of his hands on my thigh. I gathered the reins. With Stray I had good hands, but her mouth was like silk. The Other Horse shook his head and pulled, stretching his long, strong neck, and began to jiggle backward on the cobblestones and get behind the bit. I lost my balance. The Foreigner laughed.

"Walk him over the Rise."

When Stray moved into a walk from a halt, the change was slight. The Other Horse wouldn't go forward. He was prancing backward now; my leg was useless.

"Walk him over the Rise to the meadow."

Then I knew that he was going to make me jump. I bit
my lips to stop them from trembling. In a moment I would
have done what he was waiting for me to do : ask him to let
me dismount.

But "Hit him with your stick," he said. "Come on—you
can't fall farther than the ground." I remembered how
Morgan had said the same words last evening in the orchard.
I took a deep breath and tapped the horse's off shoulder
with my stick, and he walked toward the gates. The saddle
was padded for Stray's low withers. The Other Horse's
withers were high and threw my weight back. I tried to pull
my right shoulder forward. The Foreigner saw me trying,
and laughed.

"Not a very pretty sight, I must say." He stood with one
foot on the mounting block, lighting a cigarette. He threw
the match away. "I wouldn't say that much has been learned
this summer."

I kicked the horse, hard, with my heel, and we walked out
into the Lane. I looked for Jane. She wasn't in the sewing-
room window. Archibald was running up the Hill Lane from
the Village. He came toward me. He was red with running.
Suddenly he went white.

"Then it's true?" He stood looking up at me. "The devil
. . ." he began, and added something else under his breath.

The Foreigner came up to us. "You can walk alongside
to the meadow, Archibald," he said, and I thought, He
doesn't want anything to happen before he has planned it.

I kicked the horse again, and said, "I'll meet you at the
meadow gate."

"I'll walk through the wood." The Foreigner turned
away. The horse didn't move. I kicked him again.

"Come on . . . walk, please." And he did. I knew Archibald wanted to hold the bridle, but he didn't, and I was glad.

"You should have refused to ride him, Miss Catty. You don't have to ride this horse."

"I wanted to refuse. Oh, Archibald! How I wanted to." I looked down at him. His round, happy face looked thin, his well-shaped, cleanly outlined lips were tight together. "But I have to ride this horse . . . one way or another. I don't know why."

"I suppose he's going to make you jump."

"I don't think I could make this horse jump."

"You know that almost everyone in the Village is at the meadow?"

"Oh, Archibald!"

"They are, indeed . . . and they're all excited. The Foreigner's built it up like—"

"I know. Oh, Archibald!"

"That's why I came hurrying back from the Vicarage. Mrs. Eyeball told me. The *cuthrel diawl* kept all this dark from me, indeed."

"How can anyone be so mean? To plan like that?"

Archibald didn't reply, and we went the rest of the way in silence.

I seemed to have no feeling, though I was glad that Archibald was with me. When we came to the meadow gate, Codger was leaning on the stile, with Idris Williams, the post, and John Thomas Davies, the blacksmith. Dylan Price was on Merfyn Jones's milk cart with Emrys Jones, and Ellen Rhys-Evans was there with her young cousins. She smiled at me. She was the only one. Betty Eyeball was near the gate, shouting to Merfyn Jones and laughing. She stopped as the Foreigner came out of the woodland path across the road. She giggled, and he winked at her. Suddenly I thought, How quiet everyone is. There had been none of the usual greetings and exchange of news, no lively voices. I looked at Codger; he wasn't smiling. More people came. They stood about. The villagers keeping their distance from the Other Horse. No one moved. Not even the Other Horse. I sat, stiff and tense, on his back in my new habit. Head erect. Shoulders straight, I told myself, and tried not to be so stiff. Then the Foreigner went to the gate and opened it. I rode through. He followed and closed it after him. I could see Morgan coming down the hill from the Rise.

"Ride him once around the meadow, circle to the left, and keep him in a canter." The Foreigner almost shouted the words. His high-pitched voice carried well. I tried to get my weight behind the horse and collect him. I pressed my stick against his off shoulder, used the aids I knew were right, but the horse didn't respond at all. The Foreigner stood there lighting a cigarette. "You'd better try a circle to the right," he called out so that everyone could hear.

I tried again; the horse resisted me, changed his feet in front and then behind, and his quarters were displaced and wrong and awkward. I couldn't get him into a position to lead with either leg. I tried to circle him; he trotted straight ahead, bumping me up and down, changing feet, and then he shied swiftly and my right shoulder came forward. I tried to straighten it.

"I said canter. Not trot," the Foreigner shouted.

I tried to halt the horse. He stretched his neck and shook his head and went on trotting.

"Stop him, can't you?"

I shortened the reins, pulling first one and then the other. The horse stood for a moment, restive.

"Start him again. Canter this time."

Trotting again, I tried to rise, but he shifted and changed and I bobbed up and down, more clumsily off balance than before. This went on; pulling up, but never to a standstill, starting again, but never to a canter, till the horse was surly and meaner than ever, setting his jaw and pulling till my arm sockets were wrenched and sore, bending his neck in one direction and moving in the other, the horse's strong quarters following his own movements and not into the bit, rearing when I tried to halt him. I couldn't keep his hocks under me. My arms ached and my fingers were numb. I had no more strength, and I was almost sobbing.

Then the Foreigner shouted again, and there was bold mirth in his voice. "Put him at the first fence."

The horse was throwing his head back and swinging his huge quarters to the right and staggering backward. I put my utmost of mind and strength into the effort as I tried to regain my balance, get my weight on his haunches, and turn his head toward the picket fence; with surprise, I felt for a moment response. I almost said, "Good boy," then the Foreigner came up behind and cut the horse cruelly across the rump with his switch. The horse leaped forward in a furious lopsided gallop. I tried to keep him at the fence, but I had no control at all and no strength. He dug his forefeet into the ground and bucked swiftly, maliciously, to the left. I went flying to the off side and came down on my nose, hitting a stone. Stones aren't earth, I thought, and at the same moment I was pleased it was my nose and not my straight front teeth. I got up and wiped the blood from my face. The horse was standing between me and the watchers.

The Foreigner walked toward me. He took hold of the bridle. He smiled. There was a look of mean triumph in his small eyes.

"Had enough?" he asked. I was weak and stunned.

"Give me a leg up," I said. Still smiling, he gave me a strong lift. I had hardly the strength to straighten my knee. Somehow I got into the saddle. Blood was running from my nose, but my face was turned away from the gate. I was sure no one had seen that I was hurt. My mind was clear. I felt calm. I will try again to make him jump that fence, I thought. I almost had him collected. Automatically I straightened my shoulders, pulling the right shoulder level. The Foreigner stood looking at my face. I touched my stick to the horse's off shoulder, pressing with my leg; he began to pig-jump, and I was off balance again. Then he reared, high; his huge neck and head rose in front of me. My knee slid out of the top pommel, and then with head down to his forelegs, twistedly, he bucked again. I was unhooked, came off, and landed on my shoulder. This time I fell soft. I saw Archibald run toward me. It was the first movement anyone made. I was on my feet before he reached me. A cold rage steadied me. The horse had galloped away. The Foreigner hadn't moved. He was still smiling. I turned to face him fully. This time there was no hatred in my eyes. I felt only a calm authority. He started to speak.

"Catch my horse, please." My voice was clear, and carried, as I had meant it should. He didn't move. I had forgotten my bleeding nose, but he could not take his eyes away from the flowing blood. His eyes glitter, I thought. He likes to see blood. I said slowly, distinctly, using his surname:

"Jackson, did you hear me? Catch my horse."

Then he hit me. With a swift, long step forward, and with his weight behind it, he cut me across the cheek with his strong, thin switch.

The stillness was shattered. Archibald leaped at him and caught a blow on the jaw that knocked him down. I could neither move nor speak. I could only stand and see what was happening, as though I were looking through the wrong end of field glasses. I could feel the blood running from my nose. I knew it was pouring down the front of my riding jacket, but I couldn't move to wipe it. The meadow was moving like a green sea. The trees, the shouting people, whirled around me. Then I saw Morgan, straight and tall, coming toward me. I looked at his eyes. They held me until he was quite close. He lifted me before anyone knew I had fainted and carried me up the Rise to the house.

✠✠ 9 ✠✠

When I became conscious again, I was in bed. Dr. Fraser
had given me a pill, and I had slept. It was morning. Late
morning, I thought, from the lazy bird song. Jane and
Morgan were in the room. When I opened my eyes, Morgan
came and sat on the bed. I remembered, and felt my face. I
asked if it was a big weal. Morgan said it was. It felt big.

"May I have the mirror, please? I want to look." Jane
handed it to me. The weal stretched from my left ear, down
my cheek and neck. It was purple and blue, with pink swelling at each side of it. Jane looked worried. She took my
temperature and felt my forehead. It wasn't hot. I had no
fever.

"Now you must have some porridge," she said, and went
to tell Emma. Morgan held my hand, and we didn't speak.
In a few minutes Jane came back with the porridge. I didn't
want it, but I ate it and she was pleased. I asked if my habit
was very bloody, and she said that Emma had washed the
stains away with cold water and it was as good as new. My
nose was stiff and sore. I said I would like to go to sleep, and
Jane agreed.

"You should, quite the best thing for you." And she went
downstairs. I turned to Morgan.

"I don't want to sleep . . . I want to think." He leaned

over and put his cheek against mine, and said that he would
go to the cottage and work, and come back at dusk.

Jane had waited for him at the bottom of the stairs, and
I heard her say, "That odious, disgusting brute of a man
must leave immediately."

"Tomorrow will be time enough," Morgan answered.

"How can you be so calm about it? He should leave this
very moment. I shall telegraph Mr. Amphlett at once."

"And he will telegraph the guardians."

"Naturally!"

"Jane, believe me, there are reasons why we should not
be too hasty . . . also, I wish Catriona to decide his fate
for herself."

"That's ridiculous! She's far too young to decide such a
thing."

"I don't agree, Jane." Still talking, they went into the
drawing room.

I lay and thought of everything that had happened. I
knew that if the Foreigner left before his time and the guardians knew why, he would lose his job in Berkshire. I knew,
too, that things in the country weren't prosperous and that
there was a lot of unemployment. I'd heard Mr. Evans tell
Emma that in his opinion, we were headed for a depression.
I didn't know what that meant, but Emma had replied that
we were lucky to be living in a small village where things
didn't change much. The Foreigner was supposed to stay
with us until the middle of September and then return to
prepare for the hunting season. I thought, I don't hate him
any more. But I never wanted to see him again. Perhaps he
could live, for these last three weeks, in the Mochdre Village. Then he could see Betty Eyeball without riding out
every day . . . no one in Berkshire would know that he
wasn't working. I felt kind; as I'd felt when the butcher's
Airedale had rabies. I remembered him, dragging his para-

lyzed legs up the Hill Lane; his hoarse barking. No one
would go near him except Merfyn Jones, who had come
and taken him away.

I went to sleep again, and woke with the startled thought
that the Foreigner might have left. I jumped out of bed,
looked out of the window, and saw the light in his room. I
was glad. The last train left at four o'clock. The sun was
setting. I sat on the window seat and waited for Morgan,
not understanding myself at all. Soon I heard him open the
french windows in the drawing room and then his footsteps
on the stairs. He came and sat with me on the window seat,
and for a while we watched the Foreigner moving about in
his room. Now that Morgan had come, I felt sorrowful and
bruised. The weal was sore and my nose was throbbing. I
heard Stray snorting into her feeding trough. I closed the
door so that Jane wouldn't hear, and then with my head on
Morgan's shoulder, I cried so that my chest hurt and my
eyelids swelled and I couldn't breathe through my nose at
all.

"Wait a minute," Morgan said, and he brought me Jane's
smelling salts. She kept them on her dressing table in a small
heart-shaped bottle made of royal blue glass, with a silver
band around its neck.

"Here, sniff this, it will clear your nose," he said. The
smelling salts were strong, and in half a minute I could
breathe again.

"Jane wanted the Foreigner to leave, didn't she?"

"She's already written the telegram to send to Mr. Amphlett." He sat down again, next to me, and said that she had
promised not to send it till I wakened.

"Why did you ask her to wait?"

"Why do you think?"

"I can't think," I said, and Morgan chuckled.

The Foreigner had been in his room all the time, except

when he had ridden out in the morning. Archibald took his meals to him on a tray. Tessie said she wouldn't lift her little finger if he was bleeding to death.

I told Morgan I didn't want ever to see him again, but when I woke at sunset and thought that he might have gone I was glad when I saw his light and heard the Other Horse in the stable. I looked at him. "If Jane sends the telegram, he will lose his job, won't he?" Morgan put his arm about my shoulders. It was warm and hard against the one that ached. I leaned on him.

"He deserves to lose his job . . . and more. What do you want him to do?"

Quickly, without thought, I said, "I don't want her to send the telegram."

He held me close. The weal stung against the rough tweed of his jacket and the edge of the collar stuck into it, but I didn't feel the pain, only the strength of his love. I knew I had said what he wanted me to say, without truly knowing why. After a while he sat back in the corner of the window seat and lit his pipe. The tobacco in the bowl glowed. I can't smell it, I thought. He took three or four strong pulls. Each time the glow was brighter and lit up his face. "Where love most secret is . . ." I had read the lines in an old book of love poems in the library, last year, soon after climbing Moel Hebog. I remembered them almost every day.

> Cupid is blind, the reason why is this,
> Love loves most where love most secret is . . .

I tried to smile. It hurt. I knew I would never forget this moment; never forget Morgan's face in the flare of the match and the glow of the burning tobacco, against the fading light. After a while I asked, "Why are you pleased with me?"

"Because instinctively you made the right decision." And

he said that however hurt we felt, and were, however deeply we felt that justice was ours, it was never right or true to do a harmful act to another human being. Then we were quiet. Darkness seeped into the room. He got up and went to the fireplace.

"And there is something else . . . there is another reason why the Foreigner should not lose his job." I looked up at him. "Something you need never know about." Then he faced me. "Shall I see both Jane and the Foreigner? Or will you tell the Foreigner of your decision?"

I felt the quick breath catch in my throat. Morgan stood and waited for my answer. I couldn't answer. I picked up the bottle of smelling salts lying on the window-seat cushion. "I'll put these back on Jane's dressing table," I said, and went across the landing to her room.

When I came back, he was lighting the candles in the tall china candlesticks. He stood with the taper in his hand, looking down at me.

"Well, maybe tomorrow will be time enough." He blew out the flame and laid the taper on the mantelpiece. "I'll see you in the morning, Catriona." And he went downstairs.

I sat on the window seat. I felt empty and sick. Morgan was not pleased with me now. "Maybe tomorrow will be time enough." That meant it might not be. I sighed and wondered why I had to be strong all the time, when I had no strength at all. I dressed and went into the bathroom. I splashed my face with cold water. It was very sore. I looked odd. My eyes were swollen from crying, and the weal was bigger and had more red around it. My nose was more swollen, and the cut in it was deep and jagged. I went downstairs and out through the kitchen to the coachyard. I hoped I would not meet anyone, but as I came down the steps I saw Archibald; he was emptying a bucket of dirty water down one of the grids by the stables. His hair looked bright red in the light of the carriage lamp that hung on a spike over the stable door. He heard me, stopped pouring, and half the water splashed back on him. He put the bucket down and ran across the coachyard. His chin was swollen and bruised. I looked at him and he looked at me and we both laughed, and stopped because it hurt, and then laughed more than ever. When we stopped, I said, "I seem not to have laughed for so long."

"Me neither," he said, and we laughed again. Then he asked, "Where are you going? It's late." He couldn't stop looking at the weal on my face, and anger came into his eyes. He said, not believing, "You're not going to see him!" And he looked up at the lighted window over the trap room. He turned back to me. "I'm coming with you," he said.

I told him he could come as far as the door. We walked across the cobbles. I went up the wooden staircase that led to the Foreigner's room; when I came to the turn, I looked down and saw Archibald in the doorway, watching me. I was grateful, and went on up the steps. The door of the room opened onto the stairway at the top. I knocked and waited.

"Who's there?" I answered that it was Miss Catriona. The Foreigner didn't speak for a long time, and then he told me to come in. I opened the door. He was lying full length on the bed. He was in his shirt sleeves, and was wearing the yellow and black checked waistcoat. He had his boots and leggings on.

"Good evening," I said, but he didn't look at me. He put out his cigarette and dropped it into the Toby jug that was on the floor by his bed. His room was neat and tidy.

Then still lying there, he muttered, "Good evening."

I thought of how Morgan always stood up when I came into a room, even to begin my lessons. I felt weak and tongue-tied. I went over to the chair by the table and sat down. The green plush cloth on it was smooth and shiny. It had tassels around the edges of it, with plaited knobs. I was glad that he wasn't looking at me. I took a deep breath and said, "Miss Withers says that you must leave. Do you want to leave?" He lifted his arms slowly and clasped his hands behind his head. Then he recrossed his legs.

"Makes no difference to me," he said.

I didn't dare to ask him about losing his job, but I had to say something more. "Please tell me the truth, because I think you should stay here for the time you were meant to stay. Mr. Morgan does too."

He unclasped his hands and turned on his elbow. We looked at each other. He smiled cunningly and looked at the weal on my face. Again his eyes were glittering. I felt hopeless, and wanted to run out of the room. I sat still, waiting for him to answer. He pulled a packet of cigarettes from his waistcoat pocket; then he got up from the bed and stood with his feet apart. He lit the cigarette and inhaled. "Well, Miss Catriona"—he said every syllable of my name slowly —"if that's how you and the Reverend feel, I'll be happy to oblige."

I had to walk past him to the door. He didn't move. I thought he was going to touch me as I walked around him. He didn't. I got to the door. As I turned the knob, he laughed. I turned and looked at him.

"Something else you've got to say, miss?" Without speaking I opened the door and went down the stairs, to where Archibald was waiting for me. Morgan was standing behind him.

"I did it," I said. "Perhaps tomorrow would have been too late." Morgan looked at me. "Please, Morgan, couldn't we all go down to the river . . . in the moonlight?" He smiled and nodded.

We walked through the garden and the orchard and

across the river path, to the water's edge. We stood there
holding one another's hand. Archibald's was hot and sweaty,
and he held mine so tightly that it hurt. Morgan's hand was
cool, and mine felt safe and warm as he held it. I felt their
love for me and mine for them. It seemed to be all one love.
The small waves lapped against the dark river edge and
the hills on the other side were big and black and crooked;
the hills were part of the waves, and the lapping water was
as serene as the hills.

Morgan broke the silence. "Jane may be getting worried."

I thought, Oh dear, why do I always forget Jane? And
felt sorry. So I nodded and said, "We'll go back now." We
turned onto the path again and walked together through the
orchard, slowly, not talking, hearing the bustle of the world
that thrives in dark and moonlight; past the birch grove,
and across the rose garden. At the sundial Archibald said
good night, and Morgan and I walked to the drawing-room
windows. They were unlatched.

Jane came to my room about half an hour later and
brought me a glass of milk and an oatmeal biscuit. She didn't
know I'd been out. We talked for a while, and she put oint-
ment on my nose and unbraided my hair, brushed it, and
made two loose plaits. Then she said, "I don't think you'll
need a pill tonight," and blew out the candles and went downstairs.

The pain soon went out of the cut on my nose, and the
weal shrank and scarred and had rainbow colors around it,
and although my shoulder was painful I rode Stray. Care-
free we hacked about the countryside, and I began to feel
easy and natural in my skirt. We didn't jump in the meadow.
I wanted to, but Jane said, "Not for the present." She
didn't like me to ride alone, and was anxious that Archibald
ride with me. He had been riding the colt out at the Farm,
and Myfanwy Jones said that he rode "real well"; but

Merfyn Jones said that the colt was too green to be ridden, except around the meadow.

The Foreigner stayed on in the loft room, riding out each day. I never saw him. Then one day during his last week I had finished afternoon study and was in the orchard, gathering early apples, when I thought of the dun mare. She was used in the small milk cart; Stray and I often met her as we hacked about the Farm, and she was gentle and friendly and younger than Molly-fach. I was surprised that the thought had not come to me before. I ran to the stables to find Archibald. He was in the hayloft. Calling to him to saddle Stray, I ran inside to change. Emma was asleep in her chair. I didn't waken her, and I didn't see Jane. When I came down in my habit, Archibald led Stray to the mounting block.

"This is the first time you've been out riding in the afternoon, let alone by yourself." He looked doubtful. "And it's only an hour and a half to the darkness."

I mounted. Stray seemed to catch my excitement, and we trotted through the gates. "There has to be a first time," I called to Archibald. Stray broke into a canter along the grassy edge of the Lane. She was fresh as a daisy. I thought, "How happy are the wild birds; they go where they will . . . to the sea, to the mountain, and come home without rebuke." I often thought of that old Welsh verse when Jane forbade things. I could smell the stacked hay, and when we came over the Rise, I could see the Farm in the hollow, and farther away the Mochdre Hill, shadow-ridged, in the late sunlight. "There's my sweetheart, on the hill . . ." I thought of Morgan.

When we reached the meadow gate, it was open and Merfyn Jones was riding the colt around in circles. He pulled off his cap and said, "Well, indeed to goodness," and nodded his head sideways. Though he was big and broad-shouldered, when he was interested he put his head on one side, like a small bird.

"How are you, Merfyn Jones?" He was going to talk. Welshmen love to talk; over hedgerows or walls or in the lane, or in the middle of meadows. "I must hurry," I said, "because no one except Archibald knows I'm out and the sun is nearly setting."

"You must hurry, indeed," he said, "and if you could jump into the Swede turnips yonder, you'd save a lot of way." I looked at the hedge. It was thick and not very high, but the take-off was bad. I looked at him. He smiled. "The landing's even." I thanked him and put Stray at the jump. She gathered herself, changed feet, scrambled a little, and jumped. She jumped so suddenly that it threw my head back, but when I jerked it forward again we were on the other side. Stray was as proud as I was, and her feet, galloping in between the rows of Swedes were lighter than birds' feet on a rock. I was happy because we had met Merfyn Jones and jumped the fence, and because he went to the White Horse every evening.

At first the villagers had been angry and bitter when they heard we had allowed the Foreigner to stay. Even Codger, for whom Morgan could do no wrong, paid a formal call at the cottage on the bluff, and Archibald told me that he had come home and said, "That Reverend's a wise one, indeed to goodness." They had sat for more than an hour in front of the fire, and Morgan had listened and then talked to him. "Catriona will not always live here in this Village, and she must learn to deal with evil and fear, with unpleasant people and circumstances, herself, in the true way." As Stray and I came to the gate that led into the grass lane, I thought, The true way. Why was it always the hard way? Archibald had told me, too, that Morgan had gone to the White Horse, and had argued about and discussed with all the men, over their beer, the depression and how hard it was to get jobs. "He hasn't done one of you any active harm," Morgan had said. "And you would be depriving him of his livelihood."

"But he harmed Miss Catty."

"And he could have harmed her worse." There had been more high words.

"Then it was for Miss Catriona to decide," Morgan had said. He had been stern and quiet, and when he left, Merfyn Jones had ordered another round of beer and said, "Why do the bastard any more harm than he'll always do himself?"

"That he will"—Codger had the last word—"and let it be others that'll have him on their consciences, look you, for he's not worth the trouble to ours." And after that no one seemed to think about it any more, except the Vicar's wife, who was angry that her husband had agreed with Morgan.

"I think they are both quite wrong," she said at tea. " 'We have our reasons,' my husband said, 'for believing that the whole affair should be kept within the confines of the Village.' "

"Oh dear," Jane had sighed, "and Jackson seemed such a retiring sort of man. We rarely saw him."

"What reasons they could have for not sacking the wretch immediately, I can't imagine."

"Morgan's reasons." Jane's voice was acid.

"Of course! I must admit that I've always found him a little odd. I can't think why the Vicar likes him so much. Even for a monk there must be a limit to turning the other cheek."

"And he's not a monk now." Jane had patted her hair. "I shall be so glad when Jackson has left and the affair is forgotten."

And this is his last week, I thought as we came to the drinking trough.

I dismounted and tied Stray to the stump at the end of

the trough. Myfanwy Jones was in the cow shed. I called to her. She told me to come into the shed. She was milking the last cow but one. She pressed her head hard against the cow's flank, and her arms and fingers moved evenly. The sound of the spurting milk made a sound like a gong against the side of the pail. There were five pails of milk already in a row near the door, and the smell of the cow shed was strong and damp and warm. The feeling of hurry left me. There was another three-legged stool by the pails of milk. I fetched it and sat down on it and watched Myfanwy Jones and wished I could always be here, in the mountains. With Morgan. It was a deep dream. I never let it become thought. Myfanwy Jones didn't speak until she had finished the milking, then giving the last cow a hard slap on the rump, she said, "Well, and if this isn't a surprise, indeed," and lifting her skirt, wiped her hands on her petticoat. "Surely to goodness, and I wasn't thinking to have visitors today . . . but come up to the house, there's some tea and *bara-brith*. Better than Emma's, too." Her pink skin was glowing and damp, and her hazel eyes were bright and kind. I thanked her and said that it would soon be dark and I must get home.

"And how's Paddy? He doesn't come so often these days."

"He stays with Morgan up at the cottage, nearly all the time." Then I asked her if she would please lend me the dun mare. She looked surprised and asked me why I wanted her.

"You have Stray and Molly-fach—"

"For Archibald. I want him to come riding with me, and Merfyn says the colt's too green." She was carrying one of the pails to the door. I followed her. "Archibald wants to ride with me." She put the pail down while she thought. Then she put her hands on her hips.

"Archibald's a fine boy. He rides well, too. He has the feel for animals, and he profited by your lessons."

"Well then, may we borrow her, please?" She pushed a strand of hair back from her eyes.

"Let me look at you, Miss Catty-fach. I haven't seen you since you rode the Other Horse." She looked at me without smiling. "I wouldn't say that you look your best, indeed," she said.

"Wasn't it a good thing I didn't hit my teeth?"

She laughed. "When do you want the dun mare?"

I couldn't believe she meant it. "Soon, please."

She walked over to where Stray was standing and sat down on the trough. "I'll need her for the next two weeks," she said. "After that you can have the loan of her. The change will do her no harm, and I'll save on the feed bill."

I hugged her, and she nearly fell into the trough. She hugged me back, and I went to Stray.

"I must go. Will you help me up, please?"

She got up and cupped her hands and gave me a leg up. When I had arranged my skirt, I held out my hand. "Thank you, Myfanwy Jones." I felt grown-up and capable when she shook it, and then young and grateful again. "Thank you, Myfanwy Jones."

"Don't thank me," she said. "Just see the dun mare's well cared for."

When we reached the Rise again, I could see the mare in the distance, in the field beyond the Swede turnips, and as we galloped home the land was quiet. Small mountain birds, no longer soaring, nestled in the hedgerows, twittering before they slept. Soon we came to the coachyard gate.

There was no one about. I dismounted at the block and took Stray to the stall, unstrapped the saddle and bridle, and rubbed her down. When she was comfortable, I went into the house.

"You're going to catch it," Emma said as I passed through the kitchen, so I knew that Jane had missed me. I went into the drawing room. She was reading. She looked pretty in a blue georgette blouse that showed her lace camisole through it and had full, long sleeves. Then I saw. She's got her hair coiled in the nape of her neck. I felt suddenly cold, aware; but of what? I didn't know. She looked up. When she saw me in my habit, she was angrier than ever.

"Where on earth have you been riding to at this time of night?"

"It wasn't night when I started." And I told her about the dun mare and that Archibald would be able to ride with me as soon as the Foreigner left and the Other Horse's stall was free. She grew less annoyed.

"Well, that will be better than careering about the countryside alone, at any rate . . . and now you'd better go and change for dinner." She closed her book. "And take a bath . . . there's no hurry . . . Morgan is coming to dine. As you don't drink sherry, you may meet us in the dining room."

"May I go first to Nana's cottage and tell Archibald and Codger about the dun mare?"

"No," she said. I had run around enough for one day, and the next time I went to the orchard to gather apples not to leave the basket in the middle of it.

I went upstairs, bathed and changed, and waited till I heard Emma hit the small brass gong before I went downstairs to the dining room.

I couldn't wait to tell Archibald, and the next morning, early, I found him working in the garden. He was pushing a big wheelbarrow full of manure along the rose-garden path to the vegetable-marrow patch. He stopped when he saw me and sat down on one of the handles of the barrow. As I walked toward him, he said, "And what are you doing out and about at half past six in the morning?"

I sat on the other handle of the wheelbarrow and told him all about the dun mare.

"So that's where you went yesterday." He was pleased and eager. "Will we keep her here, in the stable?" he asked, and I told him everything Myfanwy Jones had said.

"I think I can ride well enough to look after you. The Foreigner was so bossy. I learned when he thought he was telling me off. I listened to everything he said about horses . . . and he knows a deal, indeed." And then he said that he must get on with his work, and I went into the kitchen. It was bread-baking day, and Emma had been up since five o'clock and was kneading dough in the large blue and white bowl. Her fat arms were white with flour.

"*Bara-brith,*" I said when I saw the currants in the dough.

"And what got you up at the crack of dawn, Miss Catty?" she asked as I walked around the other side of the table because Blodwen Price, who was taking Tessie's place while her mother was ill, was washing the floor. I avoided the part she had washed.

"Thank you, miss, indeed," she said. I looked at her. She was bending over the bucket and rubbing soap on the scrubbing brush. Her hair was black and coiled up on top of her head. She looked up. Her skin was yellow, and her eyes were black and narrow and large. She was thin. The look in her eyes didn't match her voice or her manner. She is strange, I thought. Then the wall-door bell rang. I started. Emma stopped kneading and looked at me. The bell rang again. Blodwen Price went on scrubbing and humming to herself.

"Now, who on earth can that be? At this early hour?"

"I'll go." I went out into the hall, opened the front door, and ran down the front path between the poplar trees, and as I reached the wall door the bell rang again. Someone is impatient, I thought as I turned the big iron key and pulled the bolt. "Just a minute." I opened the door, and Betty Eyeball was standing there.

Her eyes were red and swollen, she looked untidy, and her fair hair hung in wisps. I was surprised to see her. It took a moment before I could say, "Come in." She pushed back her hair and pinned it away from her face. "Good morning, Betty Eyeball," I said.

"You're up early, aren't you?" she answered. I thought, How unpleasant she is. She walked through the wall door, and past me, then she stopped. I asked her if she wanted to see Jane, but she said, "No. Emma Higgins." Then she asked if "that Blodwen Price" was anywhere about.

"She's in the kitchen," I said. "I'll show you."

"No! I'll wait in the garden, here." She sat down on the iron seat. "Tell Emma Higgins to come out," she said, and I walked away. She called me back. I turned. She put out her hand. "Don't tell Blodwen Price that I'm here. I don't want her to know . . . but I must see Emma Higgins." She looked up at me. "She's just got to talk to my mother." I turned quickly and went into the hall to call Emma.

"What is it? Who was that knocking?"

"Come here, Emma, please." She came to the kitchen door, wiping her floury hands on a towel.

"Well? What is it?"

"Betty Eyeball. She wants to see you," I whispered.

"Betty Eyeball?"

"Sh! She doesn't want Blodwen Price to know she's here." Emma was annoyed.

"Well, I don't know what all this is about, indeed, and at this time in the morning, when I'm baking."

"You'd better see her, Emma," I said. "She's been crying." I ran upstairs to change into my habit.

I jumped Stray in the meadow for a while, then feeling guilty because Jane had forbidden it, I cantered her down

the Lower Mochdre Road, to the Plas-y-Coed Wood, near
to the river. I wanted to see the leaves before they faded and
fell. It was a wood of clear streams, and we rode along the
paths that bordered them, green paths veiled with leaves
that flicked the morning sunlight from one to the other. A
late thrush, surprised, began to sing, and Stray pricked up
one ear. As we came to the heart of the wood, the grass was
a darker green.

> I shall make a new room in the grove,
> Fine and free,
> With a green top story of birches of every hue . . .

Dafydd ap Gwilym had written in the fourteenth century.
His grandfather had found one of the doors to the Fair
Land, and so his son and grandson knew the woods and the
rivers and the mountains and could write about them so that
other people knew them too.

> . . . and a summer house of bright green trees,
> A cause of fame,
> On the fringe of the green meadow . . .

Branches brushed my face. Thin birch branches, and the
twigs tangled in my hair, although it was tightly braided and
pinned up. But soon Stray became restive. She liked the open
country, so I turned her head away from the heart of the
wood and she trotted happily and faster till we came to the
edge, where Paddy met us and ran along with us, all the way
home. It was more than three miles, and Archibald later
said Paddy had been very tired and gone to his kennel and
slept all day.

I had lingered in the woods and hurried in to change for
lessons. I ran up the steps into the kitchen, and it seemed to
be full of people. Mrs. Eyeball and the Vicar's wife and
Jane and Emma. They stopped talking as I entered.

I said, "Good morning," to the Vicar's wife, and wondered why she was at Bryn Llithrig so early. Mrs. Eyeball
was crying, and didn't see me.

"We're talking, Catriona," Jane said. "Go up and change
your clothes."

As I changed, I thought, Something odd, and not nice, is
happening. But in the library everything was normal, and
we worked on *Medieval Latin Lyrics* and then read some
Shelley, and it was time for lunch. Morgan said that he was
going to the Vicarage.

"But it's Merfyn Jones's gift lamb, with onion sauce."

"I'm sorry to miss it," he said, so Jane and I were alone.
She was so worried that she forgot to say Grace. Emma
looked angry and disgusted and served the gift lamb in silence. I didn't speak, and when I had finished eating asked if
I might leave the table.

Jane said, "Yes, dear," without looking up, and still sat
in her chair with one elbow on the table and her chin in her
hand.

There was a quarter of an hour before lessons, so I went
to the coachyard to take Stray and Molly-fach some sugar,
but as I came near to the stables I heard voices. I didn't
want to meet the Foreigner, so I turned and went through
the archway into the rose garden. Archibald was spreading
the manure he'd tipped out early in the morning. He whistled, and I was about to call to him when I saw Blodwen
Price come out of the stable door, look around her, and then
run swiftly toward the kitchen.

"I have to go to my lessons," I called to Archibald, and
went through the drawing-room windows to the library.
Morgan was waiting for me.

"How was the gift lamb?"

"I don't know, I hardly tasted it."

"You look thoughtful, Catriona. What is it?"

"I don't know. And that's true . . . I don't know. I feel that something not nice is happening. Everything seems strange."

"Something has happened, but it need not affect you . . . and remember . . . curiosity is not attractive." He smiled at me. "Now let us get on with our work."

But for the first time in all the years we were interrupted. There was a knock on the door, and Jane opened it.

"Morgan, will you come here a moment, please," she said, and Morgan left me and joined her in the hall. A minute later he came to the open door.

"Finish what you are doing, Catriona, and then write an essay for me . . . on Shelley . . . and read what you like till five o'clock." He closed the library door, and from that moment, for three days, there were no lessons.

✠✠ 10 ✠✠

The next morning when I went down to the kitchen before breakfast, Emma said, "Archibald's waiting for you. You're going for a picnic. I'm just putting up the basket."

"A picnic? In the rain?"

"All day. Miss Withers says that if it rains too hard you can have lunch at Capel Curig. She's given Archibald five shillings." I thought, What about study? Emma wrapped the sandwiches in grease paper and put elastic bands around them. "Lessons have been canceled until further notice . . . riding, too." No study! Disappointment was a sharp pain. Then Archibald came up the coachyard steps and into the kitchen. He looked happy. His blue eyes were shining.

"I'm to look after you," he said, "and you'd better get ready. Miss Withers says we must leave by half past nine."

I wanted to stay at home; to know what was happening. "Curiosity is not attractive." I wasn't curious so much as hurt and angry. Angry that Morgan hadn't come back last evening. Hurt that he hadn't told me himself that study was canceled. I had never been angry with Morgan before. It was the worst feeling I had ever had. But I didn't want Archibald to see how I felt because he was smiling and pleased, so I said, "We're not going to Capel Curig even if it pours." Emma looked up. "And put some banana and raspberry jam sandwiches in, too, please." I turned to Archibald. "I'll meet you at nine o'clock in the coachyard."

I ate my breakfast without tasting it. Even Emma's burnt toast. My anger with Morgan seemed to fill my stomach up to my throat. I went into the library. The Shelley essay was on my desk, where I had left it yesterday. I went up to my room and put on long socks and brogues, thinking, We'll go to Nant Gwynant and picnic on the grass beside the Glaslyn stream and look up at Moel Hebog . . . and old Eldorai Blood may still be camped there. . . . I tied the second shoestring and knew that I didn't want to go for a picnic. I wanted to see Morgan. I went down to the kitchen. Blodwen Price was washing the breakfast dishes. Without looking up or turning around she said, "Good morning, Miss Catriona."

"Good morning." I went to the pantry to get some sugar for Stray and Molly-fach.

The air in the stable was damp and smelled of manure. I leaned over the stall door and patted Stray's strong, silky neck. He didn't even leave a note on my desk last night, I thought. She nuzzled me. I rubbed her nose. I felt cold and hard, as though there were a heavy, jagged lump of ice in my chest. I'll wait until nine o'clock. I gave her the sugar. The stiff, prickly hairs on her lips tickled the palm of my hand. He must come then, at lesson time, to tell me there is no study. I looked at her slender face and large nostrils. Her wide head and long, straight lashes. "No riding today, Stray, and no lessons." I put my cheek against her bony one, but she shook her head and stretched her neck down over the door of her stall away from me, and was no comfort at all. Then I thought of Archibald. "I'm to look after you," he had said. I didn't need looking after; I was fifteen. Then I remembered that I hadn't tied the hair ribbon around me. I had wakened and begun to think and wonder as I lay there.

Why had Betty Eyeball been crying? And why had she come to Bryn Llithrig at half past six in the morning? Why didn't she want to see Blodwen Price? I went to Molly-fach's stall, thinking of the dark-haired, strange girl. Yet she's polite, I thought as Molly-fach searched my palm with her rough tongue and rubbery lips, but even her politeness is strange. It was as though inside she were laughing at everyone. Wishing that Tessie's mother would soon be well again, I went to my room and took off my jersey. When the ribbon was tied around it, my chest looked almost flat. Anyway, it was straight across, and not divided in two. With the thick jersey on it would look the same as always. It was quarter to nine; I sat on the bed. I'll make my own bed and dust, I thought. I don't want Blodwen Price to come into my room. After the bed was made, I took the duster from the bed-table cupboard and wondered why Jane, who always thought of everything like that, had never asked what I had dusted with during punishment week, so long ago. I dusted the candlesticks and the Staffordshire hound, trying to puzzle out why I was uneasy about Blodwen Price. Then being angry with Morgan shut out all other feelings.

When I had finished, I went downstairs, took my mackintosh from the cupboard in the hall, and went to the kitchen. Blodwen Price was sweeping the floor. Tessie scrubbed it every day.

"I made my bed and dusted my room," I said. "There is no need for you to go in." She looked at me, and there was neither surprise nor amusement in her look, but a sudden knowing. Her thin yellow face was almost lifeless, yet her eyes burned, black and bright. Her hands were clasped, one over the other, on the top of the floor-brush handle. The bones of her knuckles and elbows shone white through the yellow skin. She wore sandals. She held me with her look. It was not unfriendly. It was not friendly. I'm right about my room, I thought, and broke the silence.

"Where's Emma? And I haven't seen Star and Rumpel this morning."

"Mrs. Higgins went out early . . . and I haven't seen the cats." She began to brush the floor again, and I went down the steps.

"And thank you, miss . . ." I turned and looked back into the kitchen. She was looking at me. "For saving me the work. Though it's not minding work, I am, look you."

Molly-fach was harnessed, and rugs, mackintosh blankets, the picnic basket, were all packed and ready in the governess cart. Molly-fach was impatient, and kept pulling up her bit. The Foreigner was nowhere to be seen. Archibald came through the archway.

"Emma was out, so I went to the cottage and made some hot tea. We'll need it in this damp." He went to the governess cart and put the thermos flask into the basket, and looked at everything with a responsible eye. "No sticks?"

"I put them in the harness room. Let's go to Nant Gwynant."

"It'll be easier on Molly-fach, at that." He looked at me. "You have your mackintosh. What about Paddy?"

"He's up at Morgan's cottage." Morgan hadn't come at nine o'clock. I was going away for the whole day, and he hadn't come. I found that my teeth were clenched. I took a deep breath and smiled at Archibald. He hadn't noticed anything.

"Well, we can't go for Paddy; it's all but half past nine now, so we'd best be on our way before Miss Withers comes back."

I couldn't think of any excuse to stay, so I stepped up into the governess cart and sat next to the picnic basket, leaving the reins for Archibald. He jumped in after me and took hold of them. I pretended to look in the basket to hide my tears. Molly-fach was fussing over the cobbles as she always did. We came to the gates and out onto the roadway. Tears fell on my hands. I fiddled with the basket straps.

"Catriona! Wait!" Morgan came running through the archway. Archibald pulled Molly-fach up, and Morgan came toward us. Then he stopped at the mounting block. "Come here, please, Catriona. I want to speak to you." I opened the small door at the back of the governess cart, jumped down, and ran to him.

"I was looking for you. I didn't know that you were not riding this morning. Jane didn't tell me that you were going to be away all day. I'm sorry I could not come back last evening."

I laughed. "Oh, Morgan! It's all right . . . but I'll miss studies."

"I know. I will too."

"Why can't I stay in the library and do work that you set for me?" He shook his head. "Why must I go for a picnic?"

"It's better that you are away from the house for a while."

"Morgan, what is happening?"

"I'll tell you everything, but not now, and, Catriona, please promise me not to ask anyone else about it."

"I promise."

"Now go and have a misty picnic. You like the mist, and I'm happy that you are with Archibald." We walked back to the Lane. "And don't think any more about what is happening here. You can't help."

"We're going to Nant Gwynant. Eldorai might still be there."

"Then give her my greeting and find some heart's-ease for me; they bloom late, in the damp meadows." I climbed into the governess cart, and Morgan closed the door and latched it. "Take good care of her, Archibald."

"That I will, Reverend." And we were on our way. I was happy. Archibald had not seen my tears.

The air was damp with September rain, and all trace of the sky was hidden. The outline of the Mochdre Hill was blurred and the top lost in the cloudy mist. The earth and sky were wrapped in a fleecy gray blanket that muffled the sound of Molly-fach's hoofs. Wherever color was, it glowed of itself; the dark green leather cushions, the black harness, Molly-fach's red-brown rump and jet-black tail were wet and shiny, and Archibald's hair was like a flame in the gray.

" 'How happy are the wild birds . . .' " I began.

" 'That come and go, without rebuke . . .' " Archibald added. "There'll be rebuke enough, look you, if we're not home before the darkness."

"I hope Eldorai hasn't left."

"Now, look you, Miss Catty, you're in my keeping for today . . . and you know how Miss Withers feels about Gypsies."

" 'With their clipperty-clabber and gibberish . . .' " We laughed. "I hope she's still there."

"And so do I, indeed . . . for 'tis a deal they know about horses . . . and poaching . . ."

"Never catch a salmon till the foxglove's in full bloom. Jasper Blood told that to Codger, and he tells Morgan every year when the fishing season begins."

"Except that they don't follow their own advice," Archibald said. "They fish and shoot out of season in spite of the gamekeepers."

"Oh, Archibald! The gamekeepers know they poach, and they don't mind . . . they know the Gypsies never shoot or fish more than they need to eat."

"They poison pigs, though."

"Archibald, wherever did you hear that?"

"Jasper Blood and Saiporella told Nana and Codger. Codger sings a song about it."

"I never heard him."

"You'll hear the song, though. Codger taught it to Penry Jones to sing as an encore at the Annual Concert."

"Well, it's only a song; they don't really do it."

"They used to . . . maybe they still do, look you."

"How did they poison it? And why? They couldn't eat a poisoned pig."

"They did eat it."

I put on my string gloves. "How? Here, I'll take the reins and you can talk." Archibald laughed again and handed the reins to me, and we changed seats.

"Well, to poison the pig is to '*drab the bawlo.*' Those are the only Gypsy words I know. Codger knows the whole song in Gypsy language."

"Never mind. How do they poison it? Where? . . . In the sty?"

"They use bane; three penny'worth. The Gypsy woman goes to the chemist—they call him the poisonmonger—and buys it; then with the bane in her pocket—"

"Her *putsi* . . . You know that Gypsy word, too."

"I do, indeed . . . Codger's *baccy-putsi* . . . but I don't think of it as a Gypsy word any more."

"Go on. Where does she go with the bane in her *putsi?*"

"To a farm where there is a good, fat porker . . . she goes with two or three of her people, and while the others are selling their pots and pans to the farmer's women, and telling their fortunes, the Gypsy woman flings the bane into the pig swill."

"Why don't the men like to have their fortunes told?"

"Silly stuff, indeed to goodness."

"You don't truly think that."

"I do, indeed, but look you, the pig dies in the night—"

"The bane is all that strong?"

"It is . . . and early the next morning the Gypsies come to the farm and beg the body of the dead porker."

"They'd have to wait till the farmer found out, first."

"They do . . . they're clever, indeed . . . and then they take it to their camp, cut it open, and wash its insides with boiling fresh spring water and goodly herbs till not a grain of poison is left—"

"And then they roast it and have a great feast. That's only like poaching. They needed it to eat."

"Miss Catty!"

"And then they sing and dance and play the fiddle and the harp and tell tales—"

"I'd like to play the fiddle."

"You'd be good, too. Your hands and fingers carve delicate, beautiful things. I can see them on the fiddle strings."

"Honest, Miss Catty?"

"Truly . . . and I'd like to play the harp."

"Ellen's learning, from Myfanwy Jones."

"I know, and Merfyn Jones told Emma that Myfanwy said that she had the art and the application."

"Well, and that I wouldn't be knowing, indeed," he said, and blushed. I laughed.

"If Eldorai's still there, she might tell my fortune."

He looked more at ease again. "Codger said that Eldorai doesn't dukker any more . . . and she comes no more to the villages, these days."

"She never did, unless the dukkering truly came to her. She never pretended to tell fortunes, as some of the Gypsies do."

"I hope she's still at Nant Gwynant."

I nodded, and then we talked about the dun mare and riding together until we had passed the cart road that descends steeply into the valley and Molly-fach began to shuffle and sway her rump as she went down the more gradual slope of the new road. Soon we were in the valley meadow, the gray mountains towering above us on either side. The tall, rugged grace of Moel Hebog was veiled and her summit hidden. The thin, mild rain filled the valley like smoke.

We chose a clump of dwarf oaks and sycamores near to the stream, and Archibald put one of the mackintosh horse blankets on the soft turf and lifted the picnic basket down. While I unpacked it, he loosed Molly-fach from the shafts and took off her bridle; then he gave her a slap on the rump. She tossed her head, and whinnying softly, trotted away along the edge of the stream.

"Best put your mackintosh on, Miss Catty."

"I'm not cold, and the sun may—"

"Not this day, it won't, indeed . . . it's a real misty one, and the rain will come later." He was coming to join me on the blanket.

"Please, Archibald, walk a little way across the field and see if Eldorai's *vardo* is still there . . . in the clump of oaks. You can see it if you walk upstream a little. I'll get the picnic ready."

"And the tea?"

"And the tea. You were right."

"It isn't cold, but the damp clings, indeed." Archibald walked away, and I took the sandwiches out of the napkins and put them on a big plate, and put two smaller plates for us to use. There were ham sandwiches and hard-boiled eggs. I took out the two pigs, for salt and pepper, that Archibald had carved for my birthday last year. Their tails were the stoppers and the holes were in their snouts; big ones for the salt, small ones for the pepper. They both had painted black eyes, ears that looked soft and crooked, and slim little feet, and the grain of the wood made wavy circles around their fat bodies. I thought with wonder of how he must have filed and smoothed and polished, for the wood was smooth and shiny as silk. He had begun two for Morgan, for Christmas. They were to be cone-shaped, and he had made butter patters for Emma. One day he heard her say that she was "getting that forgetful." And last Christmas he had made a blackboard for her, with a wooden frame, carved with animals and birds and a bow, to hang from the wall. I had given her a box of colored chalk and a huge sponge to wipe off the old messages. At first it had been used for grocery lists and kitchen notes, but soon Codger and Merfyn Jones and Idris Williams, the post, and Mr. Evans and Archibald and I used it, and it became known as "the message board"; and Archibald had to make one for Myfanwy Jones and one for Mr. Jones, the butcher.

Archibald whistled. I looked up, and he waved and pointed. He came running back and sat on the mackintosh blanket in front of his plate.

"Eldorai's *vardo* is still there."

I passed the sandwiches to him, and he took three and laughed.

"*Crass dy fara,*" he said.

"That's not true . . . that bread's not hard. It's Emma's bread."

"They're the only Faery words I know."

"Gypsy words . . . Faery words . . . Welsh words French words . . . Oh, Archibald, aren't words odd?" I took a hard-boiled egg, sprinkled salt on it, and then pepper.

"Faery words are queerest," he said. "Say, 'The hour is come but the man is not,' as the Faery man says at Llyn-y-Cau on New Year's Eve."

"*Daeth y awr ondd ni steath y Din.*" I sighed. "I wish I had learned more from Nana."

"This tea's good and strong."

"It's too strong. Please, open some ginger beer for me."

Archibald put three quarters of a hard-boiled egg in his mouth. It bulged out his pink cheeks. He opened the bottle and poured the ginger beer into a glass. When he'd swallowed the egg, he said, "I wouldn't be knowing why the Faery people aren't seen more often." He handed the glass to me. "Do you believe that Einion Las went to the Fair Country?"

"Yes, I do. Nana knew his great-great-great-grandchildren . . . and she said that if you are near to the Rock of the Birds, on Cader Idris, just after the sun has set and before the moon has risen, you'll see his castle."

Archibald took another egg.

"Why do you love the Faery people and stories," I asked him, "and you don't believe in the dukkering?"

"Telling fortunes is different . . . but look you"— he he laughed—"did you hear about the fight outside the Eunach's Head last Saturday night?"

"No. Who was fighting who?"

"Ifan Evans started it . . . and you know how mean that one can be with the drink in him." I nodded. "Well, he was in the pub, laughing and joking about how the three Pell brothers had camped all summer among the ruins of y Dinas, waiting for a black sheep with a speckled head to lead them to Vortigern's cave."

"And why not? The Pells should find the trasure if anyone does."

"That's what the fight was about. Ifan Evans called them Faery-bred."

"They should be proud. Proud that they are fair to look at and the best fiddlers and dancers in the whole of North Wales."

"I'd like to have a Faery forebear," Archibald said. "I

might have been able to carve Grugyn's bristles fine enough, then."

"You have a Faery grandmother . . . Nana."

"Maybe I should go and look for Vortigern's treasure." He laughed. "Do you think Merfyn Jones has a Faery forebear? He understands what the animals are saying."

"I don't know. Perhaps he knows their language. Perhaps he just loves them and understands them."

"As the Reverend understands people?"

I thought of Morgan's hand on my braids and on Paddy's head. "We were to look for some heart's-ease in the meadow."

"We will. When we walk along the edge of the Glaslyn to Eldorai's *vardo*." We had eaten the ham sandwiches and eggs, and were just beginning the raspberry jam and banana ones when the rain began to fall.

"Weather prophet!" I said as the heavy drops came through the branches and fell, bringing the fading leaves down with them on my face.

"We'd better pack up quick, look you," Archibald said, a sandwich between his teeth.

"I'll make a packet of these in a napkin. They're too good to waste."

"Well, hurry, Miss Catty. We need to cover the governess cart with this mackintosh."

He took the bridle and went to call Molly-fach. She was about halfway between us and the clump of trees where the stream curved, moving quietly, stopping to munch the sweet grass and moving again. I packed the picnic basket and then put on my mackintosh, and as I was fastening the belt I heard a whinny and looked up, and there was Molly-fach kicking her heels and bucking like a two-year-old; then she galloped away across the meadow. Archibald ran after her, the bridle in his hand. He almost caught her at the bottom of the slope near the cart road, but she twisted her neck and he lost his hold on her wet mane.

"Leave her," I shouted, and he held out his arms wide, the bridle in his hand. Molly-fach was halfway up the cart road.

We put the harness and the bridle and the picnic basket into the governess cart and pulled the mackintosh sheet we had been sitting on tightly across the top and hooked it firmly.

"That'll keep everything dry inside," Archibald said, "and look you at Molly-fach, halfway up the hill."

We laughed and took our way along the mossy edge of the coldly boiling stream, looking for wild heart's-ease as we went. We found some milkwort and meadowsweet, but there were no wild pansies. We came to the clump of trees that sheltered Eldorai's *vardo,* gaily colored in the green-gray copse. The open door of the wagon was toward us, and as we drew nearer we could see the carving and painting on the wooden porch and the fine fretwork, carved in the shape of two wheels, one on top of the other, at each side of it. The door opened in two parts, and the top half had flower-printed dimity curtains. We came to the bottom of the *vardo* steps and called to Eldorai.

"Av adray," she said. "Come in. Come in." Then, "Cul-vato, is the kettle boiling?"

We mounted the steps. Seven carved-wood painted steps up to the door of the caravan. The rug on the floor was red and thick, with bright patterns of yellow and black. Eldorai was lying in a big soft feather bed at the back of the wagon. Her face and hands were brown against the white sheets and pillowcases that were edged with fine lace and embroidered; everything shone with polishing. It was not a cold cleanness like Mrs. Evans's cottage, but a warm, glowing cleanliness of metals and bright color.

"Come in, porni Kishli . . . *besh telay* . . . sit down
. . . such a dear, beautiful day it is because you have come
. . . and you . . . *tarno mush,* young man . . . you've
grown in the two years past . . . *besh telay* . . . *besh
telay* . . ."

There was a cushioned seat under the two small dimity-
curtained windows, and thrown over it was a Spanish shawl
of heavy scarlet silk, embroidered with flowers and leaves
of many colors. I didn't want to sit on it.

"*Besh telay,*" Eldorai said, and I sat down. Archibald sat
in a deep, square wooden chair on the other side of the van.
Eldorai Blood looked at us with pleasure and welcome in
her eyes. In spite of the wrinkles crisscrossed like cobwebs
in her light brown skin, when she smiled she looked like a
young girl, and her teeth were white and strong and straight.

"You, too, Kishli . . . you've grown, and not only in
height . . . and the deep joy that it is to see you." She
looked at me. "And it's wishing I am that Nana could have
this same joy."

"Oh, Eldorai, I'm so happy to find you still here . . .
but why are you in bed?"

"The clinging damp it is, Kishli, and the years . . . but
more than the years it's the damp . . . it seeps into my
bones. . . ." She pointed through the *vardo* door with her
bony heavy-jointed finger, that had once been as slender and
long as Nana's. "But Culvato, here, is a good *chavo* and
tends me well, and tomorrow the dear sun will be out again
. . . and Eldorai along with him. . . . And now tell me
of my dear one, Codger, my soul-friend. Is he well? And if
he is well, why is he not along with you?"

"He didn't know we were coming."

"And like myself, he finds that the damp is less pleasant
than the cottage fire . . . and meetings are when meetings
are to be." And I thought of Nana and our last meeting. The

light of the fire on her face. The kettle-hook. Her bright gray eyes. Eldorai's eyes were black and shining. She looked at Archibald, sitting up as straight as he could in the wooden chair.

"You'll ne'er leave the mountains, *tarno mush,* except for once in your life . . . and that'll be when you're called. And you'll take your part against the fire from above and the sword below, and when the fighting's over it's back you'll be coming, and without a scratch to show . . . to the mountains and to the thin dark girl that'll be waiting . . ."

Ellen, I thought. "Ellen's learning the harp," Archibald had said. How strange, I thought, I know something that Archibald doesn't know himself.

"And it's the dukkerin' I'm doing." Eldorai lifted her hands.

"And Archibald doesn't believe," I said.

"He believes." Eldorai clasped her hands across her breast. "But 'tis strange that the pictures should come today. I haven't told a fortune in these long months . . . but the true dukkerin' is like the wind, that comes when it wills and none can command it." She smiled and looked beyond us both. "And on this day of welcome guests 'tis coming clear and bright on the gray mists of the west wind." She looked at me. "Come and sit near to me, Kishli, that I may touch you and know." She held out her hand, and I went and sat on the bed. I touched the cool, fine linen, and Eldorai took my hand. She looked at it, and after a while turned the palm upward. " 'Tis no common hand, Kishli . . . but then where is the hand that is? It's different as snowflakes we all are." She looked away again. "Yet one with the Spirit . . . and one in the Spirit." She looked back at me. " 'Tis the lavengro that you are, Kishli, with the gift of words." Nana's words came to my mind. "Nothing is by chance, Kishli, hear with your heart, the true hearing. Listen and

the words will come." I felt close to Nana, here in the *vardo*.
"And the gift of pain"—Eldorai held my hand in both
hers—"the gift of pain and a great love . . . and you'll
come through the fire that rains from the skies . . .
through the world's war you'll come . . . and through
your own dear fight."

"War, Eldorai?"

"War, Kishli. But not yet. . . . Fear the dear God and
do your part . . . and be not too gentle, Kishli, for you
cannot be overcome unless you yield yourself." She looked
away through the open door. " 'Tis too gentle you are, for
all the flame in you, and 'tis a great bully the world is . . .
and like all bullies, Kishli, it has a white flag in its *putsi*."

"Miss Catty certainly needs looking after," Archibald
said, and Eldorai looked at him and smiled.

"And that's a *racho bahtalo raklo*," she said, "a good
happy lad, and your true friend."

"I know, Eldorai."

"You know more than you know, Kishli." She took both
my hands and held them, and said to Archibald, "Be kind,
tarno mush, and ask Culvato to make tea for us all."

"That I will." He got up from his chair. "And it's looking for Molly-fach I'll be, for where she's taken herself off
to I wouldn't be knowing at all."

"Be back for tea," Eldorai said. "There's some good
bara-brith that Culvato made."

"I'll be back, indeed." When he had gone, Eldorai looked
at me, and she didn't smile. The look in her eyes was wise
and gentle.

"Hold the love in your heart, Kishli, for the time is not
yet . . . and yet it is forever, the love of the dear white girl
and the porno Rai . . . and the spear of love has seven
grooves that tear the heart. . . ." I thought of the moments, in my new habit, at the bottom of the stairs, of Mor-

gan's look. Eldorai's voice was low and chanting. "In the fire of your love you will touch the Unseen Fire. . . ." She smiled. "I see him, Kishli, I see you both . . . standing together, and you see only each other's eyes. . . ." It's true, I thought. There is the second sight. "Of course there is, Little Thin One, and well you know it."

"You read my thoughts."

"And more, Kishli. 'Tis not the fire of love and the parting that break the heart . . . though it comes nigh to breaking. And when the moment comes, you will be pawnie Rawnie . . . and in pain and joy, lavengro, till the day you die."

She loosed my hands and laid hers, brown and gnarled, with their polished nails, on the white sheet. I sat still. The bedcover was made of a natural-woven stuff, neither white nor fawn-colored, with strange designs on it, and signs on it in red and black and yellow. "You have already learned the gift of silence, Kishli."

"During punishment week, I think. But often I talk too much."

"Nothing is by chance, and every man is our teacher."

"Every man, Eldorai?"

"Every man, dordi Kishli. And don't give in to the gentleness when the flame should burn bright." She took my hand again and smiled. "And this is not the dukkerin' now, 'tis a piece of good advice." She laughed and was a girl again. "Don't go feeling guilty and up to your deep eyes in remorse when 'twas a just rage that filled your heart . . . and it's remembering that, always I want you to be . . . and didn't my dear Lord take a whip in His Hand?"

Then I laughed because Eldorai had heard about the library window. So long ago. Then I thought of the Foreigner—"Every man is your teacher"—and of Blodwen

Price, who, Emma said, came from the black stock in the Hollow.

"She's not bad, that one," Eldorai said, "but he, he's evil."

"You read all my thoughts."

"Today, Kishli, yes . . . but his evil cannot touch you. She, the dark one, she cannot escape it."

"Is she a witch?"

Eldorai paused, then replied, "More than you are, dordi Kishli . . . more than I am . . . but she is not bad . . . and here is Culvato."

He came up the steps, carrying a brass tray. He put it on the seat under the window and spread a lace crumb cloth on the carpet, then he put the tray on top of it. He served the tea from a silver teapot, in cups of Irish porcelain, white and delicate. There were thin slices of *bara-brith* on a porcelain plate. I took the napkin I had brought with me from my pocket and opened it.

"Eldorai, the rain came before we could eat Emma's lovely raspberry jam and banana sandwiches. Will you share them with us? You and Culvato?"

"With delight," Eldorai said. "And especially Culvato. 'Twill be a fine thing for him to eat of victuals that he has not prepared himself."

Culvato's eyes gleamed when he saw Emma's white bread and the purple and golden filling inside it. But when he took one he put it on his plate and finished pouring the tea and handing it around. His jacket was worn almost through at the elbows, and the sleeves were too short. His trousers were patched with neat, flat patches. He had sloe eyes and was thin, and sharp and supple as a wild cat. His hands were as clean as Eldorai's. Cleaner than mine, I thought.

"Go and whistle for the *tarno mush,*" his grandmother

said, and still leaving the sandwich on his plate, he went down the steps and whistled, and the sound was like the hoot owl. Archibald whistled back, and in a few minutes was at the door of the *vardo*.

"Which bucket is for hands?" he asked. The Gypsy people always have three buckets, or basins. One for the water they wash their bodies in, another to wash their clothes in, and the third they use for the cups and plates from which they eat and drink.

"I'll show you," Culvato called. He was filling a silver jug with boiling water from the kettle that hung over the fire on an iron hook that was spiked into the ground. Archibald washed his hands and came into the *vardo*. Culvato poured tea for him, and I offered him a sandwich, but he said he liked the *bara-brith,* and only then did the Gypsy boy take up his sandwich and eat it in sweet, hearty mouthfuls.

"I caught Molly-fach. She was almost at the top of the cart road."

"The moss is soft on the little roads and kind to her feet and tongue," Eldorai said.

"And she loves the nighttime . . . and the rain," I said.

"She gets real skittish, look you," Archibald chuckled, "and she's a real clever dodger. I've never had to chase her like that before . . . right up the hill slope she led me . . . frisky as a two-year-old."

"Did you harness her?"

"Surely to goodness, and it's safely between the shafts she is, with her mackintosh blanket upon her and the reins tied to a strong, low branch."

"She'll be quiet now," Eldorai said. "Let her have her way going home. 'Tis your dear sister between the shafts that she is."

And Culvato said, "Tell us a tale, Grandmother, for 'tis a long time since we had guests and a tea party."

But Eldorai answered that he should get his fiddle, and leaning back against her pillow, she said, " 'Tis Kishli here's the lavengro, and well she knows the *paramish* . . . for Nana told her all the Faery stories of the mountains."

"Tell the story of Einion Las and Olwen White-foot-print," Archibald said.

"That's Archibald's favorite story. He never tires of it."

Culvato went to his tent and came back with his fiddle. He held it carefully, as a precious thing, and began to tune it.

"Tell the story, Kishli, for 'tis an ancient tale and true . . . and the grand pleasure 'twill be for me, lying here in my bed, to hear the beautiful words, and spoken with the voice that melts my heart."

"Oh, Eldorai, you speak beautiful words."

The rain had stopped. The pale mist hung like a curtain, blurring the outlines of the trees. The leaves of the young oaks were copper-bright with wet.

"Close the bottom of the door, Culvato," Eldorai said, and we were inside the warm, shining world of her *vardo*. Culvato began to play "The Rising of the Lark," and I, sitting on the scarlet silk embroidered shawl, on the seat under the windows, began:

"The story of Einion Las and the Fair Family," and Eldorai interrupted, "And the manner in which the Twylyth Teg came by that fair name." She leaned back and closed her eyes.

"Einion Las lived in the valley beneath Cader Idris, where Arthur sleeps, and as he tended his flock on the wooded slopes that climb away in wide, shallow steps toward the moorland reaches, he thought always of the Twylyth Teg, the Faery people who live inside the mountains and the lake islands. Who can be tiny as a reed and tall as the highest tree in the forest and who can hear the ant, a hundred miles away, when she rises from her nest in the morning. Who tread so lightly that the tenderest blade of grass would not bend beneath their feet, and most of all Einion Las thought of Olwen White-footprint and was ever searching for the four white clover blooms that sprang up where she walked. And he longed to find one of the doors to the Other-world, and to go in search of her.

"It was on a May eve, when he was full-grown and as shapely a lad as had been seen in the valley, these many years, that Einion could wait no longer and he set forth up the valley path, past the Rock of the Birds, and as he climbed to the high crags he sang to himself:

> What is longing made from?
> What cloth is put into it
> That it does not wear out with use?

> Gold wears out, and silver wears out,
> Velvet wears out, and silk wears out,
> Yet longing does not wear out.

> The moon rises and the sun rises,
> The sea rises in vast waves,
> But longing never rises from the heart.

> Would that I had never heard of the Lovely Land
> Of the lake island in the green tarn depths.
> Would that I might find it before my heart breaks."

And while I spoke, Culvato played, quietly, a tune full of longing and sweet desire, and Archibald, while he listened to the words, watched Culvato's slim fingers on the strings.

"And Einion had almost given up hope, when he saw on the ground in front of him seven circles, intertwining, one with the other, and he shouted for joy and leaped into the air, and when he sat down to get his breath again, there beside him was a fat, merry little man with blue eyes. He was dressed in a short tunic

of greeny-brown color and long, tight breeches that ended in
pointed shoes at his feet. He carried a rowan branch in his hand
and pointed upward with it. They were happily met, and Einion
found that his feet were feather-light as he followed the little
man up the steep crags, till suddenly, where a moment before
there had been a rock, there was a door in the side of the mountain. They entered, and were in a country of magnificent woods,
fair and fruitful, and there were long avenues of shining trees
and crystal rivers and meadows rich with flowers. And here,
coming toward him across the fair green, he saw Olwen White-
footprint, and pure white clover flowers sprang up behind her as
she came. And she wore . . ."

I looked at Archibald and smiled.

". . . a flame-red tunic of fine silk and a collar around her neck
wrought with pearls and rubies. Her hair was more yellow than
the flower of the broom and her skin whiter than the foam of the
waves when the strong winds blow on Llyn-y-Cau. Fairer than
the eyes of all women were her eyes, and her breasts were whiter
than the swan's breast, and as she came toward him Einion's
heart melted within him, and he loved her for all time.

"And she came close to him, and with her fingers in his curly
brown hair she kissed his mouth and said:

" 'Speak to me, Einion, that I may know if your voice and
your form are of equal beauty.' And Einion spoke. And he said
the words of Dafydd ap Gwilym:

> Fair sea gull on the seething tide
> Like snow or the white moon in color
> Like a patch of sunlight, gauntlet of the sea . . ."

And I thought of Morgan on the Mochdre Hill.

> Go, sea gull, to my lovely girl
> Be tactful with my delicate girl,
> Tell her that I cannot live without her.

"And he told tales and held converse, and his Welsh eloquence charmed the Faery people and they were delighted with him and made him welcome and feasted him; and he passed his days with Olwen, in hunting and falconry, minstrelsy and dancing and the telling of the ancient tales.

"But after a while, in his heart, he felt the *hireath* for his land and the wide slopes of Cader Idris, and Olwen said:

" 'Einion-bach, follow where your heart leads. You will come back to me.'

"When the time came for him to leave, Einion felt that he could not bear the pain of parting, but Olwen laughed and gave him a richly caparisoned horse, broad-shouldered, with a flowing jet-black mane, like the horse of Finvarra, King of all the Faery Hosts, and she gave him a chest of bronze, filled with gold and silver and precious stones, and sent him on his way.

"And when Einion came to the valley of his youth, none knew him, for they thought that he had fallen from the high crags on that May eve, or died in the icy mists. But at last they believed his story, and indeed, it was difficult not to believe when they saw the richness of his clothes and the treasures he had brought with him.

" 'He was always a gentle lad.'

" 'And comely.'

" 'And indeed, all the family had the second sight and could see the Twylyth Teg.'

" 'Indeed, yes . . . Indeed, yes . . .' they all agreed, and they took him to their hearts and he stayed with them until, on a Thursday night, when the moon was full, as suddenly as he had come he went up the mountainside and disappeared.

"There was a great rejoicing in the Faery realm and a great feasting, and Einion and Olwen swore that they would never be parted again. But when Olwen told her people that she was going to live with her love in the world of mortals, 'Your beauty will fade,' the Faery people said.

" 'Your cool green eyes will shed hot tears.'

" 'Perhaps they will not be tears of sorrow,' one of her sisters said, and the other one laughed.

" 'They will not be tears of sorrow.'

"And Einion Las and Olwen White-footprint left the Lovely Land that is beyond the World's Age and they rode on two snow-white ponies, whose silver hoofs scarcely touched the rocks as they descended to Einion's house in the village.

"It was the opinion of all that Einion's wife was the most beautiful that had ever been seen, or ever been written about by the bards. And the lovers built a great castle on the mountain, near to the Rock of the Birds.

"And after a while the villagers began to ask about Olwen's family and Einion was approached by the most important magistrates. They talked for a long time about many and varied things, and then they asked the question they had come to ask.

" 'Indeed, my wife has two sisters almost as beautiful as she.' And they put it to him that his wife was of the Twylyth Teg, and he did not deny it. He thought of the beauty of the Faery people, and smiling, said, 'I would say she comes of a very Fair Family . . . a very Fair Family, indeed.'

"And Einion and Olwen lived in their castle on the slopes of Cader Idris, and the flowers bloomed in their gardens all the year and great berries grew on their trees. And Olwen grew healing herbs and was beloved throughout the land, and the mists about their dwelling were a haze of color and the winds were gentle, and on a morning in high summer the sun shone upon their bed. The covering had slipped down from Einion's breast and arms as he slept. Olwen gazed at him and marveled at the warm beauty of him, and her love dissolved her Faery heart and her tears fell upon his breast, and the ancient tale tells us that Olwen, at that moment, became a truly mortal woman. Einion, feeling her tears, awakened and looked at her, her yellow hair falling about her and her breasts like white heather, and great was the virtue of his love.

"And at this time a flock of birds flew over the Castle, and they had purple heads and beaks of gold and they made music as they flew. And the son born to Olwen was named Taliesson, and his fame is known to this day.

"And to this day the Twylyth Teg, the Faery people, in the lands around Cader Idris, are called the Fair Family."

Culvato played on, a wild, sweet stream of sound, and when the music stopped we were silent. Eldorai opened her eyes and smiled.

" 'Tis the true lavengro that you are, Kishli, and the true magic that you weave." Culvato smiled at me for the first time since we had met.

"And Culvato is the true fiddler."

"Yes. He is worthy to play on his grandfather's fiddle."

"Thank you, Culvato," I said, and then to Eldorai, "I know I can't thank you for the dukkering, but I can for everything else." She smiled. "It is late, Eldorai. We must go."

And Archibald said, "It will soon be the darkness."

Culvato took the tray, and Archibald opened the bottom half of the door for him. He carried it down the *vardo* steps. Archibald followed him. Halfway down he turned. "I'll bring Molly-fach to the edge of the road and meet you." I nodded. "And may you be up with the sun tomorrow, Eldorai," he said, and she smiled at him and made a sign of blessing with her hand. I folded the crumb cloth.

" 'Tis a great and wonderful pleasure my dear God sent to me this day . . . and it's the beauty, seen and unseen, that's His gift to you, Kishli . . . and the gifts of desire and longing." She was tired. I stood by her bed. "A blessing on you, and the *tarno mush,* your true friend . . . and a lover's blessing on the porno Rai, your love." Archibald whistled. Eldorai lay back and laughed and was young again.

"Good-by, Eldorai." Now she was not laughing.

She said, "And the end is as the beginning, Rawnie, and all causes are in a circle to their causes again." She opened her hand. I put mine into it. "Kishli is Nana's name for you. I take leave of you, pawnie Rawnie. *Mo dir develesko Rawnie* . . . my God's dear Rawnie . . . and a double blessing be on you," she said, and closed her eyes. I bent and kissed her hand and put my cheek against it. Then I went out and down the steps.

"Good-by, Culvato," I called. He was washing the cups and plates carefully, but when I spoke he stooped and picked up something from the ground and came toward me.

"Archibald told me you were looking for them," he said, and gave me a bunch of wild pansies. *"Kushti bok."*

"Kushti bok. . . . Good luck, Culvato," I said, "and thank you."

I walked under the dripping trees and out into the damp meadow. Molly-fach was waiting at the edge of the road. I got into the governess cart and pulled the mackintosh over my knees, and Molly-fach, liking the rising hill, set off at a brisk trot.

When we drove into the coachyard, the first stars were out. We went into the kitchen, and Archibald put the picnic basket on the table. The house was empty and quiet. I went into the hall and called to Jane. There was no answer. I went back to the kitchen and smiled to see that Paddy had followed us in and was stretched out on the rug in front of the fire.

"He must have known that Jane was out," I said, and sat down beside him. Star came to my lap, purring, and Archibald talked again about the rides we would have together when the Foreigner had left. All day long we had not thought of the Foreigner, nor the strangeness at Bryn Llithrig. I remembered my promise to Morgan, and said, "I don't want to know anything even if you know something . . . but do you?" He was sitting cross-legged, like a tailor. He pulled at a piece of blue rag in the rug. Paddy was asleep. Little shivers ran up and down his body, and now and then his leg twitched. "He's dreaming," I said, then, "Do you?"

"I know something, but not everything. I can guess a lot . . . but it isn't my business and I'm glad I had to look after you today."

"Oh, Archibald, wasn't it a lovely day?"

"One of the nicest in my life, indeed." And he blushed.

"We're home before Jane, too," I said, and ran upstairs and came back with the tape measure. "Let's measure you for your riding breeches." He stood up. We were sending to the Watford Riding Breeches Company for two pairs. "And Emma will knit you a yellow polo jumper. You have boots and leggings, and your Welsh tweed jacket."

"It will be good to have the Other Horse out of the stable, indeed." I felt a shiver, thinking of the Other Horse and his master, but "his evil cannot touch you," Eldorai had said.

After a while Jane came in. When he heard her open the front door, Paddy awoke with a start and ran out and down the coachyard steps to his kennel. She came into the kitchen and thanked Archibald for looking after me and said that we must think of a nice place to picnic tomorrow, so we knew that whatever was wrong had not been settled. Archibald took his cap from the hook near the board, and suddenly I remembered that yesterday had been baking day.

"Jane, has anyone taken the loaves?" Archibald turned.

"Codger said we haven't had ours," he said.

"Then they've been forgotten. Oh dear! Let's go and look in the larder." Jane was worried. I went to look, and the baskets were there, the loaves inside wrapped in white napkins.

"Archibald can take his now"—I handed the basket to

him—"and I'll take Grandma Rhys-Evans's to her tomorrow morning, before we go for our picnic."

Jane didn't say anything, and Archibald left with his basket. Then she looked around the kitchen and said, "Emma will be late. I'll make something to eat and bring it to you on a tray. You can have supper in bed; I'm sure you must be tired."

"May I take a book from the library, please?" I asked, and to my surprise, she nodded.

"And take a lamp from the drawing room; you can't read by candlelight." I thanked her and went to get the lamp. I took the one fullest of oil and put it on the table near the bed. Jane brought my supper. Two poached eggs on toast, a glass of milk, and a large piece of fruitcake. Then she left me and closed the door.

I knew that for once I could read for as long as I liked, but after a while I lay back and thought of Eldorai and Nana and Morgan. "The porno Rai, your love." And remembering how Eldorai had known what I was thinking and had seen the pictures in my mind, I fell asleep.

✥✥ II ✥✥

I took the other basket of bread from the larder and went down the coachyard steps to find Archibald. He wasn't in the stables. I went to the archway and whistled. There was no answering sound. I hadn't seen Jane or Morgan. I set out for the Village with the loaves for Grandma Rhys-Evans, and as I passed down the Hill Lane, I saw Codger sitting under the lattice porch of Nana's cottage, basking in the pale morning sunlight and smoking his old clay.

"And where might you be going, Kishli?"

"To take Grandma Rhys-Evans's bread."

"A day late."

"I know. Everyone seemed to forget."

"And yesterday you saw Eldorai, as Archibald tells me."

"Oh, Codger, yes . . . we had tea with her and Culvato, in her *vardo*."

"I wish I'd been along, indeed."

"So did Eldorai, but she said that meetings were when meetings were to be." And we smiled. Then Codger wasn't smiling. He looked at me, then spat into the flower bed.

"Well, and that's as may be, and this morning isn't the time for meetings and it's hurrying back up the Hill I'd be if I were you, look you." And he began to smoke his pipe again.

I left him, thinking, Codger is worried too, and halfway

down the Hill Lane, I noticed how quiet it was. Some of the cottage doors were open, but there was no movement inside. No early morning scullery sounds: clink of pan and clack of pot; no scrubbing noises, and some of the doors were closed.

There was no one outside the butcher's shop. It was on the Square, and there was always a merry bustle there, and chatter. But when I came nearer, I heard a low murmuring, like a growl. As I passed the butcher's window, the sound stopped. I looked in and saw that behind the marble slabs where the cuts of meat were laid the shop was full of people. I waved. I always did. Only Mr. Jones answered, saluting in his funny way, but halfheartedly. I hurried on. The street was empty except for Mary Peters and her sister's little girl, talking to Mrs. Price, from the White Horse, in the doorway of the haberdasher's. Everybody is in the butcher's, I thought, and turned into the Plas-y-Coed Lane, that leads up a hill to the right of the Square, to the Vicarage, on top of the hill and the church and the Parish Hall, farther into the woods beyond. Grandma Rhys-Evans's cottage was almost at the bottom of the hill. I thought that if she was in the butcher's too I would leave the bread inside her room, but she was there, tying her apron around her thin waist as I knocked and opened the door.

She looked after her grandchildren and her daughter's husband, although she was always in pain from her rheumatics. When she had a bad attack, Ellen came and helped in the house and with the children. Grandma Rhys-Evans was an irritable woman, and Emma said she always argued at Parish meetings and that she was very rude to the chapel people, but everyone agreed she had a heart of gold. She took the basket from me and undid the napkins; she pressed the bread hard, and then she sniffed. I knew it was a day late. She put it in the cupboard and said that no wonder everything was topsy-turvy when foreigners were allowed to come poking their noses into peaceful villages. With their uncivilized ways, and that she had never thought to see the day, and that when she was a girl he'd have been horsewhipped, and more than likely tarred and feathered. She turned me toward the window and looked at my face. Her brown eyes, in the light, were flecked with yellow, and they were bright and kind beneath the heavy wrinkled lids. She looked at the scars on my neck and face and nose.

"Tck! Tck!" she said. "The *cuthrel diawl!* The dirty *cuthrel diawl!* He might have killed the child. Did anyone think of that? I ask you, indeed, did anyone think of that? Making her ride the murdering beast." She was talking to herself. I had forgotten the scars since they stopped hurting, and Eldorai hadn't noticed them at all. Grandma Rhys-Evans turned to the sideboard. "What the child needs is a mother's love," I heard her say as she opened the glass doors. I almost said, "I'm fifteen." She took out a china mug. It had a picture of Great Orme's Head on it and written underneath it, "A Present from Llandudno." I knew, as everyone did, that her daughter Gweneth had brought it back from her honeymoon. Her daughter had died when almost everyone had the "flu," two years after we had come to Bryn Llithrig. I didn't want her to give the mug to me. She took it from the shelf and polished it with the cleanest corner of her apron. Then she closed the glass doors.

I wanted to say that I had one just like it, or that I'd be afraid to break it, or that maybe little Dafydd, who had the mumps, would like to play with it. Instead I said, "Thank you, Grandma Rhys-Evans." And suddenly I couldn't stop the tears.

"Here, use this." She gave me the corner of her apron that she'd just polished the mug with. I used it to wipe my eyes and then looked at her, but she wasn't looking at me, or far away; her eyes were empty of looking.

"It's a good mug. It's been like having a bit of my Gweneth in the house." Then she looked at me again. "Keep it in your room. It'll be good for you there. My Gweneth was a good girl."

We smiled at each other, and I felt happy again. In the cottage here, there was no strangeness. I took up the empty basket from the table and asked how little Dafydd was, and she said that he was "on the improve." And as I went out with the china mug in my hand, she said, "And don't let me hear of it's getting broken, now." She stood at the door and watched me till I had closed the gate and crossed over to the other side of the road.

I passed the butcher's shop. I didn't look in at the window, but the noise was louder. I looked at the china mug and hurried up the Hill Lane. When I reached the wall door, it was locked. It had never been locked before during the day for as long as I could remember. I went farther along to the coachyard gate. It was closed too. I heard voices inside.

"Archibald, open the gates," I called out. When he did and I came into the coachyard, I saw the Foreigner's big wooden harness box and hamper trunk, packed and ready, near the kitchen steps. The Foreigner came out of the stable. I hurried across the cobbles; he followed and took hold of my arm and swung me around.

"What are you prying around here for? Nosy little bitch." I looked at him. He held my arm twisted so that it hurt. "His evil can't touch you," Eldorai had said. I didn't move.

"And don't go telling those bloody Welsh savages what you've just seen. See?" He tightened his grip. His eyes gleamed with cold malice. And fear, I thought, and saw

Archibald coming up behind him, and there was rage in him.

"Archibald"—my voice was calm—"where's Paddy? I haven't seen him this morning."

He saw that I didn't want any more violence. "I don't know," he said. "Perhaps he's with the Reverend."

"And tell the bloody Reverend to keep his bloody mouth shut too." The Foreigner loosed my arm. The whites of his eyes were red. He turned and walked away, shouting at Archibald to clean the harness and not be so bloody lazy, standing there staring.

I went into the kitchen and left the breadbasket on the table, and without stopping, ran upstairs. I put the china mug on the mantelpiece, between the two china candlesticks, and sat on the window seat, still shuddering from the Foreigner's touch. I wondered why the wall door had been locked and why the Foreigner's traps were all strapped and labeled when he wasn't leaving for two or three days. Then I remembered the fear in his close-set pale eyes. Fear? It was fear. The people in the butcher's shop. The low, growling talk. I looked across the room at Grandma Rhys-Evans's mug. It shone, white and clean; the colors were bright and clear. The blue sky and the green hill, jutting out into a bluer sea. The golden-edged scroll with the black letters. "My Gweneth was a good girl." I turned and looked out into the garden. It was a clear day. Yesterday's mist had vanished, and the winds smelled of damp soil.

Blodwen Price had not cleaned my room. She understood, I thought. How strange. I was glad. I took off my cardigan and made the bed and dusted, thinking the while of the anger and unrest in the butcher's shop. It all began when Betty Eyeball knocked at the wall door in the early morning, when Emma was baking. The wall door. Locked. Is the anger against Bryn Llithrig? I wondered. The Foreigner? Of course, the Foreigner. Then I knew. The Foreigner and

Betty Eyeball. I sat down on the bed. She's going to have his child. He had locked the doors in fear. Fear of the villagers. But Blodwen Price? What of her? I had seen her meet him in the stables. The villagers hated the black people from the Hollow. Archibald knew. Where had he been when I called to him this morning, before I went to the Village?

My head ached with thinking. I finished dusting and went down to the kitchen to find Emma. The kitchen was empty. Then I saw the writing on the message board. Morgan's writing. I had hurried upstairs without seeing it. "Catriona," I read, "please wait for me in your room." Without looking into the coachyard, I went back to my bedroom and lay on the bed. I closed my eyes. Then Rumpel jumped up and landed on my stomach. As I sat up, he coiled backward and fell on the bedcover; then crouching low, he stalked my hand. I moved it and he pounced, then rubbed his head against my palm and mewed, asking to be stroked and tickled under the chin. He was wild and graceful, and his long fur was snow-white, except for the black spot on his back and down his left side, and his tail was fluffy as a fox's brush. His eyes were green, like emeralds.

"Oh, Rumpel! You're beautiful." Then the wall-door bell rang. I ran downstairs and along the gravel path to open it. I heard Emma's voice.

"There, now. There, now." I opened the door. It was Jane, and she was weeping. Emma was holding her arm, but as I opened the door Jane pulled her arm away and came inside.

"These impolite, savage people! These uncivilized people!" Her face was tight and angry. "Don't just stand there, Emma. Close the door. Lock it." Bursting into fresh sobs, she ran into the house and upstairs.

"Emma, what's the matter? What's happened to Jane?" Emma leaned against the wall.

"We're not savages, indeed," she said quietly, almost to herself. She was wearing her meeting hat. It was black with red ribbon ruching and cherries on it. "We're not uncivilized, Miss Catty."

"Oh, Emma! Don't be silly! Of course you're not."

"But, Miss Catty, I've never seen them so angry, at that. I'm worried. I'm frightened. I am, indeed."

"Emma, why is Jane weeping? Why are you wearing your meeting hat?"

"Because there was a meeting."

"Where?"

"In the anteroom of the Parish Hall."

"Why?"

She looked at me and shook her head. "Oh dear! It's not for you to know."

"Please, Emma, just tell me what happened to Jane."

"I can't tell you aught, except that Mrs. Eyeball and some of the girls were rude to her."

"How?"

"Well, Miss Catty, they were saying things about the Foreigner."

"The Foreigner? But he's leaving. His traps are all packed." Then I remembered that he had told me not to say anything about seeing his luggage, but Emma hadn't noticed.

"Well, something's come up. Anyway, there were ruderies about foreigners in general. . . ."

"Yes, Emma?"

"Well, land's sakes indeed, and if Miss Withers doesn't go taking the remarks for personal."

"Oh dear."

Then Emma put her hand on my arm. "I'm sorry, Miss Catty. I shouldn't have said anything."

"For goodness' sake, Emma."

"Well, Miss Withers burst into tears and said that she

had always been kind and polite . . . then someone said 'calf's-foot jelly,' and they all laughed."

"I bet that was Betty Eyeball."

" 'Twas not, indeed. That one left on the morning train. But it was awful, Miss Catty. Nobody listened to Miss Withers. They shouted her down, they did. It's excited and angry they were." She sighed. "Now, Miss Catty, you go upstairs and see if you can help."

I went, and knocked at Jane's door. She didn't answer, so I went in. She was lying on the bed, her face in the pillows. I sat on the edge of the bed and touched her shoulder. She sat up and stared at me.

"Catriona, go to your room and stay there, please." Her hair had fallen down, and she looked young and angry and sad. I wanted to put my arms around her. To tell her that I understood. Somehow I did. It wasn't her fault that she couldn't understand the Welsh people. Or was it? Anyway, she was sad and unhappy and I wanted to comfort her. I put my arm around her shoulder. She pulled away with a sharp movement.

"Jane, what's wrong?"

"Wrong?" she almost shouted. "Everything's wrong with this uncivilized village. And for goodness' sake, go to your room, Catriona. And stay there." I brought her the smelling salts and left them near to her on the bed and went out and closed the door. As soon as the latch clicked, she began to sob again.

Then the telephone rang. I ran downstairs. It was the Vicar's wife. Emma was listening; then she said, "But they'd never do aught like that." Then she listened again. "All right, I'll see she's ready . . . in about fifteen minutes, then." She put down the receiver.

"What's going to happen in about fifteen minutes, Emma?"

"You and Miss Withers are going to the Vicarage. The Vicar's wife and the Curate are coming for you." I ran into the kitchen and rubbed Morgan's message off the message board. Then I turned to Emma.

"I'm going to hide in Nana's cottage. If Morgan comes while I'm there, tell him."

"Miss Catty—"

"I can't go to the Vicarage, Emma. Morgan needs me. You saw the message?"

Emma heaved a sigh and sat in the rocking chair. She pulled the pins out of her hat, took it off, and dropped it on the rug. "I saw it. Hurry then. I've not seen sight nor sound of you." And with another sigh she added, "I must go up to Miss Withers."

I ran out of the kitchen and down the steps and across the garden to the broken hedge and climbed through. When I got to Nana's cottage, there was no one there. I went upstairs and sat in a wooden chair behind the window in the front bedroom, where I could see but not be seen. I could hear the murmurings and sometimes a shout from the Square. I thought of Nana before Dr. Fraser had said she must be downstairs all the time, here, in this tiny room. All white and yellow. The curtains were like those in Eldorai's *vardo*. Nana had died as daintily as she had lived. Her clothes set out. Her cakes baked. Emma had baked them. I thought of how a rainy day can be full of peace, like yesterday, and beauty; a bright one, like today, full of fear and violence. The sounds coming from the Square were sometimes far away, and then nearer, on the wind. It's just like growling, I thought again. After about ten minutes I saw the Vicar's wife and the Curate come up the Lane and pass the cottage. They rang the bell outside the wall door. Emma came to open it. They will be looking for me, I thought. I drew back into the shadow. After a while I heard the scrape of the wall door again and they came out. Jane was walking between them, and they went quickly past the cottage. The Vicar's wife was holding Jane's arm and Jane was leaning on her. She wouldn't let me comfort her, I thought. Then I hurried back to the house. Emma was in the kitchen, sitting in her chair with her eyes closed, but she was not asleep.

"Poor Emma," I said. She looked up at me.

"Now, Miss Catty," she said, and her voice was tired, "just you go and wait in your room, like the Reverend said."

"All right, Emma." But at that moment Morgan came up the coachyard steps.

"Catriona," he said, "come into the library." Then to Emma, "I know how tired you must be, Emma, but could you have tea ready later? It might be needed." We went into the library and closed the door. Morgan looked pale and worried. We stood before the fireplace.

"Catriona, I need your help."

"I knew you did when I read the message."

"I want you to lead the Foreigner and Blodwen Price down the river path and under the far side of the bluff, to our cave." No, Morgan! I thought. Our secret cave? The Foreigner?

"The tide is ebbing now, and will not be high again till six o'clock this afternoon."

I didn't want to see the Foreigner again. Nor Blodwen Price. Then I thought of Eldorai. "She's not bad, that one." I didn't speak.

"Come along now, there's no time to lose. They're waiting for you in the stable."

I followed Morgan out of the library, into the kitchen. Emma had picked up her hat from the rug and was tying on her cooking apron. She looked at me, but didn't speak as I followed Morgan into the coachyard. The Foreigner and

Blodwen Price were just inside the stable, near to Stray's stall.

"It's time to go," Morgan said, and they came out onto the cobbles. When I looked at them, I knew that Eldorai was right. "His evil can never touch you." They both seemed like strange children, to be helped.

"Miss Catriona will show you the way," Morgan said, "and please don't move from the cave until Archibald comes to fetch you in the motorboat. There is a train from the Junction at eight o'clock tomorrow morning."

"And what happens to my traps, I'd like to know. There's valuable stuff in these trunks . . . things that's worth a lot of money."

I remembered my first sight of him at the Station. His yellow and black checked waistcoat. He was wearing it now. And the switch. He was flicking the top of his legging.

"Anyways, I'm insured . . . except for the prize ribbons. First prize, both of them. I shouldn't like to lose them."

"You must leave them here. I will see that you get them. And now you must go."

"Well, I must say it all seems bloody silly to me . . . caves . . . boats," the Foreigner said, "but I can't say I'm sorry to leave."

"It isn't silly, look you," said Blodwen Price. "I know these people when they are angry." She looked at Morgan. "Thank you, sir, for helping us." Then to me she said, "And thank you, miss." She took his arm. "Let's get going, look you, Ted. Every minute counts." He pulled his arm away, and putting the switch under his other one and holding it against his side, he took a cigarette from his pocket and lit it, drew the smoke in slowly, and let it out through his nostrils.

Morgan said, "You must leave now." And then quietly,

"Now!" And the Foreigner turned to Blodwen Price. Morgan said to me, "Catriona, be back here within the hour, and go immediately to your room." I nodded.

"Have you anything to eat?" I asked Blodwen Price.

"Sandwiches Mrs. Higgins gave us." So Emma knew all the time, I thought.

"Come along," I said. "Let's go."

Morgan turned to Blodwen Price. "And don't move out of the cave, please. Someone—anyone—might see you."

I led them past the birch grove and through the orchard, down to the river's edge. Blodwen Price followed closely behind me along the narrow path. The Foreigner lagged behind, muttering to himself. The tide was half ebb, clean and sweet, and there were wild pansies and milkwort, like tiny blue and white butterflies in the mossy grass. I'll pick some on the way back, I thought, and hurried on. When we came to the bluff, we had to leave the river path and scramble down between a narrow cleft of rocks, steep and slippery, to the pebbly shore. Blodwen Price was lithe. She wore sandals, and was carrying her shoes around her neck. She had tied the laces together, and the shoes hung down in front of her shoulders, like Mrs. Evans's fur piece. Her stockings were stuffed inside them. The Foreigner was clumsy and scraped his polished leggings and cursed.

"Shut up, Ted," Blodwen Price said. "Mind your language." And he said that she was a stupid little slut from a mountain hovel and he didn't know why he was taking her to a civilized country or why he'd taken up with her at all. She didn't answer.

Our feet sank deep into the wet shingles, and the walking was hard. With our feet covered with damp grit, we rounded the bottom of the bluff, and then there were more rocks to climb over. They were sharp and mossy and full of slippery edges and ridges, too small to cling to or clutch, or to give a

footing. I scrambled over the smallest and as I half clambered, half slid, down the second, I could see the rock that
covered the mouth of the cave. I remembered the day we
found it; the swift, slashing storm when I was eleven. Each
year afterward we had picnicked there, made a fire on the
beach and eaten the fish Morgan had caught. The going
was harder still on the tide-washed shore. Blodwen Price
was almost over the second rock. I went to the mouth of the
cave; it looked small. Morgan got inside, I thought. I saw
that there were two blankets and a horse mackintosh in a
neat pile, just inside the opening. So that's where Archibald
was this morning when I called him. Then I saw the Foreigner. He was slipping and clutching and sliding, his long,
thin legs splayed out, and he was what Archibald called
"swearing blue." His switch was no use to him at all. He
scrambled and tore at the second rock and got to the top of
it, and then his foot slipped and he fell on his behind in the
wet gravel. The switch was still in his hand. I wanted to
laugh, but his face was scarlet with rage. He sat and sucked
a bleeding thumb.

"Come on, Ted," Blodwen Price called to him. He looked
at her with hatred. "Oh, Blodwen Price, run away from him
now." I wanted to shout the words. He staggered up and
brushed off the seat of his pants with his hands.

"You'd better go inside the cave," I said to her.

"I'll wait for him," she said. "Come on, Ted. Anyone
could see you that's around."

He swore at her, and came toward us across the silt.

"You're so tall," she said, and her voice was soft. He
stopped cursing her and turned to me.

"You wanted to laugh, didn't you?" I thought he was going to hit me again. I didn't move. He flicked his legging
with the switch, but his heels sank into the river-sodden
gravel. He regained his balance.

"I wouldn't be in this bloody mess if I hadn't had to come to this stinking Village to teach a stupid, stuck-up little—"

"Come on, Ted." Blodwen Price took his arm and looked up at him with a faint smile; then she sat down at the mouth of the cave and pulled him after her.

"Now, Ted, come on. In you go . . ." He bent down. "And don't bump your head."

I turned and walked away from them. Blodwen Price came after me.

"I know why you did your own room, miss, but you needn't worry about me putting the evil on you—not ever."

"You couldn't," I said, and there was no enmity between us. Not even dislike.

As I climbed over the two rocks and walked along the shingly edge of the river and then scrambled up the rocky cleft to the path, I thought, She's strangely beautiful. There was still time to gather a bunch of wild pansies and take them to Morgan's cottage. I climbed up the bluff. The cottage door was open. Mrs. Eyeball hadn't been there for three days, and there were cups and saucers and plates on the table, and the huge stone fireplace was full of ashes. Columbus was asleep on his seat inside the hearth. He wakened and jumped down and rubbed himself against my feet. His purr sounded like a lion cub's purr. There were more dirty dishes in the scullery sink. I put the heart's-ease pansies in a small Wedgwood cream jug and left them on the dresser. I wished there were time to clean the cottage.

Back at the house Emma was buttering slices of *bara-brith*.

"Did you leave them in the cave?" she asked, and I nodded.

"You knew all the time."

She smiled. "Indeed now, and let's pray the Good Lord that the rest of the Reverend's plan works as well."

"They have to be picked up, Emma. How will Archibald get to them in a boat? Whose boat?"

"Now, don't go asking me things that I don't know any more about than you do, Miss Catty, for it's plain dog-tired that I am." She held the currant loaf against her bosom and sliced it slowly with a long, sharp knife. "We need about five more slices. And look you, I'm still hoping that the Reverend can stop them, that crowd that's in the butcher's . . . and the others."

"They were there early this morning when I took Grandma Rhys-Evans bread."

"There's more now. All them that came for Merfyn Jones's ram sale, and that Ifan Evans from Capel Curig's there, and he bodes none any good, indeed." She buttered the bread and laid it in neat rows on the flat blue and white dish. "And that lot's all been in the White Horse." She sighed, and taking a napkin from the dresser drawer, wet it at the tap, squeezed it out, and laid it over the large plate of *bara-brith*. "And there's many of them strangers as doesn't cotton to Blodwen Price and her black brothers, either."

"The cave is small and uncomfortable for such a long time, Emma." I hoped the Foreigner wouldn't get out and stretch.

"And so it should be uncomfortable, indeed . . . and look you, they're deserving of all that's coming to them."

"Oh, Emma! Blodwen Price is not bad."

"She stole the Foreigner from right under Betty Eyeball's nose at the Midsummer Social in the Mochdre Parish Hall. Mrs. Eyeball says she bewitched him."

Emma had put a large, stiffly starched white linen table-cloth on the big table and laid out about twenty cups and saucers.

"That's what started the trouble with Miss Withers at the meeting."

"What? Blodwen Price being a witch?"

"When Mrs. Eyeball said it, Miss Withers laughed . . . and you know how nasty she can laugh when she wants to. 'Well, really, Mrs. Eyeball,' she says, 'don't be utterly ridiculous . . . a witch!' And that made them all mad, and they began to ask why Blodwen Price was working at Bryn Llithrig at all. And Miss Withers says, 'Really!' that she could engage anyone she pleased . . . and they said, 'A fine choice, indeed to goodness.' And then things went from bad to worse, as I told you."

"But Jane didn't know Blodwen Price. She just came and said that she had heard that Tessie's mother was ill, and could she fill in. She was polite."

"She'd heard, all right . . . from the Foreigner. And she's polite enough, if sneering's polite."

"Oh, Emma." I laughed. "But I hope the boat comes before high tide."

"A fine dousing they'll get if it doesn't."

"Emma Higgins!"

"And now, Miss Catty, go and wait for the Reverend in your room before I say more than I should. I'm going to brew a cup of tea for myself."

"All right, Emma. And don't worry—Morgan won't let anything happen to us."

Emma heaved a sigh and reached for the tea caddy. It was on the mantel over the kitchen range, next to the gingersnap tin. It was red and gold, with pictures of King George and Queen Mary on the front of it.

I went to my room and looked out toward the river and wondered what they were talking about, the Foreigner and Blodwen Price, out there, for hours in the small cave; and why she wanted to go with him at all. Why she spoke softly, with flattering words. Noonday stillness was on the garden. Bright, cool sunshine. I wondered where Archibald was. I

could hear Molly-fach and Stray in their stalls. The Other
Horse—what would Morgan do with him? Send him with
the Foreigner's luggage in a horse van? Then with my
thought of him there came sounds from his stall. The Other
Horse's angry whinnying, the familiar stomping, and I
heard Archibald's voice. I ran downstairs and out onto the
coachyard steps. Archibald came out of the stable. He
walked quickly across the cobbles to the Foreigner's traps
and tried to burst open the padlock on the big wooden trunk
with the harness in it. He looked up at me.

"He took the key," he said, and tried to pry the lock apart
with the fork end of a big hammer. It held fast. The murmuring voices from the Square grew louder. This time it
was not the wind that carried them. Archibald looked up
again.

"They're coming." He ran to the stable and came back
with a heavy ax, and holding it above his head with both
hands, swung it down hard against the padlock. The shouts
and voices were close now. Halfway up the Hill Lane, I
thought. Emma came out onto the steps.

"Oh, God! Miss Catty, they're coming. Come inside.
Where's the Reverend?" Then she looked at Archibald, the
ax poised above his head. She threw her apron over her
face and ran inside. Then she called to me:

"Miss Catty, come inside!"

I didn't move. The ax swung again, and this time the lock
burst open. Archibald pulled the Foreigner's saddle out of
the trunk, heaved it on his shoulder, and ran across the
coachyard and into the stable. There was stamping, and the
sound of hoofs against the hard wood of the Other Horse's
stall. The angry whinnying began again. The noise and
shouting were outside the wall door. Emma was wringing
her hands. The bell rang. Again and again. There were banging and knocking, and the bell rang without stopping, and

then Morgan came through the archway. He saw me on the steps and sighed with relief. Then he raised his eyebrows in question. I nodded.

"Good," he said. "Now go inside." Taking the Other Horse's bridle from the wooden trunk, he ran after Archibald into the stable. I stayed on the steps. Now the villagers were outside the coachyard gates. They were shouting. I could hear women's voices, high and shrill.

"Open up!" I heard Mr. Jones the butcher's hard, loud voice. And he's such a small man, I thought. There were kicking and snorting in the stable. I ran into the house and upstairs to the sewing-room window and looked into the road. Mr. Jones, the butcher, was cracking his long cart whip and shouting, and Dylan Price was carrying a bucket of tar. Tar! Mrs. Eyeball had a pillowcase in her hand. Feathers! I thought. That's what Emma meant . . . "They wouldn't do aught like that . . ." They were going to tar and feather him. I hoped that he was still inside the cave. Why is Archibald in the stable and not getting the boat? I wondered. Mrs. Eyeball was screaming:

"We want the Foreigner. Give him up . . . open up!"

"Open the gates . . ."

"Or we'll batter them down!" Caradoc Ellis and Idris Williams, the post, were carrying a small sawed-off tree trunk, and a girl whom I had seen with Tessie in church was shouting, "Where is he? I want to get a good look at him."

She was carrying another bag of feathers. A quiet-looking girl I didn't know was standing at the side of the crowd, with Mrs. Evans and Codger's daughter-in-law and Mrs. Price, from the White Horse, and her sister from Llanberis and the haberdasher's wife and Mary Peters, watching, and looking worried. The butcher's little boy, Emrys Jones, was carrying a second bucket of tar. It was only half full but it was too heavy for him, and he was straining and using both hands. There were some of the youths who sang under the oak tree at the wall corner on Sunday evenings, and Ifan Evans, from Capel Curig, was shouting and waving his cap and urging on the strangers—about twenty of them, men I had never seen before. One of them, big and red-haired, took the bucket of tar from Emrys Jones and laughed. Caradoc Ellis and Idris Williams, the post, were banging on the coachyard gates with the tree trunk, and the haberdasher—who always looks so mild, I thought—was trying to climb the right-hand gatepost.

The strangers, led by Ifan Evans, from Capel Curig, were now kicking at the gates, and Mr. Jones was beside himself with rage, cracking his whip and jumping up and down. His face was bright red. Then he and Mrs. Eyeball and the rowdy girl and Caradoc Ellis and Idris Williams, the post, and John Thomas Davies, the blacksmith, and the strangers seemed to come together with a determined strength, and with the youths behind them, they all pushed the gates together. I ran downstairs and out onto the kitchen steps.

Morgan was standing inside the gates, his hand on the iron handle of the long bolt. He was looking at the stable door. The coachyard gates were strong, but they were giving in the middle. Then Archibald and the Other Horse came out of the stable. He was rearing and kicking, but Archibald hung on to his head. I watched without breathing. He reared backward. Some strong, silent very self in Archibald seemed to force him to the mounting block, and then he was in the saddle and I couldn't see how. Morgan pulled the bolt, and the crowd surged in. But the sight of Archibald on the rearing, prancing Other Horse shocked them, and instinctively they made way. The Other Horse, wild with rage, reared again and charged into the middle of them, knocking down Mr. Jones, the butcher, and two of the strangers. The crowd parted now. Like the waters of the Red Sea, I thought.

And Archibald and the Other Horse tore through the coachyard gates at a furious gallop and away down the Hill Lane. Morgan stood behind the open gate, and then walked around the shouting crowd to the kitchen steps.

"Go inside, Catriona," he said, but I stayed on the top step. If only they don't find out where the Foreigner is, I thought. I was afraid. Morgan came up to the fifth step and waited. Mr. Jones was on his feet again, and now his face was white. He had taken off his glasses. He rushed forward, cracking his whip.

"Where is he? Fetch him out!" He was almost snarling.

"Send out the bastard!" Caradoc Ellis and Idris Williams and John Thomas Davies and Mrs. Eyeball and Tessie's friend and Ifan Evans, from Capel Curig, and the strangers were all behind him, shouting:

"Bring him out! Bring him here . . ."

"And his whoring concubine," Mrs. Eyeball screamed.

"Out of the way, Reverend," Mr. Jones shouted. "Our fight's not with you."

"Out of the way, Reverend," Ifan Evans, from Capel Curig, mimicked Mr. Jones.

And the strangers shouted, "Out of the way, Reverend."

"Out of our way!"

"You can't save him now," Caradoc Ellis called out.

Morgan held up his hand.

"Where is he?"

"Bring the bastard out!" The strangers pushed forward.

"And the black witch!" Ifan Evans yelled, and the strangers took up the cry.

"Bring out the whoring witch." The strangers were now as angry as the villagers and more drunk.

Morgan lowered his hand. He stood still. I thought Mr. Jones would lash him with the whip. There was a growling underneath the shouts, ugly and fierce.

"Where is he?"

"Where's the rutting Foreigner?"

And Caradoc Ellis, not shouting now but determined, said, "We know he's here."

"He's not here," Morgan said.

"Oh, indeed he is, look you." John Thomas Davies shook his huge fist in the air, and the roaring and shouting began again.

"We know he's here." Mr. Jones's voice was hoarse with rage. "He hasn't left the Village."

Mrs. Eyeball shrieked, "That's his room, up there." She pointed to the loft room and ran across the coachyard, trailing feathers from her pillowcase along the cobbles.

"He's not up there," Caradoc Ellis shouted, and Ifan Evans, from Capel Curig, lurched to the steps.

"It's in the house he'll be."

The big red-haired man joined him. "Search the house." He turned to the crowd and pointed. "He's in the house."

"Under the bed," someone shouted.

"In it most likely." There was growling laughter. Ifan Evans and the red-haired man started up the steps.

Morgan stood still.

"Come on! Follow us!" they shouted, and the strangers surged forward. Mr. Jones, the butcher, stopped cracking his whip.

"Come on!" they shouted. Ifan Evans had reached the fourth step. Morgan had not moved. His shoulders were tensed. Then Mr. Jones, the butcher, cracked his whip and caught Ifan Evans around the ankle, and Caradoc Ellis shouted, "Take your lousy feet off those steps."

John Thomas Davies roared, "Scum from over the mountain," and lunged at the red-haired man. While Caradoc Ellis took on Ifan Evans and the haberdasher, Idris

Williams, the post, and the Village youths tangled with the strangers, fighting with fists and feet and teeth.

"He's not up there. Tar and feather the bastard," Mrs. Eyeball came out of the traproom door, shouting, but her voice was lost in the grunting and breathing of the villagers and the strangers who were fighting with furious anger. Noses were bleeding, and two men had been knocked out, both strangers. They had been put against the wall.

I saw Morgan go around the edge of the fighting and get the two buckets of tar, which had not yet been spilled, and take them into the stable. As he came back, one of the strangers hit him. Morgan hit back, and the stranger hit him again; then Morgan socked him so hard that he fell down under the archway. Morgan came back up the steps, rubbing his knuckles and smiling. The stranger looked at him, surprised, then holding his chin for a moment, he got up and went back into the fray.

Now Mr. Jones was cracking his whip about everyone, villagers and strangers alike, until Ifan Evans, who'd been fighting the haberdasher, turned angrily and knocked him down. This time he stayed down. Dylan Price grabbed the whip and was lashing any stranger he could see, until one of them took it from him and threw it toward the open gates, where the women were standing, and returned to the fight, which was now quietly fierce and violent. There was blood on the cobbles, and havoc in the coachyard, and the women began to cry to them to stop when suddenly there was a loud shout from the Lane and Myfanwy Jones's small milk cart pulled up between the open gates, she and Penry Jones standing up in it. Like a war chariot, I thought.

She put her hands on her hips, and Penry Jones was calling out, "Clear the way! Clear the way!" His voice was deep and full. "Clear the way!" And Merfyn Jones, with his two dogs barking and working, drove fifteen strong, proud-headed rams into the middle of the coachyard. It was not their season yet, so they were fairly docile, but the sight of them stopped the fighting. Merfyn Jones stepped up onto the mounting block and held up his hands.

"There will now be a sale of rams," he said, and his clear voice carried.

The dazed fighters looked at him and sat down. Some of them staggered to the wall and leaned against it, and others sat on the cobbles, where they were. The big red-haired man came to the steps, his nose bleeding, his face scratched, and his eye black and beginning to swell. He looked up at Morgan, shrugged his shoulders, and sat down on the second step. Morgan smiled, and then slowly he laughed.

"The sale was to have been at my farm, at noontime, gentlemen . . . maybe some of you remember . . . or would you be forgetting now?" Merfyn Jones began. "None came to buy! I come to sell! Take your time. They're fine beasts, indeed."

Myfanwy Jones tied the dun mare to the right-hand gate-post and came across the coachyard. Penry Jones went to the mounting block and sat down on it behind Merfyn. Myfanwy came up the steps. She smiled at Morgan.

"Well, Miss Catty, and is it a social you're having, indeed?"

"More like a ram sale, Myfanwy Jones . . . and a timely one." Myfanwy laughed, and went past me into the kitchen.

Villagers and strangers were now looking at the rams, knowing that the animals were good, that Merfyn Jones wasn't anxious to sell, and that they needed to buy. There were five or six young rams with short white beards. The others had beards up to their ears and spiky ruffles, and their fleece was speckled with hemp, white and stiff, and water-proof. The bids were beginning.

Emma had two kettles of water boiling, and she was wearing her second-best party apron. Myfanwy Jones looked around the kitchen.

"A nice sight, Emma. A peaceful sight."

"And how would you be getting here? Rams and all?" Emma asked, and rinsed the big teapot with boiling water.

" 'Tis fate!" Myfanwy laughed. "Fate and the Reverend."

"The Reverend?"

"He came to the Farm last night and said that we just might be needed, rams and all . . . if none had come to the sale by noontime."

Emma put the tea in the pot and put the caddy back on the mantelpiece. "That Reverend! He thinks of everything —even the tea," she said.

I went to the door again. Some of the women had left. Others were comforting Mrs. Eyeball, who was leaning against the wall, holding the half-empty bag of feathers and weeping. I went to them.

"Mrs. Eyeball, come and have a cup of tea with Emma and Myfanwy and all of us."

"Tea, is it?" She straightened up and threw her shoulders back and was angry again. "Tea! 'Twas not to drink tea that I came here, look you . . . tea! The Living Jesus . . . tea!" And she began to shout again and sob.

"Well, tea sounds just the thing to me, indeed to good-ness," Mrs. Evans said. She had been trying to soothe Mrs. Eyeball, but now she and Codger's daughter-in-law and the haberdasher's wife and Tessie's friend and the quiet girl and Mrs. Price, from the White Horse, and her sister from Llanberis and Mary Peters, all came into the kitchen and accepted the cups of tea and *bara-brith* and gingersnaps that Emma served to them.

"Not that you deserve it, any of you," she said, and they looked ashamed and amused. "You look you"—she looked around at the older women—"members of the Mothers' Union . . . now, just what do you think you were doing?" She looked at the two younger girls. "And you . . . members of the Girls' Friendly . . . what were you thinking of?" She poured more boiling water into the teapot.

"We were thinking of tarring and feathering him," Tessie's friend said, and she giggled. And the others giggled. Except the quiet girl and Myfanwy Jones and Emma and Mrs. Evans.

"I've heard of this sort of thing," Mrs. Evans said, "but I never want to see anything of the kind."

"Well, he surely to goodness deserved it." Codger's daughter-in-law took her third gingersnap.

"These are real good, Emma . . . crisp and melty, too. You must let me have the secret."

"A fat lot of secrets you all let me into these past few days," Emma said.

"Now, Emma," Myfanwy Jones laughed.

"Anyways, where are they?" Tessie's friend asked the question I hoped they would forget.

"Yes . . ." Codger's daughter-in-law had a fourth gingersnap halfway to her mouth. "Yes . . . where are they? Him and that Blodwen Price?"

Myfanwy Jones handed her cup to Emma. "A little more tea, please, Emma." Then she turned, and leaning on the table, she said, "They both left last night," and took the cup from Emma, who had walked around the table and was standing next to her.

"They couldn't have." Tessie's friend was sure. I wished she weren't Tessie's friend. "They couldn't have. Every way out of the Village was watched." She giggled again. "I know. I was a watcher."

"And Caradoc Ellis, too?" Codger's daughter-in-law said, and Mrs. Evans sniffed, and Myfanwy Jones laughed.

"Well now, and it's thinking twice I'd be, indeed, before I'd hire any of you to keep watch for me," she said. Then she shook her head. "Look you now, once and for all . . . they left in Merfyn's milk cart, crouching down under the tarpaulin, in between the milk cans."

"Who drove them?"

"Cousin Penry."

"None saw the milk cart last night . . . nor Penry Jones," Tessie's friend said.

"Well now, and wasn't that just the idea, look you?" Myfanwy Jones said, and laughed again. Then she put her cup down on the table and Mrs. Evans put hers next to it.

"Thank you, Emma." She looked around. "Well, indeed to goodness, and it's a good thing that none saw the milk cart, at that." And Mrs. Evans left the house through the front door.

I went to the top of the steps, hoping that Blodwen Price and the Foreigner would keep out of sight and that no one would be walking along the river path. They really hate them, I thought, and the sight of them would start everything up again.

The sale of rams was orderly now. Mr. Jones, the butcher, had recovered and was sitting with Penry Jones on the mounting block. Mrs. Eyeball was still crying and clutching her bag of feathers in one hand and wiping her tears with a large handkerchief. The strangers were quiet and efficient, handling the rams with knowledge and giving true praise and a fair price. Soon all the handsome beasts had changed hands. Morgan went to Mrs. Eyeball, but even he couldn't calm her. She held on to the lapels of his jacket and began to sob and shout again.

"Where is he? Where is the bastard?"

The sale had ended, and one of the men near to her said, "Yes, and where did he go, at that?"

Merfyn Jones held out his arms wide, as he had done at the beginning of the sale; this time he said, "To the White Horse." But strangely there was small response. The men were talking, and Mrs. Eyeball had pulled away from Morgan and was shouting again.

"Where is he? He's somewhere about . . . he didn't leave."

And Ifan Evans said, "He's got to be hiding somewhere."

"Indeed he is, look you." Mr. Jones, the butcher, stood up.

And then Merfyn Jones began to sing, standing there on the mounting block, a song of farming and the sheep flock and return at evening: " '*A'r defaid yn dyfod i'r gwair a'r iraiddyd . . .*' " his voice high and warm and clear in the windless air. And when he came to the long, graceful phrases: " '*Chwerwed ef a chwerwo* . . . Still we'll remember . . . *dan heulwen yr awen awena arnom byth* . . . our cottage, in sunlight or moonlight . . ." Penry Jones joined in harmony, his deep voice blending and mingling, and everyone in the coachyard sat down where he was or leaned against the wall, and the women came out of the kitchen onto the steps. Mrs. Eyeball was crying quietly. When they came to the last verse, all the men sang. Then the rich and lovely sound died away and there was silence.

"There they are! Look you! His things! All his luggage!" Mr. Jones, the butcher, got up onto the mounting block beside Merfyn Jones and pointed to the Foreigner's two trunks. He lifted his arms in the air. "To the burning! To the burning!" he shouted.

"Valuable," I thought, and then that Mr. Jones hadn't said, "Let's burn them," or, "Why don't we burn them?" or,

"They should be burned." He'd said, "To the burning!"
And now almost everyone was shouting, "To the burning!"
Even Mrs. Price and her sister from Llanberis, and the
haberdasher's wife. Those who had bought rams tethered
them to the left-hand gatepost in the road and set the dogs
to watch them.

"Come and help carry," Caradoc Ellis called. "We'll
burn these things in the field." And I thought, They could
have burned them in the coachyard. Caradoc Ellis and John
Thomas Davies were lifting the big wooden harness box,
and Mrs. Eyeball was urging them on with her bag of feathers, swinging it around her head like a club.

"Burn his stinking things! Burn his stinking things!"

I heard Myfanwy Jones's quiet "Tck! Tck!" behind me,
and was glad that neither Jane nor the Vicar's wife had seen
Mrs. Eyeball today. She needed the job at the Vicarage.
Tessie's friend had followed Caradoc Ellis and the blacksmith across the road. She ran in front of them and opened
the field gate. Merfyn Jones sat down on the mounting block,
and he and Penry laughed. Mr. Jones, the butcher, put on his
glasses and went to the field. Morgan took his pipe out of
his pocket and went to sit with Merfyn and Penry Jones,
and two of the strangers were picking up the Foreigner's
hamper trunk, when Codger walked through the center of
the open coachyard gates; he was wearing his waistcoat.
The two strangers almost dropped the hamper trunk. They
put it down and sat on it and looked at him. Morgan and
Merfyn and Penry Jones stood up.

"Sit down, gentlemen, please." Codger walked down the
cobbled slope from the gate, leaning on his ash stick. I
loved to see its handle, polished and shining with long usage.
He sat down on the block and looked at the two strangers.
"Get on with it. Get on with it."

And they did. They picked up the hamper again, laughing, and soon everyone was in the field, except for the four men who sat on the mounting block, smoking.

The trunks were emptied out, and the Foreigner's belongings—boots and leggings, harness and clothes, shirts and jackets and socks and underpants and pajamas and first-prize rosettes—were heaped on top of the empty trunks.

"Faggots! . . . Dylan! Emrys! . . . Faggots! We need faggots," Mr. Jones, the butcher, shouted, and Dylan Price and Emrys Jones and some of the other children who had gathered hurried to collect dry sticks. They went into the coachyard. Archibald will have to collect some more small wood, I thought. I was standing by the field gate. Mrs. Eyeball was poking the pile of clothes and harness with a thin branch, her pillowcase still clutched in the other hand. I saw Mr. Jones coming toward me.

"Right damp it is after the rain yesterday, Miss Catty." Dylan Price and Emrys Jones came back across the road, their arms full of faggots, followed by the others, some carrying more dry small wood.

"Well, Mr. Jones, you have enough dry sticks," I said.

"Well now, and that's a fine thing . . . and from Archibald's pile, look you . . . now that's real nice . . . dry faggots and yet, Miss Catty . . . the damp . . . 'twould be a crying shame . . ." He bent his head and looked at me. His yellow lashes and the whites of his eyes were almost the same color in the white afternoon light. His eyes were china blue. I laughed.

"Why don't you ask Emma for some paraffin?"

"Well now, Miss Catty, if that isn't a fine idea. An idea I'd never have thought of, indeed to goodness . . . yes indeed . . . the very thing." And he hurried across the road.

Codger's daughter-in-law and the haberdasher's wife and Mrs. Price and her sister and the other people who had gathered were all inside the field, and Dylan Price and Emrys Jones were putting faggots all around and in between the harness and clothes and inside the upturned trunks. Everyone was laughing. Mr. Jones came back with a big copper pitcher full to the brim with paraffin. He was carrying it carefully with both hands.

"Don't drop it, look you, Mr. Jones," Tessie's friend called out as he came through the gate.

"The Foreigner's stuff will burn easy," Codger's daughter-in-law said, and everyone crowded after Mr. Jones as he carried the oil to the pile.

" 'Tis a shameful waste of good harness leather," the red-haired stranger said, and he was almost mobbed.

" 'Tis shameful you are yourself. Shame on you! Shame! Shame!"

"All right. All right . . . look you . . ." he defended himself, laughing. "To the burning! To the burning," he said, and they all began to chant the words to the tune of the Welsh National Anthem.

"To the burning . . . to the burning . . ." It fitted well, "the burning" came on the high notes. "To the burning . . . the burning . . . the burning, to the burning . . ."

Mr. Jones and Caradoc Ellis lit the faggots. Someone had put a royal blue first-prize rosette on top of the pile. I was glad I had turned away when the Foreigner crawled into the cave. I put my arm around Emma's waist. She looked at me and shook her head and smiled at the same time. The flames leaped up.

"Look you!" Codger's daughter-in-law said. "Easy burning it is. Look at that blaze." Then she saw her father-in-law. "Ye gods! Look at that! The old man's wearing his waistcoat! . . . This must be a great day, indeed."

And Codger, leaning on his stick, took his pipe out of his mouth, and looking at her with no expression in his eyes at all, said, "Indeed, and it is a great day"—he spat—"for them as understands."

And Myfanwy Jones, who was standing next to Emma, said, "Yes indeed! And 'tis a dire day it could have been, look you." She nodded and smiled at Codger. "Yes, indeed it is a great day."

And we all turned to where Caradoc Ellis had taken hold of Tessie's friend and they were dancing a Welsh jig, and Penry Jones went to the quiet girl and they began to dance. He was known for his jigs and reels, and the girl was light and lissome. They made the other two look heavy-footed and almost clumsy. Mr. Jones, the butcher, shook his fist at the flames and then gave his funny salute, two fingers to his forehead, and laughed. Mrs. Eyeball walked unsteadily to the blaze and emptied the feathers onto the fire, then she threw the pillowcase after them and sat down on the grass and wept. Dylan Price was playing his mouth organ. He always carried it in his pocket. He played well, and his father was going to give him a new one for Christmas. Now there were five couples dancing around the fire and laughing merrily.

" 'Tis a far sight better than tarring and feathering," Myfanwy Jones said, "for that would have been a sad blot on our Village." Emma and I nodded.

"And I got all my rams sold, look you . . . and at a right fair price," Merfyn Jones said, his eyes twinkling.

As the fire died down, the dancers stopped. Soon the Foreigner's belongings were a heap of charred ashes. Then I saw Myfanwy whisper to her brother. He nodded and stepped onto the first rung of the field gate and swung on it, and loudly he said, "And now, look you . . . to the White Horse it is. For it's dry as a bone I am."

And they all began to chant, "For Merfyn Jones is dry as

a bone . . . For Merfyn Jones is dry as a bone." And laughing and singing, they all came out onto the road.

The big stranger came up to Myfanwy Jones. His eye now was purple and dark blue and swelling. "The rams, Miss Jones, they'll be all right for a while, I take it?"

"Merfyn will leave the dogs with them," she said, and the red-haired man took off his cap and almost bowed to her,

She turned to me. "Well, Miss Catty, and it's good-by I'll be saying." Then under her breath she added, "Now, that was a real silly question, look you, about the rams," and went across the road to untie the dun mare. "Archibald can fetch her on Thursday," she called to me, and was about to jump up into the milk cart, but the big stranger was there to help her up. She raised an eyebrow and tossed her head, but said, "Thank you kindly." And then, "Anybody for a lift? I'm going by the Village." The stranger made to jump in. "Ladies only, this trip," said Myfanwy Jones without looking at him. "The men can walk while they can walk."

Codger's daughter-in-law, the haberdasher's wife, and Mrs. Price and her sister all climbed into the cart and rode down the Lane, laughing and talking. The others went their ways, and Merfyn Jones said, "Where's the Reverend?" And he and Codger went across to the coachyard. They came back with Morgan and stood in between the gates, and then the men, villagers and strangers, set off together down the hill, Codger and Morgan and Merfyn Jones behind them, walking slowly and talking.

"Bring Mrs. Eyeball to the kitchen," I said, and Emma nodded.

"I'll give her some hot tea. Sober her up a bit. She's surely made enough of a fool of herself for one day."

She went into the field, where Mrs. Eyeball was sitting on

the grass. I walked across the road. The breeze that had risen with the sinking sun smelled of burning and rams. I touched the horn of one of the younger ones as I passed into the coachyard. How is Archibald? And where? I wondered. I knew that he had been able to control the Other Horse. Then I thought how good it was that everyone had gone to the White Horse, it was the farthest place from the river. Morgan should have been a general—I smiled—like Alexander. He had arranged with Merfyn Jones about the White Horse, as well as everything else. I laughed to myself, and then I saw Emma bringing Mrs. Eyeball to the field gate and went through the archway to the rose garden and past the marrow patch to the birch grove.

I leaned against the young, tender birch, looking at the familiar garden, cool in the September sunlight. The marrow patch, the rose trees, resting in summer promise. I sighed. I was tired. I thought again of yesterday and today. Yesterday; Eldorai's *vardo*. Gray-green mists in the valley and white mists on Moel Hebog; the cold-rushing stream and Molly-fach's joyful gallop. Culvato's music and Eldorai's knowing, and a deep, warm delight. I looked up at the birch trees, their gleaming arms, silver-dappled in the pale sunlight. Today there had been no mists, only bright, small clouds, casting their shadows on the mountain slopes; slippery rocks and wet shingle. Violence, song, and laughter. I thought of Mr. Jones, the butcher. He had stopped Ifan Evans on the kitchen steps. And Caradoc Ellis had taken the Foreigner's belongings to be burned in the field instead of in the coachyard. I smiled, remembering the red-haired stranger, battered and bruised, sitting on the second step, and Morgan's quiet laugh. Morgan. Pansies in a blue and white jug in an untidy cottage. Jane will be coming back from the Vicarage, I thought. Have I time to go to Morgan's cottage? The tide is coming in. Has Archibald come yet?

I stood up, away from the birch tree, my mind made up, and ran down the left-hand path toward the river. When I turned the sharp bend onto the narrow mossy path I looked downriver, but there were no boats. I hurried on. The path went in a straight line, and the bluff and the cottage were all one, darker gray against the graying sky. I looked across at the mountains, darkening now, and whispered, "Thank you, Heavenly Father, that Jane was at the Vicarage . . . and that I was not." I hoped that Emma was giving Mrs. Eyeball something to eat and that she would be gone or at least more herself before Jane came home.

I began to climb the steep slope of the bluff. Columbus came to meet me, a flash of white in the gloaming. He greeted me with short, sharp mews.

"All right, Colly, you shall have your supper." He rubbed against my ankles as I opened the cottage door and went in and lit the lamp on the dresser. Then I went to the pantry and opened a tin of salmon. I washed his plate and bowl, while he purred like a tiger and wreathed about my feet. "Here you are, hungry one."

I cleared the breakfast dishes from the table and washed and dried them, along with those piled up in the scullery sink, and then folded the small lace tablecloth that Morgan used on half the table and put it in the dresser drawer; cleaned the ashes from the fireplace, and with newspapers and faggots built a fire. While it began to blaze, I dusted carefully, and then got two big logs from the heavy iron-handled chest and put them on the crackling flames. Colly came, jumped up onto his seat, and began to wash himself, licking his paw and rubbing behind his ears. His fur was short and silky, like velvet. His eyes shone like golden topaz in the firelight. His purr was loud and hoarse. He turned over on his back and stretched.

The cottage was welcoming now, and cozy, with the red-flagged floor shining-smooth and the rough dark green wool rug warm at the feet of the winged chair, in front of the wide hearth; the fading chair covers harlequin in the flickering light. I took a piece of paper from one of the notebooks on the table, and as I tore it I read some sentences from the top page of a pile of foolscap written in Morgan's academic, hard-to-understand writing: ". . . the education that gives to a man the knowledge of his own integrity as a human being will enable him to deal wisely with the matters which confront him as a member of the community. . . ."

I was about to read on when I heard the sound of a motor and ran out onto the bluff, to look along the wide curve of the river. The sound grew clearer, and a small motorboat came into view. I waited awhile, but the boat was still a dark speck on the water. I went back and wrote, "I think Archibald is coming now, but I must get back to the house. I want to see you." I propped it up against the lamp. Then I went to Colly, who was still on his back, licking his stomach. I rubbed it, and he doubled up and held my hand and wrist with his four paws, claws out, but not scratching. "Lucky Colly," I said, and wished I could wait by the fire for Morgan to come home. I closed my eyes for a moment and felt the deep dream, a school, here in the mountains, and then the deeper fear: "When I know the answer to that, I may go back to the monastery." I turned and went out of the cottage, closing the door behind me.

The sound of the motorboat was louder as I came to the path, and the sun was almost down to the tops of the mountains. The tide would soon be high. The boat came close enough for me to see, and there were two people in it. Two? My heart sank. But it was keeping to the opposite bank.

Archibald would do that. He would stay away from our side of the river till the last moment. I hoped he wasn't wearing his cap. The river was wide and the light dim. Then the boat changed course and the figure in the middle of it took off his cap and waved. I waved back. Oh, blessed Carrots. I waved again, jumping for joy; then I ran down the path and through the orchard to the house. Of course, I thought, the other man in the boat will take them back to the Junction.

Emma was alone. She was sitting in her chair, rocking gently in the firelight. She hadn't lit the lamps. Star was asleep on her lap, and her stocking feet were crossed and comfortable. Rumpel was playing with her shoes on the rug. All trace of the party had disappeared, and the kitchen was full of warm shadows. She looked at me and sighed. "And where might you have been, Miss Catty?"

"Has Jane come in?"

"No, and 'tis lucky for you that she hasn't." I nodded, smiling happily, and sat down on the rug at her feet. Star wakened and jumped down and came to me. Rumpel took no notice.

"I went to Morgan's cottage. To clean it for him."

"I'll warrant it needed tidying up a bit, at that."

"And, Emma! Archibald came in the motorboat."

"I thought I heard it. Glory be to goodness, and thank the Good Lord for that, indeed."

"Oh, Emma." I sighed and laid my head on her knee. "What a day."

" 'Tis a day that won't be soon forgotten in this Village, Miss Catty-fach," she sighed, "and it could have been a dreadful day, indeed"—she smiled and put her hand on my head—"and 'twas not, look you. 'Twas not, indeed." I looked into the fire, watching the flames light up the smooth copper of the big kettle.

"It's a great day, Emma. Codger said so"—I looked up at her—"and he wore his waistcoat."

And Emma said, "Now, and if I'd had the time to think about it, indeed, I'd have worn my Paisley for the burning, at that."

12

After the days in her stall Stray was so happy that she gave
a small gay buck as she turned into the Lane. I laughed and
we rode up over the Rise in the crisp early morning air.
Soon we left the grassy roadside path to canter over the
stubbly, cropped fields. The hay was stacked and the barns
were full. After Thursday, I thought, Archibald will have
the dun mare. His breeches had been ordered. The letter
was in the kitchen to give to Idris Williams, the post, and
Emma said that she would go, next Wednesday, on her day
off, to the haberdasher's to get the yellow wool for his
jumper. After three quarters of an hour I came home. I was
impatient to see Morgan. Archibald was waiting. He held
Stray's head while I dismounted.

"How was the Other Horse?"

"He settled down, look you, Miss Catty . . . he behaved
quite well."

"I think he hated the Foreigner. My horse books say that
owners can spoil horses . . . and I know that's true."

"It is, indeed."

"And, Archibald, he was cruel. You know, after fighting
with the Other Horse that Saturday morning in the meadow
till I was weary and sobbing, suddenly I felt he was about to

obey me . . . then the Foreigner cut him across the rump with his switch."

"He liked to hurt," Archibald said, and I remembered the strange glitter in his eyes when he watched my nose bleeding, and how he stared at the weal when I went to see him in the loft room. Then Archibald smiled.

"He was good and mad, indeed . . . and his leggings and boots all scratched and dirty . . . when he crawled out of the cave to get into the motorboat."

"They burned his traps."

"I know. And indeed to goodness, and I'm glad I won't be around when he hears about it."

"Archibald!" We looked at each other, one each side of Stray's head. "He's gone."

I went in to change, and afterward hurried down to the library to prepare the study table. Pens, pencils and blotting paper, notebooks, ink. Ink. I thought of Tessie and the bedroom rug. So long ago. Her mother was "on the mend." Emma had a postcard from her and she was returning to Bryn Llithrig today. I put the two wooden-backed chairs by the table, opposite to each other, and then sat down on the white rug in front of the dull fire. I was tired, almost sleepy. But I sighed happily and looked into the dull fire.

"Studies will commence tomorrow," Jane had said at dinner the evening before. The Curate had come back with her. She had been in high spirits. "Yes, Catriona, studies tomorrow . . . no more holidays and picnics with Archibald." Then she had talked brightly about the Harvest Social and the Curate asked her if she would arrange the altar flowers for the next Sunday. Jane had been delighted.

"We have some perfectly lovely early chrysanthemums," she replied, and they had decided to have a small whist while the Curate's sister was visiting him in October.

There at dinner with her and the Curate, listening to

their talk, I felt as though I had been dreaming; that none of it had happened—Jane's weeping, the fight, the ram sale and the burning . . .

Now as I watched the small pallid flames licking the damp logs, hovering, disappearing, and spurting up again, pale and green-edged, I thought of the roaring flames of the burning, and the dark, heavy paraffin smoke; and of Blodwen Price, and of what would have happened if they had not hidden in the cave. I shivered, took the bellows, and blew gently under the logs. The bellows were stiff, the leather was worn and cracked. Slowly the flames took hold. Rumpel came in and jumped on my shoulder; the next second he was boxing the bellows. When the flames grew stronger and I put the bellows back in their place, he lost interest, switched his tail, and crossed the room in four lopsided leaps, and swung on the curtain nearest the door. Then he scrambled to the top and picked his way carefully along the rod, slipping on the curtain rings and looking scared.

"I'm not going to help you," I said, and then I heard Morgan's steps in the hall. He came into the library, smoking his pipe.

"Good morning, Catriona."

"Good morning, Morgan." Rumpel mewed. Morgan looked up. Rumpel was crouched and stiff.

"Well, Rumpel, you got up there." He laughed and held the curtain out from the wall, and Rumpel jumped. He landed halfway down, held on for a moment with his claws, and then leaped to the ground and tore out of the room. Still laughing, Morgan closed the door. He came and stood above me, his back to the fire. He looked at the study table, and then down at me.

"Everything ready, I see." He smiled and sat down in his chair by the table. "You're an early bird." I got up from the rug and sat in mine. "And thank you for cleaning my cottage and feeding Colly"—he put his elbows on the table—"and for the heart's-ease pansies."

"I gathered them on the way back from the cave." He looked at me with deep thought in his eyes. They are gray as tarn water at dusk, I thought again, but I said, "Where was Paddy? I didn't see him all day."

"That wily one. He went to the Farm."

We sat for a while without speaking. Content. Now although I had longed to talk with him, there seemed no need for words. Morgan spoke.

"You know that Betty Eyeball is going to have a child?"

"Yes. Suddenly, yesterday morning, in my room, I knew. That was the other reason that the Foreigner shouldn't lose his job, wasn't it?"

"Yes. He must take the responsibility for his child. It is better that he has the means to do it, and do it he will. Since my talk with him he is well aware of the consequences should he try to shirk."

"I'm more sorry for Blodwen Price." Again he looked at me. "Eldorai says she's not bad."

"Of course not."

"And she said that all men are our teachers . . . even the Foreigner."

"How did you feel about him, Catriona? When you left them both in the cave?"

I thought a moment. "I wasn't sorry for him at all. When he fell, I nearly laughed . . . but when he bent down to crawl inside the cave I knew how he would hate me to watch him, and I turned away. . . ." Morgan looked at his own hands on the table, clasped around the bowl of his pipe. I had never felt so close to him. Not on Moel Hebog. Not after the Foreigner had hit me.

"What will happen to Betty Eyeball?"

"She went to stay with an aunt in Rhyl, who keeps a boardinghouse. Betty can live with her and help."

"Why did she come to see Emma that morning?"

"She thought Emma could tell Jane, and Jane would make the Foreigner marry her." He sighed, and we were quiet again. I looked at his lean hands, brown against the starched white of his shirt cuffs. "He whose hand and eye are gentle," I thought, "and strong."

"Is there anything else you would like to know?" I shook my head. "Or talk about?"

"Only that I feel happy . . . Archibald, too. We couldn't believe the Foreigner had gone."

"And soon Archibald will be riding with you." I nodded, and we began lessons.

All through the wrathful months study was a joy; and in spite of the bitter winds, when the ground was soft Archibald and I rode together. Then on a morning at the beginning of February, when every blade of grass was windfrozen above the ground, too hard for many days for the horses' legs and feet, Morgan and I sat in front of the fire in the library, before lessons. He had walked over for breakfast because Mrs. Eyeball had not come out in the wild weather. We brought our second cups of coffee with us, and Morgan was sitting on the dark green couch, facing the door. I was on the rug at his feet.

"Catriona," he said, and put his cup and saucer down on the floor, "you have studied deeply and well, and I am proud of you. Not only the legends and ancient history that you love, but mathematics and Latin, and"—he raised his eyebrows—"even geography . . . even maps!"

"Not maps!"

He chuckled and stretched out his long legs across the rug. He smoked in silence for a while.

"We have studied and we have learned, Catriona, and we

have enjoyed each hour, and now I want us to seek . . .
to think back on what, in these studies, has been for us truly
a source of delight."

"Oh, Morgan! Almost everything has."

"No, Catriona. Enjoyment is not delight. You are young
. . . you love learning . . . we both love to learn."

"Then learning is a true delight." He smiled.

"Yes, learning is a true delight, but—"

"But, what?"

"But you can't lump it all together . . . or perhaps you
can. That is not what I want us to think on."

I waited. He looked into the fire—it was bright and
crackling—then he looked at me.

"What, in all that we have studied, read, talked of, has
shifted our awareness? So that for one instant we were
beyond thought."

"I don't know what you mean, Morgan."

"Catriona, think. Why did you, as a child, love reading
so much that you fought for it? Suffered for it?"

I remembered clearly. The red plush chair . . . I turned
to look at it, deep crimson in the firelight. "It was the gateway to high adventure," I said. "And though I knew that
I was still myself, when I was reading I wasn't six, or seven,
or eight, or nine years of age. I, Catriona, was with Peredur
at Arthur's Gate; with Einion Las and Olwen as they rode
their silver-hoofed ponies down the slopes of Cader Idris.
I watched the three hundred knights of Eiddyn in gilded
armor, and the three loricated hosts. I waved my scarf from
the ramparts. I saw the shining white arm rise through
the waters of the lake . . . the jeweled sword that drew
blood from the wind."

"And your awareness was shifted . . . you were no
longer in the red plush chair?"

"Part of me was."

"But you had forgotten time and place?"

"Oh yes! The day I broke the window I had been reading for three hours before Jane opened the wall gate. It seemed like three minutes."

"So that you had stepped out of clock time . . . beyond normal thought. The world of the story was the true world, in which you moved for a brief space and had your being." I nodded.

"Like The Happening, but different."

He looked up with quick interest. "I would like you to explain to me the difference."

I thought. "In the chair . . ." I began, and thought again. "In the chair, reading, I sought for what I knew—I hoped —would happen . . . that I would be—"

"Transported?"

"Yes . . . into the world I sought . . . the bright, early world . . ."

"Go on."

"With The Happening, I didn't seek anything; it came . . . and it wasn't far away in time. It was the present, familiar world that changed around me . . . became a part of me . . . was filled with beauty and light . . . and a new, deep meaning that I can't put into words."

"Words, Catriona? We are trying to talk of things that even thought may only swiftly, tenderly touch."

"Isn't that what you wanted?"

"No. I want to seek the sources . . . the jumping-off places . . . like your chair, but in the mind . . . the imagination." He looked up. "Tell me . . . quickly. Which works—not the myths and legends that we have read —have shifted your mind to the swift awareness?"

"*The Tempest* . . . Browning . . ."

"I know which parts of *The Tempest*. What of Browning?"

"But forth one wavelet, then another curled,
Till the whole sunrise, not to be suppressed,
Rose, reddened, and its seething breast,
Flickered in bounds, grew gold, and overflowed the world . . ."

Morgan laughed, and there was joy in his laughter. I felt my mind held in balance by his mind. The feeling was solemn and exciting.

"What else?"

"I can't think. There is too much." My mind was whirling with a thousand thoughts; pictures, word-evoked through the years. I lost what I had thought to say.

"Too much for a lifetime," Morgan said, and then, "Did you and Archibald take the dun mare to have her winter shoes reset?"

"Yesterday," I replied. Morgan had released the taut strings of thought. "Stray's are good for another two or three weeks. . . . I hope the frost melts soon." I sat looking into the fire.

The dun mare had been with us since the Thursday after the burning, last autumn. Merfyn Jones had bought two more horses, and she wasn't needed at the Farm. She and Stray and Molly-fach were unclipped and shaggy as mountain ponies. They were fat and sleek with extra oats and good, fine hay and mash once a week, and Archibald was gentle and patient with the dun mare. She had never been ridden before, and was used to the shafts. His breeches fitted well, and Emma had knit him a polo jumper of thick yellow wool. Out on the dun mare, his hair flaming, with pink face and bright blue eyes, and bright yellow jumper, Archibald was like a beacon in the gray winter landscape; and when we had come in and groomed the horses, if there was time before study, Emma gave us a cup of hot tea in the kitchen. It made the warm blood tingle inside us after the exercise and the cold.

I looked away from the fire. Morgan was smoking. The smell of his tobacco was part of the room. Part of my life, I thought. He looked comfortable. Happy. I got up.

"I'll take the coffee cups to Emma. She'll be washing up. Tessie's upstairs." I took the cups and saucers to the kitchen and came back and stood in front of the fire. Morgan was still sitting with his legs stretched out, smoking. I looked at the small diamond-shaped panes between the crimson velvet curtains, their colors clear and unreflected, and the white-gray light. I thought, These windows are part of my life. They have always given me pleasure. I looked at the new pane. New? It was five years old. Penry Jones had kept his promise and replaced the plain glass one. The new one was bright yellow and had tiny bubbles in it, like beads. I always laughed when I looked at it. Morgan looked up at the sound.

"The yellow pane?"

I nodded, and he drew up his legs and leaned forward, and holding the bowl of his pipe, he pointed the stem at me. "There's a book in the cottage I want to read with you. Now . . . go and get your coat"—he jumped up—"and put on your brogues . . . we'll walk over."

"What about study?"

"This is study."

I ran upstairs and put on thick knee-length socks and brogues and ran down again to the cupboard in the hall and got my heavy rainproof Welsh tweed coat and my brown tammy and a green woolen scarf that Emma had knit for me. "To match your eyes," she had said. Morgan was waiting for me in the kitchen.

"What's all this running up and downstairs? Where on earth are you going?" Jane had come out of the sewing room and was leaning over the banister.

"To Morgan's cottage, for a book."

"On a dreadful morning like this? It can't be that important."

"Morgan says it is," I called from the door to the kitchen, and there was no answer. I turned back into the kitchen; Emma was at the stove.

"Curry!" I sniffed. "That'll warm us." Morgan laughed.

"That it will," Emma said, "and it's needing it you'll be, after being out in this weather."

We left, pulling the kitchen door together against the bitter thrust of the wind. The garden was wintry-bleak, and every stripped tree and plant was swaying like the storm-tossed sail of a ship. The birches, bending with the gale, were gray against the gray sky. We walked through the orchard, our heads down, battling the driving sleet.

"Walk behind me," Morgan said, and as we came out of the trees onto the river path we were almost blown back again. We turned toward the bluff. The soft mosses were frozen hard, and there was a sheet of paper-thin ice around the roots and the grasses at the water's edge. The wind blew us sideways. The river was flecked with foam. The mountains were towering, rocky-gray and cold. We could hardly keep our feet.

"Jane must think we're crazy," I shouted.

"We are." Morgan turned his head to shout back. When we came to the bottom of the bluff, we sheltered for a moment to get our breath; but when we began to climb up, the icy buffeting knocked us breathless again. We didn't look up till we were inside the cottage, and then without speaking we went to the stone seats at each side of the hearth and sat down, taking off our gloves and holding out our hands to the blaze.

Mrs. Eyeball was in the scullery.

"Is that you, Reverend?"

"Yes. And it's brave of you to come out on a day like this."

"Sorry I was late, indeed to goodness."

"Miss Catriona's here."

"Hello, Mrs. Eyeball. How are you?"

"Warmer than you two must be. It's a cup of tea you'll be needing."

"We are, indeed. Thank you, Mrs. Eyeball," Morgan said, and we took off our coats and hung them on the hooks near the door. I pulled off my tammy, and it fell to the floor. Colly came out of the scullery and pounced on it. I tried to pull it away from him, and we had a tug of war. Morgan was searching along the shelves of his overflowing bookcases.

"It's a small green book. . . . Now, where did I see it?" He was on his knees. I unhooked my tammy from Colly's claws, hung it up, and went to the fireplace. Colly ran in front of me and leaped onto his seat. He sat on it, looking at me with his huge golden eyes.

"All right," I said, "I'll sit on the rug." Mrs. Eyeball brought a small, round copper tray with willow-patterned cups and saucers on it, sugar, and cream in the small blue and white cream jug that I had used to put the wild pansies in on the day the Foreigner left. I took the tray from her and put it on the rug beside me. "Thank you, Mrs. Eyeball." She looked the picture of prim, happy respectability; neat in her thick gray-brown tweed skirt and woolen jumper, and efficient in her clean starched white apron. I smiled, remembering her swinging the bag of feathers around her head like a club and shouting, "Burn his stinking things. . . ." Then I thought, How many hidden things are inside us all . . . inside me. . . . Cupid is blind, the reason why is this: "Love loves most where love most secret is." I looked at Morgan's long back, and thin, square shoulders, his lean brown hands, pulling out the books and looking behind them.

"He whose hand and eye are gentle . . ." Oh, Morgan
. . . don't go back to the monastery. Stay in the world with
me.

"A small green book with gold lettering," he said.

"Come and drink your tea and look afterward." He
turned around and sat on the floor.

"I saw it two or three days ago." He put his hand to his
head and clutched the thick hair at the crown and pulled it.
He always did this when he'd made a mistake or forgotten
something. "It's in the bedroom! And it's three weeks ago
that I was reading it, not three days." Time? I thought. An
hour. A week. A day can be so long. I thought of the last
months. Months can flash by like dry lightning. I've never
been so happy. . . . The tears welled up into my eyes.
Morgan came back with the book. He held it out to me. I
looked at the gold letters, blinking.

"The Felicities of Thomas Traherne," I read. "The Felicities? . . . The Happinesses?"

"Yes. The delights . . . the shiftings. . . ." It was a
small book, bound in grass-green leather. "I'll have a cup
of tea first." Morgan sat in the big winged chair. "Then I'll
read to you. Did you bring your notebook?"

"No."

"Take one from the table." When Morgan read to me, I
always made swift notes of the words and phrases that
caught my mind. I poured the tea, giving Morgan cream,
but no sugar. I liked neither cream nor sugar. I handed the
cup to him. I wanted to put my head on his knee. I sat back
on the thick woolen rug. I was warm now. My fingers were
tingling, and my cheeks. I could feel the heat of them,
flushed with the wind and the fire and the hot tea. I looked
up. Morgan was looking at me.

"You will be very beautiful, Catriona," he said, and a
shiver passed through all my body. I blushed. But my face is

so red, he won't notice, I thought. He handed me the cup and
saucer and pulled his pipe out of his pocket. I put the cups
and saucers back on the tray and stretched out my arm to
get a notebook from the table. Morgan took a pencil out of
his waistcoat pocket and threw it to me. He smoked for a
minute or two, and then he opened the book.

"Thomas Traherne, who uses simple words." He looked
up, "and who had a Happening when he was younger than
you were . . . and who found his tutors unsatisfactory."
He began to read.

I listened. The word pictures were clear, simple, and
lovely. I wrote in the notebook as Morgan read:

> "And everything that I did see,
> Did with me talk . . ."

Morgan read on, neither too fast, nor slowly, letting the
words speak:

> "And I within did flow, with seas of life, like wine,
> I nothing in the world did know, but 'twas divine."

I remembered the strange, cool shivers, like sap in my veins,
as I had sat, naked, at the window, that day in June.

"And I within did flow." I thought of Morgan's words on
Moel Hebog. "As we learn and study, we shall meet people
who have known moments like those you knew that day
. . . and you will recognize them . . ." As I listened to
Traherne's words, the memory was more than a memory
again.

> "And all I saw, a wonder did appear
> Amazement was my bliss."

"Amazement was my bliss." Morgan stopped reading.

"Do you like him?" I looked at him. "He died when he
was thirty-eight." Morgan looked into the fire. "He took

holy orders when he was twenty," he said, and we were silent. Colly was purring hoarsely, and the fire crackled. There were scullery noises: running tap water and the sandpaper sound of scrubbing. "Turn ye to me." I thought of Lady Nairn's love song. Oh, Morgan, turn ye to me.

"When I was reading him, about three weeks ago"— Morgan turned to me—"I came on a passage about his life at Oxford." He searched the pages. "Here it is. Listen!

> "There, at Oxford, I saw the nature of the Sea, the Heavens, the Sun, the Moon and the Stars. The Elements, Minerals and Vegetables, which appeared all glorious within . . ."

"All glorious within," I thought, the hairs on the gooseberries. Morgan was reading.

> ". . . and all these things, which my nurses and parents should have talked of . . ."

He looked up. "And listen, Catriona, here's what gave me this morning's idea:

> ". . . all these things which were taught to me were good; nevertheless, some things were defective too . . ."

Morgan looked up again and said the lines from memory, smiling:

> ". . . for there never was a tutor that did expressly teach Felicitie, though that she be the mistress of all the arts . . .

"Oh, Catriona! If I could expressly teach you Felicitie . . ."

Anything I share with you is my Felicitie. I held the thought to myself and said, "I have two pleasures. Two sure ones . . . reading and The Happening." And a third, I thought. I sighed. "You will be beautiful, Catriona"; and Morgan's look when I had walked down the stairs in my new riding habit. I went on talking.

"Of course, I'm always seeking to understand, to know the meaning of The Happening." I looked up at Morgan. "Thomas Traherne—he describes simply, so that, as you said, I recognize . . . but he doesn't help toward the meaning of it either, does he?" Morgan knocked the ashes out of his pipe, against his palm, and threw them into the fire.

"Now, Catriona . . . you have asked what I hoped you would ask."

"What?"

"You seek to know the meaning of The Happening. You say that Thomas Traherne doesn't help you to the answer you seek. Yet you love him. Your memory will be clearer to you because of him. Is this not true?" I nodded and waited. "Write this in your notebook and think on it." I picked up the notebook from the rug beside me. Morgan leaned forward, holding his empty pipe in both hands; half smiling, he said:

"He who bends to himself a Joy
Doth the wingèd life destroy;
But he who kisses the Joy as it flies
Lives in Eternity's sunrise."

I looked up. "Blake."

"Another simple man. Yes, you know the lines . . . but think of them anew . . . in relation to Thomas Traherne and The Happening."

I looked at the glowing coals at the bottom of the hearth. I thought of the simple, deep words. Without looking up I said quietly, "To seek to know the meaning is to bend the joy and the wonder to myself?"

"To seek to understand it intellectually is, yes." We were quiet. Then I smiled, understanding a little.

"Amazement was my bliss," I said. "Morgan, perhaps

wonder and bliss are the same . . . and awe . . . awe is a kind of wonder . . . and bliss . . ."

"The Unknowing," Morgan said. He held out his hand and pulled me up from the rug.

I took the tray into the kitchen and thanked Mrs. Eyeball; then I put on my coat and scarf and tammy.

"May I take the book?"

Morgan gave it to me. "You may." He put his arm around my shoulder and called good-by to Mrs. Eyeball, and then he put on his old fishing cap and his overcoat and we stepped out of the warmth into the whirling, wind-driven sleet.

While the winter lasted, through the February frost and blizzards, we were happy hermits. The birds—sparrows, robins, ravens, and sometimes a wren—came to Emma's window sill. She loved the robins. "Where the redbreast lives in peace, the people know no sorrow," she said, and I thought of Nana, who told me that the robins carried drops of water in their beaks to moisten the parched tongues of the damned; and as they fly through the flames of hell, the downy feathers on their breasts get scorched. The ravens were cheeky and came inside the window, making harsh, demanding sounds. The sparrows followed them, and when it was icy-cold and there was no other food to be found even the timid robins darted in and out. At all hours of the day and evening there was someone in Emma's kitchen, drinking hot tea and thawing himself.

On St. Valentine's Day the Girls' Friendly gave a whist drive and dance at the Parish Hall, and Emma made the cakes for the refreshments and went to play whist. She wore her purple bombazine and stayed to watch the dancing, bringing back tales of Caradoc Ellis: ". . . and that silly-daft little wife of his . . . and it's a word or two I'll be having with that foolish Tessie, indeed to goodness whatever . . ." Jane had worn her new midnight-blue taffeta, with long chiffon sleeves and black satin evening shoes with a strap across the instep, and small paste buttons. As always now, her hair was coiled in a bun at the nape of her neck, and she no longer had a fringe. She had invited Morgan, but he had smiled and refused.

"You know I don't play whist, and the Curate is a good player . . . and I understand, Jane, a very good dancer." Jane had agreed.

But Morgan came to dinner, and he and Jane had sherry in the drawing room. I had a glass of Emma's rhubarb wine.

When the thaw came, and the grasses and plants were released from their frosty armor, and the rushes, supple again, were bent almost flat on the water in the strong, full currents of the streams; and the tall green ferns curved again, like arches along the brinks; the widgeon and the mallards took busy, crying flight; when the ground was soft and there was good riding, and pleasant weather for walking, Morgan and I ridge-wandered. Sometimes we walked to Capel Curig and had tea and crumpets at the Eunach's Head, or followed the woodland streams under the still bare branches, and each day and hour I thought, Oh, Morgan, you have . . . expressly taught me Felicitie, and we studied and walked and talked and understood and laughed, and planned for the long glad days of summer. For early trout in Llyn Ogwen and summer salmon in the Glaslyn stream. Morgan said that no one had discovered why, in some rivers, like the Welsh Dee, the salmon arrive even before March and their run goes on all summer, yet other streams are late-fish rivers. We planned our first day's trout fishing, and I thought, I have known true happiness.

Then on a morning in late March, I was standing at the window in my nightdress and I heard an early thrush. I leaned out. It was on a high birch branch. I could smell spring on the wet winds that blew through the pink flannel, chilling my body. My new body. I sighed. Changing was strange. It had been a whole year now. No one seemed to have noticed. Except Emma. I thought of Olwen White-footprint, whose breasts were like the swan's breast. Shivering, I turned back into the room and began to put on my usual clothes. I had my bloomers on and was tying the now quite comfortable hair ribbon around my chest when Jane came into the room.

"Catriona! What on earth are you doing?"

I started. I hadn't heard her come across the landing. She was wearing her Indian house slippers. Quickly I put on my jersey.

"Take your jersey off . . . take it off, Catriona. I want to look at you." No! Jane, please! I shuddered. "Hurry up."

She took hold of the bottom of the jersey and pulled it up over my head. I didn't hinder or help. She swung me around and looked at me.

"Well, I never!" Jane stared. "And how long has this been going on?" I stood without speaking. "Catriona, how long have you had this development? How long have you been tying this ribbon around yourself?"

"A year. I'm quite used to it."

"But why?"

"I didn't want to wobble when I was riding in my jersey, before my habit came." I thought with a shiver of how the Foreigner had looked at me and made me feel self-conscious.

"You certainly need a bust bodice." Jane kept looking at me.

"May I put my jersey on now?"

"No. Wait a minute." She went out of the room. I crossed

my arms on my chest, feeling the still strange, cool softness. Jane came back with the tape measure. "Put your hands down. Really, Catriona . . . and stand up straight. It isn't with me that you should cover yourself up . . . it's when there are boys around." She measured me. Her fingers touched me. I stood there, stiff and tense, holding my breath. "You can put your jersey on again—and the ribbon —till you get your bust bodices. We'll buy some for you in Llandudno on Saturday, before dancing class." She let the tape measure snap back with a click into the little round case. "And from now on you must wear long stockings."

"Oh, Jane! Can't I wear the long socks, to my knees?"

"And leave your thighs bare? Certainly not. I never approved of those boy's socks you buy in the Village. . . . No. On Saturday we must buy stockings, and some blouses, too." She turned. "And I must lengthen your kilts and dresses," she said, and went out of the room and across the landing as silently as she had come, in her bright blue Indian slippers, leaving me shaking.

I sat on the window seat, my hands pressed palm to palm, and to my mouth. After a while I went down to breakfast. Jane was waiting for me. As I helped myself to bacon and eggs and took my plate to the table, she got up from her chair and closed the door.

"I have something to say to you." Oh no, Jane! Please! I looked at the charred piece of toast in the toast rack. Oh, Emma! If I could have breakfast with you in the kitchen, I thought. "Now, Catriona . . ." Jane had eaten her bacon and eggs and was taking a piece of toast. "First of all, you must not be so intimate with Archibald."

"Archibald? Intimate? . . . Oh, Jane . . ."

"Don't interrupt me, Catriona. I am very angry, indeed, that you have been so secretive about this"—she looked at me—"and I am quite sure there is something else you haven't told me." She waited. When I didn't speak, she seemed relieved, and said, "Well now, about Archibald . . . you may ride with him, of course. I'm sure that he is entirely trustworthy." Trustworthy? Archibald, my true friend. Oh, Jane! She buttered the piece of toast thickly. "Only last week the Vicar's wife commented on your intimacy with him. 'She's growing up, you know,' she said. She was only too right." I took a deep breath.

"Jane . . ." I said. "Archibald . . ."

"Do stop interrupting, please, Catriona. . . . Every boy notices these things." I was glad I'd tied the ribbon around me again. "It doesn't matter how nice they may be . . . and girls must be careful . . . very careful." She put marmalade on her toast. "It's so very easy to be enticing . . . to invite indignities, and to be, well . . . in a word, unladylike." I took my piece of burnt toast. "And as you know, Catriona, I am deeply disappointed in you. You are not a ladylike girl . . . in spite of all I've tried to do." She sighed and bit into the toast and butter and marmalade with her small teeth. The marmalade bulged over, and she wiped her mouth with her napkin. "I see that now I shall have to keep a much more careful watch over you . . . watch you much more carefully. . . ." Watch me and Morgan, I thought, and I knew that she was thinking the same thing, but she said, "And just what do you and Archibald talk about when you are alone together?" Her eyes narrowed. Then she put her hand to her forehead. "Oh dear! Oh dear! And I sent you out alone with him for a whole day, last September, when there was that slight contretemps about the Foreigner. . . ." She shook her head. "You didn't know anything about it . . . and it's not important . . . but you were alone with Archibald for hours." I nearly said that

we hadn't been alone the whole day, that we had been with
Eldorai and Culvato, but I remembered in time that she
would be angry about the Gypsies. "Well? Why don't you
answer? Are you ashamed?"

"Ashamed?" Oh, Jane! Why?

"Yes, ashamed. What do you talk about, Catriona?"

"Everything, Jane. The horses, lambing, Paddy, the
cats . . . legends . . . the Farm . . . Faery tales . . .
everything."

"Not Faery tales, surely not."

I ate my toast. "They're not children's Faery tales, Jane,
though I loved them when I was a child . . . they're about
the true Faery people, who live inside Cader Idris and are as
big as we are . . . and marry mortals . . . and—"

"Sheer, utter nonsense, Catriona! Really, sometimes I
wonder about Morgan. He should have put a stop to that
sort of thing years ago." She looked around at me quickly.
"Now don't change the subject. Do you and Archibald talk
about where puppies and kittens come from?"

"Oh, Jane! I know when a bitch is in whelp."

"Please, Catriona . . ." Jane's voice rose. "Those horrible farm words." I sighed. "And don't be cheeky. Don't
pretend to sigh when I'm talking to you."

"I'm sorry, Jane. I didn't mean to."

"It's time that you know what you mean and what you
don't. You're growing up . . . at least, to all outward appearances." Then she said, the piece of toast held in her
hand, "Do you remember, when you were very young, and I
caught you"—she sucked in her breath, shuddering—"your
hands covered with blood, with that big rabbit?" Big
Brindley-Flopsy. My eyes filled with tears. Suddenly, as
though a tap had been turned on. I bent my head over my
plate. "Do you remember what you were doing?" I nearly

said that of course I did, and that Archibald and I had helped Star, too, and given her warm cream; but I didn't. I lied. I took a deep breath and shook my head.

"No. I don't remember." Jane heaved a sigh of relief.

"Thank goodness for that. It was quite revolting." She poured another cup of coffee. "But you were very young . . . you didn't even miss the rabbit." I passed the sugar to her. "And you never talk about these things—about animals—to Archibald?" I thought of him, under my window, calling to me to come quickly because Star was at her due season. I crossed my fingers.

"No. Never," I said, and I thought of Emma: "In for a penny, in for a pound." Jane put the last piece of toast in her mouth.

"Not about sex?"

"Sex, Jane?"

She dabbed her lips with the napkin and turned to me. "Yes, Catriona, sex. Don't pretend that you don't know about sex."

"I'm not pretending, Jane. I know that Paddy's a dog, and not a bitch . . . Oh, I'm sorry . . ." I wondered what a dog that wasn't a dog was called, if not a bitch. "But I've never thought of it as sex."

"Well, it is. Most decidedly so. And talking about animals is . . . suggestive."

"Suggestive? Suggestive of what? Jane—"

"Really, Catriona, how difficult you can be. Just suggestive . . . nasty, enticing"—she looked at me as she had done in the bedroom—"asking for trouble. Why, anything could happen now." I didn't speak. I was tense again. I waited, still as a small wood animal. "You do know what could happen, Catriona?" I didn't speak. I couldn't. "Of course you do. And never forget . . . if you are the least bit unladylike . . . suggestive and enticing . . . boys will commit indignities." I felt sick. Indignities . . . Oh, Morgan . . . dear Archibald. Jane put both her arms on the table. "And if anything like this happens, Catriona, it will be your own fault." She pointed a finger at me. "And you mustn't be so friendly with these Village men . . . Merfyn Jones, Penry Jones . . . so uncouth—"

"Jane!" Now I was both sick and angry.

"And please remember, Catriona, and I shall not speak of it again . . . you must never . . . but never, in any circumstances whatever . . . let a boy put his hand on your bust . . . it is extremely—"

"May I leave the table?"

"Please. Catriona, are you forgetting your manners?"

"Please, Jane." She shrugged her shoulders and looked hopeless. She sighed.

"You may. And do try to remember a little of what I have been saying to you." I was able to walk out of the room; then I ran upstairs to the bathroom and was sick.

13

All through the month of March, Jane sewed. She made three tennis dresses for herself, white, with pleated skirts and blue binding around the neck and armholes, and two dresses for me. A green one and a white, made of linen, and longer than before. When I wanted armholes too, to feel cool and free, she told me not to be absurd, and even though I wore long stockings she still bought for me the wide, square-toed, square-heeled shoes I had always worn. When I asked if I might have a pair of court shoes with low Louis heels, her face reddened with quick anger.

"Really, Catriona. You are only sixteen, you know."

Since the morning she had discovered me undressed and asked me questions, Morgan's natural talk across the dining table, harmless glances, spontaneous words and laughter had become cankers of doubt and distrust in her mind. She had never come to the stables, but now when Archibald and I came in from riding and were in the stalls she would come in and tell me to hurry and not to linger, that it was lesson time; and then during lessons she came upon Morgan and me with craft, opening the library door quietly, without knocking, and she interrupted study whenever she could. Her open disapproval and annoyance when we went fishing and ridge wandering together jarred the peace of Bryn Llithrig.

She forbade me to wear my braids on top of my head as I had always done.

"I know that you are trying in every way to look older than you are, Catriona, but I shall not allow it. You will wear your hair in two plaits, down your back." And she insisted that I tie bows of wide ribbon at the ends of them, navy blue or black. When I wore my habit, I put elastic bands instead of the bows; and Emma said once, "Jealousy's a bitter, bitter thing, indeed . . . and it's my tongue locked over my teeth I'd better be keeping."

While Jane was giving tea parties and going to the Girls' Friendly meetings and playing whist, the damp, windy days were filled with hard work for Myfanwy Jones and Merfyn and Penry, and the other Village men, who tramped for long hours in the high, wind-torn moorlands, gathering in the flock from the far reaches of the hills, and then later, in April, there was the lambing.

Myfanwy Jones borrowed both Emma's thermos flasks. She used them to keep warm the milk and water she fed, with rubber teats and sometimes with medicine droppers, to the stray and motherless lambs. Late one evening Merfyn Jones came to deliver the milk and eggs, weary and dog-tired because of the birthings, and Jane had passed through the hall to go to the drawing room before dinner.

"Emma," she had called out, "where does that dreadful smell of carbolic come from?" Emma had laughed quietly, and Merfyn Jones had looked guilty and begun to apologize, but I had put my finger to my lips.

"Just a bit of disinfecting, indeed, Miss Withers, in the hard corners," Emma had said.

"Then do please do it in the morning in future, Emma. It permeates the whole house."

"Yes, Miss Withers." Emma had closed the door into the hall.

"I get so used to the smell, indeed," Merfyn had said, and hurried to finish his tea.

At lambing time Myfanwy Jones smelled of carbolic soap too, and she loved each ewe and remembered each lamb when it grew to be a ram, or a wether, or a full-mouthed ewe; and when her flock, and the two-year-olds, and sometimes the three-year-olds, of her long-headed, lean-necked herd of black cattle were sent to the Midland pastures to be fattened, it was a deep sadness for Myfanwy Jones; and when she played the harp and sang, I felt I could hear the sorrow and the joy of birth and growing, losing and birthing again.

Archibald and I hacked about the Farm, looking each day for new lambs in the frith, small and white, seeking warmth and food among the ewes. Now the dun mare was happy, and sometimes gay. She seemed to have forgotten the fear of having someone on her back and of being away from the shafts. Archibald had trained her with love and patience, and we were proud and excited when, after months of persuasion and lumps of sugar from Emma's red tin, he first put her into a canter from a walk. We couldn't believe that she had done it without trotting first, because trotting had always been her normal gait. She watched Stray jump, and trotted and galloped about the meadow. She hadn't been bred to jump and didn't want to, but she grew to enjoy the riding as much as Stray; and Archibald was becoming known in the district for his understanding and patience with animals.

While the flock was being gathered in, fishing began in Llyn Ogwen, and later in the streams. Morgan spent his evenings preparing his tackle and the small sober flies he used in the shallow water. He had two normal rods and a smaller

one of split cane that he used when he waded in the woody
streams. I didn't fish. I sat for swift-winged hours, well out
of the way of the backward swing of his fly, quietly watching
him while, unaware, his elbow close in to his side and letting
the spring of the rod do the work, he sent the fly sailing forward to float on the glassy water. I always watched intently
for the first slight heave of the surface just before the fish
seized the fly, and afterward I would close my eyes and listen
to the wild lake sounds. The whirr and whistle of wings.
Mallards and rattle-wings and the croaking of the diving
ducks; sometimes the short, harsh quack of a goldeneye,
and in the early months the merry, watery song of the dip-
per. Once I saw him perched on a cold rock to the left of us,
with white breast and arched neck and upswept tail, and
when his short song ended he flew down to the shore and
dabbled his beak for insects in the loose top stones of the
gravelly lake edge, and then he swam out on the small wind
waves, dived, leaving scarce a ripple, and came up again,
swimming. Manfri said that the dippers and the grebe could
walk along the bottom of the lakes and streams, and they
would disappear at the smallest sound. But the coots didn't
dive, they scurried and flurried over the water, making
prime targets of themselves, and I thought of Tessie: "Why,
miss . . . you're loony as a coot," she would say. And when
the fish were not rising and we both sat without moving for
a long time, a wary water hen would come close, walking in
the mud, to take swift flight and dive when suddenly Morgan's line rattled.

When dusk fell, I watched the large trout in the center of
the lake, rising at the sedge flies that skimmed the surface of
the water, or gazed in wonder at the steep, prickly, rock-
strewn ledge of Tryfan, where the raven sailed and the buzzards mewed; changing with the changing light, black-
shadowed, yellow, pink, and pale gray; hiding the sunset

glow in deep, rough ribs of rock, to mingle with the light of the rising moon.

By the end of May the lambs were reared. In spite of the night-prowling stealthy foxes and the wild wet winds, the whole flock went to the mountains, where the streams, in spring flood, drenched the crags; and the ewes went back, each to the place she had made her own. Ridge-wandering, Morgan and I would find a lamb in a gorse thicket or in the heather under a crag, and we knew that however far the ewe had wandered, she would find her way back to it; and where the sheep hadn't cropped too closely, and there was a little soil mixed with the peat, wood anemones bloomed, rosy-pink and sometimes purple-tinged, and white heather, and at the sappy levels lichens and ferns and strong-rooted grasses.

In the valleys the hedgerows were full green and heavy with birds' nests. Thrushes and the gentle-throated blackbirds. The meadows were bright with wild flowers: buttercups, celandines with their wide golden petals, and the pale yellow melilot. The daylight hoot of the tawny owl, the whistle of the missel thrush from the high branches, and the three-toned spring call of the cuckoo were clear sounds in the medley of early summer, and on a morning in June, after study, when Morgan and I were sitting at the round table, now moved close to the open windows, he put his hand to the crown of his head, and pulling the hair hard, said, "Catriona, two weeks ago I had a letter from Sir Phillip Lockridge, and I completely forgot about it . . . and the short reply I sent to him."

"From the brother of the Vicar's wife? Morgan, why? What about?"

"About Basil."

"Basil?" I laughed. "The handsome young rascal? I've heard about him since I was six years old. And what about him?"

"He's behind in his studies."

"He always was. What's his father's letter about?"

"Our studies."

"Our studies?"

"Yes . . . he wanted to know how advanced we were, particularly in literature. I replied to him that you could hold your own in any second-year college examination. Then last evening Idris Williams came up to the cottage with this." He took a letter from his pocket and began to read.

" '. . . and thus, I am convinced that my son, Basil, who is a Cambridge undergraduate, will profit greatly, from every possible point of view, by spending the summer months in the mountains, and sitting in, as it were, at your literary studies—' "

"Morgan!"

" '—and between you and me, Mr. Morgan, I shall be vastly relieved that he is, for a while, in a quiet Welsh village. He will, of course, stay with my sister and her husband at the Vicarage. The Vicar, incidentally, has given me quite splendid reports of your character and the caliber of your work."

"Morgan! I don't believe it."

" 'I must ask you to treat what I am about to write in strict confidence, but unless some definite progress is made he is in danger of being sent down. I needn't say that I trust you to keep his nose to the grindstone. . . .' "

"Oh, Morgan! Oh, goodness! And my last summer."

He nodded and sighed. We rarely spoke of my going away, but something almost every day made us think of it.

"I'm afraid, Catriona, that we are to have an unexpected companion at our studies."

"Can't you write that it isn't feasible?"

And with another sigh he said, "But it is feasible, Catriona." And I thought of the Vicar's wife and Jane, and Sir

Phillip, who took over factories and dealt firmly with strikers, and knew that it had to be feasible.

"How old is Basil now?"

"Twenty-two."

"A year older than Archibald."

"Morgan closed his eyes for a moment, and then looked at me. I felt a shiver all through me.

"You and Archibald are grown-up." His voice was quiet and deep. I thought, Oh, Morgan, "where love most secret is."

"Does it say when he will arrive?" I asked, and he turned to the second page of the letter.

" '. . . and he should arrive, in his car, the Bentley sports model I gave him for his twenty-first birthday, and which, I must say, with pardonable pride, he handles famously. He is a splendid driver and has nerves of steel, and what I think so necessary in these days of high-powered vehicles, instantaneous reflexes. But enough of my son's merits, which I am sure you will discover for yourselves. Suffice it for me to add, once more, that I am relying on you to cram the lad full enough of the required reading to enable him to scrape through. . . .' "

" 'Scrape through . . . nerves of steel . . . pardonable pride . . .' Morgan, he sounds so pompous."

"He's a very important man."

I sighed. "When's Basil coming?"

"In the middle of June."

"But that's now."

"I know." He shook his head and ran his fingers through his hair. "I just forgot the first letter." He lit his pipe, and we sat in silence.

The June breeze came through the windows, and where they were closed the small panes broke the light into rays of orange and green, blue and crimson, on the faded chintz of the summer covers. A bumblebee flew, heavy and buzzing, to each window, then rose to the roof.

"Oh, Morgan. What a nuisance."

"This I had not foreseen."

We were silent again. I could hear Paddy barking, and the sound of clippers. Young Emrys Jones, the butcher's son, helped Archibald, and today he was working on the lawn borders. Mr. Evans had supervised them again this year, and I could smell the clove gillyflowers that I loved, the spicy scent of them. I looked at Morgan's beloved face. If I could live here with him, all my life . . . I thought. And with the thought came the longing and the pain. Then I told myself, Nothing is impossible . . . the guardians are always busy and far away. . . . I let my thoughts dwell on my desire, and my heart began to race and throb in my throat. We could have a school, up here, on the slopes of Cader Idris, where people of all ages could come. It was the old dream, dreamed since the day I walked down the stairs in my new habit. People as young as Emrys Jones and as old as Codger . . . to read and learn all the beautiful and true words that have been told and written since time began . . . where scholars who dug and found the wonders of the ancient world could rest and write and collate the notes they made in the field. Where the myths and legends of the world could be studied and the threads could be sought and unraveled . . . I remembered Krishna, and the jests he made . . . the sweet nectar of his lips, his brow and the sandal spot . . . Krishna . . . I felt the stars shooting around me. The sky fell with my dress. . . . Morgan said that the legends of the Gaelic and the Indian myths were close to each other. . . . "And Etain was loosening her hair to wash it, and her arms were white as the snow of one night

. . . long, slender, and soft, white as the foam on the wave was her side . . . And Olwen gathered goodly herbs, and was beloved in all the land. . . ."

The bumblebee flew down again, bringing me back with him to present thought. I watched him: big and black and velvety, his long, thin, tiny-pocketed legs hung limp as he flew, and I wondered how his small gossamer-narrow wings could hold him up. The cuckoo called—loud and clear. She hadn't changed her tune yet. The bumblebee hovered, buzzing, then soared aloft and left us in silence again. It was nearly noon. I wondered why some times of the day were more hushed than others. Dusk is, I thought, because it is the time between the setting of the sun and moonrise, when the earth is still and all magic stirs. But there was a noonday quiet, too, and Morgan and I were held in it. Silent. Together. Oh, Nana! I'm spellbound again. Whenever I let myself think truly of Morgan, the thought filled my whole mind and soul and body and my breath was thin and slow and my face felt white and then the blood rushed to my cheeks. We looked at each other. Morgan put his pipe on the table and the leather bookmarker in the Chaucer, at the place where we had stopped reading, of May, the young wife of January, who sat with "so benyngne a chiere" that to behold her was to be ravished; and the squire Damian was; and so began the "Merchant's Tale." Morgan closed the book.

"Farwel my book and my devocion," he said, and smiled, "and I'm afraid, Catriona, that to some extent, farwel our quiet."

And the next day, in the middle of the morning, when Jane opened the library door, I thought of his words. She was excited. Her cheeks were pink, and she was full of glee.

"Such a wonderful surprise . . . simply too exciting." She came and sat on the seat under the windows. She looked

at the books on the study table and looked away again and
clasped her hands. "Something one would never have expected . . . never even thought of . . . I'm so delighted
. . . absolutely delighted." She stopped and looked at us.

"What's happened?"

"My dear, you'll never guess. Catriona, young Basil Lockridge, you know, Sir Phillip's son, is coming to tea." My
heart sank. So soon, I thought.

"Today?"

She nodded. "Isn't it too wonderful?"

"When did he arrive?" Morgan asked.

"Yesterday. The Vicar's wife telephoned this morning."
She looked at me. "Catriona, you must wear your green
linen and"—she paused, still looking at me—"you may
put your plaits up on top of your head . . . he's twenty-two
. . . and, Morgan"—she turned to him, smiling—"you are
expected to tea too, you know."

"Am I?"

"You are." She wagged a finger at him. "Sir Phillip wants
you to coach Basil."

"I had a letter from Sir Phillip Lockridge two weeks
ago."

"Two weeks ago?" Jane was surprised and annoyed.
"And you didn't say anything about it?"

"I forgot it."

"You forgot it? Forgot anything as important as a letter
from Sir Phillip? Really, Morgan."

"I'm afraid so. Then I had another, yesterday, and I remembered the first one. I was going to tell you at lunch today."

"I should think so. Really, such secretiveness . . .
Well, anyway"—she was excited again—"you are to be
with us at tea, and you can talk about his study . . . such
a splendid idea . . . simply splendid."

"Why us?" I asked. "Why is he coming to a mountain village to study?"

"Well . . ." She gave her small tittery laugh, and then tried to be serious again. "Well, it seems that he was the perpetrator of a practical joke." She couldn't restrain her laughter. "Really rather a vulgar one. It concerned one of the more revered statues in Cambridge." She looked down, then she looked up again, at Morgan. "And he is somewhat behind in his studies, and his father thinks that it is most propitious that he can study with you and stay at the Vicar-age." She turned to me. "Catriona, I understand that he's very handsome."

"I've understood that since I was a child, Jane."

"Of course you have. Why, it's almost as though you know each other already." She looked at Morgan again. "Really, this is a most fortunate thing . . . truly heaven-sent, something one could never have foreseen. It will be so nice for Catriona to meet a young man of her own—milieu—so to speak, and"—she smoothed her skirt over her knees—"the son of a baronet." She smiled at me. Then her face changed. "And someone"—she looked at Morgan—"someone more her own age." Then she got up. "I must tell Emma to bake a cake," she said brightly. "A cake for tea on Tuesday . . . on Tuesday . . ." She laughed again, and walked to the door and turned. "The world is really chang-ing around us. What fun . . ." And she left the room.

Morgan didn't look at me. We tidied the books and pre-pared for afternoon study.

"We'll revise the Chaucer this afternoon, as we have to finish at four o'clock."

"Oh, Morgan! Oh dear."

"Yes, Catriona," he said, and I couldn't help laughing.

"It's the first time the Vicar's wife has ever been to tea on a Tuesday."

Morgan put his pipe in his pocket and got up. He stood with his hands in his jacket pockets. "As Jane said, the world is changing about us."

I was fastening the buttons down the front of my green linen dress when Jane came into my room. She was wearing her best Liberty print dress and had red lip salve on her lips. She looked at me: my hair was pinned up, and I was wearing the low, square-toed shoes. She pulled her mouth to one side, so I knew that she disapproved of how I looked.

"You'd better leave your hair down today . . . and in one plait, I think . . . and wear your skirt and blouse." She thought for a minute. "Yes, that will be a good effect . . . you will have just finished lessons. You will wear the cream-colored silk blouse."

"But, Jane, you told me—"

"I know. I've changed my mind. Until I can get you a pair of those *glacé* court shoes—you know, the ones we saw, with the low Louis heels—you will look better in a blouse and skirt." I began to unbutton the green dress. "And don't forget to scrub your hands and polish your nails with the buffer and powder—it's in the top drawer of my dressing table." She went to the middle drawer of the big chest and took out the cream silk blouse. She laid it on the bed. "I think your plaid skirt . . . not that navy one." She went to the door. "And do hurry, dear, you know how punctual the Vicar's wife always is . . . and please, Catriona, do try to be a little more ladylike."

We were waiting for the guests; Jane in her usual place behind the silver tray, I in the high chair with my back to the window. I looked at the pictures on the wall, the pink peonies and the oil of Cader Idris, and thought of all the Wednesdays. I couldn't believe this wasn't Wednesday. This is Tuesday, and Morgan is sitting in the low chair near the fire, next to me, I told myself. Morgan had never been to a

Wednesday tea. Jane was moving the cups and saucers on the tray. She stopped, and there was silence. Then suddenly it was as though hundreds of men with shotguns were standing in a row and firing, every half second, louder and louder guns. Louder and closer. Then silence again. I wanted to look at Morgan.

"The Bentley sports model," he said.

"The what?" Jane asked.

"The car his father gave him."

"Really? How exciting. How did you know? Oh yes, of course, his father's letter." Then there were steps on the flagstones in the hall and I heard a low throaty laugh. Morgan and I stood up.

"Are we late?" The Vicar's wife was breathless. Her face was red with excitement, and she was truly smiling. She stood in the middle of the drawing room, turned toward the door, and held out her left, gloved hand. "And this is my nephew, Basil," she said.

He filled the whole doorway. He was broad-shouldered and ruddy and had golden-brown wavy hair and a lighter colored mustache. He was staring at my breasts. For the first time I knew what Jane meant. I wished I had a thick sweater on, and not a thin silk blouse. Even a cotton blouse. I looked at Jane. She was beaming.

"How do you do." She held out her hand. The young man walked across the room and shook it, then turned away. "We are so delighted that you are here to visit us," she said.

"Thank you." He turned on his heel and came across the room to me.

"This is Catriona," his aunt said. She should present him to me, I thought.

He held out his hand. "How do you do." I gave him mine, but I thought, He should have waited till I held out my hand.

"You, Catty, are the nicest possible surprise." He turned to his aunt. "You said that she was a bluestocking, only interested in Latin and lit." He laughed, the rough, low laugh I had heard before I saw him. "You didn't tell me of her other charms."

His aunt sat down in her usual chair. "I thought I'd let you find out for yourself," she said, and looked at me with surprise.

Basil's eyes were big and brown, and his mouth a little open under his light brown mustache. I tried to pull my hand away. He squeezed it and let go, and went to the couch and sat down. Then he looked across at Morgan.

"And you must be the tutor extraordinary?"

Morgan smiled. "I am Catriona's tutor, yes," he said, "and I understand you want to work with us."

"Wouldn't say I want to exactly. More a case of needs must when the pater drives."

"What is the set reading for this summer?"

"Shakespeare . . . the Tragedies . . . Sonnets . . . the Elizabethans . . . all that rot."

"We can well give some time to that period." Morgan looked at me. "We have never deeply studied the Elizabethans, and you always enjoy Shakespeare."

"She always enjoys Shakespeare!" Basil Lockridge laughed outright. Then he looked at me. I wanted to go away. "She won't enjoy the Bard or anything else when she's been for a ride in the Scarlet Peril."

The Vicar's wife laughed merrily. "That's Basil's absurdly clever name for his Bentley." She turned proudly to Jane. "It's a sports model, you know . . . really a beauty . . . and bright scarlet." She looked at her nephew. "And something of a peril, too. Though Basil is a splendid driver."

"The Scarlet Peril . . . What an amusing name." Jane

was pouring tea. Tessie came in with the sandwiches and cake. Basil looked at her as he had looked at me. "Sugar, Basil?" Jane asked. He shuddered and made a face.

"Oh, Miss Withers . . . Do you think . . . ? Might Basil . . . might he possibly have a glass of sherry?"

"But of course . . . how silly of me . . . Tessie, bring the sherry tray in, will you please."

"Yes, Miss Withers."

"Catriona, hand around the sandwiches, dear." Basil should, I thought. He sat on the couch and watched me walk across the room. I handed the sandwiches to his aunt, and remembering the vulture, I chuckled.

"And what is so amusing, may I ask?" the Vicar's wife asked.

And Basil Lockridge said, "Oh, it's just a little natural nervousness—isn't it, Catty."

I thought Jane would correct him when he called me Catty, but she didn't. I handed the plate to Morgan. He looked up and winked. I put the plate back on the tray, took my cup of tea, and went back to my chair. Tessie came in with the sherry tray and put it on the small table between the door and the grand piano, against the wall. Basil looked at her again. She felt his glance and went out of the room, tossing her brown curls.

"Are you thinking to work with us every day?" Morgan asked.

"As little as possible."

"Then let us say two hours a day, either morning or afternoon, to start with."

"Oh, look here now! It's summer . . . holiday time . . ."

"Yes, Morgan," Jane said. "Basil is right . . . and I'm sure you will be willing to give Catriona more leisure time while he is here . . . and certainly to stop all that extra work you've been doing on the proofs of your book." I held my breath.

"Book?" The Vicar's wife was surprised for the second time.

"Yes," I said, "and the fellows of Magdalen College, Oxford, have asked Morgan to consider accepting a fellowship."

"Really?" The Vicar's wife was impressed, but Jane went pale. Her lips were pressed into a thin line. She had never been interested in Morgan's book, except to disapprove when I worked with him in the evenings at the cottage, before dinner. She knew nothing of the fellowship.

"Really!" the Vicar's wife said again, and Morgan stood up.

"I haven't made up my mind to accept," he said, and my heart jumped to my throat. He handed a cup of tea to her. Jane gave one to him. I sat in my chair, praying, Please let him accept . . . please.

"You will give Catriona more free time, won't you? You must . . . she's not a child any longer, you know . . . and with Basil here . . . so wonderful for her."

"No, Jane." Morgan sat down again. "I doubt if Catriona can have any more free time than she usually has. She has a lot of work to accomplish in these months, and as you know, I have never allowed her studies to be curtailed." I breathed again.

"Do help yourself to sherry, Basil," Jane said, covering her annoyance with a bright smile, and he went to the tray and poured the wine.

"Well, first things first," he said. "Catty must be allowed out on Saturdays, so I'll drive her to Llandudno next Saturday in the Scarlet Peril. I hear quite a lot goes on there at weekends . . . there must be a tea dance, or something."

"Oh yes! There is," Jane said, "at the best hotel, on the pier."

"Good!" Basil held up his glass to me.

"How lovely for you, Catriona." Jane looked at me and then at Basil, smiling. "It really is time Catriona saw something of the outside world."

"And what a lucky girl she is to have Basil to take her," his aunt said.

"So here's to you, Catty . . . and to Saturday," Basil said, and drank the sherry. He poured himself another glass and sat down again. During the last two years I had never looked at Morgan when Jane was near. Now I looked straight at him.

"I'm afraid Catriona and I have salmon fishing planned for next Saturday, all day." He smiled at the Vicar's wife and then at Basil. "The summer stream, you know, the Glaslyn." He got up and put his cup and saucer on the tea tray, and smiled at Jane. "And now, I think, if Basil will come with me to the library, we will work out a flexible schedule of work for him." He walked to the couch and stood over Basil, looking down at him. Basil hesitated. Then he stood up. He didn't want to. He drank the whole glass of sherry without swallowing. He just pours it down, I thought. He put the empty glass on the tray.

"I'll be back," he said, and followed Morgan out of the room.

That night I was uneasy. The thought of Basil Lockridge worried me in a way I didn't understand, and didn't like. Why had Jane made me wear the cream silk blouse? I had felt the way the Foreigner had made me feel at the meadow gate. I wanted to run away and hide. I didn't understand the unrest. I turned over in bed and thought of Morgan's words: "I'm afraid, to some extent, lost is our quiet."

Morgan was in the library when I went down for study

the next morning. Before I sat down, he said, "Catriona, you didn't want to go to the tea dance, did you?"

"No, Morgan. You know I didn't. Thank you for saving me."

"I wasn't saving you from anything, Catriona." I waited. "Soon now, in September, when you are seventeen, you will be going away." I won't, I thought. Couldn't Morgan feel the pain when he said it? He was speaking quietly. "I feel that your introduction to the outside world should come through your aunt and your guardians, and not through young Mr. Lockridge." And I thought, I don't care what your reasons were, Morgan. I didn't want to go to the tea dance. Morgan smiled. "Nevertheless, it will be a good thing for him to sit in at study . . . and perhaps an even better thing, for him, that he will stay awhile in the mountains. . . . And now let us get on with our work."

I opened my notebook. "Are we going salmon fishing?"

"That or something else," he said, and we began our studies.

We had a week to ourselves before Basil began to read with us, and during that time the noise of the Scarlet Peril became a familiar sound in the Village and Basil a popular and welcome customer at the White Horse. Whenever he left his car outside, the children, on holiday from school, and the youths and often the men gathered around it to talk and look and talk again; and one day when Basil came to lunch and the car was outside the wall door, young Emrys Jones had asked, with shining eyes, if he might have the honor of keeping the motorcar clean. Basil had engaged him at three shillings a week, and he went to the Vicarage every other day. He became a hero to the other children, and his father sang the praises of "the young man from the Midlands" when the Villagers met in the butcher's shop to talk and gossip. Jane had bought gin and sweet vermouth, and Basil already had the habit of what she called "dropping in for a drink" before dinner. He enjoyed and basked in the notice and admiration that the Scarlet Peril brought to him.

Emma said, "He's a hail fellow well met in the White Horse, look you, and stands more than his fair share of the drinks."

Jane had been for a spin, and came back wind-blown and laughing. "Simply marvelous . . . such speed . . . Incredible! And so exciting."

I had avoided going out with him. This last week I had been busy, apart from study and riding and French and piano practice and fishing; I had been taking cups and saucers and plates and jugs to the Farm, in the governess cart, for Myfanwy Jones's annual party, on the night of the Dawnsio Haf, the Summer Dancing, that was held on the Eve of St. John, and was an important event in the Village. The leaders of the dance, the Cadi and the Fool, were elected by ballot, and the balloting was held in the White Horse. The women took out the traditional white scarves that were carried, or made new ones for themselves and the men, and as Midsummer Eve approached everyone was eager and excited.

Basil had tried to get out of studying every morning, but Morgan, knowing his father's wishes, insisted, and at first it was difficult. He was impatient, interrupted studies, and was uninterested and sulky; but after four mornings he began to see how we worked, and was amused when Morgan asked him to seek out the anachronisms in Shakespeare's Roman historical plays.

"How strange," Morgan said to me later. "Every schoolboy knows them. He must have refused to listen . . . or read." And he gave Basil a modern translation of Ovid

and the old, bound volume of Plutarch's *Lives* and left him
to find other books in the library for himself.

Basil was settling into the life of the Village, and had
given a talk to the Girls' Friendly on modern racing cars,
which none of the girls understood but thoroughly enjoyed, and afterward he took Tessie's friend, whose name,
Emma had told me, was Caridwen Hughes, to dance in
Llandudno, after the meeting. The Vicar's wife was in a
daze of delight.

"The young rip!" she said at Wednesday tea. "He's got
the Girls' Friendly in a tizzy . . . an absolute tizzy." She
looked at me. "And, my dear . . . you, my dear . . ." She
turned to Jane. "Really, Catriona seems to have positively
blossomed." I drank my tea, and thought that Morgan
must have said to Jane what he had said to me about my aunt
and the guardians, because although Jane tried to arrange
that Basil and I saw as much of each other as possible, she
didn't insist that I go in the Scarlet Peril, nor tea dancing in
Llandudno. "And he's so well mannered"—his aunt smiled
at me—"and it is really so nice of him to take that Village
girl— What's her name?"

"Caridwen Hughes," I said.

"Yes, that's it . . . it really is nice of him to take her to
Llandudno. It makes such a good impression." She turned to
Jane. "You know what I mean."

"I know exactly," Jane said. "And he is charming . . .
and I had a letter about Catriona today." I held my breath.
Jane looked at me. "You are to stay here till sometime in
the middle of September." I breathed again. I can spend my
birthday with Morgan, I thought. "But you are to be prepared to leave at a moment's notice . . . so we must begin, gradually, to pack . . . but"—she looked at the Vicar's wife and then back at me—"I have decided that as you

will be here, and you will be seventeen, you may go to the Harvest Social."

"Wonderful! Splendid!" The Vicar's wife was enthusiastic. "And what a lucky girl you are to have my nephew as your escort to your first dance." She turned to Jane. "Really, when one thinks of it . . . up here in the wilds . . . to have an escort like Basil . . ."

"Yes," Jane said, "Catriona is most fortunate. I don't think she really appreciates how fortunate she is."

"The young rip!" the Vicar's wife said again, and pursed her lips as far as she could over her teeth. "The young rip."

"Oh no!" Jane smiled. "Boys will be boys, and he is so handsome . . ."

"Isn't he? Really . . . an Adonis."

I sighed, and then smiled to cover it up.

Jane was worried that Basil had taken Caridwen Hughes, two or three times each week, to Llandudno. Although she did not say it, I knew she was angry that I had not gone with him. She invited him to lunch almost every day after studies and had ordered beer for him; and one day, about two weeks after he had come, he put down the red Bristol glass tumbler that Jane put with his bottle of beer, refilled it, and said, "Catty, tomorrow morning I intend to ride with you." I didn't say anything. "I met your handyman . . ."

"Archibald?"

"Good Lord, is that his name?" I had never thought of the name Archibald before. "He seems to be a useful sort of fellow . . . quiet, to the point of surliness, I thought, when I said I was going to ride with you."

"We only have Stray of our own to ride," I said. "The dun mare is lent to us."

"Then you have two to ride. People are always lending horses or hiring them out." He looked at Morgan and Jane. "Who does ride the borrowed horse?"

"Archibald," I said.

"What? The handyman?"

"Archibald trained the dun mare. She'd only been used in the shafts before . . . she's timid and gentle."

"Well, I'll ride with you this summer." He looked at Jane. "Is it . . .? Well, I say . . . is it awfully *comme il faut* for Catty to go riding all the time with a servant—a young manservant, at that?"

"Oh, Basil"—Jane hesitated—"Archibald is hardly an ordinary servant."

"What's so extraordinary about him?"

"Well, Basil, when you put it like that . . ."

"If he isn't a servant, what is he?"

"He's my true friend," I said. I felt my teeth clench. I took a deep breath and ate my chocolate pudding. Jane flushed with anger and began to talk. Basil poured out more beer, held it up, and looked at it.

"Well, Catty, and what time do we ride in the morning?"

"Eight o'clock."

"What about nine o'clock? I'm going to Llandudno tonight."

"Of course not. Lessons start at nine o'clock."

"What a life!" he said. "I must say there's discipline in this house." Jane sighed and shrugged her shoulders. "Eight o'clock it is then. If studies in the summer can't be changed for an hour to ride with me . . . then I will arise at break of day and ride with you." He bowed over the table and lifted his glass to me. "So if you'd tell Archie . . ." Archie. I felt the blood come to my face. He smiled. ". . . to saddle the mare . . ."

"She's very gentle and sweet-natured, Basil. She's never had anyone but Archibald on her back. Basil, do you truly want to ride?" He stopped smiling. With surprise I thought, His face looks hard.

After a second he turned to Jane, smiling again. "I would call that a most enthusiastic invitation."

"All right, Basil, I'll tell Archibald."

"You needn't. I'll tell Archie myself."

Then Morgan said, "Come along, Catriona. It's time for afternoon study."

Jane rose from her chair. "I wish to speak to Catriona in the drawing room." I didn't look at Morgan as he held the door open for us.

"I'll wait for you in the library," he said.

Basil stood looking at us. "And I'll go and tell Archie to have the dun mare ready for tomorrow morning."

I followed Jane into the drawing room.

"Close the door," she said. I closed it and waited. "Really, Catriona! How dare you interrupt me in that disgraceful manner? When will you learn to behave? And to speak to a guest as you spoke to Basil . . . How dare you?"

"I didn't interrupt you, Jane."

"You're contradicting me!"

"I'm sorry."

"You're not sorry at all; you behaved in the rudest possible way."

"I answered a question, Jane. 'If he isn't a servant, what is he?' Basil Lockridge asked, and I answered."

"He was speaking to me."

"You hadn't an answer."

"Catriona!" Her face was white now. Her rage deeper. Her thin lips were tight. She turned and looked into my face. We were the same height. I looked at her without defiance.

"You are cheeky and rude, Catriona. Leave the room." I went out of the room and along the hall to the library.

Next morning as I was going downstairs in my habit, she called to me from her bedroom.

"Catriona." I went upstairs again. "Why don't you wear your brown bowler?"

"Oh, Jane, in the summer? It's too hot."

"Then coil up your hair on top of your head. That elastic at the end of your plaits looks ridiculous."

I went back to my room, coiled up my hair, and pinned it firmly with large black hairpins.

Archibald had saddled Stray and the dun mare. We looked at each other, but didn't speak. He brought Stray to the mounting block and I mounted, and as I was arranging my skirt the Scarlet Peril roared up the Hill and pulled up against the wall. Basil came through the coachyard gates. His legs, in jodhpurs, looked strong and big. I suppose he is handsome, I thought. He wore a checked jacket and was carrying a riding stick.

"Morning, Catty." He looked at my hair. "We're very grown-up this morning. Quite the little Amazon." He kept looking at me. I tried not to blush. When I did, he laughed. He took no notice of Archibald, who was holding the dun mare's head. Then he turned slowly, went to her, took the reins, and vaulted onto her back. He was much heavier than Archibald, and he surprised her. She made a quick movement; her hind legs splayed out and her hindquarters swung around. She staggered on the cobbles.

"Stop that now." He pulled her mouth. I saw Archibald's face redden, and rode quickly out of the coachyard.

As I came up over the Rise, Basil came galloping after me.

"Not much pep in the old girl," he said as he joined me. "Where shall we go?"

"I thought we might hack around the Farm and see the preparations for the party."

"Oh yes . . . that dancing thing. They're writing names down to be drawn at the White Horse." The dun mare was doing everything he wanted her to. Archibald would be proud of her, I thought.

"Who put the chicken coop up? Jolly good job."

"Archibald."

"He's quite the handyman."

I held the meadow gate open for him. "We'll go across the meadow and into the river fields," I said. You can close the gate." And I cantered across toward the other side of the meadow. Myfanwy Jones came to the door of the dairy and waved. She saw Basil Lockridge on the dun mare.

"That's Myfanwy Jones," I told him as he came up with me. "She owns the mare."

"I met her brother . . . and a cousin, too, in the White Horse. What do you pay for the hire of her?"

"We don't."

"You mean she lends you the mare for nothing?"

"Yes—so long as we love her and look after her well-being."

"Her well-being! Catty . . . the words you use . . ." He laughed. "Her well-being . . . Come on, let's see you go over the picket fence, and I'll follow you."

"No! Basil, she's not a jumper . . . she doesn't jump . . . she doesn't know how."

"She'll learn. She'll jump for me."

"Basil, please."

"Don't be silly," he said, and galloped the dun mare around the edges of the field. Stray was fussy and impatient. She wanted to jump.

"Quiet, Stray. Quiet."

"Come on . . . get going." He galloped toward us. He didn't look for bumps or rabbit holes.

"Mind the potholes," I called out when he came closer.

He didn't reply, and turned the dun mare toward the picket.

"No!" I shouted. He laughed and hit her with the riding stick. She had never been hit like that before. She was hurt and bewildered. She shied.

"Stop that," he said, and hit her again and put her at the fence.

"Basil! Stop it! Stop it!"

He galloped her up to the fence and put her to it. She went head first into it, and Basil nearly went over without her. He recovered himself, and in a rage he pulled her head around, jagging her bit. She staggered about, her eyes rolling with fear. He hit her again. She went around and around, terrified. She would hurt herself. She was crossing her forelegs. I was as frantic as she was. He turned her away from the picket, and she bolted sideways, lost, changing from one foot to the other. Then he pulled her head around and put her at the fence again.

No! I said the word inside myself. I galloped toward them. I didn't know what I was going to do, but I knew that she must not be put at the fence a second time. She was mad with fear and whinnying. Myfanwy Jones will hear her, I thought, and with the thought came another. The noise of the churning will cover the noises in the meadow. I rode in front of them. The dun mare lifted her front feet a little off the ground, shuddered her coat, and shied away from me. "Stop it, Basil." I slipped down out of my saddle and ran to them. The dun mare was going around in circles, crazy with pain and fright. I hit Basil Lockridge across the thigh as hard as I could with my riding stick, and before he had time to recover from his surprise I pulled him, with all my strength, off her back. When he was on the ground, I went to her slowly. She was trembling, and jumped away from me. "Sweetie . . . come here . . . come along, it's all right, come on, sweetie. . . ." She stood still. Quietly I took hold of her bridle and stroked her neck and whispered to her and stroked her nose. "It's all right, sweetie. . . ." I almost sang the words, and she quietened a little. Then Basil Lockridge was walking toward us. I turned slowly, not to startle her again, let go of the bridle gently, and walked to meet him so that he should not come near her. I stood in front of him. The light brown hairs of his mustache seemed to stand straight up out of a white skin. His eyes were blazing.

"Don't go near her, Basil," I said quietly. "I told you she had only been used to the shafts, that she was timid and had only been ridden carefully." He flushed and went white again. "I'm going to lead her home. Please walk behind me, leading Stray, and we'll tell Archibald that she put her foot in a rabbit hole and that we didn't want to risk anything. Do you understand?" He was looking at me as though he were deaf. "I hope Archibald won't be in the stables yet, anyway." I looked at the dairy. "And Myfanwy Jones hasn't seen anything." I looked at him. "I'm sorry . . ."

"You hit me," he said.

Myfanwy Jones came out of the dairy. "What's up? Taking a rest?" she called out. "Like some buttermilk?"

"No, thank you, Myfanwy," I called back. "And I'll bring the rest of the crockery this afternoon."

"Thank you, Miss Catty . . . and I hope the weather holds." She went back into the dairy.

"Go and get Stray. Please, Basil."

Without speaking he went to where she was browsing, eating the meadow grass. I went back to the dun mare. She shied, and her eye was wild, but she let me take her head. I walked her across the meadow, talking to her and stroking her neck and patting her as we went. Basil met us at the gate. He held it open for me and waited while I led the dun mare through, and then he closed it and followed us up

the Rise, leading Stray. Archibald wasn't in the coachyard.
We were half an hour early. Stray trotted into her stall.

"Basil, I'm going to groom the dun mare. It may make
her forget her fear . . . she likes to be groomed more than
anything." He walked away while I was talking to him. I
tied the mare to the post by the mounting block and went
in to tell Morgan that I should be late for study. Basil
was already in the library. "It's important, Morgan," I
said.

He looked at me. "I'll wait for you, Catriona. Basil and I
will prepare some work."

As I was leaving the library, Basil said, "Interesting!
Very interesting. Lessons can be altered for a horse . . .
and what a horse."

I went into the coachyard and unsaddled the dun mare
and put a halter on her and tied her again to the post. I used
the currycomb lightly, around and around, from her stiff
held-back ears to her rump, talking to her and crooning. She
was still shaking. I used the dandy brush gently—she wasn't
muddy or dirty, and it soothed her—and then brushed her
mane with long, slow strokes, and after that her tail. Then
I used the soft brush, and she moved her head toward me.

"Good girl . . . dear, good girl . . . dear sister," I
murmured. I thought of Eldorai. I pulled her ears, and she
didn't put them down again and back; and wiped her eyes
with a soft damp cloth, and then polished her with a
rough towel till she shone. I was wet with sweat when I
finished, but she had stopped trembling. I put her in her
stall and gave her some sugar and rubbed her nose. Stray
put out her hairy lips; I gave some to Molly-fach first, and
then came to her and stroked her nose. She nuzzled me. Then
I emptied the dirty water down the drain outside the stable
door and put the bucket back in its place, cleaned the curry-

comb and the brushes, and decided, for the moment, not to tell Archibald that anything untoward had happened. I went upstairs to change, and joined Morgan and Basil in the library.

14

The day of the Dawnsio Haf dawned fair and windless. Archibald and I rode out to the Farm and helped Myfanwy and Merfyn Jones to put up the long, narrow table for the refreshments, and the heavy plank that they put across two big milk cans, without their lids, that was the beer counter. Mr. Jones, from the White Horse, had already left five barrels of beer, and Archibald helped Merfyn Jones to clean and fill the acetylene lamps that would be on the table and the beer counter. Myfanwy and I brought all the crockery from the house in a large wheelbarrow. Myfanwy pushed it, and I carried the big starched white tablecloth.

Penry Jones was chosen to be the Cadi and to lead the Summer Dancing. Basil was the Fool. He had been elected unanimously in the secret balloting that was held with ceremony in the White Horse.

"Solemn as a conclave of cardinals, it was," Morgan said, and laughed.

"And 'tis an honor, indeed, for a stranger," Codger said. He was in the kitchen, rocking himself in Emma's chair, with Star on his lap, "resting up" for the evening's celebrations. "And 'tis a shame, look you, that the younger needs to take so much to drink." And he told us that Basil had treated everyone, and they in turn had treated him, to toast the result of the balloting. "For 'tis a darkly different young man he is, indeed, after five beers."

"And that along with the whisky, look you," Emma said, "from the flask that he keeps in his back pocket."

Basil was pleased to have been chosen, and entered into the spirit of the Midsummer Eve party. He borrowed his aunt's red lip salve and some colored chalk from Emma for his make-up, and in the afternoon went out with the men to gather the birch branches that everyone carried in the dance. They were called St. John's branches.

In olden days fires were built on the hilltops, and the men leaped through the flames, singeing their branches, three times forward and three times back. First the unmarried, then the married, and after them the bravest of the maidens made their leaps as the flames died down. The married women only held out their birches over the fire, and then everybody danced. They took the singed branches home with them, and kept them all year in the house, to guard them from evil.

We carried our branches and danced with them, waving our white scarves; torches, held in high iron stands that were spiked into the earth in a wide circle, had taken the place of the hill fires.

The procession formed at dusk in Myfanwy Jones's meadow, and the shadows were lengthening as we walked down from the Rise toward the gate. On either side of us the hedgerows, blurred in the half-light, were full of twittering movement. Away to the left the edges of the Mochdre Hill were black-sharp in the gloaming. We came to the gate and walked across the dew-wet grass toward the crowd, gathered at the other end of the meadow, near to the stile. Dense clusters of midges and gnats hovered, some as high as the tops of the dwarf oaks and others low to the ground, and each fell prey to the wing-silent, wide-gaped nightjars, two of them, swooping and gliding, soaring upward and diving. "The Deryn Corff." Codger called them the Corpse Birds, and he said their eerie whispering was heard when a spirit passed into the Otherworld; but Archibald said it was the male bird's mating song. As we came nearer, the outlines of the moving, laughing figures near to the stile grew darker as the dusk light faded and their voices were clear on the still air.

Penry Jones, the Cadi, was dressed as half woman and half man. He had a man's trouser leg on his right leg and one of Myfanwy's frilly white lace petticoats on the other. He wore a starched white ruffle, the kind the women wear, under his tall Welsh hat, and a man's waistcoat. The crowd around him was laughing and teasing.

"And 'tis all in an upset we are, just a-looking at you," Merfyn Jones said, and his cousin laughed.

"And it's real daft that I'm feeling, look you." But he was enjoying himself, and had a mug of beer in his hand. Myfanwy Jones was serving her guests from behind the large plank.

"No more than two mugs each before the dancing," she said as Mr. Morris, the plumber, held out his for more. "And you have to play the violin at the head of the procession, look you, Mr. Morris." She gave the District Nurse her beer in a tumbler. "And you've had two already, indeed."

"Myfanwy's right! No more beer for you till your playing's done." The District Nurse took Mr. Morris's arm. They had both taken their summer holiday at the same time and there had been talk in the Village, and Emma said, "'Tis no one's business but their own . . . and no one knows for sure, anyway, look you." Mr. Morris put his empty mug on the plank and went to get his violin from its case, which was on the grass near to the stile.

"And it's more than your fair share that you've had,"

Myfanwy was saying to the red-haired stranger who had been in the fight in the coachyard. Then I remembered; he had been at the Farm to help with the flock-gathering, last March. He smiled down at Myfanwy and shrugged his big shoulders.

Dylan Price had been sitting on the stile, playing his new mouth organ. He brought rich tone from the small instrument and often came on Sunday evenings to play for the youths who sang outside the wall, under the oak tree. He jumped down as Basil and Merfyn Jones came to the stile. They climbed over it, into the grassy lane. I looked for Archibald. He was talking to Ellen. She was almost as tall as he, and her dark straight hair was in one plait. She wore a red and white checked dress with a small white collar. I knew her eyes were violet-blue, but they seemed dark and deep as she looked at him.

Jane was talking to the Curate, and Tessie was with Caradoc Ellis. Her friend Caridwen Hughes was standing quite still. She was watching Basil. Like Star watching a bird, I thought as he and Merfyn Jones went along the Lane to the house. She wore a tight red dress with a low-cut round neck, and no bust bodice. I wished again that she weren't Tessie's friend. Mr. Morris had tuned his violin, and he and Dylan Price and a tall dark youth who played the accordion for the jigs and reels at the smaller socials were standing near to the stile, waiting for the Cadi's command to start the Summer Dancing; and then I saw Emma and Codger come slowly across the field. He was wearing his waistcoat and she her summer silk. It was lavender-colored, with a Bertha collar of Maltese lace. Tears came into my eyes. Wherever I go, I thought, I shall never see truer dignity. And then the word *grace* came to my mind. I wiped my eyes with the back of my hand.

The quiet girl who had danced with Penry Jones at the

burning was among the jolly, chattering crowd around the
Cadi. She had flaxen hair, tied with a green ribbon and
brushed back from her small face. She was watching Penry
Jones with a smile. Then Mr. Jones, the butcher, came running with a mug of beer in one hand and his birch branch in
the other, his white scarf hanging around his neck.

"Come on, Cadi! Let's get started . . . Lead on! Lead
on!" he shouted. "Let the procession start . . . Lead the
way." And everyone took up the cry. I went to Emma and
the District Nurse at the edge of the crowd.

"No more beer till we all get back here, look you," Myfanwy Jones said, and came and stood next to me.

"Lead on! Lead on!" they all shouted.

"Wait a minute." Penry Jones held up his hand. "The
Fool! We can't start without the Fool." He put his empty
beer mug on the grass.

"Where's the Fool?" the shout went up.

"We want the Fool."

"Here I am," Basil called out, and almost leaped over
the stile, followed by Merfyn Jones. He bounded toward
us like a huge stag, and he was wearing a white Pierrot suit,
with baggy pants and sleeves with frills on them.

"Made of two sheets," Myfanwy Jones whispered.
There were big red woolen pompons down the front of it,
and he wore a tall pointed hat.

"He made himself up," Merfyn Jones said. "He's a live
one, indeed to goodness." I watched Basil. He was holding
one side of his baggy pants out with his left hand and a
birch branch with bells on it and colored ribbons with the
other. He had drawn red circles around his eyes and dark
purple lines from his nose to his mouth, and he had darkened his fair mustache with soot. He jumped up to the
Cadi and then bowed. And bowed again. Everyone cheered.

"Bravo!"

"Hurrah!"

"Hurrah for the Fool!"

Raising both his arms, the Cadi said loud and clear, "Now is the moment." And he sprang into the air and came to earth, to stand with his feet apart. He held up his birch branch and waved it about his head, and his voice was deep and strong. He almost chanted the words. "Let the Dawnsio Haf begin." And he leaped forward to the music of Mr. Morris's violin and Dylan Price's mouth organ and the accordion, to the head of the procession, and led us across the meadow.

Basil was weaving in and out among us, and the girls were giggling as he switched their legs and behinds with his belled branch. When we came to the meadow gate, he swung on it and then jumped down and leaped in the air and swung on it again, switching us all as we passed through onto the road.

Then he danced the Vicar's wife around and around in a jig and left her to take both Jane's hands and whirl her almost off her feet, leaving her dizzy in the Curate's arms, and was away to dance with one girl and then another, gamboling merrily through the laughing crowd. He separated Myfanwy Jones from the red-haired stranger and pulled her, in a wild run, to the front of the procession, where the quiet girl and the Cadi and Idris Williams, the post, were doing a three-handed reel. After a minute they stopped and Penry Jones raced on ahead, followed by the Fool, who had given Myfanwy Jones back to her partner and was close on the Cadi's heels.

At the top of the Rise they waited for us all to catch up, and the Fool was dancing around the Cadi, pulling his trousered leg and leaning back and holding his stomach with mirth and then pointing to the petticoat leg and doubling up forward with laughter. We all stopped dancing to watch the performance, waving our branches and scarves and cheering, while Mr. Morris tuned a string on his violin and Dylan Price wiped his lips on his white scarf. Then the comedy ended and the Cadi and the Fool ran forward again, the musicians after them, over the Rise and down the Hill Lane. We all followed, running and hopping and switching one another's legs and laughing. Archibald and Ellen were dancing with Myfanwy Jones between them, and Tessie and Caradoc Ellis and the quiet girl and the big stranger were doing a Welsh jig at the side of the road, near to the wall door.

When we came to the bottom of the Lane, the Square was full of people. A crowd of summer visitors and people from the other villages who knew of the St. John's dancing had come to watch. Grandma Rhys-Evans was standing on the steps of the butcher's shop. I left the procession and went to talk to her.

" 'Tis a fine Fool we have this year, indeed to goodness," she said as young Dafydd and his sister joined the merry throng. "And who might it be? He has the build of John Thomas Davies . . . but is of lighter movement . . . and I see the blacksmith . . . over there, dancing."

"It's Basil Lockridge. He's staying at the Vicarage," I said, and she looked down at me.

"Is it now? And it's wild tales I'm hearing about this young man from the Midlands . . . and his red motorcar, indeed." She turned toward the Square. "And land's sakes . . . look you at him now." I stepped up onto the step above and looked.

Everyone was watching the Fool. He was doing the Charleston in the middle of the road, opposite the haber-dasher's, and Mr. Morris and Dylan Price and the accordion player had quickly changed the rhythm of "Y Hufen Melyn," "The Yellow Cream," to suit the new dance. His feet made swift patterns. Basil did learn to dance, I thought, remembering; and then all the people took up the rhythm, and some tried to copy the movements of Basil's feet and some of the visitors knew the dance well, and soon everyone in the Square was jiggling and moving; then Basil stopped. He stood still. The music ceased. After a few seconds he put his finger to his head in comic thought, then he jumped in the air and ran to the Cadi and pretended to knock him down. Penry Jones lay flat on the roadway, his arms outstretched, and a huge shout arose. The Fool, standing over him, waved his arms and hands as though he were bringing him to life again. The crowd moaned with each urging, and as the Cadi rose to his feet the music started again, and shouting and laughing, he jumped in the air, and taking the Fool's hand, led the crowd, dancing, toward the lane that led through the Mochdre Wood and back to Myfanwy Jones's meadow.

"'Tis a fine Fool . . . and light as a feather on his feet . . . whatever the tales. Yes indeed," Grandma Rhys-Evans said, and Myfanwy Jones came across the Square.

"Well, and if it isn't just fine you're looking, Grandma."

"And 'tis a fine Dawnsio Haf, indeed."

"And good weather, for once." When it rained, Myfanwy's St. John's party was held in the barn. "And I hope the rheumatics aren't too bothersome."

"Not so bad when the weather's dry, like this last week or two."

Then the children came running back, and Myfanwy said, "The men'll soon be through the wood. Let's get back to the meadow and see what's happening." I nodded and stepped down.

"Good-by, Grandma Rhys-Evans. I'll see you on Tuesday morning with the bread." She was smiling and watching the crowd as we walked away up the Hill Lane, behind

Tessie and Caridwen Hughes and the quiet girl, who were talking and doing Charleston steps and giggling. We passed Jane and the Vicar's wife. The Curate had left. A little way ahead of us Archibald and Ellen were walking together. Archibald didn't go with the other men, I thought.

Myfanwy Jones said, "That will be a fine thing, indeed," and looked at them, smiling.

"I've known since the day we had tea with Eldorai."

She looked around at me. "And how is she? How is Eldorai these days? She has ninety-odd years, look you."

"She was in her bed, in the *vardo* . . . she's beautiful." Myfanwy smiled again, and nodded. The road down from the Rise was gray in the moonlight. Archibald and Ellen, still walking in front of us, came to the gate. Archibald held it open for us. I thought of his gentleness and kindness. Of his carvings. Grugyn and his bristles. The stoat. Emma's message board and the salt and pepper pigs. The swallows, one in full flight and one lying limp.

"They're the only birds who do this . . . that I know of," he had told me, and one day he had called to me from the coachyard steps. I had gone down and he was holding a bird in his hands. "Look!" he said. "This young swallow is full-grown and it can fly . . . but it is feigning dead. Their nest's up in the eaves . . . there, in the corner near the oak tree." He had pointed upward to the stable roof, and when he took his hand from over it the bird had not moved, but stayed still in his other hand. He said that it was lucky to have swallows nest in the walls:

> "Swallows and starlings find honest eaves
> But the jackdaw nests where the house beds thieves."

It was Codger's rhyme. The bird had lain on Archibald's palm, its wings falling over the sides of his hand as though they were broken.

"Look, Miss Catty." He had spread out the strong, smooth feathers in a shining blue-black fan. "The quills are as hard as those of an old bird." I had been filled with wonder. "Let's take him to the road and put him in the dust," Archibald said, and as we walked to the coachyard gates he told me that their parents push them out of the nest as soon as they are full-grown, and they are never taught to fly. "Often they fall to the ground like a stone . . . till the knowledge comes to them." He was stroking the bird. It wasn't fluttering or frightened. Its eyes were not darting like those of other birds we had rescued. The young swallow didn't move. "Do you want to hold it?" Archibald had asked, and I held out my hand.

Walking across the meadow with Myfanwy Jones, I still remembered the sharp, cool feel of its thin, wiry feet on my palm, the soft warmth of its underfeathers, and the quick, tiny thud of its beating heart. I had stroked its shining feathers and touched its head with my finger, between the calm, undarting eyes. When we came to the gates, Archibald looked along the wall. "Put it down there," he said, and showed me where the dust was thick, near the wall. "Not too near . . . give him room."

I put the swallow, still limp, on the ground, and we stood back and watched. For a while it didn't move. If I hadn't held it in my hand, I would have thought it a dead bird; Archibald had remembered, and carved it, just as it looked lying in the dust before it suddenly raised its wings, high above its head, and held them poised; then without a flutter the wings descended in a swift, strong arc, and in a whirl of dust the swallow was away, circling and gathering speed until he soared out of sight.

Remembering, I smiled.

"Why are you smiling?" Myfanwy Jones asked as we reached the refreshment table.

"I was remembering Archibald and a swallow," I said.

The torches were shining, and the long wooden table was covered with the white cloth. It glowed, rose-colored in the torchlight and yellow-gold in the light of the acetylene lamps. Three of them, one at either end and one in the center of the table, and there were large platters of beef and ham sandwiches and oatmeal cakes and *bara-brith* and seedcakes. "Look!" I said. "Five of Emma's spongecakes with lemon-cheese filling!"

Myfanwy nodded. "And it's dearly grateful I am . . . and Emma's a love of a woman." I turned to look for her. She was sitting with Codger and the District Nurse about six yards away from the end of the table, near the dairy. Then faintly the sound of music and voices came from the wood. I listened. The thin sweet strains of the violin carried on the air, sharp, apart. The mouth organ and accordion music mingled with the talking and the singing. As the sounds came nearer, the hand lamps flickered in between the trees beyond the road like elf lights. I went over to Emma.

"You know what I am going to eat?"

"That I do." She looked up and laughed.

"Me too," the District Nurse said. "My mouth's watering."

Emma said, "Well, look you, if you want a slice of my cake, don't take it from the one that's second to this end."

"Why?" we both asked.

"Because that one has next to no filling in it. I ran out."

"Thank you kindly for the warning," the District Nurse said.

"And unless someone is kind enough to bring me something to eat, it's fainting I'll be," Emma said. "And my poor legs won't move another inch . . . for the time being."

"You stay here." I went to the table and put two beef sandwiches, a slice of *bara-brith,* and a large piece of spongecake on a plate, then to where Myfanwy Jones was serving tea from an urn, and took a cup to Emma with her food.

"Thank you, indeed, Miss Catty."

"The same for you, Codger?"

"Except for the tea, Kishli."

"Beer?"

"And whatever else would I be drinking, now look you . . . and the sun down these many hours?" As I turned to go, he said, "And just *bara-brith* and cake, please, Kishli, no sandwiches." I went to the table again, filled his plate, and took it to him, and as I went to the beer counters the Cadi and the Fool and all the merry throng came dancing and chattering out of the wood. Once they were all in the meadow, they broke ranks. Some of them sat on the grass to get their breath and others rushed to the beer plank.

"Give me one for Codger before the rush."

Merfyn Jones said, "Hurry! Here they come!" I hurried. Codger put his plate on the ground and drank the beer slowly and with enjoyment.

"Thank you, Kishli," he said, wiping his tidy bristly beard with a white handkerchief.

"Catriona!" the Vicar's wife called. "Do be a dear . . ." She and Jane were sitting on two chairs nearby. "Be a dear and bring me just a tiny piece of Emma's spongecake. I'd know it anywhere . . . that delicious filling." I went to the table, cut a piece from the cake next to the end, and looked at Emma to see if she had noticed. She had.

"Would you like tea?" I asked. The Vicar's wife took the plate. She looked at Jane.

"I should like some beer," Jane said.

"Splendid! Splendid idea! I should too. And how clever of you to think of it, Miss Withers . . . just the very thing."

"And a piece of cake for me, too, dear." Jane smiled.

All the men were around the beer plank. I'll get Jane's cake first, I thought, and while I was cutting a slice for her I found Morgan was at my elbow.

"You're a busy one."

"Jane and the Vicar's wife want beer . . . not tea."

"You take the plate. I'll get the beer."

"Thank you." I went back with the cake. "Morgan's bringing the beer."

"Thank you, Catriona. Where's Basil?"

"I don't know." I looked around and saw Myfanwy Jones sitting on the grass. She had stopped pouring tea, and everyone was helping himself. I went and sat down with her.

" 'Tis a real fine St. John's Eve, indeed," she said, "and not a breath of wind." She looked toward the house. "The Cadi and the clown went to change," she laughed, "and the Fool would want to wash his face, at that."

"Here they are," I said, and Penry Jones and Basil came over the stile dressed in their normal clothes. There were cheers and shouts, and everyone followed them to the beer counter and Merfyn gave them mugs of beer and they were cheered again and toasted, and then they went to the table for food. Basil was surrounded. Caridwen Hughes left Caradoc Ellis and joined the girls who were crowding around him. Tessie went to Caradoc Ellis, and they sat down on the grass. Archibald and Ellen were sitting a little farther away, eating their sandwiches and talking, the plates on the grass between them. Morgan came across to us with a full plate. Beef sandwiches, *bara-brith,* and cake.

"We can share this," he said to me. "Would you like some beer?"

"I don't want a whole mug."

"I'll bring you a half of one . . . and for you, Myfanwy?"

"I'll wait awhile, thank you, Reverend . . . I've just

had some tea." He went to the plank and came back with
two mugs and sat down next to me on the grass, and then the
Vicar's wife stood up and Merfyn Jones left the beer
counter and called for silence. We all stopped talking.

"While we are all together here, I should like to announce
the date of the Harvest Social," she began. There was a
murmur of interest, and then there were shouts of applause
from Mr. Morris, the plumber, and Mr. Jones, the butcher,
and some of the youths. "It will be held on the fifteenth of
September."

"Hurray! Bravo!" Now everybody shouted.

"And"—she held up her hand for silence—"and this year
the committee has a surprise for you . . . this year we
have decided to have . . . now, what do you think?" She
paused, smiling. "What do you think?"

"Beer served in the Parish Hall if it rains," Mr. Morris
shouted, and there were chuckles, but the smile faded from
the face of the Vicar's wife. It looked thin and irritable in
the light of the acetylene lamp. Then she smiled again, ig-
noring him.

"What do you think"—there was silence—"the committee has decided to have?" The silence held. "The Merry
Music Men," she said. "The Merry Music Men, from
Llandudno, to play for the dancing." And then there was a
great shout of approval.

"Bravo!"

"Hurrah!"

"Here's to the Merry Music Men." Mr. Morris, the
plumber, raised his mug. The District Nurse took his arm
and drew him aside.

"Can they play the Charleston?" Basil Lockridge called
out. He was sitting on the grass with Caridwen Hughes, in
the shadow of the dairy. The Vicar's wife beamed.

"I'm sure they can! Oh yes, Basil. Of course they can
. . . Llandudno's very forward, you know." She shook a
finger at him. "It isn't only in New York that they dance
the Charleston, you mustn't think that."

"Good!" Basil got up from the grass. "Then I'll conduct
a class in the Charleston. Free."

"A splendid idea, Basil . . . splendid," she said, "and
we'll have it in the Parish Hall." Everyone began to cheer
again, and some of them tried to remember the steps Basil
had done in the Square, and Dylan Price and the thin accordion player played "Y Hufen Melyn" in Charleston
time, and Basil pulled Caridwen Hughes up from the grass
and they gave an exhibition dance to applause and shouting.

" 'Tis an energetic dance at that," Myfanwy said. "And I
hear tell that young Basil went to America."

"Yes. His father took him on a business trip last year."

" 'Tis a fine thing, to travel," Myfanwy said, and was
about to get up when the red-haired stranger came and held
out his hand.

"Thank you, kindly," Myfanwy Jones said, and they
went together to the refreshment table. Then the dance
ended, and Jane and the Vicar's wife left Merfyn Jones
and went to his sister. They insisted on shaking hands with
her, so I knew they were leaving. Jane looked around for
me, and then I saw Penry Jones and the big stranger handling Myfanwy's harp carefully over the stile.

"Look, Morgan! Myfanwy's going to play."

Jane came across to us. "Come along, Catriona, we're
leaving. It's getting late."

"Oh, Jane! Myfanwy's going to play the harp . . . and
we don't know if I'll be here for the Annual Concert."

"Of course you may be here."

"Please mayn't I stay?"

And Morgan said, "I think Catriona should stay for a while, Jane . . . it may be the last time she'll hear Myfanwy play the harp."

"Oh, really, Morgan . . . the last time . . . you know as well as I do that we don't know when she will leave. This indecision . . . such a nuisance, one can't make any personal plans at all." She looked around. "Where's Basil?" Then she looked at Morgan again. "All right, she may stay for a while and Basil can bring her home. I'll just go and tell him."

"I'll see Catriona safely home, Jane," Morgan said, and her face tightened. Then she shrugged.

"Well, don't be late."

Morgan got up from the grass. "Why don't you stay too, Jane?"

"No, thank you. I really don't care for this kind of music . . . especially the singing, as you know."

"Are you coming?" the Vicar's wife called, and came toward us. "Remember, we said we would meet Dr. Fraser and the Curate at nine o'clock for a game of whist?"

"Of course I do." Jane turned to join her. "Now, don't be late," she said again, and they walked away together.

Morgan took the plate back to the table, and Penry Jones brought one of the chairs for Myfanwy and everyone sat down on the grass, inside the circle of torches, in front of her. The youths were gathered together near to the stile with Dylan Price and the accordion player. Morgan came back. Basil and Caridwen Hughes came closer into the circle, and Archibald and Ellen were sitting near to us. Merfyn Jones brought two of the lamps from the table and put them at his sister's feet, and the big red-haired man carried two torches in their iron holders and spiked them into the ground behind her chair. Then he sat as near to her as he could.

The torchlight goldened her light brown hair, and the lamps low down lit up the polished wood of the telyn. Her waiting hands looked gold-white and her hazel eyes shone. She was beautiful, with a whole-souled beauty, timeless as music. She settled, raised her arms, and then her strong, gentle fingers touched the strings and the sounds of night were hushed and mingled with the ancient wellspring of the harp music. She played at will, each rippling chord a thought. "I bathe thy palms in showers of wine . . ." Oh, Morgan. ". . . in showers of silvery sound." Her arms moved in the age-old rhythm, and we were held in solemn thrall. Until with a familiar chord she released us and Merfyn Jones began to sing, sitting on the grass, leaning against one of the big milk cans that held up the beer plank. *"Am danat ti mae son, Wenaf Wen. Wenaf Wen* . . . You are like a star o'er Cymru, Brightest Gwen. Whitest Gwen . . ."

Morgan lay back on the grass, his hands behind his head, and I remembered the first day, when he had lain so, on the slope of the Mochdre Hill, and said, "When you are happy, be silent, that the birds of happiness may nest in your hair." And I thought, Oh, Morgan . . . you have truly taught me Felicitie. And Merfyn Jones's clear, high voice grew warm and full, and in his song was yearning, ". . . *O'th flaen mae mynydd maith, Wenaf Wen. Wenaf Wen* . . . Far better here to bide, Whitest Gwen. Brightest Gwen . . ." O Heavenly Father, must I leave? . . . The tears came silently. Flooded and fell. "Far better here to bide . . ." I closed my eyes, and the music deepened my wound.

Archibald and Ellen were sitting side by side, still apart. Not even their hands touched, but their faces were rapt. I felt their deep content. For the first time in my life I know what envy could be like, I thought. But I felt none. To see them was a strange, deep happiness, in which I shared. The

tears came again. Eldorai . . . help me to be a pawnie
Rawnie. Morgan sat up, and I turned away to hide my face,
and now Penry Jones moved. He sat up straight and
breathed. He was near to Emma and Codger in their chairs,
and the quiet girl was with him, but when he began to sing
she moved a little way behind him. "Men of Harlech . . .
Cymru fydd fel Cymru fu, Yn glodus ym mysg gwledydd . . ."
And his deep-throated voice held the thunder of mountain
ambush: "On the rocky crag flies freedom's flag, The trum-
pet still is sounded." And Merfyn Jones and the other men
and the youths sang with him, *"Rwystro bar yr estron . . .*
Smite as he was smitten . . .*"* in a swelling surge of sound
that rang through the valleys and along the mountain slopes,
strong and wild, to the ringing climax, *"Gwalia'i fyny . . .
Rhyddid aiff a hi."*

I wanted to touch Morgan, to hold his hand as we shared
the tales the mountains told in goodly praise of race and
courage. But I sat still, listening as I had listened to Nana;
as I listened to Morgan when he looked up from a book and
spoke his own thoughts; not with my ears alone, but with
every pore and heartbeat, to remember for always the sound
of the music, and the strong, clear human voices in the windless mountain peace.

Now Myfanwy rested. The red-haired stranger came to
her and spoke. She nodded her head and smiled, and Dylan
Price, sitting atop the stile, began to play Caradoc's trump
in a good fast tempo, the tones clear and true, and all the
men sang in harmony, *"Fe ddaw'r frenhines deg i'w plith
. . . I edrych an Garadog . . .* And Caradoc's Queen
across the field, a fiery roan, came riding . . .*"* And before
they had time to breathe, the tall accordion player began the
blithe and merry tune of "Gone Away Jack." Faster and
faster, till it was a race between the singers and the musician.
Morgan took out his pipe, and the big stranger brought a

mug of beer to Myfanwy. She sipped it and handed it back to him and sat still until the lusty chasing-song ended in laughter. She waited awhile; and then slowly lifted her hands and the sweet, long, familiar chords of "The Rising of the Lark" rippled and flowed and Merfyn Jones sang, *"Canu mae, a'r byd a glyw . . . Cyfyd hireath dynolrw . . ."*

"Nana's song," I whispered to Morgan, and he smiled. "Sing and let the whole world hear . . . Wake the longing in mankind . . ." Nana . . . Suddenly the stress and the longing, the sorrow-parting to come, the fear of a life new and strange, all dissolved in the thought of Nana and the sound of the music under the proud stars; Morgan, the dark trees, and the spellbound faces; the glow of the torches. I looked around me. We are all part of Nana. The thought slid away. I tried to hold it. William Blake meant this, ". . . eternity in an hour." Again the thought slipped away, but the feeling stayed. I looked at Morgan's face. He looked up. We listened to the words of the song. "Wake in men's hearts the longing to know joy . . . Rise, rise, O Lark . . ." I turned away from his eyes and sat still while the echoes of Merfyn Jones's voice were gathered into the night. Myfanwy played the closing chords. No one moved.

Then Merfyn Jones got up and went behind the beer plank.

"Beer, anybody?" he asked. Only Basil and Caridwen Hughes and Mr. Morris, the plumber, rose from the circle. When they had gone back to their places again, Myfanwy waited, and then gently she played the opening chords of the lullaby that the grass blades whisper, and that all Wales knows: "Sleep my babe, be still and slumber, All through the night." And the other women sang in harmony with her, crooning softly. I listened, resting. Then I looked up and found that Basil Lockridge was staring at me. Puzzled by his look, I smiled. He turned away. I wondered why he didn't smile back at me, and then forgot him because Myfanwy was singing her own lullaby, as I had heard her when she sang to the lost lambs and the newborn calves. Now I listened, remembering.

"Tell Miss Catty that Myfanwy has two stray lambs she's cherishing in the kitchen," Merfyn Jones had said to Emma one day last May, and after lessons Morgan and I had walked across the blossoming meadow to the Farm. He and Merfyn had smoked, sitting on the bench under the window in the kitchen, and talked, drinking mugs of beer, and I had gone to the basket in front of the fireplace and lifted the blanket. Two tiny, thin, yellow-white lambs were lying side by side with their eyes closed. I touched the fluffy, wavy pelt of one of them. It didn't move. I touched the curls on its forehead. Little lamb, who made thee? I was thinking, when Merfyn Jones said to Morgan:

"Those sneaking weasels . . . Scarce a drop of blood left in them." And Myfanwy Jones had come in from the milking.

"Are they not beautiful, Miss Catty?" She had turned to greet Morgan, and then knelt down by the basket. She stroked them gently. "They'll not die." She stood up, looking down at them. "They'll live, indeed." And she had gone to the pantry.

She came back with warm milk and water, mixed, and a medicine dropper. I sat on the floor beside her while she wakened them, first one and then the other, took it in her arms and fed it, drop by drop, crooning the lullaby. I had looked at Morgan, on the wooden bench with Merfyn Jones, and he had turned to me. We had listened, the three of us, in the firelight, in the big farm kitchen. *"Huna 'n fwyn, y tlws ei lun . . . Pam yr wyt yn awr in gwenu . . ."* She had sung then as she was singing now. But here she sang to the souls of earth. "Little nestlings in the trees now are sleeping. But the blossom of my bosom has a warmer nest than these . . ." The spell of Nana left me, and the longing and the sorrow came back. I wanted to put my hand on Morgan's knee and say, "Please, Morgan, tell me . . ." I would try to be a pawnie Rawnie. I closed my eyes. "Tell me, that I may know . . . Morgan . . ." The fear darkened all my thoughts and dreams. "Are you going to stay in my world? Are you going to accept the fellowship?" The fear held me, as Myfanwy's voice, low and full, died away, a whisper on the still air.

Then she looked at the red-haired stranger and smiled. He came and took the harp from her hands. She sat for a moment longer, then she stood up; and though some of us leaped up and helped others, and some got up slowly, it seemed that we all rose from the grass in one movement. As though she were a queen, I thought, and looked at Morgan. He was looking at Myfanwy too. Then he turned and looked down at me.

There were no farewells. We went our ways. Only Basil and Caridwen Hughes were left sitting on the ground, drinking their beer. Codger and Emma were walking slowly toward the gate; he was leaning on his ash stick and she on his arm. Penry Jones and the quiet girl, and Myfanwy and Merfyn and the big stranger, were clearing away the cups and saucers and beer mugs and plates into two wheelbarrows. The torches had gone out, and the acetylene lamps were flickering low.

"Morgan, I want to go to the clump of dwarf oaks and find a sprig of mistletoe on the whitethorn near the center."

"Plucked before dawn on the Eve of St. John." He laughed quietly. "And you will have true dreams for a twelve-month." We walked together to the deeper dark of the copse.

As we passed between the sturdy trees, I tried to keep the

fear and the question deep down in my heart. I felt the ringed trunks as I passed each tree, and wondered why they grew in Wales, in hardy companies, giving shelter to man and beast and breaking the surge of the mountain winds. Suddenly my hand on the rough cool bark, I was speaking. "Morgan?"

"Yes, Catriona?"

"Are you going to accept the fellowship?"

He walked on slowly, his head down. He's angry, I thought. I walked behind him. I wanted to cut my tongue out. Pawnie Rawnie! I thought, and wanted to die. He stopped.

"Here we are." He went closer and looked. "And here is some mistletoe." He stretched out his arm and pulled a sprig, turned, and gave it to me. "I may accept, Catriona . . ." I stood waiting. I felt the smooth sappy leaves with the tips of my fingers. "Either that, or something else to do with education."

I thought my heart would burst. "When you are happy, be silent . . ."

"May I have my sprig now?" Morgan's voice was deep and warm. I went to the tree, and with my left hand against the trunk, I stood on my toes and pulled a small sprig.

"Now we shall dream true for a whole year," I said.

"And forget, in waking, what we were in dream."

"I remember my dreams."

Morgan stood silent, tall. "Do you, Catriona?"

The copse was a place of night-thriving creatures that rustled at us as we stood among them, made small flutterings in the branches above, and whisperings in the grasses at our feet and in the low bush-clumps around us. A thin, pale shaft of moonlight pierced the darkness, and I saw Morgan's eyes. They were dark, and the look in them answered my longing. We stood, silent. The night rustling stilled, listening. To my singing heart, I thought, and the oak trees stretched out their leafy arms and entwined us and drew us together with strong, gentle hands. Then Morgan moved.

"Do you remember, Catriona? Or do you forget the majesty that was yours in the world beyond dream?" He touched my cheek with his hand, a moth wing in the darkness. Then he turned swiftly and went to the edge of the copse. I followed him slowly. He was waiting for me at the meadow gate.

We closed it and stepped onto the roadway, and in front of us, black and clear in the moonlight, I saw two figures. ". . . and it's coming back to the mountains you'll be . . ." Eldorai had said, "to the thin dark girl that'll be waiting for you." I turned to Morgan and touched his arm. "Look," I whispered, and we stood still. Morgan smiled, and my eyes filled with tears. Archibald and Ellen were walking, hand in hand, up the Rise.

� 15 ✳✳

Basil grew more interested in study. He looked around for himself and found the works of Christopher Marlowe. He liked what he called "the earthy bits," and discovered that Marlowe had been up at Cambridge. Since he had come to the Vicarage, I understood more clearly Jane's talk about being enticing, and I wore the thickest, loosest jumpers I had for morning lessons.

"Aren't you absolutely sweltering in that heavy sweater?" Basil asked one morning in July.

"Sweater?"

"Yes. Sweater! They're called sweaters in America. Jumpers is an old-fashioned word." He laughed—the throaty laugh that made me uncomfortable. "And you use plenty of odd enough words. Anyway, why do you always wear these woolen things?" And I replied that the Arabs wore loose heavy woolen robes to keep them cool in the desert.

"Ah! Method in the madness," he said, and I smiled.

He was interested in anachronisms. "Old Shakespeare's mistakes," he called them. "Who'd have thought it? Really, the things one learns." Morgan laughed, and five study periods later, when we were again working on Marlowe, he lit his pipe and talked to us.

"It is essential," he said, "that classical learning is maintained, or the continuity of English literature will be in jeopardy." Basil wrote it in his notebook.

"Great idea, the notebook idea. Something to fall back on when you're stuck."

"And if the young people of future generations are not taught classical lore and the ancient literatures they will study Shakespeare's works, act his plays in school and college, see them performed in the theaters and hear the greatest actors speak the words, but they will be unaware of his deepest beauty." He looked at Basil and smiled. "Don't call what you have been seeking, and finding, mistakes, Basil . . . the Greek and Roman myths, to this man"—and he held up the volume of Christopher Marlowe—"meant simply beauty . . . erotic beauty, I think, symbolized by Venus . . . and without doubt Marlowe gave to the Elizabethans, in his translations of Ovid, a gift rich in lore and legend, but"—he put the book on the table—"to Shakespeare the myths of the ancient world meant beauty and wisdom. The wisdom of power, rightly used, and the tragedy of it, used for evil. These myths sank deep into some waiting crucible of his mind, to well up not only in the Roman plays, but throughout all his works." Morgan leaned back in his chair and looked at us. "And what matters is that the ancient beauty and wisdom come to us in our own language, bearing, if not in exact context, the true essence of the allusion, in words eternally fresh, and alive with the fire of his genius."

"What was the fire of his genius?" Basil asked. "What is genius, really?" Morgan and I were surprised. It was the first time Basil had asked a question.

"That's hard to answer, Basil." Morgan thought for a while. "Genius?" He leaned forward with his arms on the table, holding the bowl of his pipe with both hands. "Is it a strangely pure vision of natural things? Is it a noble, ever seeking passion for beauty?" He looked up. "Is it to be able to give to others a blazing glimpse of inner truth in a world of outward appearances? A genius"—he paused—"is, I think"—he paused again—"one who knows the stern inner beauty of reality and has direct intuition of its enchantment."

"Holy Moses! I started something." Basil looked at his watch. He stood up. "I'm late. I'll see you tomorrow," he said, "and I won't ask any more questions. Let's stick to old Marlowe—he had the right ideas."

When he had gone, Morgan said, "He has something of the lusty Elizabethan temper himself."

"Morgan, what did you mean by the stern inner beauty of reality? What is reality? Is it God? Is it love? Is it this table"—I rapped the hard wood with my knuckles—"that I can touch? Or is it thought . . . imagination that creates but we cannot see? And why stern?"

Morgan looked at me across the table. "Stern . . ." He rose from his chair and went to the window seat. When he sat down, the sunlight shone through the gold, green, and red panes and made patches of color on the side of his face and the sleeve and shoulder of his tweed jacket. He leaned his arm on the wide sill. "The word, for me, has nothing of harshness or severity." He looked up. "You love our mountains?" I nodded slowly. "They are stern . . . and they are beautiful. Do you remember, Catriona, on Moel Hebog, what I said to you?"

"Yes"—I thought of the words anew—"that when the storms and blizzards had passed, and the soft snow melted away . . . the mountain would stand, tall and fair, with only the changing light for a mantle."

"You have remembered."

"And I thought of Nana, in the mingling lights of fire and sun, on the day she died." Morgan leaned forward, but he did not speak. "Now I think I know why you used the word," I said.

"And love, Catriona, love is stern."

"Love is also understanding, and kind."

"No!" He shook his head. "Understanding, perhaps, in its deepest sense, but never kind." His eyes were cool and steady, urging me to deeper thought. "No, Catriona, love is not kind. 'Love is stern and splendid.' A modern philosopher said that, and he is right."

"Now again, I don't understand."

"Kindness gives no thought to whether its object be good or bad. Love desires beauty and strength in the beloved." And I thought, Morgan has desired this for me . . . the Other Horse . . . going to talk with the Foreigner. He has always demanded from me the utmost I could do, and sometimes more.

"But, Morgan," I said, "God is gentle and kind. . . . 'Gentle Jesus, meek and mild . . .' I used to pray when I was small."

"Gentle, yes . . . kindness is not the same thing at all. It is possible to be gentle and yet very stern." I thought, That's true. Morgan has never been kind to me. He whose hand and eye are gentle . . . he is stern. Felicitie? That has nothing to do with kindness.

"And God, Catriona . . . I don't believe that God is kind. He pays us the incredible compliment of not holding us in easeful bondage, but freeing us to adventurous liberty. His Arms are open, wide, leaving us free, and waiting, if so we desire, to embrace us." He shook his head again. "No, God does not dissolve the image of Himself in us with a kindness that asks less of us than we are capable of giving."

His pipe had gone out. He put it in his pocket. Love is stern and splendid, I thought. I didn't want it to be. I wanted it to be kind, to ask less of me than I could give. I wanted to touch him. I ached to feel his arm about my shoulder, as I had felt it on the window seat in my room, after the Other Horse had thrown me. I sat still in my chair. "Stern and splendid." The words were a whisper.

"Yes, Catriona . . . and warm and passionate, and beautiful beyond words . . ." He stood up and looked out of the open window. "And sometimes love can be immeasurable pain," he sighed, and came to the table. He closed the books and stood looking down at me. "I'm going to the Village before lunch."

"May I come with you?"

"No." The swift flash of his eyes pierced me with a shaft of live light. I didn't move. I heard him open the wall door and close it behind him. He will never be a monk again, I thought. The longing was deeper now. The dream closer. I thought of Nana. "What is longing made of, that it never wears out? Gold wears out, and silver wears out . . . but not iron . . . iron glows when touched by fire. . . . Perhaps longing is made of iron . . ." After a while I went to the window and looked out at the full-summer borders, all waste and sweetness.

During the days that followed, Basil studied without grumbling and asked more questions. He enjoyed reading of Drake, old Hawkins, and Frobisher; Raleigh, turbulent, fierce, and gentle. I liked Raleigh. He had marched, with black-plumed helmet, beside the coffin of his Queen and written of her on that day:

> . . . a durable fire,
> In the mind ever burning,
> Never sick, never old, never dead.
> From itself never turning.

Morgan said that Raleigh had been only one year at Oxford, before he was seventeen, and his leaning toward philosophy and oratory had made him the pride of the Oriel students.

"One year," Basil said, "and oratory and philosophy. Queer sort of education . . ."

"Is it, Basil?" Morgan asked. "He learned a way of thinking and a love of beauty that he never lost."

"Is that what we're supposed to learn? Shouldn't we learn a few facts?"

"That's not learning, that's instruction," I said. "Morgan says that in his book."

"Now, Catty, you stick to your legends and fairy tales." I was going to protest, but I saw that Basil was serious. I didn't speak again. "That book of yours," he said to Morgan, "what was the name of it?"

"So far, *Education, the Weapon of Progress.*"

"Weapon? Why weapon? Progress doesn't need weapons . . . and why education, anyway?"

"Because progress without true education is a mockery."

"Now it's true education." Basil shrugged and lit a cigarette. "I would say that facts were facts. What's your idea of true education, anyway?"

Morgan leaned forward, his elbow on the table, chin in hand. He was absorbed, trying to put his abundant ideas into a few words. "Basil," he said quietly, "you asked for it." Basil put out his cigarette half smoked and lit another. "True education"—Morgan paused—"is the learning that reveals to a man the order, the co-operation and beauty, the harmony and discipline, that exists in nature . . . in the universe . . . and teaches him, through his own disciplines, his reason, imagination, and eventually his wisdom, to play his part in creating a higher order and a deeper harmony. This kind of education, Basil, is man's weapon, so that the magnitude of his own inventions and discoveries shall not overwhelm him."

"I get it." Basil put out the other cigarette. "Now I won't have to read your book."

Morgan laughed. "Let's get back to the Elizabethans," he said, and we worked till noon.

Basil didn't stay for lunch. He roared away down the Hill Lane in the Scarlet Peril, and Morgan leaned back in his chair, smiling. "He'll write a reasonable paper this autumn," he said, and sighed a little because Basil would work only before lunch, and although we asked him to join afternoon studies he went to Llandudno and other seacoast towns and didn't get back to the Vicarage till the early hours of the morning. He often had a headache during study.

He was polite and almost thoughtful to Jane, and thanked her whenever he lunched with us, in a way that brought an immediate invitation to gin and vermouth before dinner, and he flattered his aunt shamelessly. He had taken them both once, with the Curate, to a tea dance in Llandudno, and they talked about it at Wednesday teas and planned to have a social tea dance for the Mothers' Union instead of the usual whist drive.

"New ideas, Miss Withers . . . progress. . . ." The Vicar's wife was full of plans. "Basil's visit has been a wonderful tonic for all of us." They had hoped to be taken again, but Basil took Caridwen Hughes. She was the envy of all the other girls, except Tessie, who was incapable of malice and proud of her friend's success. Basil helped with the harvest, raking and stacking and working as hard as everyone else.

"Lots of chat about tumbling in the hay," he had said. "Never thought I'd be working in it." And he drank his fair share of Mr. Price's free beer. He and Caridwen Hughes and Penry Jones and the quiet girl and Tessie and Caradoc Ellis practiced the Charleston in the coachyard, to the music of Dylan Price's mouth organ and the accordion, and then gave their class in the Parish Hall. All the villagers who could walk came, and almost everyone learned. They were used to dancing the quick, intricate steps of the Welsh reels and jigs, and the swift turning and kicking movements were not alien to them; another lesson before the day of the Harvest Social was unanimously voted, and the villagers went about their daily tasks like puppets on the ends of strings. Basil had called on the leader of the Merry Music Men to make sure they could play the Charleston.

"They can," he told us, "as good as I've ever heard. Even in New York." And everyone grew more and more excited about the Harvest Social. When Merfyn Jones came with the butter and eggs, even Emma attempted a few steps.

"This is not the dance for them as has varicose veins," she said, and held her sides when Idris Williams, the post, danced it for her while she poured him a glass of lemon barley water for his bladder troubles. "Who'd have thought it? That old sobersides, indeed to goodness. Why, he's light as a grasshopper on those two flat feet of his." And at Mr. Jones the butcher's, only Grandma Rhys-Evans and Codger stood still and talked. Mr. Jones jiggled and sold his good meat and told everyone how the "young spark of a lad from the Midlands" had livened up the Village, "look you," and kicked the wooden counter with his flying heels.

Codger, sitting out under the lattice porch of Nana's cottage, said, "Kishli, I've seen some mighty peculiar things in my time, look you . . . but I never thought to see this Village, the whole Village, suffering from the St. Vitus's dance." He chuckled and spat. "And 'tis a fine surprise all the visitors from over the Mochdre Hill will be having, at that." And he sat there laughing quietly, his clay in his hand, turning his toes in and out and his feet from left to right, his bones cracking like fireworks.

My own feet I hardly recognized in the soft black leather

court shoes with the low Louis heels. They looked small and slender, and now Jane said I might wear my plaits pinned up. I had a new, semi-evening dress for the Social. It was pale yellow, almost cream-colored, with a full skirt and a tucked bodice, with a high round neck, short sleeves, and pearl buttons down the back.

"I think I'll let the bodice out a little," Jane had said when it came from Chester, and I had nodded, but it didn't seem to make any difference.

Tessie didn't go home on the night of the Harvest Social. She stayed in the little room off the pantry, next to Emma. She helped Jane to dress, and everyone felt festive and excited. Jane wore her new, electric-blue taffeta, with a low square neck, and wide shoulder straps, and a skirt with two tiers. She wore her hair in the bun she had worn for nearly three years—she called it a chignon—and long paste earrings. She looked young and pretty. Tessie helped me to fasten the buttons at the back of my dress.

"Pusterkin's had three kittens again."

"Oh, Tessie! When?"

"Last week . . . one's all white, like Colly, look you."

"What are the others like?"

"Like Star, black and white, and . . ." She giggled. She was wearing a brown velvet dress, and her brown curls were shining and clean. She no longer had pimples.

". . . and . . . Oh, Miss Catty! That Mr. Basil, he's real fast, look you . . . and not only when he's in that red motorcar. He's—"

"Now, Tessie . . ." I knew she had been wanting to talk about Basil, while she talked of the kittens.

"I'm sorry, miss . . . but Caridwen—"

"Tessie!"

"All right, miss." She fastened the last button and the

hook at the waist. "But he's got his eye on you, miss . . . good and proper, Caridwen says."

"Tessie, please!"

"Beg pardon, Miss Catty. Here, let me." She fastened the clasp of the pearls my aunt had sent to me for my fourteenth birthday. They were small and even. I loved to wear them and to feel them, warm, when I took them off. I wrote to my aunt once a month, and she sent postcards to me from far places and gifts on my birthday. "Oh, Miss Catty!" Tessie stood back and looked at me. "Miss Catty, you're real beautiful—indeed you are."

"Thank you, Tessie. I'm the same as ever I was." Then I thought, How silly. I'm not the same.

"Well now, and I wouldn't be saying that, miss," Tessie said, and left the room happily.

Jane had a sherry party before we went to the Parish Hall. The Vicar and his wife came, and the Curate, who because he had incipient consumption and needed to work in a small parish had stayed on in the mountains; Dr. Fraser and his sister and the English artist, with his Cornish wife, who had again taken the first prize for the best vegetable marrow away from Mr. Evans; Basil and I, and Morgan. Everyone was talking gaily. Dr. Fraser's sister wore a fawn lace dress, almost the color of her hair, and her eyes were blue. When she smiled, she looked like a little girl. I should like her if I knew her, I thought, and tried to think of something to say to the Curate. I could never feel there was anyone inside him. He said the right thing, in the right tone of voice, with the right expression on his face.

"Your first dance, Catriona. A memorable occasion."

"Yes, it is. How is your sister?"

"Quite well now."

"Has she been ill?"

"Just a nasty summer cold, you know—most disagreeable."

"Oh, I'm so sorry."

"Quite . . . quite. . . ."

"Would you like a glass of sherry?"

He looked at his empty glass. "Perhaps, a little . . .
just a little."

I took it and went to the tray on the small table. The
Vicar was congratulating Basil on his game. Basil was a
strong temporary member of the Village Fives team, and
there was to be a final next Sunday.

"The honor of the Village is at stake, Basil," he said, and
added that it might be better if Basil didn't go to Llandudno
on Saturday night.

"Honor at stake or not," the Vicar's wife said, "you'll
be in your greenhouse." She turned and smiled at her
nephew. "And going to Llandudno has never spoiled Basil's
game before." Jane was smiling up at Morgan, and as I
turned to give the Curate his sherry Basil was at my elbow.

"You're a charming hostess, Catty." He held my elbow.
"Mine needs filling too, you know."

I pulled my arm away gently and went to the Curate. I
was about to stop and talk to the artist's wife, who was
wearing a flowered dress with puff sleeves and her hair in a
round bun on top of her head, and who was talkative and
jolly, but Basil said, "I need some sherry-red wine," and his
voice was louder and throatier. He's beginning to be drunk,
I thought, and went to the tray.

"Is this your glass?" He nodded and put his arm around
my waist.

I stiffened and poured the wine. "Basil, please take your
arm away," I whispered, and turned to give him the glass of
sherry, and Morgan was there.

"Catriona, will you take a sherry to the doctor's sister,

please?" I nodded, filled a glass, and went across the room. She was talking to her brother and the English artist, who was not tall and thin, and was angry-looking till he smiled.

"Catriona," he said, "I would like to paint you in your jersey and kilt, as I have always known you."

"Before I get too old?"

"Before you go away," the artist said, and the pain seared through my heart. Although Jane reminded me every day that the telegram might come, I put it out of my mind and thought, Morgan will not let me go, but I couldn't stop the feeling at the top of my stomach. I turned to Dr. Fraser.

"You look very lovely tonight, Catriona. If I were a painter, I'd like to paint you now."

"The girl in the kilt and jersey will always be there," the artist said, and I laughed. But I felt sad and looked around at Morgan. He had his back to me. Jane was beside him again, smiling up at him and talking.

"Can you dance the Charleston?" the doctor asked me.

"Yes, but I like to waltz . . . around and around . . . fast."

"Then save a waltz for me."

"I will, thank you."

The artist said, "This Social will surely be different from any other we've ever had."

"I hear that more tickets had to be printed." The doctor's sister had a soft voice, but the Vicar's wife heard her.

"Yes! Yes! A hundred more. Imagine . . . people are coming from all over. Isn't it wonderful?"

"It most certainly is, my dear." The Vicar was beaming; he looked at the doctor. "It should mean two, perhaps three, new beds for the Maternity Clinic." He turned to Basil. "And to a great extent due to you, my boy."

"Not at all, Uncle." Basil poured himself another glass of sherry.

"Oh, yes it is. You've been quite wonderful . . . the Charleston lessons . . . so original. Basil learned the Charleston in New York, you know," the Vicar's wife told us, "in one of those—illicit easy places."

"A speakeasy, Aunt Gladys . . . and even you would never believe that place." He put his empty glass on the tray. "The Animal Room, on Fifty-eighth Street. It has to be seen . . ." Her answer was lost in the chatter and laughing, and soon we all left the drawing room to walk to the Parish Hall.

I walked with the doctor's sister, and we were almost at the wall door when Basil called:

"Catty! You're coming with me in the Scarlet Peril."

Tessie came to me with a scarf. "You'll need this, Miss Catty. I'll bet he takes you the long way around."

"Thank you, Tessie." I looked at her. "But how did you know I'd be needing it?"

"Because he's talked to Miss Withers already. I heard him."

I didn't want to go with Basil. I looked at Morgan, but he and Dr. Fraser were standing on the front doorstep, talking, and Jane was looking at me. Doesn't she know he's had too much to drink? I thought.

"Yes, go along, dear," she was saying. "And we'll all meet at the Parish Hall." Basil was walking toward me. "Now, don't be too late," she called after him. Basil came and took my arm.

"Basil, it's such a short way—why don't we walk?"

"Walk! Sacrilege! Come, wench." And holding my arm, he opened the wall door and we went through it. The Scarlet Peril was outside, against the wall between the door and the coachyard gates. I put the scarf over my head and tied it under my chin. He opened the door and I got into the low seat; then he went around the other side, and sitting down, leaned over me, touching me, to see that my door was safely closed.

"Can't have you falling out, Catty," he said. "Now! Hold everything." Morgan and the doctor were at the wall door, watching. The others were walking down the Hill Lane. Basil pressed his horn, and the harsh cracking sound pierced the twilight quiet. The engine roared, and everyone leaped to the sides of the road as we hurtled past. I kept my hands folded on my lap. We sped on, down through the Square and up the Plas-y-Coed Road and past the Parish Hall.

"You've passed it, Basil," I shouted in his ear.

"Silly girl, didn't you know? You're going for a spin," he shouted back. "And about time, too." I sat back. We tore along the Old Roman Road and way around the other side of the Mochdre Hill. Two miles ahead there was a fork in the road. I knew that if he took the left road we should be an hour late.

"Basil, take the right-hand turning," I shouted, and he laughed and put his hand on my knee. I knew he hadn't heard me, and I knew, strangely, that he would do the opposite of anything I said.

"What you say?" He squeezed my knee, threw his head back, and laughed.

I waited a moment, then I leaned toward him and shouted as loudly as I could, close to his ear, "Take the left-hand turning." He laughed again. We were coming to the fork.

"For you'll take the left-hand and I'll take the right-hand . . ." he sang, and took the right-hand road on two wheels. I held on to the rim of the door and sighed with relief. "And they'll all get to the Social before us. . . ." He had taken his hand from my knee when we turned the corner. He put it back again, halfway up my thigh. "We're going for a spin," he said, and patted me. Then we came around by the wood and he saw the meadow gate. The brakes screamed, we skidded sideways and stopped. I was thrown forward and knocked my head on the hard metal underneath the inside of the windshield. I was stunned.

"You fooled me!" he said. "Blast you, Catty! You fooled me." Then, "I say, are you hurt?" I took my hands from my forehead and blinked. I saw double. I shook my head. It hurt. "You're going to have one hell of a duck egg," he said, "and it serves you right . . . you shouldn't have fooled me." His anger was rising again.

"Oh, Basil, Jane would be angry if we were an hour late for the Social."

"She wouldn't." He looked at me. "She wants you to go out with me." I knew he was right. "She's got a crush on the tutor extraordinary herself." No! Then I thought, Is that true? I remembered Emma: "Jealousy's a bitter, bitter thing." I had known for years that Jane was jealous of the things Morgan and I did together. I sat still. I felt as I had felt the day I came into the drawing room and saw her for the first time with her hair coiled in the nape of her neck. It is true, I thought. I felt sick, and sorry. I closed my eyes.

"I say, are you all right?"

"Yes, thank you, Basil. Will it show?"

"It's showing now."

"Oh dear. Never mind, I'll pull my hair over it." I took off the scarf and pulled my hair down, slantways, across my forehead. "Better?" I asked. Basil still looked annoyed.

"Fine sort of ending to our first spin," he said, and I laughed a little.

"Come on, let's go to the Parish Hall." The bump had begun to throb, but I could see straight again. We drove up the Rise and down the Lane at normal speed to the Hall.

The Merry Music Men were playing a fox trot as we drove up, and some of the men and youths were standing around the door. There were welcoming cheers as the red motorcar came to a standstill. Dylan Price came and opened the door for me before Basil had time to get out.

"Thank you, Dylan Price," I said, and then, "Good evening," to the others, and went in to find Jane. I wondered if I would show what I knew. I hoped not. I felt shocked and angry and sad.

She was sitting with the doctor's sister, halfway down the room. There were chairs around the walls, and all the girls seemed to be sitting on the right side as I went in. I walked to Jane.

"You were a long time," she said, and I thought, I'm imagining the look in her eyes. "And your hair is all loose and untidy. Really, Catriona, you can't be trusted to behave for a minute."

"It was the wind."

"I thought when you started out you were wearing a scarf." And now I knew that I had not imagined the look in her eyes.

"Where is Basil?"

"He's coming in."

"Please go and comb your hair."

I knew I couldn't change the way I had it, so I said, "In a minute, Jane. I want to look."

The Parish Hall was decorated with autumn flowers and paper hangings and flags. A huge Union Jack was spread across the front of the double doors to the anteroom, behind the refreshment table, and the big banner, bearing the Welsh Dragon, was over the center of the stage. There was powder strewn about on the floor to make it slippery. The Merry Music Men, five of them, the pianist and leader, the cellist, violinist, the accordion player, and the drummer, were dressed in red and white striped blazers and black trousers. They wore red bow ties and patent leather shoes. Everyone stood about in his best dress and suit. It doesn't look very gay, I thought. They all seem to be uncomfortable. The blacksmith was putting his finger between his neck and the stiff white collar he was wearing. He was standing with Mr. Jones, the butcher, who never feels uncomfortable, I thought to myself. He was talking to the leader of the band, who nodded and then settled into his seat at the piano and raised his hand, and they began to play a waltz. I longed to dance. The Curate asked Jane. He danced quite well. Jane did the steps correctly, but she looked stiff. Caradoc Ellis was dancing with the haberdasher's wife. She was quite good-looking. I was surprised. I had never noticed her tall, supple figure before. She looked at Caradoc Ellis with an odd smile as they danced. The haberdasher was dancing with a short, plump woman who had thin, wispy hair and a small, fretful face. Caradoc Ellis's daft little wife, I thought, remembering Emma's words, and looked for her, but she and Codger hadn't arrived. Now there were a lot of people I didn't know, men and girls together, sitting along the left side of the room; they were laughing and talking. They must be from the Mochdre Village, I thought, and the blacksmith asked one of them to dance. A thin girl with large black eyes. Llewellyn Davies, from the Mochdre Village, asked Tessie. Myfanwy and Merfyn had not yet come, nor Penry, nor Archibald and Ellen. Mr. Jones, the butcher, was waltzing all over the floor with Codger's daughter-in-law, who was wearing a bright pink dress, the color of her cheeks, and her hair was frizzed and stiff.

I decided to go and look at my forehead. I wondered where Basil was. When I looked through the window of the ladies' room, I saw him. He was at Mr. Price's beer stall, drinking with some of the men. I saw him take a flat silver bottle from the back pocket of his trousers and pour some-

thing from it into his mug of beer. Mr. Price served one
round of free beer, and the money he took for the rest he
gave to the Mothers' Union and the Nursing Fund. Only
tea and lemonade and ginger beer could be served in the
Parish Hall. I wondered where Morgan was. I looked at
the bump on my head. It was the size of a plover's egg, with
a purple ring around it and a pink one around that. Like a
sunrise, I thought, and pulled my hair as neatly as I could
down over it. I looked odd, but tidy. I went into the Hall
again and saw Myfanwy Jones and Merfyn and the red-
haired stranger. I must ask her his name, I thought. I
walked toward her, then the Merry Music Men played a
schottische and Penry Jones met me and asked me to dance.

"Thank you, Penry Jones," I said. "You are my first
dancing partner—except at dancing class." He looked
pleased, his yellow-brown eyes twinkled.

" 'Tis a truly great honor, Miss Catty . . . a signal
honor, indeed." And away we danced. After a while he said,
"And 'tis a fine and easy dancer you are, at that . . . fine,
indeed," and we didn't talk any more. I didn't even think.
Then I saw Morgan standing by the big door, watching me.
I waved to him over Penry's shoulder. I didn't want the
merry dance to come to an end. When it did, Penry Jones
said, "Thank you, Miss Catty . . . Thank you. And will
you have a waltz with me later?"

"Oh yes! I will!" He laughed and left me with Jane on a
seat near the wall.

"What on earth are you doing with your hair like that?
It's not in the least becoming . . . and looks rather common."

I didn't say anything; she hadn't noticed the lump. Then
I saw Emma in her purple bombazine and I almost ran
across the room, but remembered in time, and walked over
to sit with her and Myfanwy Jones.

"Myfanwy, what's the big red-haired man's name?"

She looked at me and blushed, then she tossed her head. "That great, staring good-for-nothing?" she said. "His name's Gwilym Evans."

"And he's real light on his feet for one so heavy-built, look you," Emma said.

"And he's lightheaded, too," said Myfanwy Jones. She was wearing a gray silk dress with a pleated skirt, and her fair brown hair was in a bun at the back of her head. The music began again, and Merfyn Jones came across to us.

"May I have the pleasure of this dance, Miss Catty?" he asked.

Emma and Myfanwy Jones smiled, and Penry came up and said, "Come on, Cousin," and Emma was left alone, nodding happily to the music and watching us.

Merfyn Jones hadn't the lightness and rhythm of Penry, but he danced well and I enjoyed every moment. Jane looked disapproving when he took me back to her. She gave him her cold smile and then turned to me.

"You'd better sit quietly for a while, Catriona," she said, and peered about the room.

"Basil's outside," I said.

"He should be dancing. Did you upset him? Did you quarrel? I hope not; Basil is a very eligible young man. Did you quarrel?"

I shook my head and felt the bump throb. While I had been dancing, I had forgotten it and felt no pain at all. When the music began again, the doctor asked Jane to dance. I looked around, enjoying the music. The people were gay and comfortable now, and happy; dancing, sitting and talking, girls and men together on either side of the Hall; almost everyone was dancing. Then I saw Archibald and Ellen, and suddenly my eyes filled with tears as I

watched them together. Archibald's strength and gentleness.
Her eyes when she looked at him. Morgan came and sat
with me, and together we watched them as they danced.

"Morgan, can you dance?"

"Of course I can."

"Dance with me." He laughed and stood up. He held out
his hand. It was a waltz. He put his arm about my waist and
held me away from him, but when we began to dance it
would not have mattered if only the tips of our fingers had
touched, at arm's length. I was no longer me, dancing; I lost
myself, aware only of Morgan's touch and the strong,
smooth flow of his rhythm. I closed my eyes.

"Open your eyes, Catriona," Morgan warned. "Look at
your thumbnail, and you will never get dizzy, however
swiftly we spin." I looked at his lean brown fingers, holding
my hand as we danced. If only this waltz would never end.
Now, after the dances, people had begun to clap and the
band to play encores. When the waltz ended, I clapped,
Morgan clapped, and others joined in. Morgan put his hand
on my waist again, and then I saw Jane. She was standing
at the other side of the room, with the doctor, and the look
in her eyes sent a cold shiver through me. Morgan raised an
eyebrow.

"A goose walking over my grave," I said. The music
started again, and Morgan and I came together, dancing.
It was "The Blue Danube." I shall always remember this
waltz. This tune. Then I thought, I won't have to remember . . . I shall be here, with Morgan, all my life. And I
smiled while I danced, my feet skimmed the powdered floor
boards and the strong, joyous rhythm seemed to have taken
us both up into itself, so that we were a part of everyone
who had ever danced to that waltz and a part of the melody,
in the place where it had been, before it danced into the wait-

ing mind of Johann Strauss. Love and laughter; laughter and dancing; love and dancing. The music stopped. We stood a moment, still. It was as it had been at the bottom of the stairs, in my new habit. Then he said, "You dance beautifully, Catriona."

I couldn't speak. I wanted to stay close to him, touching his fingers. To move away from him was a sharp pain in a deep joy. I could barely do it. We were walking slowly to the chairs.

"Catriona"—Jane came up to us—"it's time for refreshments; you'd better come with me."

"Will you have another waltz with me, Catriona?"

"I will."

"I'll come for you," he said, and left me with Jane.

"You're dancing far too much, Catriona . . . and never with your escort. You should behave more quietly . . . this is your first dance. . . ." We went to the refreshment table. It was an excuse, I thought. No one had refreshments at a special time. They went to the table when they felt hungry or thirsty. The long table was laden with Mrs. Price's sandwiches and Emma's cakes and scones and tartlets, and she always made an orange spongecake for the Harvest Social. I had often seen it in the kitchen, but never before in its place of honor, in the center of the table. I was looking at it and thinking of Emma when I felt a touch on my arm. It was Archibald.

"Look at Emma's cake."

"It's wonderful, indeed," he said. "Miss Catty, will you dance with me?"

"Oh, Archibald, I will." Jane was at the end of the table, talking to the English artist. It was a fox trot. Archibald danced well, and we were happy.

"I can't believe it, Miss Catty-fach . . . I just can't believe it, look you. . . ." His blue eyes were bright, and he looked scrubbed and clean, all through.

Then he smiled over my head, and when we turned I saw Morgan and Codger watching us from the door. "Codger's wearing his waistcoat," I said, and Archibald nodded.

"I got it out of the mothballs and hung it up to air this morning." We waved to Morgan and Codger as we danced.

When the fox trot ended, the Merry Music Men, without pausing, began to play the fast, merry tune for "Strip the Willow." Everyone formed into two lines, partners opposite each other, and the merry country dance began. Archibald and I stayed partners, and almost everybody joined in. When it came to an end, we were all hot and thirsty. Archibald and I, breathless, went to sit down. After a minute or two he said, "I'll bring you a lemonade."

"Bring one for Emma, too." I was still breathless. "I'm going to sit with her." I went across the room to where Emma sat in the corner. The band began to play another schottische, and I saw Caradoc Ellis ask Jane to dance. He swept her into the middle of the room. She looked uncomfortable, and haughty.

"That Caradoc Ellis," Emma said, "you can't help liking him . . . reprobate though he is, look you. . . ." When the people clapped for an encore, Jane put her hand to her head, and Caradoc Ellis took her to her seat and bowed. Emma turned to me, happy.

"Well, Miss Catty-fach, and it's surely to goodness a fine time that you're having at your first dance . . . and so you should, indeed." She nodded her head, and I wanted to hug her. "And it's a real bit of fluff that you are when you're dancing, indeed to goodness." She looked proud. Oh, Emma . . . I felt the tears again. My nose tingled.

"Myfanwy Jones likes the red-haired man," I said, and she nodded slowly.

"That she does." And she gave a big sigh. "At last." Archibald came with our lemonade. He was going to sit down with us, but I stopped him and said:

"Thank you, Archibald . . . and please ask me to dance again." So that he knew that he needn't stay with us. He smiled and went to where Ellen was sitting with the haberdasher's wife and took her to the refreshment table. She was wearing a soft silk dress of dark blue. Her eyes looked violet-colored, and her skin was pale. She had wound the dark braid over the top of her head. The tears came again.

"Oh, Emma, Ellen's beautiful." Emma looked at her, walking across the room with Archibald.

"She is, at that . . . and what's more, she's a good girl." I thought of Nana, and what she had said of her grandson so long ago, when he had come to her cottage door on the day she died: "A gentle, understanding boy."

"And Archibald is a good man," I said, and Emma smiled.

"And it's a man he is. Indeed, and it's hard to believe." She drank her lemonade. Then she looked at me. "And you don't know how good you are to look at, yourself, Miss Catty . . . and I don't know as I ever want you to, at that." Now there were tears in Emma's eyes.

"But am I a good girl, Emma? Like Ellen?" She sniffed and sighed.

"Now, there's grave doubts about that, I'm thinking . . . indeed I am." And we were laughing when I saw Basil Lockridge come to the big door and look around. Caridwen Hughes got up from her chair, and I gave a sigh of relief, but just as she came up to him he saw me and walked by her. He came across the room. I felt Emma stiffen. The band was playing a fox trot. Basil took no notice of Emma.

"Come on, let's dance," he said, and pulled me up from the chair. He put his arm around my waist and held me tightly, so that my body was close to his. I tried to pull away. I saw Emma's face. Her lips were pressed together. She looked angry and worried. And we were having such fun, I thought.

"Come on, Catty. Dance . . . You've been dancing all the time . . . dance now . . . blast you."

"I can't. You don't give me any room."

"This is how a fox trot should be danced. Close." He laughed and pulled me closer to him. I had never hated his throaty laugh so much. I looked for Morgan. I couldn't see him anywhere. If only Jane would see us. She would disapprove of Basil's holding me close like this, I thought.

She saw us, but she turned away and pretended that she hadn't. I felt hopeless. Basil was dancing quietly, but all his body moved as he held me against him, and he smelled of drink. I turned my head away. I almost hated him for spoiling my first dance. Then I thought, He hasn't spoiled it. This dance will end . . . and then Morgan will dance with me again, and Archibald and Penry Jones . . . I wished the music would stop, but the dances were getting to be longer and longer. "You're not a cold little bluestocking . . . I've been watching you," Basil whispered in my ear. I clenched my teeth and breathed slowly, and at last the music stopped. Basil didn't let me go.

"Basil, please, the music has stopped."

"Come outside and get cool."

"I am cool." But he held my arm so that it hurt if I tried to pull away, and walked me out through the side door of the Hall.

"Let's go for a spin."

"Certainly not, Basil." I was angry. We were beside the wall that looked toward the old well and the Plas-y-Coed Wood. Everyone else was at the other side of the Hall. It was moonlight. Swiftly, before I knew, he pressed me against the wall and his strong arms held me. I fought. He pinioned my arms to my sides, and when I put my head down he stood, hard, against me and pushed his chin up underneath mine, so that I had to raise my head. Then he held the roots of my plaits at the back of my head and covered my mouth with his mouth. It felt huge and wet. He pressed against my clenched teeth. I couldn't breathe. My teeth parted, and his tongue, foul-tasting of drink, thrust into my mouth, and almost down my throat. I couldn't fight any more. He felt my weakness and loosed his hold on my hair. He put his hand on my left breast. Rage filled me. My arms were still held. I was weak and sobbing with fury.

"You hit me," he said against my mouth, and then I felt his tongue again, and his hand kneading my breast.

"Basil!" Morgan's voice was like a whiplash. Basil stood still against me, his mouth on mine. He stopped kissing me. I closed my eyes to shut out his face. Slowly he stepped back, away from me. "Go inside," Morgan said.

"What the hell—"

"Go inside." In the light from the door Morgan's eyes were flaming, his face was white. Basil turned away from me to Morgan, but he couldn't meet his eyes. He pulled his cigarette case from his pocket, took a cigarette, and shut the case with a snap. He put it back in his pocket, struck a match, and lit the cigarette. Go away. Oh, go away, I prayed. He drew on the cigarette and turned on his heel, then he stopped, turned, and looked at me.

"Can't say you're sweet sixteen and never been kissed, eh, Catty?" My stomach came up into my throat. "Or is it seventeen?" Then he walked past Morgan without looking at him and went into the Hall.

A shuddering breath came out of me. I turned to the wall and big, empty retchings tore at the muscles of my stomach. Again and again I heaved. I tried to breathe slowly, but my lips were stuck in a grimace. I leaned against the wall. My

left breast felt bruised and sore. I straightened up. Now.
Eight in. Hold. Eight out. I couldn't. Each breath was a
choking gasp. I tried again. I must. I looked up. I could see
Morgan standing in the light of the well lamp. I pulled the
hair over the bump on my head and went to him, running,
across the grass. When I was close, he held out his arms. I
didn't look at him. He held me against his heart.

"Catriona." He held my head. The bump hurt against
his jacket. I was shaking. He pressed my head against him,
and I remembered the other weal, against his collar, after
the Foreigner had hit me. "Morgan." Shuddering sobs came
with the thought, He touched me. Morgan stroked my hair.
"Catriona. Catriona." I felt the touch of his lips on my
braids. His gentle, tender kisses. I held my breath, and the
trembling stopped. Quiet, I could hear his heart, and feel it,
thudding against his ribs. He was trembling. I lifted my
face. He bent his head till our cheeks touched. I put my
arms around his neck, and we stood, holding each other, and
after a while he was still. For long moments he held me.
Then he put me away from him. But I lay my head on his
breast, and again he held me, bending so that his chin
touched the top of my head. "Catriona." I felt his strength
and passion, his tenderness, and a strange thought came to
me, his grace. I knew I would love him till I died. I sighed,
a long, trembling sigh, and looked up, and saw Jane. She
was standing in the lighted side doorway. I knew she could
see us clearly in the light of the well lamp.

"Morgan, Jane is there."

"Never mind." He held me, and then held me away from
him, firmly, his hands on my shoulders.

"I want to go home."

"No, Catriona."

"Morgan . . . I must! I can't see Jane . . . or Basil
. . . not anybody." I began to shake again.

"Catriona, we must go back into the Hall." He put his arm around my shoulder. "Come along; no one knows what has happened. Only you and Basil and I." I stopped. We were halfway across the grass.

"Morgan, I can't." I couldn't stop shaking, and I had pins and needles all over my body. "I can't face Jane . . . she saw us."

"Catriona." His voice was stern. "Catriona, behave yourself." He held me tightly by the shoulder and walked me across the grass. I took a deep breath, and then another, and we came to the stiff, furious figure in the doorway. The band was playing the Charleston.

"We mustn't miss this," Morgan said to Jane. "How kind of you to come and look for us. This is what the whole Village has been waiting for."

"And the Mochdre Village, too," I said, surprised that I could speak; more surprised that my voice sounded natural, even gay.

"What were you doing by the well?"

"I bumped my head." I moved the hair back from my forehead. "I didn't feel well, and Morgan came to see what was wrong." Morgan hadn't seen the lump. He winced. "It's much better now," I said quickly, and pulled my hair over it again. "Let's go in and watch." I waited for Jane to move. Slowly she turned and walked into the Hall. Morgan and I followed her.

"Catriona, that bump?"

"Never mind."

Then he said, "Catriona, I'm going to leave you with Jane."

"No! Morgan, please."

"Go to Jane," he said, and left me. I watched him walk around the sides of the Hall to avoid the dancers, then I went to sit with Jane, who had found a chair next to the

artist's wife. The villagers were all around Basil and Caridwen Hughes, dancing the Charleston with boisterous
energy. The artist's wife looked at me and said, "Aren't
they wonderful, Catriona? Such rhythm . . . They've
picked it up so quickly." She laughed. "It's catchy. If I can
find my husband, I want to try it."

I sat down next to Jane. She turned and looked at me.
Her eyes were cold and glistened. Like the marcasite earrings, I thought. Her face was hard as stone. She turned
away as though it were distasteful to look at me. I sat still.
Then I saw Archibald and Ellen in a corner by the big door.
They were keeping time, turning their heels out and laughing, but not kicking their legs up. Mr. Jones, the butcher,
was almost doing a solo, and he was kicking his legs up and
around, while Codger's daughter-in-law shuffled at his side,
her face now brighter pink than her dress and her hair un-
frizzed and limp. Idris Williams, the post, was enjoying his
dance with the haberdasher's wife, and Myfanwy and Gwilym Evans were as good as Penry and the quiet girl. I saw
everything clearly, as though I were looking at a moving
water color, clearly painted, like Nana's. The blacksmith
was again with the thin girl from the Mochdre Village, and
Caradoc Ellis was with Tessie. All the villagers, dancing
with frolic and zest, were a moving mass of turning heads
and swinging arms, jiggling feet and kicking heels, to the
amazement of the Mochdre villagers and the other strangers, who were clapping their hands and moving their feet
and then getting up to try it in the corners. Soon some of
them moved out on the floor.

The artist's wife said, "Really and truly! Who would
ever have believed that there'd be a scene like this at the
Harvest Social?" I nodded and tried to smile. Then I saw
Emma and Codger, sitting together in the corner near the
main door. Emma looked drawn and pale. Like the day I

broke the library window, I thought. What has happened? They were talking with their heads together, and Codger was holding Emma's hand. I wanted to go across the room and sit with them, but Jane turned to me again. I felt her bitter rage. I wanted to go far away from her.

"How did you get that lump on your forehead?"

"I bumped it."

"Where? When?"

"Someone pushed open the ladies' room door just as I was coming out."

"So that's why you have been draping your hair across your forehead. Really, you have behaved . . ." She shrugged with disgust. "You have disgraced yourself . . . dancing all over the place with these farmers . . . and only one dance with Basil." She spoke through her teeth. "I'm ashamed of you." I didn't answer. "I don't seem to have taught you a thing in all these years, and heaven knows I've tried." Jane was sitting up straight with a smile on her face, as though she were saying normal things. Only I heard the scrape in her voice and felt her fury. "If anyone ever tried . . . I tried." Her hands were clenched on her gold-chain handbag. "And meeting Morgan by the well . . ." She turned full to me, her pale blue eyes blazing-cold. "Catriona, you were disgusting. I saw it all . . . everything. Poor Morgan, poor, dear Morgan . . . to embarrass him like that. Shameless! Shameless!" The music stopped. There was a burst of laughter, and then wild applause.

"Exhibition! Exhibition!" Mr. Jones, the butcher, shouted, still breathless, and everyone took up the cry.

"Come on! Come on! Exhibition from the champions . . . exhibition . . ." And everyone either sat down or stood around to watch, except Basil and Caridwen Hughes, Penry Jones and the quiet girl and Caradoc Ellis and Tessie.

The Merry Music Men began to play, and the three champion pairs began to Charleston, and the English artist and his wife came to sit next to us.

"For verve and energy the like of this can rarely have been seen," he said.

"Even at the Animal Room on Fifty-eighth Street," his wife called across to Jane, and they watched with surprise and laughter. Then the other pairs left the floor and Basil and Caridwen were alone. Soon she, too, sat down, and Basil was left in the center of the floor. All the watchers began to stamp and clap. Basil bowed and began to dance; all kinds of steps, faster and faster, flinging his legs out, high and wide, his hands touching his side-kicking toes and then whirling around and around, his heels flying and his feet twisting as he turned in circles, and soon the hand clapping changed to loud and enthusiastic applause. He doesn't look drunk now, I thought. Then the others, refreshed, all joined in again, dancing with more fervor than before.

The English artist said to his wife, "All right, come on . . . let's try." And they went out onto the dance floor. I watched them for a moment, and then Jane said, "We must go home."

I wanted to walk home with Morgan. I wanted to waltz with Morgan again. But I seemed to have no strength and no feeling.

"All right, Jane." We went to where the Vicar's wife was sitting with Dr. Fraser and his sister, and the Curate. She was clapping her hands.

"Isn't Basil stupendous? . . . Absolutely stupendous? Just look at them all. Have you ever seen such a fantastic sight? . . . Miss Withers . . . come and sit down here." Jane sat down.

"It's all due to your nephew . . . he really is wonderful," she said, and the Vicar's wife looked around proudly.

"So many people from the other villages came to look"— she clasped her hands—"and look what they are seeing . . . and doing. Oh, my dear! And so much more money than ever before. The Vicar will be delighted. Dear, dear Basil . . ."

"It's certainly a great success," Jane said.

"More than that! More than that!"

"Yes, really quite splendid . . . and now we must be—"

"Oh no! You mustn't . . . You can't leave . . . the fun's just beginning."

"Catriona must."

"Must she? I suppose she must. Well, Basil can take her home, and . . ." Oh no! ". . . then he can come back . . . and of course, you'll stay." She turned and put her hand on Jane's knee. "You mustn't go, Miss Withers, of course you mustn't go."

"Very well then, if Basil takes Catriona home."

"Miss Catty, it isn't a waltz, but I know you dance it." Penry Jones was standing in front of me, smiling. "Will you allow Miss Catty to dance a Charleston with me, Miss Withers?"

"It's rather late, she was just about to—"

"Of course she can," the Vicar's wife said. "Go along, dear." And Penry Jones took my hand and we joined in the dancing.

I found I could move to the rhythm without lifting my feet from the floor. I danced without thinking, without feeling. Penry Jones looked far away. The schottische I had danced with him earlier seemed to have been at another Harvest Social, in another world. A gay young world. He smiled at me, dancing. I remembered his high sweet whistle as he walked down the Hill Lane with his tool bag on his back. The yellow pane with the bubbles in it. Our feet moved to the music. Penry Jones danced with quiet rhythmic ease. The music stopped. We stood while the Merry Music Men put new sheets on their wobbly stands.

"Shall we go on dancing? Or shall I take you back? You look tired, Miss Catty." Then Morgan was at my side.

"That was a good dance, Penry Jones," he said, "and I think the Village has proved itself to be abreast of the times."

"Indeed it has! But a good Welsh reel, look you, that's the best of all." Penry Jones smiled at us. He was as tall as Morgan. "And Miss Catty here's a fine dancer . . . and it's leaving her in your hands, I'll be."

"Good night, Penry Jones," I said. "And thank you."

"Good night, Miss Catty . . . and it was most truly a pleasure."

Morgan stood with me while the violinist changed a string. "We'll dance the next dance, Catriona. It will be easier to talk." And I thought, Penry Jones said I looked tired—but Morgan looks ashen. The music started. It was a waltz. Morgan put his hand on my waist, and we danced, as we had danced before. I came alive. Morgan didn't speak for a while. I was almost happy again; my hand held in his, his arm was around my waist.

Then he said, "Catriona, you must go home with Basil." I went out of step. Morgan's rhythm didn't falter. I was in step again.

"No!" Morgan didn't speak. "I won't . . . I won't be alone with him. Please, I couldn't." His fingers closed more tightly around my hand. His eyes held a tenderness that brought the tears, stinging, to mine. "I can't!"

"Catriona, you came with him. Everyone saw that you arrived together . . . and he will not touch you again. If I were not sure of this, Catriona, I would not ask you to go home with him." We danced, around and around, so that it seemed that we were still and the world was spinning. "The Village people would think it rude indeed of Basil if he did not take you home . . . and I want you to leave with him for another reason, Catriona." He danced more quickly, then reversing, he swung me around. "Catriona, you are to leave tomorrow." He didn't let me lose step. He held my hand tightly, and his hold on my waist kept me on my feet. I'm dead, I thought. My heart has stopped. He whirled me around and around in a strong, swift rhythm till the end of the dance. Then he held me for a moment, looking down at me. I couldn't raise my head. "Catriona." I looked up at him. His hands dropped to his sides. We stood facing each other. His eyes were deep and dark in his white face. I could see his bones under the skin.

"Good night," he said, "dear heart." And we turned and walked to where Jane was sitting.

The blood was rushing through my veins. I'm not dead! I thought. I'm alive. I felt the blush rise to my throat and face. He won't let me go . . . ever. I heard his words with every pulse of my blood: "Good night, dear heart." Now he was saying, "Basil will take Catriona home."

"Yes, yes," the Vicar's wife said. "But he is coming back. . . . Basil! Basil!" she called, and Basil left Caridwen Hughes and came toward us. "We can spare you for ten minutes, Basil . . . to take Catriona home." She laughed. "Perhaps only five minutes . . . in the Scarlet Peril."

"Delighted. Five minutes it is! Come on, Catty. Time for little girls to be in bed."

I looked at Morgan, but his eyes held no message. "I'll see you in the morning," he said.

"Come on, Catty." Basil didn't take my arm or touch me.

"And put a damp towel on your forehead." Jane turned to Basil. "The silly girl bumped into a door." She looked older and thin. Morgan stood without speaking. I looked at him again, then I said "Good night" to the Vicar's wife and the others, and she got up just as I was turning away.

"Dear, dear child," she said, and to my surprise, she kissed me on the cheek. "I hear that the telegram came and that you are leaving us tomorrow. . . . Well, we've been expecting it." She looked sorry. "Dear child . . . good night. It's not good-by . . . of course not. You'll be back. It isn't as though you were going to a far country. . . ." And I thought as I listened to her, I never expected to be kissed by the Vicar's wife.

"Catriona may be going to many foreign countries," Jane was saying. "The guardians want her to travel for a year." The Vicar's wife sat down again.

"Really? How interesting. You must send us postcards, Catriona." She turned to Jane. "I love those ridiculous highly colored continental postcards . . . Vesuvius in eruption . . . you know . . ." She was laughing again. The music started.

"Come on, Catty," Basil said.

Without looking at me, because she was searching in her evening bag, Jane said, "Idris Williams gave me the telegram." She raised her head. "That's why I came to look for you . . . at the well." She shrugged. "You leave tomorrow at noon. They are sending a car for you."

I had no other words. "Good night, Jane," I said, thinking, Morgan won't let me leave. I looked at him again.

"I'll see you in the morning, Catriona." This time he was stern. Jane watched and smiled, a thin, satisfied smile.

"Now, hurry back, dear boy, the party can't go on without you," his aunt said, and Basil and I walked across the room.

I looked at Emma. Her face was pinched and small. She knows, I thought. That's what she and Codger were talking

about. I was about to go to her, when Myfanwy Jones met
us. Basil went on to the door, and Myfanwy and I stood together. The tears stayed behind our eyes, filling up the lumps
in our throats. There was deep wisdom in her, and a tender
strength.

"We all know, Miss Catty-fach." And I knew she didn't
mean only that I was going away. "We've known, look you,
that you were going to leave . . . but 'tis always a shock
when the moment comes . . . but 'tis a rich adventure,
Catty-fach, to travel and to see the world. . . ." The tears
began to fill our eyes. " 'Tis not good-by that we're saying,
Merfyn and Penry and me . . ."

"And Gwilym Evans?" I asked, and we smiled at each
other.

"Nor Gwilym Evans, neither," she said, and turned away
and walked toward the refreshment table.

As I walked to the door, there were shouts:

"Good night, Miss Catty."

"Take care, Miss Catty."

"Ffarwel, Miss Catty."

And then I knew why Morgan had said that I must go
home with Basil.

As I reached the big door, Ellen and Archibald came running and sliding across the room.

"Miss Catty . . . Oh, Miss Catty . . . good-by," Ellen
said, and Archibald stood silent. The lump in my throat almost choked me.

"You remember?" I asked them both. "A loving wife. A
cushion on his chair. And a well-tuned harp." They turned
to each other, and then to me again. "Well, Archibald,
you'll have the loving wife and the well-tuned harp . . .
and wherever I am in the whole world I'll send you the most
beautiful cushion ever seen."

"Oh, Miss Catty . . ." Ellen's eyes filled with tears and spilled over. I kissed her cheek. Archibald didn't move. "He is your true friend," Eldorai had said. There were no words between us.

"Come on, Catty," Basil called from the door. I turned and walked out of the Parish Hall.

We came to Bryn Llithrig without speaking. Basil got out and opened the car door. He opened the wall door and stood aside while I passed him. He followed me up the path. I went up the porch steps and turned around.

"Good night, Basil." He pulled my scarf out of his pocket.

"You left this in the Scarlet Peril."

"Thank you." He stood with one foot on the bottom step, looking at me.

"And I don't think you'll forget your first dance . . . or your first kiss, eh, Catty?"

"Good night, Basil." I turned and walked to the front door.

As I opened it, he said, "Good night, Catty. I'll see you when you grow up."

I went to my room and sat on the window seat, and leaned my head against the hard sill. I felt no pain. "Good night, dear heart," the garden whispered, and the birch grove; the dark mountains and the silver river; and the quiet stars. "Good night, dear heart." I fell asleep where I was.

The roar of the Scarlet Peril's engine broke my sleep. I wakened as the sound stopped. The wall door scraped on the gravel, and in a minute I heard Jane say, "Good night, Basil. Thank you for bringing me home."

"Not at all . . . A pleasure . . . Splendid party, wasn't it?"

"Yes. Splendid. . . . Good night."

370 of the Rising of the Lark

"Good night, Jane. Sleep tight." Jane closed the front door and came upstairs, and the Scarlet Peril roared away down the Hill Lane.

Neither lamps nor candles were lit in my room, but there was moonlight and the door was open. Jane passed without looking in. She closed her bedroom door. I wanted to see her, to talk to her, to talk with her. To tell her how grateful I was for her care of me. To ask her forgiveness for my wickedness and disobedience. To thank her for her patience; a hundred things; most of all, to thank her; and to tell her that I couldn't help loving Morgan. I went across the landing and knocked on her door.

"Jane, may I come in, please?" There was silence.

Then, "Catriona! You should be asleep."

"I was, and then I heard you. I'd like to talk for a while."

"Don't be absurd, Catriona . . . I'm tired . . . and as for you . . . you should be exhausted. Don't you know what time it is?"

"No . . . and I'm not tired."

"Well, I am, Catriona. Go to bed now. We must be up early in the morning, you know . . . you leave at noon. . . . Good night."

Oh, Jane, please . . . her words left all the years empty between us. Jane . . . I waited. I heard the metallic sound as she put her marcasite earrings on the silver tray on her big three-mirrored dressing table. Then the rustle of the taffeta as she took off her dress. One shoe fell to the floor, and then I could hear the hairpins dropping on the tray.

I went back to my room and sat again on the window seat. The river was a sheet of moving glass, gray in the fading moonlight. "Good night, dear heart." I stood up. The thought of Morgan filled my heart and mind. I took off my dress and put on a pleated skirt and jersey. Smiling, I coiled my hair in the nape of my neck. I looked at myself. I was a dark shape in the mirror. And with my sandals in my hand I crept downstairs.

When I opened the kitchen door, I heard Emma. Though she was in her room, beyond the pantry, I could hear her sobbing. I went to her door, stood a moment, and opened it.

"Emma." She was sitting on the edge of her bed, still dressed in her purple bombazine, her elbows on her knees and her hands covering her face. The tears were streaming through her fingers, onto her bosom, making dark spots and splashes on the tightly stretched stiff silk. "Oh, Emma . . . please, Emma . . ."

"Miss Catty . . . Miss Catty-fach . . . Oh, Miss Catty," she said through her hands, "I can't be facing the day that's dawning . . . I just can't . . . and all the other days that'll be without you." She lowered her hands and looked at me. Her face was tear-stained, peaked and old. I put my arms around her and held her. Dear, kind, laughing Emma was old. I held her tightly and put my cheek against hers. All my life, I thought, loving her, Emma has cared for me . . . truly cared.

After a while she drew herself away and looked at me, blinking back her tears and pushing her hair from her face.

"Well, and indeed to goodness whatever, and if it isn't a fine pair of Harvest Socialers we are . . ." And she stood up. "And it's laying the breakfast things I'll be . . . for there's nothing like getting busy with what comes next to keep you from brooding." She looked down at me. "And just what might you be doing at this time in the early hours in your kilt and jersey? Now, look you . . ." I stooped and put my sandals on, and then stood up. "And with a new hair fashion, too." She shook her head. "And quite the young lady, at that." She laughed.

"I'm nearly eighteen, Emma." I was taller than she.

"And, Emma, I'm not going away." Her eyes opened wide.

"Don't exaggerate, Miss Catty." She put her hand slowly to her mouth, understanding my words, then she clasped her hands in front of her bosom, beaming with joy, and looked young again. I put my arm around her waist, and we went into the kitchen.

The coals were still glowing in the grate, and Emma's warmth was in every corner and dark shadow. We stood a moment, looking into the embers; then she picked up the poker and raked the fire into new flame. I ran out and down the coachyard steps.

My feet were wet with night dew as I passed the birch grove and ran through the orchard. The river mist, blown landward, was damp and clinging. It cooled the sweet fever in my blood. When I turned onto the river path, I could see the firelight, pale flame-gold, through Morgan's window. Like the morning star, I thought, and stayed still. The river lapped the rush-grown grass, singing his name, and the dark hills made music. Each one has its own . . . Moel Hebog . . . I laughed. O Heavenly Father, let me be beautiful for Morgan, I prayed. I remembered the first day on the Mochdre Hill. "O sea gull, like the snow-white moon in color . . . let us keep countenance and laugh together . . . Winged gauntlet of the sea . . ." I stood looking at the window light and let the memories fall like the rills of a mountain stream till the last bright memory, "Good night, dear heart." Each heartbeat spoke the words. The blood sang them in my veins. He is waiting. I began to run, and didn't stop till I came to the bluff. I wasn't out of breath. Soon I shall feel his arms around me. I shall sit on the rug with my head on his knee. I climbed, running, till I came to the window.

Morgan was in his chair. The fire was dead. I went icy-cold with the thought, It was the lamplight I saw. Paddy and Colly were lying close together on the rug. Morgan's face was gray. He was staring at the dark, empty fire grate. I saw and felt everything in the room. He held his cold pipe in his right hand. His left hand was limp on the arm of the chair, "and sometimes love can be immeasurable pain." I felt his wound and fell back, away from the window, against the stone wall.

After a long while I felt the hard stone, cold, through my jersey, shivered, and came back to thought. He was not waiting for me. . . . Morgan . . . why? I was glad of his hurt. I wanted to go in to him and tear him with the words he had taught me to use. I stayed there with my back against the damp stones, the lump between my breasts, and the hot pain between my eyebrows, sick with longing, until the dusk of dawn crept along the edges of the mountains. Then I scrambled, blind and dry-eyed, down the bluff, onto the dark river path.

Slowly, unaware, I came to the orchard and leaned against the tall pear tree. Morgan was not waiting for me. He will let me go away. While I stood, the trees lost their apartness, as the light gnawed away the shadows between them. I looked up through the branches, to the crooked hills. It was almost morning. Suddenly Morgan's words came to me clearly, twice-spoken. "I'll see you in the morning," he had said, standing there with Jane and the Vicar's wife and Basil, saying good-by in the Parish Hall. He had said, "Good night, dear heart," and, "I'll see you in the morning." I slid down to the grass at the foot of the tree. This morning he would wait for me, the fire blazing, with Paddy and Colly, the smell of bacon cooking, and Mrs. Eyeball's wheat cakes. The tears came in a flood. "The heart does not break, though it comes nigh to it," Eldorai had said, and I knew, "The heart holds its pain and its love, as the kettle-hook holds the flame." I lay face down on the dew-wet grass and wept, and my tears bathed our hurt. "Longing can never be where love is not." I thought of Nana. *"Sili fritt, Leisa bela,"* the Faery woman sings in the Llithrig Wood at twilight. I lay still awhile, and then sat up. It was full daylight. I must bathe and change before I breakfasted with Morgan. I rose from the grass and walked to the birch grove. I leaned my cheek against the cool-smooth bark of the sapling birch and knew the depth of Morgan's love for me, and his wisdom. O Heavenly Father, give me strength to be as he would have me be. I felt a strange quiet. Almost a joyful quiet. I knew that I must leave, but Eldorai's words sang in my heart. "Meetings are when meetings are to be." I walked past the vegetable-marrow patch and across the rose garden, to the archway, up the kitchen steps, and into the house.